DIVINITY 36

BY GAIL CARRIGER

The Tinkered Stars
Crudrat

The Finishing School Series
Etiquette & Espionage | *Curtsies & Conspiracies*
Waistcoats & Weaponry | *Manners & Mutiny*

The Parasol Protectorate Series
Soulless | *Changeless* | *Blameless* | *Heartless* | *Timeless*
prequel: *Meat Cute*

The Custard Protocol Series
Prudence | *Imprudence* | *Competence* | *Reticence*

Parasolverse Tie-in Books & Novellas
Poison or Protect | *Defy or Defend* | *Ambush or Adore*
Romancing the Werewolf | *Romancing the Inventor*
How to Marry a Werewolf

AS G. L. CARRIGER

A Tinkered Stars Mystery
The 5th Gender

The San Andreas Shifters Series
The Sumage Solution | *The Omega Objection*
The Enforcer Enigma | *The Dratsie Dilemma*
Newsletter exclusives: *Marine Biology* | *Vixen Ecology*

DIVINITY 36

TINKERED STARSONG BOOK 1

GAIL CARRIGER

In the beginning, the Dyesi created the domes and the divinity…

DIVINE INTERVENTION

Phex never wanted to be a god. But not everyone chooses divinity. Some have divinity foisted upon them by aliens in cafes.

It was a very ordinary evening in every way. There was a revival scheduled for the next night, but that was the *next* night, so the cafe was calm. It was half-full with the usual teenage malcontents pacified by caffeine or sugar or song. They were talking and flirting, and Phex had little to do but see to their whims and keep the place clean. The dome overhead showed its customary display of gods performing reruns in an endless loop of colorful charm. It was a pattern so ingrained into Phex's daily life that he knew where he was in his shift just from which godsong was playing.

Tillam was singing "Day Gone" with Missit belting out the chorus in his smooth, syrupy voice (which meant Phex had forgotten to take his break) when the alien came into his cafe.

Not that it was really *his* cafe, more just his domain. At school, Phex was the tall, glum refugee that no one liked. At the cafe, he was still all those things except that he perked a

mean coffee and bubbled the perfect tea, and no teen would
ever risk offending a barista in any corner of the galaxy.
Especially not under a dome. So, it was Phex's cafe and he
ruled over it with silent glares. In school, he was a lump in
the corner, not trying to fit in, just trying to get through. After
school, he had something they wanted, even if it was only a
cup of some overpriced, overhyped slurp.

He had his regulars. The lingering elderly crowd who
were still there when he first came on shift, and then, as it got
later, the teens stopped doing whatever it was that normal
teenagers did after school (who weren't mandated workers
like him) and started to arrive. The adults ceded the territory
with tolerant smiles and careful movements, and the young
people took over – louder, sprawling, and high-strung. It was
like when one of the slower godsongs on the dome gave way
to a faster, more lively performance. Phex knew all their
drinks, just like he knew all their names, but he asked for
both every single time because they never asked for his.

Tillam was sifting the dome, Missit belting out high
cantor in that insanely beautiful voice, a regular refrain that
marked the start of Phex's last hour on shift. Phex was
singing along, not high cantor but low, inventing a harmony
none of the real gods bothered with. He did that sometimes
with the older songs because he heard them so often, he
wanted something different even if he had to come up with it
himself.

The Dyesi that entered Phex's cafe was not a regular and
did not immediately approach the counter. Phex only saw it
when it made itself known, moving forward as if birthed by
the dome. Phex was usually more observant than that, but this
was a *Dyesi*.

The creature shimmered into existence, iridescent and
shining as if stepping out of Tillam's performance and into

reality. The dome was Dyesi tech. Phex supposed the Dyesi might be afforded some natural camouflage as a result.

The cafe hushed in the presence of greatness. Even adolescents knew to be cowed when a Dyesi walked among them. *Especially* adolescents. This one was average-sized, bigger than every human there, but narrow about it – not thin, just lean and bendy. Like all its kind, it had smooth hairless skin on the blue end of the spectrum, all the colors of the cafe and the cupola reflecting and shimmering over it, like the surface of highly polished metal.

Phex moved quickly over to the retail port to take the alien's order. He worked hard to control his reaction. Almost every Sapien found the Dyesi wildly attractive with their glowing skin, willowy elegance, and huge eyes. Someone more poetic than Phex had once called them *the nymphs of the stars*.

This one had purple eyes.

Purple.

"What will it be?" Phex asked, colonist-level polite, Galactic Common.

"Beautiful greetings," it said, in Dyesi, staring at him.

Phex understood because everyone understood at least a little Dyesi. It was the language of divine entertainment, after all.

It continued to stare, cataloguing Phex's features – blue hair, black eyes, high cheeks, arched brows, and precision lips. A blueprint for human symmetry, an amalgam of cross-breeding for genetic superiority. Phex knew what his face was: the combination of many faces made into a simplistic ideal average, forgettable in its perfection.

"Would you like to place an order?" Phex switched to full Galactic Formal, diplomat's tongue, careful with his pronouns.

"You're quite lovely," the Dyesi said after a long pause, voice flat and sharp when speaking Galactic.

What could Phex say to that? *Thank you – I'm the product of a long tradition of gene manipulation that failed me in every way but pretty.* Something more self-effacing? *I'm base human issue, nothing compared to the Dyesi.* Which was true because the Dyesi were unattainably gorgeous.

What he went with was "Can I take your order? Citizen? Visitor?"

"Would it be intrusive to ask for the title of *friend*?"

"I'm here to make you a beverage, not an emotional contract." Phex dropped to Galactic Common since it was rude of the alien to have asked.

The Dyesi did not acknowledge the reprimand. "I think we should be friends."

Phex was silent, confused by this social aggression. It was too strange even for Dyesi. Not that he'd had much personal experience with the species. He'd watched an interview once with a Dyesi cultural anthropologist who said they preferred the *it* pronoun because they liked both the distance it provided and the objectification it emphasized. The Dyesi specialized in being different, being something *other* and *better*. They liked to be thought of not just as custodians of art but as art themselves. The Dyesi did not *make friends*. Certainly not with common baristas on common little moons.

They had a reputation for being cool and aloof. Powerful in a way that wasn't physical but manipulative. Everyone wanted something from the Dyesi – fame, influence, sex, attention. To be the object of desire was to control all the air in a room. Under bubbles of artificial atmosphere, *that* was real power.

Phex said, "Would you like saposi juice or corrosive dark?" He was a barista and a good one, so he knew that

Dyesi went two ways with beverages – overly sour or overly bitter.

"You have interfaced with my people before?" The alien's expression was hard to read because, well, *alien*. But it felt almost flirtatious because of its crests. Phex was a little fascinated – he'd never seen those infamous crests up close before. They were made of an accordion of thin membrane that rose off the top and back of the Dyesi's large, pointed ears, like a fish fin. Those crests could open and flap about, wiggle and droop, and generally seemed to indicate emotion and reactions in the way that whiskers did in some species. Right now, they were unfurled and arched towards Phex, like a probe's feelers intent on him.

Still, this was beginning to get frustrating. Did the creature actually *want* a beverage?

Attacon 7 had a diverse population. Phex was no stranger to being a decent interstellar barista to alien life. The moon saw a lot of spaceship traffic. This Dyesi should know that. Why wasn't it just ordering a damn drink?

Phex wasn't one for polite small talk, so he said, "I know Dyesi taste."

"And you engage with our music?" It gestured with one six-fingered hand to the dome that formed the structure of the cafe. Tillam's performance had ended and Errata had taken over. Their style was more percussive, less lyrical, but easier for Sapiens to dance to. Phex always found himself swaying his hips when Errata performed.

"Doesn't everyone?" Phex asked. Thinking about the sheer number of cupola entertainment units in his hawker center alone. Domes were the best way to showcase gods, and young people these days demanded gods. His cafe screamed divinity all day and all night, and no one ever complained. When he'd first arrived five years prior, Phex had hated it – the constant sound and sensory overload. But like everything else off Wheel, he'd eventually become accustomed to the sensation. The fact that his cafe made sure to always install the latest updates to its dome was a big draw.

"Unfortunately, not *everyone*," replied the Dyesi.

"Greedy much?" said Phex, he thought under his breath.

"Is the divinity not to your taste? You were singing along just now. You have a pretty voice."

Phex flinched. That was not a compliment the Dyesi paid lightly. Telling someone they looked lovely was Dyesi-cheap. Small talk. A social nicety. Telling someone they *sounded* good came with a cost. Phex might not know any Dyesi personally, but he knew the warning signs of recruitment. Everyone did. Mostly because *they* wanted it.

But Phex didn't want to matter. He only wanted to survive.

He panicked and looked around. A good thing, too, because he caught that one kid who was always causing trouble scooping an expensive god statue off a side counter. The relic disappeared like magic into the kid's wide sleeves, and she stood smoothly and sauntered out of the cafe.

Phex put both hands on the high counter and vaulted over it.

The kid took off across the hawker center.

Phex bolted out of the cafe after her.

It was no contest. Phex had long legs, legs that had almost gotten him killed on the Wheel but had served him well since then in sports or dance. Those legs made easy work of catching a petty thief. Phex hadn't run the blades for years, but he never stopped training as if he needed to. When survival meant speed and dexterity, you didn't stop even when you found yourself safe. Especially then. Because safe wasn't something you trusted. The song of a refugee was carried in Phex's speed.

The kid dodged a noodle stall, dove through a group of gossiping locals, and rounded a bench. That was her undoing. Phex simply springboarded off the bench, flip-twisted midair, and landed facing her.

He slapped his hands to her shoulders. "Give it back."

She struggled, trying to wrench free of his grasp.

"I'll return it to the cafe and no one need know. We'll both forget this ever happened." Phex hated her for putting him in this position.

"I don't have anything." Scared eyes glared at him.

"You stole a god statue. If we do this quick, I won't file a report with the cops."

"You're crazy!"

Phex shook her in frustration, bony shoulders small and sharp under his hands. "Give."

"I don't know what you're talking about."

He let go of one shoulder and poked at the weight in her sleeve. "Give it back and I'll leave you alone."

"Why would you be nice to me?" She pouted but looked a little less wary. Perhaps she thought she could still get away with it.

"I'm not nice. I just hate cops. Give over or I *will* call them." Phex had no way to know if she believed him. He'd never threatened anyone before.

The kid tightened her lips, examined his face, feared whatever she saw there. She fished about in her sleeve and handed him the statue.

It was Missit.

Phex sneered at the tiny god in his hand. She didn't even have good taste. "You couldn't be original?"

The girl made to grab it back.

Phex just held the stupid thing above his head, well out of her reach.

She screeched at him. "Have you ever seen him live? With Tillam? He's amazing. The best thing ever. Missit is the *greatest god* of all! I love him. I worship him!"

Phex looked her dead in the eyes and said the most cutting thing he could think of: "He's overrated."

"Oh, my god! You can't say that. He can cantor and grace. He's the most multitalented god ever to exist. Ever! He's the absolute eternal."

"Can't skinsift, though, can he?"

She made a dismissive noise. "He's still only a Sapien."

"Aren't you too young to like a first-gen god?"

"He's not *that* old! He was the youngest ever recruited! I can't believe this. How could you? You don't deserve the statue. I should have stolen it sooner."

Phex rolled his eyes. "You think it's mine? I'm still a minor. How could I own a licensed god statue?"

"Then why do you care to chase me down and get it back?"

"Lost items are docked from my pay. This crap is expensive. Plus, I need the exercise. Breaks up the monotony of my day."

Suddenly, Phex wondered why he was still standing in the middle of the hawker center, making a spectacle of yelling at a kid, holding a statue of a god he didn't like high above his head.

He snorted at the ridiculousness of it all and turned to leave. They'd attracted a small crowd. He glared at the bystanders until they moved out of his way.

He found the cafe untroubled by his absence, the patrons still held somewhat in thrall by a Dyesi among them.

Phex brought the statue to the counter with him in case it

needed reprogramming after its little adventure. Trouble-maker. He put it within line of sight on top of the pastry display case and told it firmly to stay.

Missit's gorgeous face winked at him. Knowing Missit's personality insert, the statue had probably started flirting with the girl and that's why she'd stolen it.

"You're very *pretty*," said the statue in Missit's warm, golden voice, confirming Phex's guess. It used the Dyesi word for *pretty*, but everyone knew that translation. Quite a few Dyesi terms were part of Galactic Common these days.

Really, Phex loathed the interface statues. They were more trouble than they were worth. Except that they made small talk with customers so Phex didn't have to.

Phex scowled at the Dyesi. The alien was still standing in the same place. Its crests still pointed at Phex in a clear indi-cation of interest. So was a small recording device on the first finger of one bluish hand.

"The statue is correct. You are *pretty*. And you are also *graceful* for a Sapien of your size." *Grace* was another Dyesi word. Another term never to be applied lightly.

Phex figured this Dyesi had observed, and probably recorded, his little run through the hawker center. He wrin-kled his nose. He wasn't *that* big – there were plenty of aliens taller than he, and many adult Sapien variants were bulkier. He *was* tallish for a human off-world. Someone had tinkered with his genetics in favor of intimidation. His brows were heavier than fashionable, and his nose had a bit of hook to it. He'd shot up starting young and was pretty certain he hadn't stopped yet. He figured eventually he'd put on muscle, too. Right now, he had that annoying hormonal thing where he had to fight to be comfortable in his own frame. Sometimes he forgot his elbows, and sometimes all his joints ached as they tried to accommodate new length. He was always hungry. But none of that was new to Phex. His childhood was one of aches and hunger. He kept up with his crudrat training – running and climbing and flips every day, partly because it was *his* body and it better yield to his control. Partly to defy the hunger. But also because it was one way to get back at his unknown family for triggering his genes. It was his body, in the end, not theirs.

"Have you finally decided what you want to drink?" he asked the alien, intentionally rude.

But the Dyesi was riveted by the playback on its recorder, not whatever had initially brought it into the cafe.

"You just flipped as if it were part of your movements every day. Just flipped in the air. Like a grace."

"There was an obstacle." For Phex, that was explanation enough.

"You have a lovely voice. Your appearance is striking. And you are *graceful*."

The repeated compliments were freaking Phex out. "My hair is not long enough," he protested.

"True, but it *is* an unusual color. We can give you extensions. And your face shape is adequate. Have you never wanted to become a god?"

That was covetous, and it genuinely scared Phex. "You're an *acolyte*?"

The Dyesi's large purple eyes shimmered in amusement. "All Dyesi off-world represent the divinity in some capacity. Why else would we leave Dyesid Prime? We all keep our crests peeled for potentials, especially among Sapiens. Your kind make for very popular gods."

Phex pointed an accusing finger at the statue of Missit, which was pretending to be coy. "I know."

The Dyesi snaked out a hand and picked the statue up. Twirled the shimmery, metallic bit of tech with equally shimmery blue fingers. "Missit is still one of the most worshiped. Would that we could repeat the magic that made him." It sounded wistful.

Phex didn't believe in any gods. He didn't consider himself a worshiper of the divinity at all, but he still knew most of Missit's songs and his history with the Dyesi. Everyone did. Missit was just that popular. "Sapiens will never let you recruit a child that young again."

"You think it's his youth that did it?"

"I don't worship. I have no feelings on the matter."

"Good. How old are you?"

"Sixteen, maybe seventeen."

"You don't know?" The Dyesi's crests wiggled in a cute way. Phex suspected that it meant confusion.

"I know very little about my birth." Plus, Phex was never certain how the years matched up across the galaxy, or how time morphed in alien minds. His age was in his bones, he supposed. Someday, he could have them sampled for stardust-striation if he cared to know the truth. But by the time he could afford such a thing, his age wouldn't matter anymore.

He caught a couple of kids out of the corner of his eye, standing and skulking toward the cafe door in a slightly suspicious manner. "Sit!" he barked at them.

"You don't control us, refuse," objected one.

Phex gestured autocratically for them to retake their stools. He didn't want to know what they were up to, but they were better where he could keep an eye on them.

They sat back down.

Phex returned his attention to the Dyesi.

It was looking at him, intrigued. "You're an odd sort, even for a Sapien."

That was a better compliment than *pretty* or *graceful*.

"Do you actually want a drink? This is a cafe, after all."

"No. I want to talk to you." The Dyesi slow blinked, large purple eyes intent.

"I don't talk."

"That one called you *refuse* in a tone of contempt. Why?"

Phex sighed. He supposed he better answer the alien's questions if he ever wanted it to leave his cafe. "*Refuse* is slang for *refugee*. There are quite a few of us on this little moon, and we struggle to adapt. As a result, we have a certain reputation."

"Isn't that prejudice?"

Phex considered the question. "You Dyesi don't like gender pronouns. You don't like sweet things. You talk first to appearances. Is that prejudice?"

"Yes. For we are not *all* like that."

Phex lifted his chin. "Then yes. Prejudice." He was what he was, and that meant he struggled to fit in. He didn't take *refuse* as a slight, because he didn't care. On the Wheel he hadn't even been considered a person. To be taunted because he actually existed was better. At least on Attacon 7, people noticed him enough to insult him.

The Dyesi's ears were still fully crested. More questions were coming. "You are a Sapien, but here, you too are an alien?"

"I've lived on Attacon for years. They've fed and educated me. I try to be a good citizen. But yes, as alien as you, in the end."

Though most Sapiens balked at calling a Dyesi *it*, Phex did not. He grew up in a place where anything not Wheel was enemy, and all planetary aliens were beastly and dangerous and it *it* IT. Six years as an exile, meeting all kinds and sorts, drifting in and out of culture, and Phex still flinched when he met an alien he'd never seen before. He still thought of them as something *other*. Something to be feared. He was still wary of their strangeness. The Wheel had hated him, when it thought of him at all, while simultaneously training him to hate and to fear everyone else. He worked hard to suppress those instincts, but they still bubbled up, and this annoyed him. He resented a past that had built fear into his subconscious, and he resented aliens for reminding him of that past.

"Would you consider leaving Attacon?" the Dyesi asked.

"Where else could I possibly go?"

The Dyesi cocked its head, imitating him. "I think you should become a god."

"Because I am *pretty*?"

"You are *graceful*. It was a pleasure to watch you run and jump. And your voice has *power*."

Phex took a chance, leaning over the counter. Curious to see if he could elicit a real reaction from a Dyesi.

Gods were performing on the dome overhead, so the Dyesi's skin was shimmering and speckled with skinsift, matching the music, syncing with the display on the dome. It was a thing of incredible beauty that inspired true awe. Even Phex could acknowledge that. But this Dyesi was not inside the performance, only passively receiving it, so its colors were muted. Or perhaps this Dyesi simply wasn't god-level, and a god's skinsift was a talent possessed by only a rare few of the species.

Phex had always wondered about skinsift. So, he decided to test it.

He sang a refrain from one of Tillam's biggest hits. One of Fortew's lines. Distinct from the godsong above them. It had a contrasting cadence and different notes. He sang it soft but true, pushing it toward the Dyesi's bare skin with his breath. Phex's vocal cords had been altered just like the rest of him. It's what the Wheel did – messed around with human genes, hunting for some impossible version of perfection. He

may not have the training, but his voice had been modified
pre-birth into harmony with itself.

The Dyesi's skin shimmered with new specks of light,
dusted with purples and pinks, like bubbles on the surface of
a fancy drink. Skinsift. Much more intense than before. It was
beautiful, just as it was above them on the dome. But definitely different.

The alien flinched and jerked away, abrupt and almost
clumsy. Then it changed its stance, growing taller, defensive.
"Are you trying to injure me with song?"

Phex dipped his head, ashamed but intrigued. "Could I?"

The Dyesi's body language was now wary. Phex was a
tiny bit proud of that. But also embarrassed. Had he
committed a cultural violation of some kind? But if this Dyesi
wanted to take him away and turn him into something else,
Phex needed to know who had the real power in their
dynamic.

"You're sure it is me and not just my voice that you
want?"

The Dyesi's crests flared and vibrated. "There is something more important than your voice?"

Phex took a chance. "Is there something more important
than your skinsift?"

"You are a little cruel, aren't you? You'll do very well as a
god."

Phex worried that might be true.

The Dyesi looked him up and down. "There is a Tillam
revival tomorrow. Will your cafe be hosting it?"

"Of course." That was a stupid question. Tillam was
performing a new song as an apology for ending their recent
tour early – every dome in the galaxy that could afford the fee
would be hosting it. Tillam may not be the most popular
pantheon at the moment, but they were one of the most

famous and well-established of all time. They were never
without worshipers. The cafe would profit nicely.

"I'll return tomorrow," said the Dyesi. It turned, all liquid
elegance, and left Phex's cafe.

The alien never had ordered a drink.

Phex finished his shift and ran home, leaping and wall-
walking just because he could. When he was alone in his pod,
he looked up everything anyone had posted about Dyesi
recruiting, auditions, and the path to godhood. The infonet
had notably little to say on the subject. Being recruited was
the dream of many, but the process and reason some Sapiens
were chosen over others eluded everyone who hadn't gone
through it. And those who had clearly labored under gag
orders.

Phex didn't like the idea of becoming a god – performing
for millions, transforming into an object of worship. A statue
in a cafe. A song on rotation. But he couldn't deny a strange
joy at being wanted. And he had to consider the fact that his
life was already repetitive and statue-like and trapped under a
dome. Would it be so different to be a god instead of a
barista?

He didn't sleep that night. He wasn't certain if it was fear
or anticipation or both.

2

O GREAT BARISTA

Phex's boss was a space-born Sapien, slender and light on her feet. Most people called her Del, but Phex stuck to *boss*. She never smiled, but everyone waited eagerly to be grumbled at because her complaints poured forth with as much bitter deliciousness as her coffee. Between them, Phex and Del might win prizes for glowering. She'd taught him everything he knew about customer service, which was nothing at all. It was a policy that served them both well. The regulars had decided that grumpy baristas were part of the cost of caffeination at the best cafe on Attacon 7.

On revival nights, Phex and Del performed a smooth dance of humorless drink production. Del operated the port and dispensers, while Phex circled the cafe, collecting the empties, taking sit-down orders, and relocating stools and tables to their proper places. Phex did also keep an eye on the dispensers – he tried to jump in and rotate the flavor casks, because Del would do it if he didn't get to it first, and she was small enough to get injured.

When Phex came back on shift that revival night, his Dyesi had already arrived with friends and was actually ordering something at the counter. The other customers had all fallen back into that reverent hush, which clearly caused the Dyesi a certain amount of self-satisfaction. It was as if by visiting this cafe, the Dyesi were authenticating it as the best cupola for a Tillam revival. Phex gave the aliens a nod and left his boss to do her thing.

Del was pleased. Dyesi in the audience only added to the experience for everyone, since they would reflect the dome. Phex wasn't surprised to see her settle the aliens at a central table, where they might provide a low visual point and amplify the beauty of the performance. All three had their crests up and open and alert to the cafe around them. Like the rest of them, those crests were multifaceted and reflective, but because they were so thin, light could also pass through them. With the cupola shining brightly for seating and revival preparation, those crests dispersed that light into rainbows like prisms.

The revival officially opened with a minor pantheon, a new set of gods who'd been touring with Tillam. They were good – original songs, beautiful colors and patterns – if a touch mass-produced. But they were stiff in a way that Tillam was not. Certainly, their cantors harmonized beautifully, their skinsift was stunning, and their graces were rhythmic in all the right ways. Phex enjoyed their performance and hummed along happily while focusing on his duties. Perhaps that was the thing. Were these major gods, Phex would not have been able to pull his gaze away from the dome. But they were not, so he was unaffected.

The baby pantheon did have some worshipers at the cafe, though – synth stickers on their cheeks making crude mockery of the skinsift. Even those who were just there for Tillam seemed happy enough while they waited for their great gods to take the dais. Some wore full metallic makeup and body paint in a crude simulation of their beloved metallic gods. Some of the diehards probably had tinting surgery done or iridescent tattoos – permanently altering their skin to be more like the gods they adored.

Everyone was always calm and well behaved during a live beaming. There would be no statue-stealing or discipline issues for Phex tonight. Just worshipful silence.

The three Dyesi sitting among them skinsifted to the music in a relaxed way, as if their skin were absentmindedly humming along. They exchanged a few words with each other between songs but mostly seemed to be analyzing the performance and assessing the reaction of the people in the cafe around them, crests open and swiveling about, in time with the graces' beat.

But everything changed when Tillam took over the dome.

These were major gods.

Phex had experienced a few of Tillam's revivals before, so he was somewhat prepared. But even he could admit to being awed.

He still had his duties and his boss was right there, yet Phex found himself pausing to absorb the performance. He'd heard most of Tillam's godsongs many times before, but he still could barely look away. Several were on rotation in that very cafe, and yet Phex had to stop and experience how different they were when performed live for a beam.

This performance was newly choreographed just for this tour. And when gods changed their movements, the sounds changed too. The pacing shifted and, of course, so did the colors and patterns on the dome. Every micro alteration in cantor tone changed the subtleties of skinsift and therefore the images around them. Every new movement the graces made, each spin or catch, each leap slightly higher than before, changed the beats and the pauses, interrupting the cantors' voices, remaking the patterns of skinsift. A live performance was a thing entirely new every single time. And Tillam were the best ever to take over any dome, anytime, anywhere.

More than once Phex found himself standing, stunned into awed stillness by the sound and the look – by the grace of it all. Missit's high cantor, the sharp spikes of color that resulted, Fortew's low cantor and the darker, swirling, smooth vibrancy that accompanied his tone. The way the sound pigments interacted over the skin of their Dyesi. The darkening, slow color-shifts driven by their graces interrupting the sound waves and the cadence they beat out with their feet – becoming both the throbbing backbone of the godsong and the means by which the verses ended. Tillam was formed of six gods in truth, come together to create a thing so close to magic, it was a drug for the senses, an experience that transported human consciousness the way it sifted Dyesi skin.

As one of Tillam's songs came to an end, Phex shook himself, looked around, dazed. He forced himself to make sure everything was okay in the cafe but also to see if anyone had observed his momentary weakness. He caught the eyes of his Dyesi friend – purple interest sharp and sure.

The next song started and the alien gestured him over.

No one spoke during a live godsong. It simply wasn't done. Phex found it difficult, sometimes, not to sing along with the ones he knew, but this was not a regular day under the cupola. This was a revival, so Phex held his tongue.

He nodded to the Dyesi at the table, moving his head with the beat. During a revival, he did everything as if it were a dance. He had to move around to do his job, but he wasn't a monster – he would not spoil the experience for others.

The Dyesi gestured with its ear crests at the show overhead, a question in those purple eyes.

Phex gave a tight nod of approval. It was a good perfor-

mance. He would not deny the Dyesi their right to self-satisfaction over their art. Especially when the divinity had put so
much work into taking over the galaxy with it.

He did not know what the alien wanted from him. Why
summon him? Their drinks were still full.

The godsong came to an end, and there was a pause while
everyone returned to the reality of their sad little lives on a
sad little moon that was not large enough to earn a true dome
and real revival of its own.

Voices hummed briefly as people shared their excitement
over the fact that the next song was Tillam's *new* one.

The cupola positively vibrated with anticipation.

There was rush of orders at the counter. Phex turned to
help.

A blue hand on his wrist stopped him. Contact. No one
had touched Phex in a very long time. Certainly not an alien.
Its skin was cool and soft – for some reason, Phex had
thought they would be damp. He jerked away but turned back
to the table.

"Yes?"

"You will come to us for the next godsong."

"Why?"

"We want to watch you react."

Phex considered. What reaction did they expect? What
reaction did they want? Was he being judged? "I'd rather
not."

"Oh, but we insist." Galactic Formal but a mandate.

Phex pushed back. "How is that?"

"We can cut this cupola off at any time. How do you think
your boss would react, or your customers, if we shut it down
just after the new godsong started? Or in the middle?"

Beneath this statement was the implicit threat that Phex
would be blamed. That it would go badly, not just for Phex

but for everyone. Domes dropping out mid-revival had caused panic and despair. One did not interrupt worship. One did not curtail the divine.

The Dyesi had won for now.

Phex nodded and fled to the counter. Spent a few busy minutes serving drinks and snacks and trying not to think about how easy it was for these aliens to manipulate him.

A crash of sound and color on the cupola heralded Tillam's return, and even those in the middle of ordering ran back to their stools or standing spots in hushed anticipation.

Phex made his way reluctantly to the table of Dyesi. He stood next to them, feeling tall and awkward.

The new song opened with stillness and lines of light, not born of the dome but of artifice. The gods stood on their dais inside these white streaks – the Dyesi silent iridescent blue, the Sapiens metallic golds, the graces shadow dark and pearlescent.

Missit sang first, his sweet warm voice spun over the dome. He'd made his tone round and breathy and somehow plaintive and very sad. The color it wrought was a misty turquoise sheen. It moved over the Dyesi's skin in rays, like sun through water. The turquoise spiraled and spiked outward. The artificial lights cut out and the dome took over.

Phex felt very small, as if he were microscopic, trapped inside someone's teardrop – looking out through salted sorrow at a colorless world.

The godsong drove the turquoise forward in a pattern of simple spiraling beauty. Missit's voice was pushing out skinsift and nothing more. Then, Phex realized, as did all the congregation at once, that the graces were moving, dancing between Missit and his Dyesi sifters, cutting shadows in and interrupting the rays, shivering the song with a low pulsing beat. They made slow turns every few

words. It was haunting. As if they were stalking the
sadness.

Then Fortew's voice joined Missit's, providing a low
cantor's foundation – support and affection to mitigate the
sorrow. At the same time, all of Tillam twirled and leapt in
unison, and a crash of dark blue shot out, the teardrop
bursting open.

This was a lament, praise of a thing so important, its
absence could cause misery. It was like experiencing grief in
retrospect, knowing what was gone while still loving it. Phex
wondered if Tillam was disbanding, if this was their goodbye
or just the end of the tour. Or was it an ode to a loved one
whom one of the gods had lost?

Phex could not look away from the dome. He did not
think to check the cafe or see if the Dyesi were as absorbed as
he. He could only let the godsong, its colors and beauty, roll
over him. He'd never held anyone or anything close enough
to feel this kind of loss. Phex had fled his whole world, but
that place was unremitting and cold. He felt no grief over it.
He had no fond memories to balance the clear turquoise rays
with navy. The song was making him feel something he had
not even known existed before.

Then, in the last verse, Fortew's low cantor drifted away.
The graces stopped moving. The dome became a swirling
turquoise carried once again only by Missit's clear, warm
voice. Then the sound and color ended.

The dome died to grey.

Phex returned to his own body with a shiver, found
himself standing dumbfounded and wet-faced. The victim of
godfix. He jerked a little, coming back and looking around to
see if anyone would mock him for his fixation.

Fortunately, everyone in the cafe was equally impacted.
They had just experienced ecstasy, the revelation of true

divinity. Phex found it wonderful and terrifying at the same time.

On the cupola above, the image changed. In some massive performance dome light-years away, someone switched off the dome sensors and returned them all to an old-fashioned projector-style view. Suddenly, they could see the massive congregation, and Tillam on their dais at the center of it, looking tiny and not at all godlike. Just a collection of six ordinary people who did extraordinary things.

They graced their last. Tillam's standard goodbye was a simple elegant curl of the right hand, a fluttery benediction. The performance was officially over.

Missit curled an arm about Fortew's back, in comfort or support or solidarity. Zil, Tillam's dark grace, held hands with one of the Dyesi – difficult to tell which when their skin was made chaotic by the roar of the congregation. As if sensing the ambient noise for the first time, the gods on the dais reacted. Cantors and graces huddled protectively around their sifters. The congregation grew louder, transported by that last godsong into hysterical sobbing approval.

Phex wondered if Tillam faced danger, trapped in a dome with that loud crowd. If their Dyesi gods might be injured by sound as easily as they were made magic by music.

Then, all around the galaxy, the beam was killed.

The revival had ended.

The cafe was stunned silent, only a few sniffles here and there. People with wet faces and mouths bowed in wonder. The manifest awe of godfix.

Phex looked down at the three seated Dyesi. They seemed unmoved.

He asked, "Tillam's sifters. Is the dome dangerous for them? At the end like that, with all that noise from the congregation?"

The aliens blinked up at him, dark blue and green and purple eyes.

"What an interesting reaction," said the one with the navy eyes.

"*That* is what you took from it? Concern for two of our gods?" asked Green Eyes.

"Did you *feel* nothing?" asked Purple, his friend from yesterday.

"Of course I felt it."

"What do you think the godsong was about?" it pressed, crested ears curious.

"Loss."

"What for?"

Phex knew that was a trick question. "Ah, no. That is not for me to say. I would only reveal what I fear losing if I answered. I need to know more about who wrote it to understand what they grieved."

The Dyesi looked at each other.

"It is one of Missit's pieces," said Purple.

Phex nodded. "Did someone he loved die? Or is it a different kind of loss?"

One of them said, "A remarkable talent, to be able to transmit such feeling. Sorrow for absence is not a sensation we ourselves experience."

"Dyesi do not grieve?" Phex was intrigued.

"Not like that. Not in that way."

Phex nodded. "Then that's probably why he wrote it, isn't it?" He gestured around the somber cafe. "Not so that we would feel his sorrow" —he turned back to stare down the at the Dyesi— "but so that *you* would."

People were talking again. A few were getting drinks, warm comforting beverages. But they were moving and speaking quietly, contemplative, as was the custom for those who have been recently transformed by art.

"Explain," demanded his purple-eyed friend.

"Missit has lived among Dyesi his whole life. Perhaps the song was to share some of his humanity with *you*, not share his grief with us."

"A fascinating perspective," said the navy-eyed Dyesi, looking at Phex with renewed interest.

Phex dismissed his own whimsy. "I only speculate. I've never met a god."

"Perhaps if you meet Missit, you will ask him?" The suggestion was somehow sly.

Phex shook his head. "To ask an artist to explain is to return a gift unopened. If you wish to know Missit's intent, then *you* should ask him. May I resume my work now?"

All three Dyesi made a funny clicking noise and inclined their heads in unison – grace.

Phex paused a moment, genuinely curious. "What is it named, that song?"

"'Tillam's Lament.'" The one with the purple eyes gestured with its ident ring. "Can you get to our audition dome tomorrow morning, first shift?"

"Is it this side of the moon?"

"It is."

Phex calculated. He would not get much sleep, but why not? He was curious. They had lured him with that last song, if nothing else. Plus, he should consider godsong itself. Could he maybe someday create such a thing? Make others feel that way, on distant moons with foreign minds? The idea was both preposterous and tempting.

The Dyesi beamed him the coordinates of the audition space.

Phex's wrist ident vibrated softly.

"We will see you there."

"Will you?"

"We will remove this cafe's divinity license if you do not attend."

"I see," said Phex, because he did.

Del was his boss, not his friend, but he would not risk her livelihood by being stubborn. He wasn't perverse – he wouldn't refuse simply because he didn't like the tone of Dyesi regard. Besides he had to admit to an interest in what their auditions would be like. What exactly would the divinity demand of those who wanted to be gods?

That night in his sleeping pod, Phex wondered what the others were feeling. Others like him who had been told to audition. Probably, they were talking excitedly with their friends via ident chips, or practicing long into the night. He wondered if it was possible to regret something he'd not yet done and wasn't sure he could.

Fortunately, at the official auditions, Phex was somewhere in the middle of the lineup. There were maybe sixty hopefuls on Attacon 7, all his age or younger, all nervous and scared. Phex was glad not to be going first.

The same three Dyesi from his cafe the night before sat in judgment this morning. They had spectator seats front and center, affording them the best view of the dais, a table set before them. Two additional Dyesi stood on the dais to skin-sift, and a third facilitated the proceedings. It was not a very big dome, but Phex suspected it was the biggest on Attacon 7.

"Name? Nomenclature? Gender?" said the facilitator.

The first person to take the dais gave their respective identifiers in a clear if shaken voice. Like most of those auditioning, this one had very long hair, indicating a desire for godhood from an early age. They sang a third-generation godsong in a sweet, breathy voice. That audible airiness was rare in gods. Phex assumed it was not desirable and wondered if something like that could be trained out.

The two sifting Dyesi stood on either side of the Sapien, and then walked about the dais, changing the direction of the sound waves and the reaction of their skin. They had pretty sifts that translated to the dome overhead in appealing ways, but their fuzzy, ill-defined patterns paled when compared to the vibrancy of true gods.

Phex wondered if this was because this dome was not made for live performances, or if there was a natural range in skinsift, or if it all came down to the quality of the cantor.

The Dyesi judges politely asked each cantor to dance, since all cantors must demonstrate at least a little grace. A few aliens and one Sapien auditioned for grace roles. They were tested for rhythm and acrobatic ability but were also made to sing. In the best pantheons, graces sometimes gave voice and cantors sometimes took wing.

Most of those auditioning were dismissed after less than nine minutes on the dais. It was impossible for Phex to understand why, but the Dyesi clearly found it easy to eliminate based on seemingly arbitrary nuance.

Phex spent most of the morning trying to understand and predict flaws. He also spent it avoiding eye contact with other contenders and trying to be smaller than he was.

Only one high cantor made it through by the time Phex's turn came around. Unable to determine why, Phex had no choice but to climb onto the dais and sing, no better prepared than he had been at the beginning.

Phex chose one of Errata's songs because he loved their style. Errata boasted a particularly strong low cantor, and they'd built many of their performances around her. If Phex were forced to pick a favorite godsong, it would be Orlol singing Errata's "Riverrun." So, that was what he sang.

"Name? Nomenclature? Gender?"

"Phex. Singular name, no extension. Male."

"One name? Like a god already," said his Dyesi, the one with purple eyes.

"It is a *grace's* name," objected Green, crests twitching.

"And we will test him for grace," replied Purple, firmly.

The crowd of wannabe gods murmured. No one had yet tested for more than one position.

"I'm here for cantor," Phex objected. He didn't like surprises.

Purple Dyesi's face speckled with opacity, which Phex suspected was smugness. "*You* will *also* test for grace."

Phex tried not to roll his eyes. "Dark or light?" Dark graces focused on interrupting godsong. Their movements were larger and broader, and their stances were held for longer. Light graces were all about rhythm – sharp pauses, complex footwork, short tumbles and tricks. Phex didn't think crudrat runs and flips really suited either role. But this Dyesi had seen him move. Maybe it would tell him.

No such luck. "Neither. I just want to watch you grace a dome."

Phex nodded. He suspected it had more to do with admiring his physical form than actually testing him. There was a certain covetousness about the purple-eyed Dyesi. It wanted to show off the little Sapien it had found.

"Can I touch it?" Phex asked.

"What?"

"The dome."

The three judges looked at each other, crests wiggling.

"Without causing damage." Phex clarified. "Can I climb

and push against the dome itself? Physically." At the cafe, he wasn't allowed to even clean the thing. There were divine specialists assigned for maintenance, even if it was only a cupola receiver. He got the impression that domes were delicate things.

"You want to use the dome itself for gracing," Purple clarified.

"Yes."

"That will be interesting. You may. But sing first."

So, Phex open his mouth and sang. It was odd. He'd only ever sung with a prerecorded pantheon on the dome above him. His solo voice sounded strange, projected alone at the two Dyesi on the dais.

He sang Orlol's part of "Riverrun," but it wasn't the same.

It wasn't right.

Of course, there was no high cantor harmonizing with him, no graces providing beat or break. But ignoring that, his actual voice didn't *sound* like Orlol's. Even when he really tried. She was emitting *cantor* – he was just… singing. By the end of the first verse, he decided to play rather than be annoyed by his own failure at mimicry. Phex let himself stretch some notes. When the high cantor role took point, he switched to singing that instead. He could go high – he just didn't enjoy it. His vocal cords had been triggered to give him a wide range. He let himself be flexible, taking unexpected pauses and pushing lyrics into the breaks. He enjoyed himself. Why not?

Phex thought he would find it embarrassing – everyone watching him sing in a language he did not know, using a skill he'd never been taught. But it didn't bother him at all. Even the fact that he was being judged by aliens against standards he could not comprehend. What did it matter? It was all just noise coming out of his mouth. He may have been forced to audition, but he wasn't the type to intentionally fail. He would do it, but on his terms.

It was fascinating to see how his voice affected the Dyesi sifters. Whenever they were in his line of sight, Phex could not resist staring at them.

He was causing that. Skinsift.

He was doing it. The vibrant swirls and blooms of brightness. The complex patterns and spikes of color. There were lots of pinks in Errata's pieces. His version was no different, yet the way it coiled over flesh and dome was distinct.

He was *creating* something unique.

Unlike with previous cantors, the judges didn't stop his audition.

So, Phex stopped himself after the second chorus. He was there under duress, after all. No point in giving them too much of what they wanted.

3

SOFTSKIN GRACE

"Did we tell you to end the song?"

"Have you not heard enough?" Phex stayed on the dais and stared down at the three Dyesi judges.

Navy looked at Purple. "His personality. Will it work?"

"You know we can only test *that* as a potential. Sifters, how did he feel?" asked Purple.

"Overly strong color," said one of the Dyesi on the dais.

"Dangerous pattern," said the other.

Phex was pretty darn certain neither was a compliment.

"I want to see him grace," said Green Eyes.

Navy gestured at Phex with an elegant six-fingered hand. "You will grace us now. What do we play for you?"

"This was your idea. Why don't you choose?" Phex registered his displeasure the only way he could.

"That is not how this works." Navy was clearly annoyed by Phex's attitude.

Phex took the easy option. "The same Errata song, then."

There was a brief pause, presumably while they loaded the dome.

Phex considered the two Dyesi sharing the dais with him.

They were now no longer something to watch and sing for –
they were something to avoid. They were physical elements
to become part of his movements, obstacles and props.

Orlol's low, throbbing cantor speared out, and the familiar
smooth magentas of "Riverrun" swirled over the dome. They
were playing the official recording.

Phex began to move.

Phex knew the basics of traditional Sapien dance forms
from his schooling on Attacon 7, but he instinctively fell back
on the blade-dodging of his youth. Once a crudrat, always a
crudrat.

This time, he ignored the cantor's part, although he
allowed himself to hum along, since that was what he did
when it played in the cafe. Instead, he moved with the grace's
beat, pretended that it was the rhythm of blades.

Back on the Wheel, the blades he ran were solid and
steady, the unchanging heartbeat of a space station. Dyesi
music wasn't like that. It shifted its cadence – slowed,
paused, sped up in prescribed patterns of threes and sixes and
nines. Nuanced in a way that appealed to the psyche. Addic-
tive to humans and aliens alike.

That beat was not reliable like the blades. Phex could get
himself into motion, running and flipping. He could sprint up
the side of the dome and twist as if he were dodging the sharp
edge of death. He could turn the two Dyesi on the dais into
phantom blades, moving around them as if they cut. But it
wasn't *right*. The dance of his youth was made for survival,
not entertainment.

It wasn't, in fact, a dance at all. It was speed and tricks.
Phex didn't know what to do with his arms, since during a
crudrat run, he used them to scoop crud and nothing else.
There was no way to move them that looked pretty.

He was able to change his foot pattern to match the music

sometimes. He pretended in his head that the blades changed their rhythm and modified his steps accordingly. But mostly, he needed momentum for his flips more than he needed timing.

It felt weird to put his feet and hands on the dome, but he did it. It was part of running the blades, to leap up and push off curved walls. Of course, the tunnels of his childhood were much smaller than this dome, but Phex had been much smaller then, too. He knew sometimes when he pushed off and landed that it broke the godsong, because he could not land on a beat. But he did land all his jumps and flips without falling, and mostly his feet hit the dais in cadence with the song, which he thought was pretty good for a first attempt.

As he had with cantor, Phex stopped partway through the song. He'd shown them all of his moves. He wasn't inclined to push, repeat, or damage himself for their entertainment.

The Dyesi judges showed no reaction. Phex had ended with one knee down, panting. He was definitely not as good as he had been as a child. He thought he'd been keeping himself fit with his daily runs, but apparently not.

The Dyesi signaled for the music to cut. The dome went grey and Phex stood up, sweating.

"That was no grace," said Navy.

"It was remarkable, though, in a weird way," objected Green.

Phex hid his amusement. That was a compliment. No other audition had gotten a compliment.

"Does it matter, if it has no actual grace to it?" Navy sounded annoyed, its crests flattened slightly.

"What is grace if it cannot turn to something new?"

"This is *too* new."

Phex was fascinated. Somehow, he'd never considered

that the Dyesi might argue with each other. Certainly not
over him.

"Grace or not, it must be counted as an asset. A unique
skill," Purple interrupted firmly.

"We take him for cantor, though," said Green.

"Yes," agreed the other two.

Purple said, "You are to stay, Phex." An order, not a
request.

Phex considered. It was midday and he was thirsty,
getting hungry as well. He thought the others would be too. A
few were quite small and fragile-looking – they obviously
needed a break and nourishment even if they'd only been
sitting and waiting. "Will you feed us?"

"Demanding as any god."

Phex crossed his arms. "We play this stage at your will."

"Payment in kind?" Purple looked amused.

Phex was no one's joke. "So, you will sing and dance for
us now, Dyesi?" There was insult there because everyone
knew that among all the gods, the Dyesi were the least effective graces and they *never* sang.

All six Dyesi in the room emitted the puffed breath and
silent open-mouthed laughs of their species.

Apparently, Phex's annoyance was hilarious.

To Dyesi.

Purple said, "You *are* a funny one. We will break now and
provide food. It is interesting, Phex, that you have the name
of a grace. Do not worry, if you become a god, we can always
change your name."

Phex frowned. His name was the only thing he'd kept. Or,
to be more precise, it was the only thing that had stuck with
him all along. He supposed the Dyesi could give him a
second one – in many cultures, people had more than one
name. But he refused to let *Phex* go and surprised himself

with his own vehemence. He hadn't realized he felt possessive over anything. Let alone something as banal as a name.

"Fine." There was no point arguing over an uncertain
future.

The others still waiting to audition and the one who, like
him, had been told to wait all stood and stretched.

Phex made to leave the dais.

One of the Dyesi sifters stopped him. "It was a pleasure to
risk you singing my skin."

The other one nodded. "Softskins like us rarely get the joy
of color from a god."

"I am not a god."

"You have their beauty."

"Your confidence in me is flattering." What else could
Phex say?

The second one crested at him. "You have the talent but
not the ambition?"

Phex considered. "Must I want it?" He looked at the
eager faces of the others milling around below. Scared but
hungry for fame, or music, or art, or worship. He knew
without looking in a mirror that his face showed none of
those things. Hungry for lunch at the moment, of course, but
nothing else.

"No, but it helps," said the one who had given him the
compliment.

"Where there is no love, at least you look the part," said
the other.

"Will that be enough?" Phex wondered.

"We Dyesi draw no distinction between love and beauty."

Phex nodded, filed that bit of information away.

"Thank you for sharing the dome with me," he said,
because they had just been his partners in cantor and grace,
and it seemed only polite.

The two Dyesi's cheeks flushed with clouds of embarrassment. "We are only softskins, but thank you."

That was the second time that term had been used. Phex had not heard it before. "What does *softskin* mean?"

"Oh. That we are sensitive to sound but not beautiful about it."

"I see." That answered Phex's initial question. It was not the dome that made the performance lackluster – it was the Dyesi who transmitted to it.

Not knowing what else to do, he gave a little bow and left the dais.

Lunch was an awkward thing. Phex did not know what to do with his hands or the right phrases to say when there was no cafe counter between him and his peers. They also seemed wary of him, for some reason. At school, no one really noticed him. Here, they noticed but pretended not to.

The Dyesi provided basic ration cubes designed for ease of digestion across species and high nutritional value, which, therefore, were appealing to no species anywhere, ever. Phex had grown up on the Wheel version, so he did not mind them. He ate his fill and made sure to drink plenty of water.

Even when he had to touch them in the press for cubes or water, the others jerked away from him. He supposed they regarded him with envy as one of the two to make it through. Phex had never been envied for anything before. The other blessed Sapien gave him an inviting smile, but Phex did not know how to make friends. He nodded at her but ate by himself and was grateful when auditions resumed, for she promptly fell asleep and he didn't have to worry about her eyes on the side of his neck.

By the end of the day, it was still only him and that one girl.

They ate a few more ration cubes for dinner, and then they were both asked to sing again. This time, different songs. They were allowed ones they knew well but would not have had a chance to practice. Not that Phex had practiced the first one. He was assigned another Errata piece where Orlol's part dominated. The girl was given another Tillam song to test her high cantor. Phex thought that was unfair. Missit's parts were notoriously difficult, and she should never have chosen Tillam in the first place.

On an apparent lark, the Dyesi then had Phex sing the same Tillam piece in Missit's role.

Phex loved Missit's singing, but it was much harder to imitate than Orlol's. Orlol's voice, like Phex's, was clear and true but it wasn't *special*. Missit had sugar syrup pouring from his mouth, warmed to elevate any partner. Missit's voice was unique where Phex's voice was simply perfect – manufactured perfect, no less. Missit's voice rolled and soothed. He shaped his cantor with an emotional quality Phex could not hope to imitate. So he didn't. He sang the part by contrast, making it pristine, precise, and sparkling clean. He sang Missit's cantor correct and exact. It was a different performance and it was not as good. Phex knew it never would be.

"Interesting," said Navy at the end.

"Is there no love in him for high cantor, or is it Missit's voice that breaks his spirit?" wondered Green.

"Missit brings out the worst and the best in equal measure. We cannot guess at Sapien motivation."

The three Dyesi exchanged looks.

Finally, Navy said, "We will take you both. Come, sit with us. We have contracts to discuss."

Phex balked. It was one thing to force him to audition,

especially as, in the end, he'd almost enjoyed himself. But it was quite another thing to force him to leave the static safety of this moon and his daily routine of school and cafe. For what? Celebrity? Notoriety? Fame? He'd never wanted any such a thing. Plenty of people had left the audition crying today, hearts sore for a dream that Phex had never even contemplated. Yet there the Dyesi sat, offering it to him instead. Phex, who knew better than most that to want a thing did not automatically mean you got to have it.

Then again, Phex *had* stayed. Stayed until the very end.

So, he sat down in front of them, still feeling judged.

"What now?" he asked.

"You sign a contract and come with me," said Purple.

"Where?"

"Home. Back to Dyesid Prime. Where else?"

"To become a god?"

"To become a potential god. To train and compete with others for the chance. And then to test and try to form a pantheon. And then, maybe, if you are good enough, if you give beauty, if you match with others, to become a demigod."

"And if I don't make it, like most don't, what then?"

"We send you back here, no different than you are now."

Phex thought that was unlikely. Oh, not that they would return him. But that he would remain unchanged by the process.

But did he fear change?

Phex ran his tongue over his teeth. Dry. He hadn't been hydrating properly. He was tired. He suspected that was part of it. Easier to sign contracts without reading them properly when tired. But then again, those who really wanted godhood probably asked no questions. From the corner of his eye he saw the girl already signing. Then she stood, bowed in gratitude to the green-eyed Dyesi, and left the dome. Going, Phex assumed, to hug her waiting family, to celebrate a victory, to pack for an adventure.

Phex really wasn't sure he wanted it, but what else was he doing with his life?

He stared deep into the large purple eyes of possibility.

The Dyesi wanted him.

True, they looked at him like he was something to be owned. But they also looked at him like he had *value*.

No one had ever wanted Phex before. And these aliens were offering him the chance to become wanted not just by them but by millions. That had to count for something.

Phex nodded. "Okay. Let's talk terms. What do I get?"

This startled all three Dyesi. They became crested and speckled with confusion.

"The chance to be a god, of course."

Phex shook his head. "Even gods need food and a place to sleep. Here on this moon, I have my own pod, three rationed meals a day, and mandated work to earn a little something and give back to the society that took me in. At the very least, you must match that."

"Such a small thing as this keeps you from godhood?" Navy was clearly confused.

Phex tried not to be upset. "My survival is a *small thing*?"

"Oh, he is angry. How remarkable."

Purple, his advocate of sorts, seemed a little more comfortable with Sapien foibles. It explained, "The divinity feeds you regularly and with a range of food suitable to a variety of preferences and constitutions. We can supply Sapien ration cubes if you prefer. We provide accommodation, hygiene chambers, a team of medics and aestheticists, and acolytes to see to all your daily needs. You will want for nothing. It is in our best interest to keep you as fit and healthy as possible."

That Phex understood. Gods were highly trained and highly valued for how they looked as well as what they did. The divinity would be invested in keeping them nutritionally bolstered and well rested for the sake of fluffy hair and vibrant skin.

"Am I paid as well?" He would, after all, have to give up his cafe job.

Purple wordlessly swiped the contract around and pointed to a number.

"Per year?" asked Phex, surprised.

"Per month," the alien corrected him.

Phex tried not to show his shock. Why hadn't they said so from the beginning? Why threaten his job and his boss and her livelihood when they could buy his loyalty at two times a month what he made in a year? Were they crazy? Of course he would do it. Phex had come to Attacon 7 a child with nothing but the rags on his back, burned and stinking from exposure to toxins. He wasn't a proud person. He would do almost anything to survive. He had done it. Money was, in the end, his best chance of survival. Why had they not simply said that the divinity paid well? Even if he only lasted a few months as a potential, he would be able to save up quite a bit.

"Oh, I'll sign," said Phex.

The Dyesi did not show joy or gratitude, not so far as Phex could see.

Purple looked at the contract screen. "Let us fill this in, then. We have all your initial information from the audition. But we need more for your travel authorization. This contract is for one year, Dyesi time. If you level up to demigod status, we renew for three years. If you attain pantheon status, your god contract will be for six years."

Navy added, watching him closely, "Of course we increase remuneration with each level achieved."

Phex guarded his reaction this time so as not to appear greedy or too easily swayed by money. He only nodded.

"You could be away from your family for a very long time," the alien cautioned, testing him. Different type of blade.

Phex tapped the tabletop near the contract screen. "Does it not say? No family."

Purple tilted its head, scanned the information in front of it. "Interesting. Very well, then, shall we proceed?"

Phex waited.

"What's your status?"

"Status?"

"Here on this little moon? Were you born here? If not, what's your planet of origin? Are you a resident, visitor, or temporary occupant?"

"Oh. Refugee."

"What?" All three Dyesi stared at him, their huge eyes intrigued.

"Refugee? Why? Is it affiliative?" Green asked.

"What?" Phex hadn't known that there were nuances to refugee status.

"Were you escaping persecution? Discrimination? Was it political? Religious?"

Phex considered how to classify what the Wheel thought of him. "Cultural, I guess. My status in my home quadrant is nonexistent."

"Well, of course. You are here, not there."

"No. I literally do not exist to them. I am not person in that culture."

"Are you a cyborg or a carborg?" The Dyesi didn't look disgusted, merely intrigued. Not everyone had Attacon's abhorrence for extensive body mods.

Phex shook his head. "No."

The green-eyed Dyesi scooted over to read Purple's screen. "Oh, I see. Mark him as planetless."

"But that is for those whose home worlds have been destroyed," objected Purple.

Green pointed at the screen. "He's Wheel-born. See there? They have no home world that we know of."

"How peculiar. He is pretty and physically skilled, plus his range is admirable. Should we send missionaries to this Wheel? If he proves to be an asset and survives training, of course. Should I make a note?" Purple sounded covetous.

Phex was about to warn them that that was a *very* bad idea, but the green-eyed Dyesi, who clearly had some passing familiarity with the Wheel, said, "No. The culture is considered nonviable on the basis of extreme xenophobia and highly violent tendencies. It is impossible to make contact to recruit. They kill aliens on sight. No one goes into the Wheel. No one comes out of it, either. Our potential god here is an aberrant."

Phex knew that somewhere in the galaxy, there must be others who had escaped. Perhaps not many. But he was living proof that it was possible. It had involved toxic-waste disposal units and alien scavengers who shouldn't have been where they found him. Certainly a good dose of luck and chance, but still he couldn't be entirely alone in a Wheel-less universe, could he? But it wasn't worth arguing with Dyesi on the subject, so he remained silent.

Purple moved them along. "*Planetless* it is."

Green said, "It may be difficult to alter your status to potential god. Normally, we recruit under work or performance permits, allowing the potential to maintain nationality and status with their home sector. As a refugee, you have none. Have you a guardian?"

"No. I was deemed capable of autonomy as an introverted isolate without need for family."

"Your status is both refugee and emancipated minor?"

That sounded close enough. "Yes."

The Dyesi looked at each other, uncomfortable for some reason.

"That is sad."

"We are sorry for you."

Phex was confused. What an odd reaction. Aliens were so strange.

"When do you legally gain whole personhood?" asked Navy.

Phex knew those regs by heart. "Attacon triggers adulthood based on education level and emotional maturity."

"Then are you a legal adult already?"

Phex was a little flattered by that question. "I have not yet completed basic education. I have about three Attacon months left."

The Dyesi scrolled through his records. "You are a good student, though. Your marks seem solid, not brilliant, but passing."

Phex agreed. He did enough to get by because it was required of him. That was how he played out his whole existence. Expend only the necessary energy. Conserve the rest, hoard resources in case he needed to escape again.

"Then who has the authority to release you into Dyesi care?" asked Purple.

"Care?" Phex was offended by the term.

"Stewardship?" suggested the green-eyed Dyesi.

"Shouldn't you say *employment*?" Phex asked, perhaps injudiciously.

"You think becoming a god is work?" Purple was… what? Affronted? Amused?

"Is it not?"

The three Dyesi all crested their ears at him. Maybe a little offended, but also intrigued by the notion.

"It is beauty and art and love and passion and metamorphosis," said the Dyesi with the navy eyes.

"And a *job*," pressed Phex.

"I suppose, from your perspective, it might appear so."

"When Del hired me, she talked to my monitor, so why not do the same?" Phex suggested, a little annoyed by how long this was taking. Now that it was decided he would be leaving Attacon 7, he needed to give Del his notice, pack, and then quietly freak out for the rest of the night.

He tapped his ident band and flicked it to transfer his monitor's contact info. He'd had the same government rep since assuming residency but had contacted them only a handful of times. He worked hard to be self-sufficient. He thought if he talked to them too much, he might get noticed in a bad way.

The Dyesi pinged them instantly. The monitor looked annoyed until they realized who was contacting them.

"Yes, Dyesi?" Galactic Formal and full respect. "What can I do on this bright day for the divinity?"

"We would like to recruit a minor from your jurisdiction."

"You hardly need my help with that."

"This one is a refugee."

"Ah. Well. That is strange. Record-locator number?"

The Dyesi transmitted Phex's information.

"Oh, yes. Our crudrat. To your taste, is he? How interesting. You know the Wheel-born are odd, right? What am I saying? I'm talking to the gods' blessed Dyesi. You define *odd*."

Purple ignored all side talk. "What steps do we take to secure Phex's work permits or performance rights?"

"I should imagine it is the standard contract for your lot."

"Yes, we have one prepared. But who signs for the releasing nationality when he is a minor and has no planet?"

"Good question. We've never had a refugee recruited by the divinity before. Let me consult with my superior."

Silence descended.

Phex looked around.

The Dyesi were all still crested at him.

"Sorry to be a bother," he said, because he thought it was the right thing to say.

"It is fine," said Navy. "It is good to know what to do under these circumstances. In case it happens again."

"It would be a lot easier if you recruited adults for godhood, wouldn't it?" suggested Phex.

"We tried at the beginning. The pantheons were not strong enough. Personalities were too fixed. They did not harmonize or hold steady."

"Nor were they pretty enough," Green added. "Youth is better. Especially with Sapiens."

That struck Phex as a little creepy.

The screen buzzed with the monitor's reappearance. "He can't be released on a work contract of any kind. Not to go off moon."

"Can we buy his indenture?"

"Refugees cannot be indentured under the Intergalactic Antislavery Act. And Attacon does not allow for the indenture of minors under any circumstances, anyway."

"Impasse," said the Dyesi.

Phex considered. "Can my refugee status be transferred?"

The monitor did not seem to care that the refugee being discussed had involved himself in his own future. "Is Dyesid Prime cleared to take interplanetary refugees?"

"Yes, but none have elected to go there," Purple replied.

The monitor made a humming noise of amused agree-

ment. "Dyesid Prime is in the middle of nowhere with underground habitation, megafauna, and Class Nine surface danger.
All your trade is tailored to the entertainment industry. It's not
exactly paradise for an ordinary citizen who desires a normal
life."

The three Dyesi flattened their crests, clearly offended by
the monitor's bluntness.

Phex was amused. He didn't know anything about the
Dyesi home world, but he did know most aliens were proud
of their planets. Attacon 7, being a mere moon, tended to
have attitude on the subject.

The monitor consulted something. "Are you sure, kid?
The Dyesi are odd about keeping Sapiens."

Phex felt a thud of fear. Risk. "Can I come back here even
if I'm their refugee?"

"So long as they cover expenses and you aren't a dead-
weight to our society."

Phex looked at the Dyesi opposite him.

"Resettlement is in the contract," said Navy.

Phex resolved to read that part carefully.

The monitor was in a hurry. "If you're decided, do you
remember what to say?"

Phex did. He'd memorized the words when he first
arrived on Attacon 7. They hadn't wanted him, but they
needed colonists, and he had no criminal record. It was the
first time Phex had to recite a vow. He memorized it so hard,
it became a mantra he never forgot. Like a favorite godsong.

This time, he was sitting with iridescent blue aliens
instead of elderly disinterested immigration officials. But the
words were the same.

"I would like to formally request asylum of the Dyesi and
their planet, Dyesid Prime. I will work to ensure I am no
burden to your resources. I will strive to become a

contributing member of your culture, should I be offered the privilege of citizenship. Until such a time, may I please take status as refugee in your sector?"

He didn't get all the words exactly right, but he hoped it was good enough.

The purple-eyed Dyesi's face speckled opaque, whitish clouds sliding across its cheeks and neck. Phex wondered if that meant he had made the alien unhappy or embarrassed or if that was smugness. It turned to its green-eyed companion. Phex got the impression Green was a kind of divine legal representative.

"Is the divinity authorized to speak for the home world in this?" asked the monitor.

"It is our destiny to recruit," Green said. "It will clear with the imagoes. I will ensure it. They will appreciate the idea that if he makes it through, he'll last forever."

Phex didn't like the implication of that. It sounded proprietary. But it was also, apparently, done.

The monitor on the screen said, "Refugee transfer complete. I will send it to the Dyesi embassy for authorization. They will need to issue his travel permits and make his new status official."

"No need," said Green. "I carry the necessary authority."

"Very well. Show me the seal."

Green flicked its finger ident.

"Approved. I trust that all transport costs, filing fees, and resettlement payments will be absorbed by the divinity?"

"Of course. You understand that divine gag restrictions are now in effect?" asked Purple.

"Yes, but as a refugee, his status and location are not a matter of public record, anyway. Do not fret, I will say nothing. I know how your lot gets." The monitor glanced back at

Phex. "Congratulations, refugee. Good luck with the whole god thing. Have a nice trip."

The monitor buzzed off.

Phex was left wondering what had just happened. He had shown up to do what? To audition. To be a performer. To put on a show. And now he had been passed off to aliens.

The one across from him slowly blinked its huge purple eyes. "You are ours now, Wheel-child."

Navy added, "We always take care of our own."

Phex wasn't certain if he felt threatened or comforted, so all he said was "Thank you."

4

ALL ALIENS GREAT & SMALL

Transport to the Dyesid sector was excessively dull. Phex slept most of the way. He was good like that – able to sleep anywhere. His travel companions included the Dyesi with the purple eyes and the Sapien girl from Attacon. But they stopped to pick up other potentials in other parts of the galaxy as they went.

The others were nervous with each other but chatty. They even tried talking to Phex. But he had no information worth offering, either about their situation or himself. In the case of the first, they were probably better informed than he. And with the second, he knew from past experience his history caused others discomfort. Better to say nothing. So, even when he wasn't asleep, he mostly pretended that he was.

It probably took them a week to flit between stars, but Phex lost track of time in the haze of FTL and stasis. At some point, Purple left them and a sanctified acolyte took over. Phex felt oddly bereft.

Dyesid Prime was a ringed world surrounded by satellite moons. The planet itself was rough – small and fierce with enormous vegetation and massive destructive dracohors roaming the habitable zone. The Dyesi occupied a vast network of underground caves that had become both their major cities and the original domes. Much of the population still lived there, but acolytes had long since migrated to the satellite rings, particularly the three largest moons.

At some point, those moons became artificially linked with tubes and bridges. The Divine Three: Divinity 12, Divinity 24, and Divinity 36. Dome-covered and diminutive, they made a busy hive of entertainment and the associated tech industry, housing some thirty million Dyesi acolytes who promoted gods – their main export – with devout fervor and strict discipline.

Phex was a little disappointed to learn that he and his fellow potentials would never get to visit Dyesid Prime. It would have been his first planet. His first feel of real gravity. His first breath of natural air. Phex supposed if he became a god, he would get to visit other worlds and foreign domes on tour. Apparently, some part of him looked forward to planets full of aliens. He didn't like that part. His own optimism had a bitter taste.

Phex and his five travel companions disembarked onto a dock, only to be joined by some two dozen more potentials. An acolyte ordered them, in Galactic Formal, to stick together and follow any instructions, and then added in a curt manner, "Welcome, potential gods, to Divinity 36."

They were loaded onto a ground crawler, which transported them across the moon to their housing facility. The topography was uninspiring, moondust and asteroid aesthetic. There was a massive atmosphere and gravity bubble around Divinity 36, just like on Attacon 7. In fact, the only thing that seemed special or unique was the tube system connecting the three moons, which looked like nothing so much as a mixed metallic, plastic, and ceramic noodle, bubble-wrapped and clumsy.

Bored by the moon itself, Phex took the opportunity to assess the other potentials.

The Dyesi were the easiest to spot – twelve iridescent blue-tinged heads, crests alert and interested – potential sifters. Being younger, these were mostly about Phex's size. Like the older ones he'd met, these had the general body shape of S-class Sapien, what Phex had learned as a child to call *human*, although Attacon 7 had told him not to use that word. Except that the Dyesi were not S-class – they were leaner, stretched-looking, with graceful bones, and joints that seemed to bend in various directions, giving them their liquid way of moving.

Eleven Sapiens sat around Phex, all cantors. They were a range of S-classes, some more familiar to Phex than others.

A dozen assorted Hominins made up the grace contingent. They varied wildly in appearance, and Phex found them the most interesting. These the Wheel of his childhood had called *alien* and *monster*, and Attacon had instructed him sharply never to use those words. Phex still did sometimes, but only in his head when he forgot the rules.

Everyone looked travel-worn and nervous, even the Dyesi.

The building they drew up to had three columns of multiple stories, with a bean-pod-shaped roof composed of three massive domes. Each dome was big enough to hold an actual revival.

The potentials climbed out of the crawler and collected their various luggage. A few, like Phex, traveled only with small packs. He suspected they too came from moons or space stations where people simply did not collect stuff.

They assembled in a large, chattering group. Well, mostly

chattering. Phex didn't partake of chatter. He maintained an aura of impassive aloofness, and no one approached him. The Dyesi potentials glanced at him with interest, and one of the graces stared openly, but his fellow Sapiens ignored him.

A crowd of reporters lined either side of the entrance, wrist beamers at the ready in case some great god worthy of their attention happened by. Sacerdotes, priors, other high-up acolytes, and even the occasional demigod walked quickly in and out. The new batch of potentials was of little interest to the reporters, though a few of Phex's companions primped and smiled as if they should be.

Phex glanced around to see if he recognized anyone.

"Oh, *my gods*! Is that Tillam? They stopped their tour, right? Are they home?" The girl from Attacon 7 sidled up to Phex. Her name was Gemma – he'd learned this during their transport together. She was *very excited* because she'd wanted to be a god *her whole life*. She liked arbitrary word emphasis and she blinked a lot. Phex found her extremely annoying.

"I absolutely *worship* Tillam."

"I know," said Phex. Because she'd chosen to sing a Tillam song for her audition, even though Missit's part was obviously too difficult for her.

"Missit is *my* belief."

Phex didn't say anything to that because of course she believed in Missit. Half the galaxy believed in Missit. Gemma obviously didn't have an original bone in her body. He looked away from her so as not to provide any kind of encouragement, but she would keep talking.

"This is so exciting! I can't believe we'll be living in the same building as *real live gods*."

What did she expect, dead gods? What an antiquated notion. Phex sighed and helped her pull her massive case across the road toward the entrance.

A new voice said, "We will not be on the same floor or even in the same section. They separate potentials from demigods, and demigods from great gods. It is not like we will actually run into any of them." One of the potential sifters was talking to them, and being Dyesi, it should know.

"Hi, I'm Gemma," said Gemma brightly.

Phex was not so stupid as to hand out his name to an alien without formality.

The Dyesi seemed appropriately taken aback by Gemma's rudeness. Its crests flattened.

"Hello, Sapien Gemma," it said but did not offer up its name in return.

Phex took a moment to be grateful for the fact that he'd been in food service and therefore trained in alien first-comment.

Gemma didn't seem to notice she'd committed a socio-cultural gaffe, just prattled on. "It's *too* bad. I would love to meet them in person. Do you think they smell like normal people? Gods, I mean."

"Smell." The Dyesi was confused. "What does smell have to do with *anything*?"

"Just wondering. Do you know how we will be housed? Do we get solo pods? Do we share with others? Are we grouped by—?"

Phex stopped listening. He didn't need speculation. Presumably, they would find out soon enough. He let the poor Dyesi deal with Gemma and refocused his attention. The acolytes at the front were consulting with one another. The crowd of reporters, now surrounding them, swayed and shifted, melding in with the potentials, more annoyed by the size of their group than actively interested in them. Phex found this unsettling.

"Are we going inside anytime soon?" asked a sweet, warm voice.

A potential was standing next to Phex wearing a full-coverage cape, dark glasses, and a rather silly hat. Photo sensitivity, perhaps? Divinity 36 was very bright.

Phex didn't answer because he didn't know.

"Hi," said the newcomer. Not introducing himself.

Phex arched his brows at the pretty voice, probably a high-cantor potential. He seemed very young. "Hi, kid."

The Sapien boy grinned hugely at that. His teeth were very white, and he was painted or tinted very gold, like a god already.

They were instructed by acolytes in how to greet a space Dyesi-style. Apparently, potentials could not enter a divine building without according it all due honor.

The acolytes then gestured for the group to follow them inside.

Phex and his caped companion hovered near the back. As they moved, Phex noticed an enormous alien lurking in the crowd of bystanders. It stared in their direction, focused on Phex's new friend.

Phex's stomach dropped. Its mouth was slightly open, red tongue licking again and again over wide lips. It violently pushed a reporter aside and lurched in their direction. Its hands were out and grasping. It did not look sane. Fanaticism had crumbled its face into avarice.

It was one of the *fixed*.

Phex moved fast, interposing himself between the caped boy and the monster. He modified his speed by instinct and threw an arm around the kid's back, guiding him forcefully toward the center of the group, where they could use the other potentials as shields.

But the fixed were nothing if not persistent. Fixed did not respond to social cues. Fixed did not see *no* in body language.

The boy felt slight but strong under Phex's arm. But his shoulders were stiff and his body tense – he was frightened.

The fixed lurched again, jerky and desperate. Mouth wide and breath loud. It broke free of the crowd and got far too close.

Phex had no patience for this. He kicked out fast and hard, hitting what amounted to, apparently, a kneecap.

The alien stumbled back.

Phex hustled his new companion forward, assessing him out of the corner of his eye. There was something familiar about the boy's face shape, what little Phex could see of it, and certainly his voice was *special*. And the skin was very perfectly metallic gold. But it was the way the kid walked that triggered Phex's memory.

The thing that made Missit a god was his voice. But the thing that made Missit unique was the way he moved. A Sapien who'd spent most of his life among the Dyesi, Missit no longer moved like a Sapien at all. He had that oily-smooth Dyesi walk – the skeletal manifestation of iridescent skin. There were Sapiens who were elegant, but it was never the same as true Dyesi elegance. Except in Missit.

Which meant that Phex had his arm around a major god.

A very stupid god who had, for some reason, shunned his bodyguards in favor of trying to sneak inside his own home with a bunch of dumb potentials. As if potentials weren't *also* likely to be worshipers. As if a potential couldn't go mad with proximity and obsession just like anyone else.

Annoyed, Phex practically dragged the god inside the building. The fixed couldn't follow them there. Security forcibly prevented that.

He let the god go as soon as it became clear Missit was no

longer in any danger and then took up position shielding him from the other potentials by virtue of size and unpleasant expression.

Missit muttered a greeting phrase to the space similar to the one they'd just been instructed to learn, but different enough to distinguish him as no mere potential, Phex suspected.

Phex wanted to give Missit a lecture on security and taking threats seriously. But Missit was obviously a capricious god. He was now smiling cheerfully up at Phex, as if being threatened by an insane alien were a pleasant experience. His grin was endearingly crooked, which Phex found extremely upsetting.

So, Phex just repeated the Dyesi greeting phrase in a grumpy tone.

"You're very protective," said the golden voice.

Phex scowled. He had no idea why he'd done that. Probably some weird instinct activated by proximity to the divine.

"And you're clearly an idiot," Phex replied. If even Phex, who wasn't a worshiper, knew how dangerous the fixed could be, surely a long-standing god like Missit had tons of first-hand experience.

Missit pouted at him. Even his lips had been made metallic, or was that wet-look makeup? Troublesome, like one of those teenage brats at Phex's cafe. Phex bet, given half a chance, that Missit would steal his own statue.

That idea made him smile. And Phex never smiled.

"Oh," said Missit, his breath hitched.

They now stood to one side of the group of potentials, which had assembled in a large lobby space. Phex continued to shield Missit but moved them both subtly so that the god had access to a side hallway and could go away and do whatever gods did when they were at home.

Missit, however, appeared to enjoy pretending to be a potential too much and just stood there, grinning at him.

Phex gestured with his chin at the hallway, as much as to say *Shove off*.

The god shook his head and hissed slightly.

Did this kid have no sense of self-preservation? Phex supposed he owed Missit respect, even in his own head. Missit was older in age and his senior professionally, but he looked like a baby, and he was behaving like a child. And no alien had yet been able to read Phex's thoughts.

From the front of the group, the acolytes began announcing dorm assignments. Apparently, all twelve potentials of each type roomed together. Phex was appalled at the idea. Twelve artistically minded singers who wanted to be celebrities, sharing one living space? A travesty was about to take place on the sixth floor of the middle building.

"Are you going to join us there too?" Phex asked. Perhaps that would snap the god out of his grinning stupor.

It did. Missit's eyes widened. "Oh. Uh. Yeah. No, I'm this way." He darted off down the hall, presumably toward another set of elevators. The cape flapped out behind him but didn't disguise the Dyesi elegance of his limbs.

What an odd encounter.

Phex was left shaking his head in exasperation. "Weirdo," he muttered under his breath, for his own satisfaction.

A fierce-looking cyborg with a military air and a glower to rival Phex's was now standing where Missit had recently been. The metal of this cyborg's skin was *real* metal, not tinted flesh, but there were also panels of ceramic, plastics, and silica tech. Expensive mods, powerful, and placed each where they would do the most good in a fight, creating a body that was a patchwork of physical prowess. Phex's own skin prickled in aching respect.

"Where'd he go?" growled the cyborg.

"Lost something, have you?" Phex could be cheeky too.

Missit's bodyguard grunted at him.

"Does that a lot, does he?"

The cyborg grunted again.

Phex gestured down the hallway.

The bodyguard gave him a funny half-salute and trotted after.

———

As a crudrat, Phex had owned one set of clothing, relieved himself in waste ducts and gutters, and stripped down without shame among other crudrats so they might tend to his injuries. Modesty and privacy were the privilege of the wealthy and the elite.

On Attacon 7, he'd lived in a pod big enough to hold him, his bed, and a set of shelves. There'd been a private hygiene box, slightly too small for his frame, that efficiently dealt with all biological needs and that he'd regarded as a luxury. Each day, he left that pod fully dressed and returned to it the same way.

Apparently not so on Divinity 36.

The potentials were allowed very little time to settle into their room, which was comprised of one large living space plus kitchen and separate hygiene facilities. There were pod-like beds set into the wall that offered some measure of privacy via thick, oily-looking, green curtains. *Everything* was communal except those bed niches.

Anthropologists hypothesized that because the Dyesi had no obvious secondary sex characteristics, they had no concept of body shame. Their groin areas were usually covered by something simple – a short skirt or loincloth – but skinsift combined with the capacity for controlled body temperature meant they rarely wore more than that. Out of common courtesy, they wore local apparel when visiting other cultures, and some Dyesi covered themselves with robes, but the majority were mostly naked most of the time. Anyone who worshiped the divinity already knew this. They saw it under the dome regularly.

Few potentials seemed to have realized how this might directly impact them. Apparently, there was some panic over the fact that the hygiene facilities were communal.

Phex had known he would have to learn the Dyesi language. He had not thought much on other aspects of Dyesi society like food preparation, sleep schedules, cleanliness, or modesty – but he was not surprised.

He threw his pack into the bed niche nearest the door, because he liked to be close to exits, and glared at anyone who looked like they might object. He was intrigued by the kitchen, having never had access to one before, but didn't go inside it.

For a species that eschewed clothing, the Dyesi used a remarkable number of textiles in their decoration. In addition to the curtains over the sleeping niches, doorways were also covered by drapes, and walls decorated with fiber art. There were a few little tables scattered about and several stools at the kitchen counter made of woven plant fiber, but otherwise, the chairs and couches were puffy, pillowish things into which one had to cast oneself and hope for the best – like the furniture version of a trust fall. Pillows and blankets lay everywhere, as if someone had reminded the Dyesi many times over that Sapiens were delicate creatures who easily got bruised and cold. Most everything was coordinated in blues and greens and woven in patterns clearly inspired by the domes. It gave the whole place an aura of plant-based softness. Phex wondered if Dyesi fiber art was generally influenced by skinsift or if this was a consequence of Divinity 36 being a center of worship.

The entrance to their dorm had no door, only yet another thick fabric flap. Phex wondered if this was why the Dyesi had a tradition of spoken words upon entering a space – it was a means of announcing oneself.

One large window at the far side of the kitchen looked out over the street they'd arrived on and the lunar city beyond. Dyesi architecture, at least on this moon, seemed predominantly round and organic but also somewhat crude, rough-hewn from the rocky surface, monochromatic and minimalist. Clearly, the Dyesi aesthetic and obsession with beauty did not extend to their cities.

One of the potentials made the mistake of sitting in a couch puff. He sank fast, flailed indelicately, and needed help getting out.

The acolyte who accompanied them huffed in amusement. "You will learn to love them, very comfortable."

"If you say so," replied the potential, mussed and embarrassed.

The acolyte gave them no time to do more than assess the space, drop their bags, and get nearly eaten by a couch.

"Medical screenings now," it ordered.

Obediently, they all followed it back out into the hall.

They were taken to a waiting area. About half of them remembered the spoken phrase required to enter. The other half were made to leave and come back in until they got it right. Phex used the same phrase Missit used when entering the building, presuming the same pronouns applied to him. Unless gods had different pronouns, in which case he was self-aggrandizing.

Shortly after, three names were announced, and it became

clear that those three were expected to go into their medical exam together and get naked.

This came as an additional shock to the potentials. Except to Phex, who was just amused. Perhaps because he found all cultural discomfort somewhat entertaining. He was grateful not to be in the first group, though.

Those three returned some half hour later looking a bit shellshocked.

Phex was called with the second group.

Inside, standing next to a medical chair, Phex stripped without hesitation. Not that he was accustomed to group exhibitionism or medical exams – it was just that there was a principle in play. He refused to be shy like other Sapiens.

"Are you okay?" asked one of the others.

Phex looked down at himself, confused. Same body he'd always had, no weird rashes or anything out of the ordinary.

"Yes."

"But you have, you know…"

Phex didn't know. "What?" He looked again. From what he'd learned in school, his genitalia matched to that of other Sapien biological males – annoying extra floppy bits.

"Scars."

Phex shrugged. He ran the blades. Scars happened. He supposed these Sapiens weren't crudrats, but it couldn't be *that* weird. Human skin was delicate and damaged easily.

"Doesn't everyone?" he asked, not actually curious.

"Not really," said the potential cantor, looking embarrassed for Phex, his own body smooth and blemish-free.

"We won't tell," added the other.

"Thank you?" said Phex, confused but accepting.

A Sapien medic gave him an amused look, gestured him into the exam chair, then dialed it into position. There were other medics and technicians, and one Dyesi acolyte supervising everything. The medic gave Phex's body a cursory glance, then beckoned the acolyte over.

The Dyesi glided to them and bent to look at Phex's skin.

Phex had a number of small nicks and cuts, which were now just faint whitish lines. But that wasn't what caught everyone's interest. He also had three big scars – rough, raised striations, stretched and dark-tinged at the edges. He'd never been a very good crudrat, and these proved it. He was lucky not to have lost limb or life.

The acolyte's gentle touch was startling. Phex wasn't accustomed to being touched and never when naked. The Dyesi traced the largest scar on Phex's side with its sixth finger, followed the rough texture down over Phex's ribs. It wasn't care or pity, just curiosity. Phex raised his right arm to show his other scar underneath.

"I have a third one on my left shoulder blade." His back was pressed to the chair.

The medic apprised the acolyte. "Blade wounds. Deep and old. Large enough to have been stitched, stapled, or sealed at the time, but these weren't tended correctly. They should have been repaired into invisibility at the time." She turned back to Phex. "It will be difficult to fade them completely now." She returned to setting up her machine.

"Were you a warrior of some kind?" the acolyte asked.

"No. They're from cleaning the blades of an air-filtration system."

The Dyesi speckled white along the cheeks. "This is from some kind of *work*?"

Phex supposed that was one way to think of it. "When I was a child."

"Child labor?" The acolyte was not pleased.

Phex thought that was rich, coming from aliens who actively recruited youngsters from other species to perform in their entertainment industry. Of the thirty-six who'd arrived with Phex, he would have labeled most of them still children and all of them younger than he was. Missit had entered the divinity at age ten.

Phex said simply, "Yes."

"An injury on the job was not considered sufficient grounds for adequate skin repair?"

Phex remembered every one of his slashes. The flip that he'd mis-landed when his shoulder met the blade. The late reach behind his head that caused the one on his arm. The not-quite dodge that resulted in the rib wound. He remembered what it was like to bleed, how the pain was different in each spot. He'd been so angry at himself for the mistake, for the damage the blood did to his meager clothing. He'd had to beg a fellow crudrat to wrap him with dirty rags. He'd missed meals because he'd traded for the care.

Phex said, "This is the second time in my life I've visited a medic. Never for an injury." The first was when he'd been assessed and accepted as a refugee. His scars had stood him in good stead then. Attacon's medics had been impressed, validating his refugee status partly on the basis of something they termed *societal neglect*.

The acolyte made a funny hissing sound, crests wilted. "Should you pass into godhood, we will make them disappear. The divinity will approve the expense."

"You would require it?" Phex didn't like his scars, but they were old friends, of a kind.

"They are ugly things. Gods are *never* ugly. Why would you wish to keep them?" This was clearly coming from a place of curiosity. Which Phex found easier to tolerate than sympathy.

He looked covertly around. The two other potentials were still staring at him and listening in. He couldn't read their thoughts, but they seemed to pity him more than anything else. *That* was definitely worse than sympathy.

He glared at them until they looked away. "My scars are a record of all the times I wasn't fast enough."

"And you require the memento?"

"Yes." Phex's scars were memories scraped into his skin. They were all he had. These aliens could push him as much as they liked, test him all they wished, make him perform all hours to their will, but they would never be as bad as the blades. He thought that maybe, occasionally, he might need that reminder.

"You are a strange creature," said the acolyte. "But do not challenge us on standards of beauty."

Phex said nothing. He knew they would not spend time, tech, or skill on a mere potential. His scars were safe unless he made it through to demigod status. If he made it through.

The medic made some abrupt adjustment to the chair, flopping Phex back and continuing the exam.

The acolyte watched.

It made Phex uncomfortable to be the focus when there were two other potentials to question as well.

"Your hair is interesting. Is that a dye, a genetic mutation, or something else?" the Dyesi asked.

"Environmental chemical alteration. The effect is permanent." Crud did strange things the kids who worked with it every day. All crudrats had blue hair.

"The color cannot be altered?"

"Will that affect my chances?" Phex knew there were major gods who had no hair, or short fuzz that could not be grown or dyed. But none of those gods were Sapien. Sapiens were particularly valued by the Dyesi for their long hair and for the fact that it might be shaped and colored. His would prove difficult in that regard. Phex could grow it out or get extensions, but it would always be blue.

"Our aestheticists will enjoy the uniqueness but may become annoyed by a stubborn shade."

"I can always wear a wig or spray over the color."

The acolyte clicked. "Your arms need definition. I will assign exercises. Your second toe is longer than your first. It is unfortunate that you can also grace or we would take off the tip, but that might impact your balance. Your ears are misshapen. Your brows require plucking, and you'll need eyelash extensions. Why must Sapiens have such small eyes? Let me see your teeth."

Phex grimaced.

"Whitening serum," ordered the acolyte.

"Nothing nice to say?" replied Phex, thinking that his controversial ears would seem too round and stick out too far compared to the Dyesi. Dyesi ears were easily twice as big as his but close to the head and pointed with the crests up off the top and down the back. Phex thought those ears were pretty enough but also, occasionally, quite comical-looking. But the Dyesi definitely did not want his opinion on matters of beauty.

The Dyesi blinked at him. "Your face and body show excellent symmetry. Your collar bones are well formed. You have ten of all the digits you should have ten of, two of all the limbs and organs you should have two of, and one of everything else."

"Up to Sapien standards but not exceeding them?" suggested Phex, amused.

"Mmm." The acolyte abruptly turned and moved away, attention on one of the other potentials.

"And now let's look inside, shall we?" The medic began Phex's internal exam. Various monitors, instruments, micro needles, and testing apparatuses clicked out and wrapped over or snapped into different parts of Phex's body. It didn't hurt, but Phex held very still in case it might. A tech moved to assist.

The medic's impassive face showed unexpected shock at something on her readout. "Wait, what is…?"

She and the tech went into a flurry of activity, dancing about and chatting in some alien tongue. Apparently, Phex's insides were a doozie. Much worse than his ears.

5

ALL THINGS BERRIL &
BEAUTIFUL

"What is wrong with the potential?" The acolyte glided back over.

"You misconstrue. There is nothing *wrong* with him. That's my confusion. How is it possible to be so damaged on the exterior yet so perfect inside?" The medic checked the monitoring screens again, looking increasingly confused. "He clearly had a childhood of hard physical labor. I can see that in his bones. Yet his S1 genome is pristine."

Phex found that interesting. He knew that what the Wheel had done to his genetics was extensive, but he had no idea life as a crudrat could actually impact his skeletal structure.

"Explain," the acolyte demanded.

"Look at the density here and here. It's like he came from a mining colony or a planetfall survivalist cult. Yet his genetic code is almost too perfect. Precision-engineered. If I were to design a base-level S-class human from the skeletal structure out, it would probably look something like this boy. Manufactured to exact specifications. Organs and everything."

Phex decided to help them out a bit. "Because I was."

The medic seemed to remember at that juncture that Phex was, in fact, able to listen and talk back.

"You were *made*, not born?" She whispered this for some reason, something like disgust in her tone.

"Bit of both, I suspect. I can't recall the event myself."

"How cute. He thinks he's funny," said the tech, who spoke Galactic Common as if the language abraded on the way out. The tech was some species Phex had never encountered before – diminutive with a sheen of yellow fur poking through a mass of wearables.

The medic glanced furtively around, looking suddenly very Sapien. The other two potentials were finishing up, unstrapping. Phex was the only one still under examination.

The medic said, "Hold the next batch." Then, once the others were safely out of the room, she lowered her voice and explained to the acolyte, "If other Sapiens know this, it could cause unstable pantheon formation."

The acolyte's crests flattened. "Sub-species violence? Ostracism? Phobia? Bias?"

"Prejudice." The medic turned back to Phex. "What is your home world?"

Phex wondered if that information really was absent from his Attacon medical records. It was certainly part of his refugee status. "I'm Wheel."

The medic looked away from her screen. "Tech head? Explain."

The tech consulted system records. "Wheel. Xenophobic. Class S1. Prime uncut *Homo sapiens*. No somaform adaptations."

The technician had extensive integration augments, which Phex found weird. The Wheel buried its tech deep inside the brain. Because his brain had rejected the implant, Phex ended up a crudrat. The idea that he might have had something external and become one with the Wheel was frightening in its desirability.

The medic was staring at Phex. "Why the tinkered genes?"

"Let the professional finish," suggested Phex.

The tech continued. "The Wheel has a cultural propensity for genetic tinkering at the fetal stage to elevate social status through aesthetics. They call it *triggering traits*. How cute. Plus, there is a single cyborg enhancement required of all members of the population – one cortex implant, a socially mandated controller device."

The medic went back to her screen to check the veracity of this statement. "But this boy has no such implant."

"Exactly." Phex made a face.

"I don't understand," said the acolyte.

"Neither do I." That was an order for clarification from the medic, and Phex knew it.

Phex explained, annoyed at having to talk so much. "I was probably born to progenetor stock – that's what the Wheel calls the ruling elite. Whoever mine were, they cared about physical ability more than appearance, although that was probably important too." Phex knew what he looked like, even though the acolyte had insulted his ear shape. "Wheel puts the implant in us when we're six. A small number of kids can't integrate it. As there's no alternative, we're rejected from the entire social structure."

Phex had been through multiple anthropological inter-views – he knew the right lingo to use. Attacon's academics, politicians, and diplomats were all interested in the Wheel. Since the Wheel was a closed society and allowed no outside observation, Phex was a desirable source of primary informa-tion. Early on, Phex had been surprised by the stuff they found shocking. He'd become terse and uncommunicative the more he had to repeat himself. Now he just liked to get it over with, so he tried to give them all the necessary info up front. "Without an implant, we're not considered people. Those of us who survive become crudrats, hence the blue hair. And, apparently, dense bones."

"But why?" The acolyte was still confused.

"You want me to explain the Wheel's entire social structure to you during a medical exam?" Phex let the blade enter his voice. "Don't you have thirty-six of us to get through today?"

"What's your status now that you've left this Wheel?" the medic pressed.

"Potential godhood." Phex thought that was obvious.

The medic was not pleased. "Hasn't anyone ever told you not to be intentionally evasive with a medical professional?"

"Because you pass out honesty, you expect it in return?" Phex looked away. He'd only been a crudrat for four years, but it had engraved certain characteristics into his psyche that were permanent, like the blue hair. Being intentionally evasive with authority was one of those things.

"You act frustratingly older than you are, Wheel-child," the medic whined.

Phex felt weirdly pleased to have needled her so successfully.

The tech jumped in, having called up Phex's records. "His status prior to being recruited was refugee on Attacon 7. Wheel refugees are rare even in bordering sectors. Less so now since the Kill'ki Coalition began their extraction program, but that operates nowhere near Attacon." The tech focused on Phex. "Were you rescued?"

What a preposterous idea. Who cared about crudrats? "No. I escaped."

"How?"

Phex shifted under the stabilization bands. "Now you want my life story as well as a lesson in Wheel cultural programming? Am I to be here all night?"

The acolyte's crests perked and it made a clicking noise. "We can look into it later if it becomes necessary."

The medic began to cycle down the exam instruments, with more force and sharp movement than they strictly required.

"Wait," said the tech. "How is his hormone regulation?"

"Ah." The medic consulted her scans. "Balanced. Just like the rest of him. They left nothing to chance."

Phex huffed a laugh. "The Wheel doesn't believe in chance."

"Believe?" The acolyte's ear crests swiveled to point at Phex.

"*Believe*," replied Phex, emphasizing the word, knowing it had divine power.

The medic interrupted. "His body's childhood rejection of the brain implant is my only medical concern. It likely indicates an overactive immune system. If we attempted an implant, organic or artificial – vital-organ replacement, for example – the same thing might occur again. Excessive genetic manipulation of the fetus can do that sometimes. It can also render patients overly asymptomatic."

"What does *that* mean?" asked Phex.

"You can get sick, but you're unlikely to *show* that you are sick. Instead, you're more likely to infect others."

"Charming," said Phex.

"With regards to godhood, your genetic enhancements, hormone regulation, and bone strength are assets. You should be more fit than most Sapiens for grace." Turning to the acolyte, the medic said, "I recommend putting a physical push into the training regime for this potential. Even if he isn't slated for grace, he could be very beautiful with grace as a secondary skill. He is designed to tolerate high levels of physical fitness. Also, the divinity should know that his vocal cords are extremely strong. I put a warning into the system."

"Isn't that a good thing?" Phex asked.

"Dangerous voice. I imagine it's why you were recruited." Now the medic was being evasive.

Phex dressed and left the chamber, glad to have the exam over and done with. In the waiting room, the potentials were all staring at him with varied expressions of horror, pity, and disgust. So much for not talking about his scars. Sapiens really were the worst gossips in the universe.

After everyone completed their medical exams, the potential cantors met up with the other twenty-four potentials in a small dome, where important-seeming acolytes with very perky crests waited for them. The other cantors were noticeably avoiding Phex. It was like being right back at school on Attacon 7.

Phex supposed it was indoctrination time. He lurked at the back, trying not to be noticed, conscious of his height when compared to all the other Sapiens.

The speech of welcome was made in Dyesi. Phex could pick out some words from years of listening to godsong, but he didn't actually understand what was said.

Fortunately, they repeated the whole thing in Galactic Formal.

It was absolutely *not* a speech of welcome.

"Potentials, let me be the first to enlighten you. Your primary objective in being here is to form a pantheon. For the first several months, during training and assessments, you will be recorded but not beamed. You are of no interest to anyone until you begin to function properly under the dome. We have only three rules here on Divinity 36. One, if you are not good enough, you will be eliminated. Two, if you form a sexual or romantic liaison with another potential, you will be expelled. Three, if you cannot tolerate or survive Dyesi culture, you will fail or you will die."

The Sapiens in the crowd were shocked into silence by the sharp, direct brutality of the strictures. The grace potentials reacted in mixed ways, but most took it seriously. Only the Dyesi potentials remained unaffected, their crests puffy and alert.

After the speech, food and drink trays were brought in, offering a range of interesting-looking delicacies, obviously representing many different alien cuisines.

Everyone stood in awkward silence for a long moment.

Then the Dyesi potentials made their way forward and began selecting nibbles.

"Better eat as much as we can," Phex overheard one Sapien say in Galactic Common. "After this, it'll be Dyesi vegetables until the bitter end. Operative word being *bitter*."

Phex watched what the sifter potentials ate, and then he chose what they did. Might as well get used to it right away.

It seemed like they were expected to circulate and chat with each other while they ate, which made Phex highly uncomfortable. He was accustomed to the cafe, where he was the one distributing food. He didn't know what to do or say when he was not serving. Idling about like one of his former useless customers wasn't his natural state.

He gravitated to the outskirts of the small dome and entertained himself by watching his fellow Sapiens interact with the aliens. The cantors were good at talking with each other but not so with the potential sifters or graces. The Dyesi, on the other hand, seemed to be making a conscious effort to mingle. Phex found it interesting that the potential sifters had to go through the same training process as everyone else, as if they were aliens to their own divinity. But then, the acolyte had said, *Your primary objective is to form a pantheon.* Sifters would be the only potentials who really knew what that entailed.

A small – very small – part of Phex wanted one of the Dyesi potentials to approach him. Self-isolated though he may be.

Phex became fascinated by the diffident posturing the potential sifters displayed around any given acolyte. It was all body language and could be transmitted at a distance. He tested his own spine curve and shoulder position to see if he could do it too. Curious, he caught the eye of one of the acolytes and imitated the subtle motion. The acolyte's crests flattened back. Was that shock? Phex had no idea what he'd just said, or intimated, but he was pleased with himself. The acolytes struck him as somewhat self-satisfied.

He smelled something tasty, like one of the spiced nut pastries from his cafe, and then…

"Ooof," he huffed, looking down. A smallish alien had wrapped her arms about his waist and was squeezing him.

"What? Who?"

"Hi!" She had a sharp, sweet face, smiling eyes, and short, fuzzy hair. She was also the source of the pleasant smell.

"Do we know each other?" was all Phex could think to say, even though he was well aware that they did not. He would have remembered.

"No. I'm Berril," said, evidently, Berril.

"I'm Phex. What are you doing?"

"I'm not flirting with you, I promise. You just looked like you needed a hug."

"I did?"

A vigorous nod met that.

"Well, that would be a first."

"I doubt that."

"No I mean, it's actually my first."

"First what?"

"Hug," Phex said, honestly.

The little alien was clearly startled by this information. "You've never been hugged before?"

"Not as I can remember."

"Is it your culture? Should I not?" She relaxed her grip slightly but didn't lower her arms.

Phex tilted his head, considering. "No. Is this yours? Hugging strangers?"

"I'm Shawalee."

Phex hadn't heard of the species, but she was bone-thin and light enough to be chiropteran, even though he couldn't tell if she had wings or just wore a very fluffy cape. He had no doubt she was there for light grace.

Her smile was pointy like her nose. "We are a bit more touch-driven than most species. You don't mind?"

Phex considered her soft, warm weight. The sensation was odd. Not unpleasant but definitely *odd*. It was kind of nice to be leaned on as if he were something useful and solid. The hug was awkward because he wasn't sure what to do in return – where did he put his hands? – but not unwelcome.

"May I have my arms back?"

She relaxed enough that he could extract both arms without hurting her. He crossed them because what else could he do with them? Surely not touch her in return. He leaned his upper back against the dome, feeling daring, and she shuf-

fled a bit so she could stay wrapped around his waist and lean
completely against his side. Phex was reminded a little of the
murmels – the blue space-born creatures he once wore
wrapped around his neck who ate the crud while he ran the
blades. It'd been years since he'd had one coiled around him,
and he hadn't realized he missed it until that moment.

"I'm here for a grace," Berril announced.

"Mmm," Phex agreed.

"I knew you wouldn't be the talkative type. Can I talk,
though? You don't mind?"

Phex didn't. He liked chatty people so long as they had
interesting things to say. He'd had a few regulars like that at
the cafe, mostly elderly folks who came in the early hours
before the students took over. They'd tell him long stories of
neighbors or partners, friends or lovers, people he didn't
know and never would. There were two types of humans at
his cafe. The kids who postured and played but really only
cared for flirting and friendship and made little distinction
between the two. And those near the ends of their lives, who
spoke about the relationships they'd made and the people
they'd lost. As if life was, at either end, entirely about the
other people who shared it.

"Mmm," said Phex again, in what he hoped was an
encouraging manner.

So, this new person, this tiny fuzzy thing, leaned against
him, all her weight, which was nothing at all, and told him
about herself, the friends and family she'd left behind, what
she thought of becoming a god.

Her Galactic Common was accent-inflected in a pleasing
way, like a trill, and she didn't bother with formalities.

At some point, she fluttered her cape at someone. Another
grace came over – taller, bigger-boned, but still elegant and
slender. Like Berril, they seemed to be the only representative

of their species. They had long metallic hair with a coppery
sheen that would reflect the dome beautifully, and silvery
skin covered in a feather-like indented texture. Phex thought
maybe the somaform was for an aquatic world, which would
also explain the alien's languid movements.

They introduced themselves as a Dorien who went by the
moniker Sharm.

Less than a day on this alien moon, most of that time
spent with medics, yet Berril was clearly the type of person
who collected others. Because a short time later, one of the
Dyesi potentials came over too.

"How did medical go, Berril?" it asked, clearly already on
friendly terms.

"Good, I think. I'm not sure I'll be pretty enough,
though."

Dyesi never sugarcoated appearance. They were religious
about their aesthetics. "Your hair is a deficit," agreed the
sifter potential. "But if they let you come all the way here,
that means you have something the divinity admirers
greatly."

"You're pretty, Berril," objected Sharm.

Berril made a funny face. "Thank you, but I'm not pretty
by Dyesi standards. And that works against godhood."

The Dyesi clicked and then said, "You are correct, Berril.
Your friend here is more to our taste." It gave Phex a brief
glance out of huge eyes.

Phex grunted. He knew very well what Sapien gods
tended to look like and that he fit the mold. Although the
acolyte at medical had a long list of objections, Phex
suspected his list was shorter than everybody else's.

The Dyesi squared its body and faced Phex full on. "I'm
Jinyesun." Phex was honored by the name and wondered if
younger Dyesi were more free with names. Except earlier,

that one with Gemma had been offended. So, maybe it was
only Jinyesun who behaved so openly.

"Phex," he replied.

He was allowed his preferred silence then, while Berril,
Sharm, and Jinyesun talked animatedly with each other. He
enjoyed their conversation. The aliens each had different
perspectives on the training they were about to endure.
Jinyesun had valuable insight, having been raised with
godhood in mind.

"You were tapped early?" Phex was moved to ask.

"Of course. I have excellent sift."

"It's a birth trait?" wondered Berril.

"Like all skin." Sharm flashed their pattern proudly.

"Yours is lovely," praised Berril.

"Do you think so?" The Dorien was delighted by the
compliment.

Phex jerked his chin in agreement.

Sharm made a pleased little warble noise.

"What age does it begin for you, Jinyesun?" asked Berril.

The Dyesi explained that they were under surveillance
starting six years after their first instar. Which Phex assumed
meant *birth*. That was the same age that the Wheel had tried
to insert his implant. The same age he'd become a crudrat.
The same age memories began.

Phex was content to listen, enjoying Berril's thin arms
around him. He had no idea why she'd decided to adopt him
and he didn't like feeling confused, but he wasn't opposed to
her casual affection. It was novel but pleasing, like one of
those warm drinks from an alien planet that Del occasionally
imported for the cafe staff to try. She did feel awfully small
and frail against him. And hadn't he read somewhere that
chiropterans ate less but more regularly than most species?

"Have you had enough to eat, little Berril?" he found

himself asking abruptly and perhaps a little sharply. He was
immediately embarrassed by the intrusive nature of the
question.

Berril didn't seem to mind or find it odd at all. "Yes,
thank you, they had hedgehog nectar, from my homeworld.
I'd offer to fetch you some but's it's already all gone. Popular
export, you know?"

Phex did not know, so he only grunted again.

Berril being Berril, soon enough, even more people joined
their group. Two Sapiens and another Dyesi wandered over,
assured of their welcome.

Or *maybe* two Sapiens. One of them was extremely odd-
looking – small and slight with a lovely sculpted facial structure almost pretty enough to be an alien. But his ear shape,
general proportions, and movements screamed *Sapien*, except
everything about him was grey – soft grey skin, silvery-grey
hair, grey eyes. It was as if someone had washed away all his
color saturation. It wasn't artifice like the gods got, either.
This was real. A tinkering of some kind? A somaform adapta-
tion? Carborg mods? Phex had never seen the like. It was so
subtle, it could be trigger traits done by the Wheel. But this
kid wasn't Wheel-born. No progenetor family would have
permitted those natural flaws in facial symmetry and body
proportion.

The three newcomers looked at Phex with interest. The
grey one's wide eyes were intent and assessing, possibly
envious. Phex didn't know if that was because of his appearance or because he had a chiropteran embracing him.

"We aren't supposed to flirt," said the boy during a lull in
conversation. He had the clear, syrupy voice of a high cantor.

Jinyesun said, "Berril is Shawalee. They are like that."

"It's not a courting ritual?"

Phex shifted, suddenly uncomfortable with the scrutiny

and the hug. He didn't mind it when he was furniture, but now he was focus.

Berril frowned. "You're scaring him, and he only just relaxed." One of her thin little hands patted Phex's hip. "It's okay, big guy."

Phex narrowed his eyes because Berril shouldn't have to justify her culture.

"Are you jealous?" asked Sharm. This seemed to be genuine curiosity rather than accusation.

"No!" The grey boy took offense. He held up delicate hands as if to ward off a blow. His fingers were covered in silver rings.

"Then why?" Berril asked.

"It was meant as a genuine warning. The acolytes don't like it. We're expelled if we form a relationship, right?" Grey eyes pleaded with Jinyesun for confirmation.

"Dyesi understand physical contact between friends. We know there are some species that require a greater amount of touch than others. We understand the nature of intent. It is not necessarily flirting that the divinity restricts – it is sexual and romantic intimacy."

"Why?" asked Sharm.

Jinyesun looked uncomfortable.

"Oh, oh, I know!" Berril chirped. "Because that can damage a group dynamic. Violate the first objective."

"We are here to form pantheons, so don't mess with the team?" The other Sapien made her statement a question.

"No drama?" suggested the grey boy, smiling humorlessly. "I get that." He did seem like a practical type – for all his rings, his attire wasn't fancy. A basic jumpsuit of some kind, cut well and reinforced in places, a high-tech flexible fabric but not flashy. It was patterned but also in shades of grey. It looked like it faded into urban environments easily.

Phex agreed with the principle. If the Dyesi wanted solid pantheons, ones that would last and bring in new worshipers for years to come, they'd need to put a damper on drama, particularly Sapien drama. From working at the cafe, Phex knew kids his age were overly invested in the turmoil of relationships, sexual or otherwise, and the parting that inevitably resulted. The Dyesi would have their work cut out for them with thirty-six teenagers.

He looked down at Berril. "Either way, us flirting would be unlikely." Phex wasn't settled on a sexual preference, but he was pretty certain his scope didn't include Berril. He suspected she felt the same way.

"Oh, he speaks," said the grey boy.

"I'm Phex." Phex introduced himself to the three newcomers.

"Kagee." The boy was spiky and grumpy, but Phex understood that. No one liked when others made assumptions about them.

Phex tilted his head and then looked at the other Sapien.

"Villi." She gave him a tentative smile.

Phex gave her a more distinct nod of acknowledgement. He was careful not to disturb Berril, who was once more leaning against him.

"What colony are you from?" Berril asked Kagee, curious about his coloring.

Phex was equally interested.

"I'm not." Kagee looked resigned. He probably had to answer this question a lot.

"What planet, then?" she pressed.

Kagee's sculpted lips firmed and then relaxed with effort. "A dumb one."

"Are you actually Sapien?" Berril didn't really know when to stop.

"I'm Sapien enough." Kagee made a slightly helpless gesture with his hands – they were slim and fine-boned, seemingly weighted unnecessarily by so many thick silver rings. In a clear effort to change the subject, he asked Phex, "Why is your hair blue?"

Phex considered the quickest way to handle this question. His initial approach hadn't worked with the medic. "It's been permanently dyed since I was a child," was what he came up with.

"It is *pretty*," said Jinyesun, using the Dyesi word.

Phex looked at the potential sifter and wondered if that was an actual flirt. Dyesi never used the word *pretty* lightly.

"It's not long enough." Kagee tossed his own very long silvery hair.

Phex tightened his lips briefly over his teeth, then said, "I grew it out of laziness, not ambition."

"Don't you *want* to be a god?" Berril asked.

"I'm here, aren't I?"

"Low cantor, right? Your voice is cool, when you bother to use it." Villi smiled again. She smiled a lot. Phex wasn't sure yet if that meant he should like her or dislike her.

"Maybe grace," he replied, because they'd mentioned that during his medical exam. He knew what the acolytes actually recruited him for, but he wasn't above messing with his fellow potentials' sense of entitlement.

Everyone looked at him askance.

"But they never take Sapiens for grace." Berril sounded almost hurt.

"And that would throw the numbers out of balance," added Jinyesun.

Phex gave a half-shrug. "One of them saw me run."

"And that was enough to challenge your position?"

"Apparently."

Berril craned her neck to try and see his back. "You're flightless, though."

"Not all graces have wings," said Sharm.

Berril was instantly contrite. "Sorry, Sharm. I forget, since for us there is only one way."

"Welcome to the multifaceted nature of godhood." Kagee popped something into his mouth that looked like actual dead animal meat. Disgusting.

The party, or orientation, or whatever it was, seemed to be breaking up. Phex gently extracted himself from Berril, careful when unwinding her arms, and wondered what they were in for next.

6

TRAINING WHEELS

Phex found himself walking back from the party with the other Sapiens, forced to navigate the vast building without an acolyte. He hadn't memorized the way.

They found themselves at the end of a hallway in front of a curtain to what they thought was the right dorm. But a set of guards, one of whom looked like a certain cyborg Phex had met before, ordered them away. Apparently, they were on the correct level but in the wrong building.

Eventually, they found themselves a slightly annoyed acolyte who led them safely home.

They said their greetings to the space, which amused the acolyte because apparently if it was your own room, you didn't have to greet it. So many rules.

Phex sat in his niche, watching the other potential cantors unpack. He wondered if he was supposed to offer to help. He wished there were guides to interacting with other people. For interacting with other Sapiens, even.

For lack of anything better to do, he moved his own small bag onto the shelf at the foot of his bed niche and went to investigate the kitchen.

"Do you cook?" Villi asked, coming to sit at the counter facing him and leaning her chin into her hand.

"No."

"But you know your way around a kitchen?"

"I worked at a cafe."

"Oh."

Phex was unfamiliar with Dyesi appliances, so he left those alone. He managed to find cold storage and dry staples and figured out how to turn on the water.

"Can you make me a drink?" Villi asked, even though they'd all just eaten.

"Not at the moment." But Phex found some kind of light-weight drinking vessel and filled it with water for her.

Silence descended.

One of the others perched on a stool next to Villi, staring at Phex. He gave them water, too.

"Where you from, then?"

"Attacon 7."

"Moon, huh? Was it nice there?"

"Not really."

"You're not very friendly."

To Phex, *friendly* seemed more exhausting than gracing a dome.

"Where are you from?" asked Villi of the newcomer, either trying to peace-keep by diverting attention or protecting Phex from unwanted conversation.

This last would have been a weird and near-impossible task, as Phex *never* wanted conversation.

He continued puttering. He felt oddly comfortable in the alien kitchen. Probably because there was a counter between him and everyone else, like at the cafe. He enjoyed that. No one seemed inclined to join him, which he enjoyed even more. It was as if he had claimed territory. It was unlikely any

of the other cantors had kitchen experience. Any Sapien rich
enough to come from a planet with a house big enough to
boast its own kitchen could probably also afford to hire others
to use it. And if any other cantors came from moons or spaceships or space stations, they would have grown up without
private cooking facilities. It was entirely possible that he was
the only one there who'd been in food service.

Eventually, six of the counter chairs were occupied by
chattering Sapiens getting to know one another, Gemma
among them. Fortunately, she seemed to find everyone else
more interesting than Phex. Kagee lay in his niche with some
kind of personal immersion device over his head. Two of the
others were in bed, asleep. Phex didn't know where the last
two had gone. Maybe into the hygiene chamber.

Phex used his wrist ident to translate some of the Dyesi
labels on the food cubes. He ended up with a good idea of
what most everything was *called* but not necessarily what it
was *for*. He was able, at least, to serve water to those sitting
at the counter. Then he began trying to figure out how to boil
water for drinks, since it was now nighttime, and as far as
Phex was concerned, that meant cafe hours.

He wondered idly if some of the powders on the shelf
were caffeinated or sweet and water-soluble, or if they were
some form of grain for baking. He sniffed a few baggies but
hesitated to put anything in his mouth. He found some
familiar dried black beads, which he knew he could turn into
the Dyesi's beloved corrosive dark. But he'd never met a
Sapien who could tolerate the stuff.

Fortunately for Phex, there came a ritual room greeting
from the curtained entrance, and two familiar faces peeked in
– Berril and Jinyesun.

Phex gave them a curt nod from his kitchen sanctuary.
They took that as permission to enter.

Villi turned around. "Oh, hi! Welcome, welcome. How's your room? Is it a big open one like ours?"

The other Sapiens seemed startled by the presence of aliens but not entirely opposed to continued socialization.

Berril, who had no respect for Phex's space with regards to kitchens or otherwise, came over to hug him. Jinyesun followed her but did not try to hug, which was a relief.

"Got a girlfriend already?" said one of the Sapiens, watching with interest.

"She is Shawalee," explained Villi, sounding a little wistful. "They're like that."

"Are they?"

Villi nodded. "Big huggers."

Phex extracted himself. Turned Berril about and gave her a tiny push. "Go hug Villi."

Berril trotted around the counter and squirmed in between Villi and one of the others, putting an arm around each.

"Hi," she said grinning at the new Sapien on her left. "I'm Berril."

The Sapien smiled back. "Hello, Berril, I'm Kallow. Welcome to the cantor dorm." She had a low, mellow voice and long, curly dark hair.

"Hi, cutie," said Villi, obviously pleased to have Berril touching her. She probably came from a high-physical-contact society, too.

"Oh, I get a nickname already?" Berril chirped. "Sapiens are so cool."

Phex looked at Jinyesun, who was standing in his kitchen, face speckled with shifting pale blues. Mild embarrassment, maybe? The alien's presence did not feel that intrusive. More like a coworker. It was careful about physical contact and spatial autonomy.

Apparently, no ritual greeting of the space was required

when entering a zone like the kitchen. Which Phex was relieved to know. He'd been a little disgruntled by the notion of having to call out his identity and recite ritual words every time he got up to use the facilities in the middle of the night.

Phex said to the Dyesi, "Good. You're here. I have questions."

Jinyesun lost the speckles and crested eagerly at him. "Do you? How nice."

"First, the greeting. What does it mean?"

"Greeting?"

Phex said the Dyesi words as Missit had done upon entering the building.

"Oh! That is not a greeting. That is an acknowledgment. There is no direct translation to Galactic, but it is like *I am coming inside*. Only it also acknowledges the space and your relationship to that space."

"And the pronoun *I*? Do I change it for gender like in Galactic, or does it indicate social status?"

"That is complicated. The words you just spoke would be used by someone returning to a familiar space. When entering a new space, it's best to use your own name instead of a pronoun. You will be taught the correct forms in language class, I imagine."

"Thank you. Now, this kitchen – please explain it to me."

"With pleasure," said the Dyesi, much to Phex's relief.

While Berril and the others chatted, Jinyesun went over everything Phex hadn't figured out yet and taught him the Dyesi words for the different foods and tools.

Together they sourced a bag of bright-green powdered leaf that had a fragrant smell and a malty grassy flavor, which Jinyesun said the Dyesi used mostly as a colorant. Phex mixed it with a sweetener and hot water, and it became a passably tasty tea. He made seven cups and set them before everyone at his counter. Watched with interest as some drank it and some did not. Berril pushed hers away after an aborted sniff. Phex refilled her water instead.

Jinyesun assured everyone that the kitchen wouldn't be stocked with anything dangerous for Sapien digestion. It was meant for them to use – hence, the presence of sweetener.

Phex waggled the bag of corrosive dark at the Dyesi as an objection.

Jinyesun gave one of those soundless laughs. "Fair. Although corrosive dark will not actually *hurt* you. That is for times like this, when we Dyesi visit you."

"It's okay with the acolytes that you and Berril are visiting our dorm?" asked Kallow.

"Socialization and cultural sharing are strongly encouraged," explained Jinyesun. "How else will we form solid pantheons?"

Phex hid his discomfort at the notion.

"Just no fraternization," said Kagee, walking into Phex's kitchen. He wore a pale blue robe thing with what looked like an elaborate hand-painted design on it and trailing sleeves, that Phex thought was decidedly *not* kitchen-safe attire.

Phex put more water into the heating device for him.

Jinyesun crested at Kagee. "You mean sexual or romantic relations? No, those are not permitted."

"Bummer," said Gemma with a wide-eyed expression. "There's a Dorien grace who is super hot."

"Oh, my gods, Doriens are so sexy," one of the others agreed.

"Do you think a Dorien can really make godhood?" wondered Gemma. The Doriens were one of the earliest aliens to convert to the divinity, yet there had never been a Dorien god.

"It'll be fun to watch, either way."

"*They* are named Sharm, and *they* are very nice." Berril's smiling eyes turned quite calculating all of a sudden.

Kagee clattered about the kitchen, annoying Phex with his presence, but he was no more able to figure anything out than Phex had been. But he was remarkably careful with his sleeves. He didn't seem inclined to ask Jinyesun for help, so he ended up leaning against one of the larger appliances, arms crossed, sleeves trailing, ring-covered fingers tapping against the delicate bones of his wrist, glaring at everyone.

Phex made more green powdered tea and offered it to him. The grey boy took it with a curt nod of thanks, the silver fall of his hair catching a bright beam of light as the moon rotated. Their one window now gave them a spectacular view of the planetary rings and the Dyesi's sun beyond.

Phex checked to see if the others needed top-ups. Everyone seemed to be fine, so he wiggled the bag of corrosive at Jinyesun again.

"No, thank you," Jinyesun declined politely. "I should sleep soon. Training starts tomorrow, and it will not be easy." The sun's rays hit its open crests, making rainbows dart about the kitchen in a cheerful way.

Phex figured they all should get some rest and wondered if he would be able to sleep at all. He'd never bedded down with so many other people in the same room.

Accordingly, their little gathering broke up a short while later. Phex put all the cups into the cleaning compartment. Jinyesun had insisted on showing him how that worked. Phex assumed cleanliness was important to Dyesi. Or at least to Jinyesun.

Kagee figured out how to block the kitchen window and dim the lights, thank goodness.

Phex somewhat wished the Dyesi had stayed to guide him

through the hygiene process. Fortunately, there was a diagram on the wall. According to the illustration, which was an amusing blue stick figure, squatting seemed to be required. Phex figured he'd get the hang of it eventually.

Phex was the last one to use the body-cleaning facilities. It was designed for three at once, but he was happy to have it to himself – not because of modesty but because he hardly needed people staring at his scars again. Once more, blue stick figures showed him what to do. The sharp-misted spray seemed to sanitize sufficiently. At least he didn't smell afterwards. Phex amused himself wondering what Attacon 7's sonic cleansers would do to Dyesi skin.

Robes were provided – very Sapien and thoughtful of them – with one still waiting for Phex. He figured he'd just sleep in that, since he hadn't anything else.

Phex was the last one still up, so he turned off the ambient lighting with his ident. A few voices murmured to each other in the dimness but not loudly. He climbed into his niche and drew the stiff curtain closed. It turned out to be thick enough to block out some sound as well as light. He wondered idly if it was made of animal hide. Dyesid Prime's surface was home to massive dracohors – highly prized for their thick skins. He wasn't entirely sure how he felt about sleeping behind a dead creature – as if he had been swallowed whole. Then again, wasn't that a good metaphor for the divinity?

He was fast asleep before he had time to worry about it further.

Ambient sound and a sunlight alarm woke them the next morning. An acolyte arrived soon after with food and beverages. The food was a puck-shaped spongy protein substance into which vegetables had been cooked. Phex found it tasty if oddly chewy. He thought it could have been improved upon with something pickled or spicy, but he wasn't one to complain over free food. The drink tasted like a halfway point between green tea and black coffee. It was sweet, which suggested it was designed specifically for non-Dyesi. Phex wasn't wild about it, but he drank it anyway.

Kallow said that it came from her home world, which was relatively close to Dyesid Prime.

"We'll probably be eating quite a few things from there," said Villi. "Since it's the nearest Sapien colony. You'll teach us the names of stuff?"

"Of course."

"What's this called, then?" asked Kagee, sipping the hot drink with a wince.

"Tea," said Kallow, as if that were obvious.

"It comes from a leaf?" Villi examined her cup with interest, as if it might reveal all the secrets of the universe.

"No, a seed pod."

"Then shouldn't it be called coffee?" Kagee frowned.

"We call it *tea*," Kallow repeated, clearly annoyed with the grey boy.

Kagee wiggled his rings at her insistence, dismissively.

Phex thought Kagee put admirable effort into pissing people off.

The acolyte interrupted to say that they had very little time to eat, dress, and get to their first class. Perhaps they could argue over the naming of beverages another time?

The Dyesi continued issuing curt instructions while the potential cantors scuttled around, preparing to leave.

"We will provide you with this exact first meal, or something quite similar, for the duration of your stay with us. It is nutritionally calibrated to meet your needs during your training regime. We have learned that Sapiens in particular do best with healthy food and unhealthy beverages to start their days. Midday, we provide another high-protein and vegetable meal with added starch. You will always have access to adequate hydration. It is important that you remain physically fit to meet the standards of godhood. You may petition for additional calories if your growth structure, home-planet density, or somaform tinkering requires such." The acolyte looked pointedly at Phex, who was the largest there. However, the little puck thing had filled him up, so he didn't think he'd need more than the others.

"After training, your third meal is up to you, within the scope of what can be provided on Divinity 36. You will need to prepare it for yourself. There are ingredients in your kitchen as well as boxed meals of high nutritional value from various Sapien worlds that need only be hydrated and heated. You may choose whatever you prefer."

Everyone, now dressed and assembled in the middle of the room, turned and looked at Phex.

Phex crossed his arms and glowered back. He would make them drinks, not food.

"Let me see you all." The acolyte assessed the twelve of them, one after another, as if it were an image consultant. This was amusing, since it wore a short plain green skirt and nothing else.

"You must wear clothing that allows you to move freely yet is fit tightly to the body. We must see your movements and physique at all times. It should not flop, if you were to go upside-down, for example. For the sake of Sapien shame hormones."

A few of the potentials hurried back to their niches to change into something else.

Phex owned only three outfits – his school uniform, his cafe uniform, and an old maintenance uniform he'd inherited because it was durable and easy to clean. They were all full-coverage jumpsuits made of ultra-tech wicking fiber – soft, stretchy, stain-resistant, and comfortable. Ugly as all get-out, but what did he care? For lack of any other option, he was wearing the one required for school.

Gemma, at least, knew an Attacon 7 uniform when she saw one and seemed amused by his choice.

She sidled over. "Don't you have any workout clothing, Phex?"

"No."

The acolyte overheard. "Will his attire not suffice?"

"It's a bit odd, since it's intended for basic education," explained Gemma.

"Are we not getting educated?" Phex gave her a hard stare.

Gemma ignored him in favor of the acolyte, "You see, on Attacon we have this—"

"She doesn't like the way the style looks. But it functions to your parameters," Phex interrupted. He didn't want to have to explain the social status of Attacon clothing to a Dyesi who probably cared little about clothing beyond the fact that it kept thin-skinned Sapiens warm.

The acolyte said, "Ah, fashion. I never could see the nuances."

"Why should you?" Phex agreed.

"Someone has to dress cantors and graces for the dome, I suppose." The acolyte looked thoughtful. Its ear crests didn't seem to know where to point. "I do hope I do not get *that* assignment."

Everyone was finally ready, and the Dyesi led them out

into the hallway and up to a different floor to begin their training.

There they found the other two groups of potentials under a small cupola about twice the size of Phex's old cafe. Phex said the ritual greeting as he entered, using his own name.

"Phex is coming inside." It felt awkward, and he was the only one of the Sapiens who remembered to do it. The others had to go out and come back in again, saying the right words. They glared at him. He supposed he should have reminded them, but how could they forget something so simple so soon?

All thirty-six potentials sat on the floor while three acolytes took to the dais and explained their daily schedules.

It seemed not unlike school. There were language lessons for those who did not speak Dyesi fluently. Sensitivity training and outreach for those who did. After that they divided into specialties – sifter, cantor, grace – for what the Dyesi called conditioning. Then everyone had some kind of physical training.

After that, it was lunch, then divine indoctrination and performance theory. And then the rest of the afternoon would be spent once more perfecting their specific roles – skinsift, grace, or cantor.

Every thirty-six days, they would be brought before a panel of acolytes and judged.

"An exam every month," said Villi fretfully, as they walked from their first cantor conditioning to physical training.

"Why worry? We only just started," replied Phex.

Kagee came up on Villi's other side, staring at Phex. "Your stoicism is very annoying. Did you know that?"

Phex gave the boy a *glare*. Kagee should practice more stoicism and less sarcastic commentary.

Kagee returned the glare with interest, then sped on ahead of them.

An acolyte was assigned to guide them from room to room, but only for the first day. Phex focused on memorizing where to go this time. The building was confusing, each level exactly resembling the other. He thought maybe the colorful tapestries provided guidance, but he hadn't figured out how exactly. A morning of language and then cantor on top if it, and Phex's brain felt full and stretched. Asking him to also develop a sense of direction amid alien interior design seemed unfair.

"How did we find our first cantor lesson?" asked Kallow of everyone as they walked.

"It's nothing like voice training," said someone behind Phex.

"The way they describe music using the Dyesi words for color and pattern is confusing and hard," complained Kagee. His language skills were among the weakest.

Villi lengthened her stride to overtake Phex. He moved quickly to one side, conscious of his bulk taking up so much of the hallway, not wanting to crowd anyone.

Villi was apparently eager to join Kagee in complaining. "And the way they focus on two tones at once. Harmony is everything. It's nothing like the vocal work I'm accustomed to."

Phex held his tongue and his opinion. That had been his first-ever music lesson of any kind. He had no voice training to compare it to. But it had all made sense to him, under the context of the dome. The cantors around him were now all complaining freely, as if the acolyte leading them wasn't even there.

Phex thought that might become too easily habit. Was it a

good idea, forgetting that the eyes and ears of the divinity were everywhere?

"Even though we all know there are times when cantors sing solo," said Kallow, "It's like the acolytes are ignoring that."

Phex thought about Missit's warm voice scrawling turquoise sorrow on the cupola back on Attacon 7. How alone it had sounded during "Tillam's Lament"? That was clearly never meant to be – a high cantor alone. *Any* cantor alone under a dome seemed impossibly sad and an anathema to godsong. Therefore, it was likely the hardest thing to execute well. Of course they wouldn't start potentials singing alone – this wasn't really *singing* after all, it was *cantor* work.

The Sapiens' exercise chamber turned out to be a cavernous dome full of resistance equipment and cardiac machinery. There was also a dais, which Phex assumed would be used for dance and grace training. Even cantors must know how to move prettily. Missit and Fortew of Tillam danced their dais regularly. Missit had even taken on the role of light grace in one memorable moment of godfix. But then again, Tillam's graces, Zil and Tern, had been known to sing on occasion too. There was a reason Tillam were considered the most innovative of the first-gen pantheons.

The acolyte in charge was busy explaining how the cantor potentials would rotate from one machine to the next when another acolyte entered the room.

The two engaged in a hurried exchange full of crest wiggles, and then the new Dyesi approached Phex.

"I understand that you are here for low cantor, but there's a note in both your intake and medical assessments that you should join the graces during this time slot. There's never been a Sapien grace. It would be unique."

"I don't believe the intent is for me to actually grace," explained Phex.

"Then why the grace addendum?" the Dyesi asked sharply, as if Phex were at fault for its confusion.

Phex twitched his lips. He considered explaining, but it was easier just to show them. Everyone else was already on their first machine, exercising.

So, Phex took a quick run around the edge of the space, vaulted over one piece of equipment with a twist, then ran up the side of the dome and sprang into a backflip to land in a crouch. He'd missed his morning runs, and this was the best he was going to get, trapped inside a building.

Maybe he was showing off a little. But he enjoyed how impressed the Dyesi had been at his audition, and he wanted the acolytes of Divinity 36 to be impressed too. Of course, he hadn't considered the Sapien response.

Kagee clapped sarcastically. Villi and Kallow hooted. The others stopped whatever they were doing and just stared at him.

"What *was* that?" asked one of them.

"It wasn't grace and it wasn't dancing. Is it a sport?" Kallow asked.

"Of course you're like this," said Kagee as if Phex's physical abilities were designed specifically to annoy him.

The two acolytes crested at Phex, looking thoughtful rather than shocked. They were less impressed than comprehending. To them, Phex was an alien not to be underestimated.

"I see. An additional skill set worth cultivating," said the one in charge.

The other added, "We might be able to tint him with grace. Definitely better off training with the grace potentials during this time allotment."

Phex took in the somewhat-envious faces of the other potentials and winced. Now they all thought he was being given special treatment. Which he supposed he was.

"It's not unprecedented," he said, so everyone could hear. "I can name at least one other cantor god who regularly plays grace." He didn't say who. Because why should that boy be mentioned all the time?

Gemma was not so reticent. "Missit," she piped up, all smiles. "I believe in him," she explained, as if that hadn't been made obvious when she unpacked a Missit statue and put it on display in her niche. She added, "But he came to it later in his career. At the beginning, he only ever sang."

The acolyte who'd come to take Phex away said to him, "In truth, you have something of Missit about you."

Phex was offended. "We are *nothing* alike."

The acolyte emitted one of those silent Dyesi laughs. Why did these aliens aways find him so funny? "Come with me, then, graceful cantor."

―――――――

"Phex is coming inside," Phex said in Dyesi as he pulled aside the flap aside and followed the acolyte into the graces' exercise chamber. It was entirely different, nearly three times the size of the cantors', and felt a lot more like a real dome.

"What are you doing here?" Berril bounced over, leaping and skipping through the dead space where a congregation might stand. She was obviously delighted to see him.

"They want me to train with you graces during this part of the schedule." Phex held up his arms dutifully so she could slide her skinny ones around his waist, squeeze, then bounce away again.

Berril stood, looking between him and the acolyte with

big eyes and quick head flips. She was wearing much less because of exercise, and Phex could see her wings for the first time, which were draped back in soft leathery folds from her elbows dipping down in the back almost to her ankles.

Phex took another long moment to look around, finally deciding that this must be a midsized performance dome of some kind, not an exercise chamber. It wasn't stadium-sized or made to hold a full congregation and disseminate mass godfix, but it boasted a full-sized dais. This made sense – graces needed to practice as much as possible on the kind of dais they would eventually use when performing. And winged graces needed space for aerial maneuvers.

Phex nodded at Sharm. The Dorien looked at him with curiosity but not hostility. Phex felt more comfortable among this mixed group of aliens than he had with his fellow Sapiens. He suspected that said a lot more about his personality than anyone else's.

The acolyte trainer put all thirteen up on the dais and through the basic steps and moves of dark grace first – bold and interrupting. Dark graces existed to formulate pauses, breaking sound patterns with stillness, shading the colors as a base for strong, bold rhythms and patterns. It was all big, broad movements and large muscle use.

It made for a great warm-up.

Then they all worked on light gracing – footwork and sharp, rapid beats, creating rhythm and motion, disturbing sound waves in a way designed to enhance the song and brighten skinsift rather than pause or interrupt it.

Phex enjoyed the activity a lot, but he was definitely better at dark grace.

After a break for hydration, during which Phex was introduced to the others by Berril, they focused on trick moves –

flips and the like. This was their opportunity to show off what they could do and learn unusual techniques from each other.

The three chiropterans unfurled their wings and made use of the full volume of the dome. The remaining land-bound graces were acrobats, dancers, or martial artists. Interestingly, Sharm seemed to be relying on a fighting technique, fluid and beautiful. But Phex thought he remembered learning once that the Dorien were a pacifist species.

Berril's wings were amazing, much bigger than Phex expected, leathery but covered in a fine fuzz, like her head. Since her wings were a yellowish color, Phex suspected the acolytes would want to dye her. The Dyesi loved to augment what nature had provided with artifice.

He watched Berril move for a bit, swooping and coiling. Most graces worked by interposing themselves between sifters and cantors, but a grace like Berril could interrupt the sifter and the dome as well. He marveled at the differences in patterns she could create.

His thoughts were interrupted by the acolyte instructing him to practice a wall-flip until he could land it exactly on one specific part of the dais. Once he had that down, he had to do it until he could land it on a specific beat. And then until he could land and hit a specific depth of vibration. He'd never done that many wall flips in his life. He was soon drenched in sweat and utterly exhausted.

Phex was taking a break, drinking water and watching chiropterans, when he noticed they had an audience beyond the acolytes.

Standing within the open entrance of the dome were two figures. One was all too familiar – Dyesi movements but not Dyesi, shining gold and grinning. The other was Zil, Tillam's dark grace, a shimmering metallic red. Phex caught both their eyes, one after another. He lifted a flask of water at them in inquiry. Zil held up a hand in rejection. His hands were oddly shaped, each finger widening toward the tip with no fingernails. Phex didn't know what planet or part of space Tillam's dark grace came from, but he'd always thought Zil quite beautiful. He was as tall as a Dyesi with red skin so dark it was almost black. He had the obligatory long hair, also bright red and both had been tinted to a high-shine metallic by Dyesi aestheticists. He was not a chiropteran, but when he leaped, Zil moved through the air as if he were floating. He had this way of jumping so high, it was as if he hovered. Phex wondered if he could learn how to do that.

The supervising acolyte came over to Phex, presumably to get him back on the dais. It noticed what Phex was staring at.

"The gods walk among us," said Phex.

"When a pantheon is home, they occasionally check in on potentials. It is encouraged."

"Why?" It seemed beneath the old gods to visit new ones.

"It is important for potentials to learn that gods are, as you Sapiens might put it, *only human*."

Phex thought about Gemma. "Gods should not themselves experience godfix?"

"It is more that gods should not worship other gods. Incestuous adoration is neither healthy nor divine."

Phex thought he understood. "They are encouraged to interact with us to remind us that they are people too?"

The acolyte looked pointedly at the two in the doorway. "They are encouraged to model appropriate behavior. And you should ask *them* questions."

Phex thought of approaching Zil to ask for guidance in how to improve his jumps, but that felt presumptuous, especially with Missit right there... smirking. "I think, perhaps, us approaching them is a bit much, if all you provide is Tillam."

The acolyte huffed in amusement. "They *are* quite advanced as these things go. But fear not, there are many demigods who regularly return to Divinity 36. Less popular and younger pantheons. Not every visitor will be Tillam. We understand how ego works."

"Good," said Phex. Then he nodded to both the gods and the acolyte and returned to his wall flips. He would be very sore that night, but there was no way he was going to look like a slacker in front of Missit.

7

HOLY MISSIT, GOD OF BLANKETS

The first few weeks of training blurred together in Phex's head. Each night when he climbed into bed, exhausted, he could feel the memory of grace in his muscles and godsong in his throat, like he had done something real for the first time in his life.

Gracing was fun, but cantor training was tough. The Sapiens were competitive, and Phex knew less than everyone else about vocal work. They were made to harmonize over and over again, working in pairs or groups. Phex had more range at his disposal than anyone, going from whistle register all the way to fry, but no education in how to appropriately apply it. He also had perfect pitch and zero patience, so he could never not hear when any of the others around him messed up. This meant that sometimes he tried to sing louder to cover over the dissonance. Other times, he would simply switch to their part, trying to show them with his own voice how it was *supposed* to sound. Which meant he was often jumping between high cantor and low in the same godsong. Then everyone would blame him for not sticking to his assigned role. The others all had formal training, but all Phex had ever done was sing along in a cafe. A fact some never let him forget, like it gave them license for the hostility they'd felt towards him from the start.

But the acolytes also got annoyed with him. Sometimes, he opened his mouth and their ear crests snapped all the way back, Dyesi horror. This was always followed by an order to shut up.

By the end of the second week, when most of the other cantors advanced to working with softskins, only Phex and Kallow were held back for remedial training. It was embarrassing.

But by the end of the third week, they were allowed to work with Dyesi, too – no domes, just one-on-one in private booths the acolytes called *amplification chambers.* Phex assumed these were lined with dome tech, because otherwise, skinsift wouldn't work. After all, the Dyesi only sifted under a dome. They didn't walk around changing colors whenever anyone had a conversation with them. Although that would be amusing.

"Why are we given these *softskins* to work with and not real sifters?" asked Villi one night.

"Much harder to damage and less of a loss to the divinity if you do," explained Jinyesun, who had become a valuable resource on all things Dyesi. A few other aliens had taken to joining Berril in the cantors' dorm of an evening, but Jinyesun was the only Dyesi to visit regularly.

"They are expendable," said Kagee, deadpan. His expression was flat, but something about his voice made Phex think he was very angry.

Kallow looked sad. She liked her softskin practice partner a little too much.

"They are not gods and never can be." Jinyesun's tone was soft, and Phex wished he could understand Dyesi crests.

He wondered if the Dyesi looked down on softskins the way Sapiens looked down on crudrats. He hoped not.

After weeks of dome-performance theory class, Phex was getting better at identifying the nuances of skinsift. He could tell how very poor the softskins were at it, even compared to the weakest of the sifter potentials. The potentials hadn't been taught why some Dyesi were so much better at skinsift than others. Phex was beginning to suspect they never would be. The Dyesi liked to keep their secrets – even Jinyesun held its tongue and controlled its crests on occasion.

Jinyesun, perhaps upset by Kagee's words, left. With a startled look and a tiny wave, Berril followed.

Most of the cantors sat in a loose circle on the floor, a few in bed niches. No one trusted the couch puffs yet.

Phex sat apart from everyone else, at the head of his bed, cross-legged and pretending to read his ident but mostly keeping an eye on the others. They left him alone. They always did. At the beginning, some of them had tried to casually touch or talk to him during social times. It hadn't been unwelcome, but it had been confusing and suspicious. Berril, Phex didn't mind, maybe because she made it clear what she wanted – cuddles only. But with his fellow cantors, Phex didn't know what he was supposed to do, what they really wanted or expected in response. All too often, he froze or panicked and retreated alone to the kitchen or his niche.

"We probably have to be trained before we can have an effect on Dyesi who aren't softskinned." Kallow munched on a crisp the size of her head that was made from some Dyesi starch.

"Or maybe if we aren't careful, we can really hurt them," suggested Kagee.

Phex thought this was probably right. He would never forget learning that a song could wound. But Kagee would get annoyed if Phex agreed with him out loud, so he said nothing.

Phex suspected that the range genetic manipulation had given his own voice made him particularly dangerous. He didn't mind. Not that he *wanted* to hurt anyone, but the fact that he *could?* That was currently the only advantage he had, stuck on this alien moon, in an alien industry, at the whims of an alien culture. If his voice could harm the Dyesi, so be it. Maybe someday he would need to use that to escape.

"Do you think it's us cantors or the potential sifters who aren't ready to team up yet?" wondered Villi.

Phex hadn't considered that angle. He'd just assumed it was the cantors at fault. He might ask Jinyesun later.

The heavy curtain to the hallway suddenly snapped open. Everyone turned to stare.

"I'm coming inside." Missit stumbled into the room, announcing his relationship to the space in rapid, perfect Dyesi. The god leapt to one side and flattened his back against the wall, looking around with bright eyes.

Their startled Sapien faces clearly delighted him.

Phex, on the other side of the doorway, had enough time to school his own countenance.

Missit noticed him and grinned, then darted over to stand outside Phex's niche, hopping from foot to foot.

"Hide me."

Phex crossed his arms. "What are you *doing* here?"

"Hiding. Quick. Help." Missit dove for the end of Phex's bed.

Phex curled himself out of the way, trying to hide his amusement. Missit wrapped himself in Phex's blanket, turning into a tube of fabric. His sock-covered feet wiggled near Phex's knees, and his hair stuck out the other end so that he looked like some kind of gold-fronded noodle… with sparkly gold socks.

Phex turned away from the spectacle of Missit in his bed to find the other potentials not so sanguine about the situation. They were all staring at him and his newly acquired god-noodle with awed eyes.

Gemma was hyperventilating.

Villi, never at a loss for words, gaped in dumb silence.

Kallow inhaled crisps and began coughing.

Kagee looked annoyed. But that was his default expression.

Still, it was Kagee who said, "Phex, is that Missit?"

"Seems like."

"*The* Missit? Tillam's high cantor? God of gods?"

"Is there another one?" Phex wondered.

"Do you two *know* each other?" Villi found her voice at last, although it was squeakier than usual.

"No." Phex replied, because they didn't.

"Then why is he in your bed?" demanded Kagee.

"Apparently because it's closest to the door."

"What's he doing?" Kallow recovered from her coughing fit.

Phex thought that was obvious. "Hiding. Badly."

"Hey!" said muffled Missit.

"Your hair is sticking out," explained Phex. He contemplated tweaking one sock-covered toe but suspected that was too irreverent for anyone to take. Gemma might actually faint.

"Why is he hiding?" asked Villi. Apparently, the other cantors were going to continue to quiz Phex since they were too afraid to directly address a god. Despite the fact that said god was obviously a ridiculous infant.

"It would appear to be his *thing*," replied Phex.

"What's he hiding from?" Kallow demanded.

Phex could only guess at that one. "His bodyguard? His pantheon? Responsibility? Life?"

"Why?"

"Because he's insane or a brat. Or both."

Missit's head popped out from the blanket tube, and he craned his neck to look at Phex. "Hey, now. We don't know each other well enough for you to be mean. Yet."

"You're in *my* bed," Phex pointed out. "And we've met before."

"You knew that was me?"

"Of course."

"But half my face was covered. How?"

"You walk like Dyesi. You're Sapien, but you don't move like one. It's like you have double joints." Phex narrowed his eyes. "What are you *doing* here?"

"I wanted to see you." Missit's beautiful golden face was briefly shadowed by a frown. "Took me forever to find you. I thought you were training for grace. So, I went to the wrong dorm."

"They think I have a knack, but training a Sapien to be an actual grace is taking things too far," explained Phex.

"Too bad, really. I was excited by the idea. There's never been a Sapien grace." Missit focused on Phex's eyes.

The intensity made him uncomfortable. "Is that why you're looking for me? Curiosity?"

Missit's eyes were brown but flecked with something like gold. Phex wondered if, like Missit's skin and hair, that was Dyesi artifice, or if the god had been born with eyes like that. On the Wheel, that would indicate a trigger trait, but here, who knew?

Missit suddenly sat up, still wrapped in Phex's blanket. He wriggled back so he could lean on the shelves at the end of the niche. "Wait. We haven't formally introduced ourselves. I'm Missit."

"So the universe knows."

"You're Phex."

"Which you bothered to find out. I'm flattered."

Missit gave him a pleased smile. "You're interesting. For a potential."

Phex let his exasperation show. "And you're a lot like your interface." *As shiny gold in skin and mannerisms, and possibly even more annoying.*

Missit was delighted. "You owned one of my statues? You *believe* in me?"

Phex made a disgusted face. "Of course not. I worked at a divine cafe. Someone tried to steal you."

"I'm *very* popular." Missit wiggled his eyebrows. Even they had been threaded with gold – the Dyesi were very meticulous about godly appearance.

Phex decided he was in danger of giving Missit too much attention. The god was oddly hypnotic for a frenetic nitwit. He supposed most gods were like that or they wouldn't be gods.

"What are you doing here?" Phex pressed.

"Hiding, remember?"

"No. What are you doing inside a potential dorm, in an acolyte building, on Divinity 36? Aren't you supposed to be on tour or practicing new songs or relaxing in some fancy mansion on a private moon somewhere?"

"We're home for a bit."

"And they make Tillam stay in the same place as us lowly potentials?"

"Technically, we have our own floor."

"Of course you have a whole floor."

Missit laughed, a bright, tinkling sound. "Pantheons like to stay together, even when we aren't performing."

"Even after so long." Phex tried to remember how long Tillam had been together. "A decade?"

"Even after that." Missit's face briefly fell and his eyes went sad. Then he grinned again. Phex wondered why Tillam was *really* on Divinity 36 and what could make a great god like Missit so unhappy, he became careless with his own safety.

Missit wiggled out of the blanket, elegant even while squirming. He left it in a rumpled pile and climbed out of Phex's niche.

Phex felt oddly bereft.

The sudden absence of the divine like the cold void of space.

Missit was wearing satin pajamas. Phex wondered if the god hadn't bothered to dress that day or if this was loungewear and gods didn't have to wear tight jumpsuits like potentials. He also suspected they felt as silky as Missit's voice sounded. His fingers twitched.

The pajamas were gold, of course. Missit was always all gold.

Phex couldn't stop staring at the reflected shine in the skin at the hollow of Missit's throat, like sunlight off asteroids.

"Best if no one knows I visited you," Missit said to Phex, then looked around at the rest of the potentials, none of whom had moved or spoken to him, and all of whom were staring at him in varying states of shock. "Okay?"

They all nodded, mute.

"You're leaving?" wondered Phex.

"You want me to stay?" Missit looked hopeful.

"You made a mess of my bed," pointed out Phex.

He watched in approval as the god obediently shook out the blanket and spread it neatly. He tucked it around Phex's feet. Did the boy inside the god never stop? That close, he smelled of something warm, metallic, and salted sweet. Phex shook his head at the presumption and to clear his mind of the smell.

"Enough," he said, a little sharply. He didn't like to be played. Missit knew his power all too well.

Missit backed off, still smiling. Still shining silken gold.

Then, with another wild flap of the heavy entranceway curtain, Missit vanished into the hall.

Everyone charged at Phex, gathering around his niche and asking him questions at once. It was exactly the kind of thing Phex hated most.

How had they met?

How could he speak to a god so casually?

How dare he order a god around? Not just any god, but *Missit*.

What could he tell them about what Missit was *really* like?

Phex felt unmoored, dizzy, and baffled. He wonder if this was the lingering effect of direct god exposure or if he hadn't eaten enough that day.

Phex was seized by the sudden need to make tea. He pushed through the crowd and marched into the kitchen. He didn't answer their questions, of course, because he didn't have any answers. He was just as confused as they were. Only, he was better at hiding it.

"Will he be back to visit again?" Gemma leaned on the counter, eyes desperate.

Phex put some fruit juice in front of her. Gemma liked it better than tea.

"You're so mean, Phex, telling us nothing." She grabbed the cup with both hands and sipped it aggressively.

"Phex never talks," said Villi. "Not even about gods."

"Apparently, specifically *not* about gods."

"He talks *to* gods, though." Kagee was glaring and sharp-toned. "No one else finds that curious?"

"It *is* the most I've ever heard Phex say." Villi sipped the tea Phex handed her. "He almost smiled. Never seen him do *that* before, either."

"Well, it's Missit. Everyone gives Missit what he wants. Not even Phex can resist," said Gemma with confidence.

Phex didn't like that assessment. He considered taking the juice away from her, but she seemed to be enjoying it.

"You're weaker than I thought," said Kagee, sounding genuinely disappointed in Phex.

"Maybe if Missit visits again, I could tell him how much I love him." Gemma's voice was all hope.

Phex thought that was something Gemma wanted to do for herself, not something she wanted to do for Missit. Because what kind of reaction did she expect when she meted out adoration to a god? Love in return? It didn't work that way. Missit didn't owe Gemma anything.

Phex thought it unlikely that Missit would visit their dorm again. He'd only wanted to confirm where Phex was and *what* Phex was. Now that his curiosity had been satisfied, he would leave Phex alone.

In a way, Phex was right.

Because Tillam departed Divinity 36 the next day, going on something the acolytes called *a creative retreat*. It would be many months before Phex saw Missit again.

Enough time, as it turned out, for everything to change.

Phex started dreaming in Dyesi. He hadn't realized the Dyesi language was an insidious thing. The Wheel spoke a root version of Galactic, and Attacon 7 spoke Galactic Standard, so Dyesi was the first language Phex had to actually learn. He wasn't sure how he felt about it now nesting inside him, slowly taking over his brain. If he started to think *in* Dyesi, would he think *like* a Dyesi, too? Would that be so bad, when he sometimes felt as if he understood them better than he did his own species?

As if to prove his own confusion about the human condition, Phex awoke in the middle of the night to some muffled sound that wasn't conversation or release. Something suspicious and out of the ordinary for the cantor dorm. He moved his curtain aside, straining his ears. Someone was crying.

He slipped out of bed and padded softly around, listening at each curtain until he identified the culprit. Kallow.

He went to the kitchen, found the tea from her home world, and made a cup – weak because it was the middle of the night. It wasn't ever pitch-black in their dorm, but he knew the kitchen well enough now either way. Tea was the only thing he could think of that might help. Hot beverages, the only language he really spoke fluently. Or should that be *fluidly*?

He carried it to her niche, tapped his nails softly against the stiff drape.

Kallow drew the curtain aside, sniffing.

He pressed the cup into her hand but bent and blew on it so she knew it was hot.

He considered his duty discharged, but when he began moving away, she grabbed his wrist, tugged him to sit, scooting back so he had a spot.

He perched awkwardly while she hunched over the drink and continued to sniffle. Maybe he should have brought her a towel rather than a drink. Not that he'd seen a towel anywhere on Divinity 36.

The beverage clearly hadn't helped, because she seemed to be getting worse, her face glistening with tears. She inhaled the tea's steam. "The smell reminds me of home," she whispered, a hiccough on the last word.

"You miss it?" Phex guessed.

"So much. Do you miss yours?" she asked, finally sipping.

"No." Because he didn't – neither Attacon 7 nor the Wheel, assuming either qualified as *home*. If pressed, he would probably say he liked Divinity 36 best. At least there he got to do something interesting and the food was good.

"Yes, we all get it. You're unflappable. Even with a god in your bed." Kallow rolled her eyes, which Phex took as a good sign.

"Thank you?" questioned Phex, not sure if it was a compliment. He thought she might want to talk about her home more, and that was better than talking about him. Or Missit. Missit, whom he weirdly *did* miss, like some ache for a memory that hadn't fully formed. Lingering divine influence, he supposed. "What bits do you miss most?"

"The smell of forest air. Food that hasn't been processed for space transport and preservation. Baths."

"You'll be on a planet again someday. Yours is close. You might even go home for a visit if you earn godhood."

"But that could be *years*. We're barely at the beginning, and the end seems so far away."

"Homesickness?" suggested Phex, remembering the word from somewhere – an old word.

"I do feel ill."

"The implication being that you can recover from it."

"But do I *want* to stop missing it? It's my home, after all."

Phex couldn't imagine such a thing – to pine for a place. A person, maybe. But not a place.

She seemed to be crying less now. Perhaps talking really did help. Remarkable.

"What else do you miss?"

"My family. My friends. The way people greet me when I walk anywhere, even if they don't know me. That's what my hometown was like. What about yours?"

How to describe the Wheel without incurring pity? "Cold."

"Like you."

Did he come off as cold?

"I'm sorry, that was mean. Perhaps you're just shy and guarded."

"*Cold* is fine."

"What kind of place made a creature like you?" Kallow wondered.

Phex was trying to be helpful or at least manufacture sympathy. He could hardly see how his past would facilitate connection, but Sapiens seemed to enjoy sharing bits of themselves. Portioning out personal information as if knowledge told were somehow better than knowledge learned. So, he said, "Space station. Forced air and dehydrated ration cubes do not nostalgia make."

"I thought you came from Attacon with Gemma."

"Attacon 7, moon colony, forced air, also some ration cubes, but that's not where I was born."

"Will you regret it, do you think?"

Phex was confused. "Regret what?" *The ration cubes?*

"The part of yourself you're giving up to become a god."

"I have nothing to give up."

Kallow's tone was wistful. "Oh, I think you'll find that you did, in the end."

Phex wondered if she knew something about the divinity that he did not. Or if she, who missed her home, could never comprehend the regrets of a person who'd never had one. Or the *lack* of regrets.

Kallow finished her tea. Fortunately, she was no longer crying.

"That was very weak," she griped.

"You need to sleep."

"As if tea would keep me awake. Do you know how much of this stuff I drank every day before coming here?"

"No."

"So much. All the time. There was always this big pot bubbling away, help yourself all day or night." Her voice hitched.

"Don't start again," admonished Phex, who didn't want to feel like he'd wasted effort.

"How do I stop missing it?" she asked, plaintive.

Phex said nothing. He had no idea.

"How do I become stoic, like you? Nothing seems to ruffle you, Phex. Not this place. Not the crazy routine they put us through. Not the terrible food. They take you away and make you practice with graces until you're limping and your feet are covered in blisters or bleeding. Then they hold you back, like me, because you aren't a trained singer and can't cantor well enough. But you're never upset by any of it. Kagee needles you. Berril drapes herself all over you. Gemma whines at you, complaining about everything. Most of us cantors resent you for your looks. None of it gets to you. How do you *do* that?"

Phex considered. "I've nowhere else to go."

"Does that make you lucky or pathetic?"

"At least I'm not homesick," he pointed out.

She gave a watery chuckle. "You're funny. Why don't you talk more?"

"Easier not to." Which made him what, actually? A coward?

"If you say so." Kallow handed him back the cup, now empty.

"Feel better? Or should I make more tea?"

"If I said *more tea*, would you do it?"

"Of course."

"If I said I wanted it stronger, would you make it stronger?"

"I know how you take your tea, Kallow. As I said, you need sleep. You see, that's why I don't say much. When I do, I have to repeat myself."

"Funny again. So, your solution to every crisis is a hot drink?"

Phex considered. "It seems like a decent solution."

Kallow shook her head. "You might be right. I do feel better. Might be the tea, but it's more likely the company."

Phex was startled. Imagine *that* being true.

"You really should talk more. You're maybe even nice."

Phex did not like that suggestion at all. Neither niceness nor talking seemed sensible. "No, thank you."

Kallow patted his arm.

He stood quickly, taking that as a dismissal. Worried she might want to hug. Worried he did. Worried he might be mistaken for flirting.

He paused, holding back the flap. "I think it's better to have something to miss," he said, hoping that could be interpreted as comfort.

He thought it was probably true, too, but he was still grateful it didn't apply to him. He returned the cup to the kitchen and went back to his own bed, annoyed at losing

precious sleep but feeling somehow warmer on the inside.
Which was odd, since he hadn't drunk any of the tea.

Up until the fourth week, Phex liked gracing best. He almost
asked to switch. Would the Dyesi let him audition for dark
grace? To be fair, at first, he simply liked the graces better
than the cantors. He understood them, even though they were
a mixed group of aliens and the cantors were, ostensibly, just
like him – Sapien.

The cantors, with their constant chatter and petty gossip
and revolving rivalries, felt incomprehensible to him, like the
people on the other side of the counter at the cafe.

But soon enough, he liked gracing better, too. The way he
inhabited his own body during dance practice – it made him
feel useful. It reminded him of blade-running, which should
have turned him off. He didn't think he had enjoyed crudrat
work, but it turned out that when he felt safe, or safe enough,
in a place where he slept in an actual bed and owned three
whole outfits and ate three whole meals and got clean each
night – then? Well, then he liked it. Or at least enjoyed the art
that the Dyesi made of his former life.

But the fourth week was when the cantors got to practice
with potential sifters under real domes. No more softskins.
No more amplification chambers.

That was an entirely different experience.

Phex hadn't realized that the sluggishness of softskins fed
back into a cantor. They had made not just the colors but his
notes dull, his song muddied and formless. Causing true skinsift was another experience entirely. It was the difference
between singing and cantor, music and godsong.

It was as if the sifter's skin *saw* his voice. The Dyesi

absorbed the sounds that he created and turned them into not just color and pattern but something more like passion or yearning. A thing that started from air and raw nothingness deep inside his chest was woven into star shine. Nothing could be more wonderful than making the formlessness of the universe manifest as beauty. What he could draw across their skin – it was the opposite of pain.

No wonder they could be gods.

Cantor became his favorite part of every day. Standing with one Dyesi potential under one small dome on that alien moon. He could not wait for the time when it would be two sifters.

He awoke hungry for that each morning rather than food.

He fell asleep wondering what it was like for the great gods who were actually *good* at it. How long would it take for him to get to their level?

Phex had barely begun, and already he wanted to push himself. He, who had never craved anything, wondered if this was love or obsession.

The acolytes noticed, if not his affection, then the colors that resulted. They were pleased. Approval puffed their crests during Phex's sessions. They were not the type to compliment, but they could not hide their pride in a low cantor with such potential. It was enough for even the other cantors to notice.

What Phex hoped neither saw was the caution that lurked under his joy and his newfound skill.

Phex felt like he *had* to be careful with the potential sifters. He was convinced he might hurt them if he let himself sing for only the colors and patterns that he wanted to see. The acolytes gave them existing godsongs to work with, but Phex would have liked to experiment, sing rifts just to know what they did to Dyesi skin. But Purple Eyes had said he could *injure with song*, and the medic said he had a *dangerous voice.* The fear of what that meant lurked inside him, like an ugly color under his stubbornly blank Sapien flesh.

Phex didn't care which potential sifter he was paired with. The other cantors were prone to discussing their preferences in the evenings before bed, which felt strangely dirty. Like he was back in the cafe with those kids and their petty relationships. As if this were a warped kind of dating. Which he supposed it was. Only, they were dating for a unit of six. Still, Phex didn't like discussing the Dyesi with Sapiens as if they were pastry to select from a display case.

The most popular potential sifter, and the one all the cantors wanted to end up with, was Yislofei. Phex genuinely didn't understand what was so appealing about Yislofei compared to the others.

To Phex, each sifter was different. Skinsift was no prettier or easier with, for example, Jinyesun than it was with Yislofei. Jinyesun did lovely sifting – curved organic patterns with deep colors – but that didn't mean Phex preferred Jinyesun. When Phex worked with Yislofei, the pattern was more angled, spiky and sparkling. It was flashy, and there was something to be said for flashy, but the rich curves that Jinyesun brought to the dome were just as pretty in their own subtle way.

To say he liked one sifter over another was like having a favorite color or musical note. Why? When the sifting range was the point? Still, it made him cautious with his joy.

"Phex, do you have a preference?"

"No."

"But everyone has a preference."

Phex turned the question around. "Why do we always talk about sifters but never graces?"

"Well, we work primarily with sifters, don't we?" said Kagee, pursing sculpted lips.

So far, yes. But from what Phex had seen under the dome, gracing was just as important. There was no rhythm, there was no heartbeat, there was no stopping, without grace.

"Are you avoiding the question?" Villi's smile was pointed.

Phex considered. "Must I choose?"

"No, but it's weird you aren't bonding with any of them," pointed out Gemma.

"Must I *bond*?" Phex wondered if he'd somehow missed a lesson on pantheon structure.

"No," Kallow frowned. "I guess we just assumed. I mean, isn't the point to build relationships? So we can become pantheons. So we can be gods."

"You think it's up to us?" Phex was genuinely curious.

"Who else?" Kagee looked like he thought Phex was being intentionally annoying. Those grey eyes of his ought to have been soft, but they always seemed sharp and disappointed in Phex. Phex felt like he was perennially missing something Kagee thought he should notice.

"Them," said Phex.

"Them, who?"

"The acolytes. The divinity. Isn't this their game?"

Villi grinned suddenly. "And we're all playing it, even though we don't know the rules?"

Phex flicked his hands open. *Exactly*. Of course that was what was going on. Did they actually believe they would get to pick? That this would be fair? That potentials had any kind of power?

"Don't be silly," said Kagee, his face pinched. "We just have to be talented enough to make it. That's how we play the game."

"Yes," said Kallow, looking sad, "but it's *talented* by *their* cantor standards, isn't it? And we haven't been told those. Except maybe that Phex is one possible pinnacle." There was bitterness in her voice.

Phex felt guilty. He hadn't meant to make her unhappy.

"Then how do we win?" Kagee asked.

Phex thought that was a crazy question. This was like running the blades. There wasn't winning or losing – there was surviving or not. As if there could be any other kind of game.

"Well, Phex has neatly avoided answering the question, as usual." Gemma suddenly leaned close.

Phex jerked away from her. Too close.

"You really don't have a preference?"

Phex thought about the twelve potential sifters. Some he'd worked with a few times, some only briefly. "No. I just like singing the colors." Pushing skinsift out over a dome. Phex lived for that moment. And he'd never had anything to live for before.

"Okay." Kagee drew out the word like Phex was the weirdo for saying he enjoyed the very thing that they'd all been recruited to do. "Anyone ever tell you that sometimes you act like an old man?"

Phex looked down at feet. Admitting that he liked it now seemed foolish. As if his enjoyment were a secret thing he should have held close and kept guarded for fear of losing. Mentioning it had cheapened it – since none of the others seemed to feel the same way.

They were more focused on finding the right fit, learning the correct skills, becoming the best at godsong. They didn't seem to enjoy cantor very much. This thing that they could do with their voices that became something magical, something beyond just a song – Phex was now afraid that his love for it would make him even more different from these strange human creatures he was supposed to belong with.

And while love was an alien sensation to Phex, fear was awfully familiar.

Unfortunately, that fear, and the companion feeling of not belonging with his fellow cantors, only got worse when the next day, grace training kicked Phex out earlier than usual, and he heard them all talking without him.

His shoe had rubbed his heel raw, worse than normal, so he'd started bleeding but not noticed. After a run and flip, he'd gotten blood on the dome. The acolyte in charge told him in disgust to go back to the dorm and bandage it properly, no need to trouble a medic for something so trivial. Phex was reminded of being yelled at for bleeding on the blades those times he'd been cut on a crudrat run. Seemed his blood was always a problem for others whenever it left his body. But then when Berril teased him for being a thin-skinned Sapien, Phex didn't mind so much.

Phex took off his shoes and walked barefoot through the hallways, stopping occasionally to wipe the back of his foot on the opposite calf, so his jumpsuit, and not the floor, caught the blood that dripped there.

He paused at the threshold to the cantor dorm, hearing raised voices from within.

Gemma's voice was shrill. "He gets special treatment."

Kallow's voice came next. "He is good at gracing, but that seems like extra work. I wouldn't call it *special* treatment."

"And now we pair up with Dyesi and he's good at that, too."

Phex wondered if he should announce himself and enter the room. But that was Dyesi socialization. What was the correct Sapien thing to do? He didn't know. So, he did the crudrat thing and stayed hidden and listening.

"The acolytes like him better than the rest of us. So do the graces and the sifters. Even gods like him," Gemma was still bitter about the Missit incident. "Everyone likes him best. It's not fair."

Phex shifted his weight, brushing his heel against his calf again. Hoped the Dyesi cleaning machines could get Sapien blood out of Attacon wicking cloth.

"Did I miss the part where they said this would be fair?" That was Kagee, of course.

One of the others whose voice Phex couldn't identify said, "It's not so much that he's so good at everything, it's more that he doesn't seem to care about how good he is."

"It's like he doesn't want to be here," said Villi.

Phex shivered slightly, the sweat cooling on his body. He felt queasy, stomach suddenly unhappy about something he'd eaten. Except he'd eaten the same thing that they'd eaten every day since they arrived. It had never upset his stomach before.

"He said he had nowhere else to go," volunteered Kallow.

"Why should it be easier for the only one of us who doesn't actually care?" Gemma again, the whine in her tone.

Kagee sounded bored. "Maybe that's *why* it's easier."

"I think he's arrogant," said another unknown voice. "Off dancing with aliens and skipping the hard bits."

"Except he wouldn't find it hard."

"Just makes the rest of us look bad by doing it perfectly and without comment."

Phex wondered if he was wrong to be so quiet and hide in the kitchen all the time. But he had nothing to say and was of no use to them in the living room, smiling and playing games. He didn't know how to play games – or smile, for that matter.

"Just imagine if he was in our last lesson. He would have switched octaves like it was nothing, while running."

Phex slid down the wall, sat in the hall, looked at the raw spot on the back of his heel. Tried to stop getting sick from other people's words. His belly seemed to be translating his confusion over their contempt and jealousy into bile.

Gemma sniffed. "Of course it'd be easy for Mister Perfect."

Phex closed his eyes. He could do what he could do because of who he was and how he'd been triggered. It wasn't superiority. It was just genetics.

"He never seems to get tired, either, always staying awake later than the rest of us."

Why would they pick that as another thing that upset them? He liked to make sure the kitchen was clean and everything was shut down properly. And he preferred to use the hygiene chamber alone, so no one got upset by his scars.

"Like he doesn't want us to see him sleep."

Kagee said, "You hating on a man because of insomnia?"

"It's creepy."

Someone snorted. Probably Kagee.

"And there's that, too. I mean he's a *boy*, right, not a *man*. But when he deigns to speak, it's like he's older than us, even though he can't possibly be. Like he's better and finds our conversation boring."

Would they be shocked or embarrassed if Phex pushed through the curtain? Would they realize he'd overheard? Would they resent him even more for it?

Phex wished more than anything in that moment that he could leave and hide in Missit's bed, roll himself up in Missit's blanket. *Odd wish.* But the god was light-years away, and even if he were home, Phex didn't have that kind of courage. Apparently, even he had limits to his abilities.

He couldn't go to the grace dorm – they were still in practice.

So Phex stood slowly, padded quietly toward the sifter dorm, his shoes in one hand, blood on his heel. At least he knew the Dyesi wouldn't be talking about him behind his back. He didn't know how he knew that – he just did. The Dyesi weren't like that.

Or maybe he just hoped that they weren't.

8

BATTLE NOODLE OF THE
REFUGEE

Thirty-six days as potentials, and the first round of eliminations was imminent.

An aura of desperation colored the social gatherings leading up to it. The cantors were even more critical and full of complaints, lashing out not just at Phex but also each other. Phex retreated more and more to his kitchen – got quieter and quieter, especially around his fellow Sapiens. Jinyesun got more chatty. Berril got more clingy. Whenever they were together and not gracing, she was hugging Phex or leaning against him. Phex was flattered. As if this flighty little chiropteran with her amazing wings had spotted a stability in him that made her feel safe.

She still came to the cantor dorm in the evenings, dragging other graces along. Sharm came regularly, which was odd, as the Dorien seemed about as antisocial as Phex. Phex supposed Berril was inexplicably taken with that kind of personality. Jinyesun was always welcome, endlessly willing to explain some point of Dyesi culture or kitchen confusion. Phex didn't mind asking questions, so long as the end result was the other person doing the talking.

Phex was in the kitchen, Jinyesun sitting at the end of counter, sipping corrosive dark. Behind them the cantors and a few graces and sifters were playing some kind of language game. Everyone spoke Dyesi most of the time now. But this game was not Dyesi in origin, so everyone was feeling challenged by it. The Sapiens in the cantor dorm still defaulted to Galactic Common when tired, but Phex was starting to resent his old language. It didn't contain the right vocabulary to talk about the divine. And divinity was all that mattered anymore. He wondered if the Dyesi language would influence what he could see, since there were so many more words in Dyesi to describe color and pattern. He wondered if the dome might leak into his brain and reform how he perceived the universe.

"Did you grow up speaking the Dyesi we are learning or a different language?" Phex asked, feeling like this was the first full sentence he'd said in days. But this was Jinyesun, who had bandaged his heel and was always kind.

Jinyesun's crests remained neutral, so it was not an intrusive or unusual question. "Dyesid Prime has only one language. We are not a very large population, and planetfall only colonized one continent."

"I suppose your cave style of occupation limits linguistic diversity too?"

"Maybe." Jinyesun clearly had never thought about it. For the Dyesi, the caves were the only way to live.

Phex made a face. He had no idea how language evolved on planets.

Jinyesun offered more. "I am from the south caves, so by some standards, I have a strong accent. I think it sounds normal, of course."

Phex huffed. Only realizing after he did it that was the way to express amusement in Dyesi. So, he added quickly, to avoid giving offense, "I have one too, in Galactic Common, I mean." The kids at school had teased him a lot about it when he first arrived on Attacon 7. It was one of the many reasons he spoke so little.

"Because of living on a moon or because of being from Attacon?" asked the Dyesi. "I cannot hear accents in Galactic."

Phex suppressed a wince, wondered how to phrase this delicately. "I grew up speaking an old-fashioned version of Galactic Formal. They say I sound stilted and stiff. Like I am trying to be a diplomat."

Jinyesun's crests twitched. "Like a child speaking the language of adults?"

The Dyesi seemed to have a lot of linguistic formalities, so Phex hazarded a guess, "Is there a different register for children in Dyesi?"

Jinyesun clicked affirmation. "It is almost a completely different dialect. It is only spoken prior to instar. You will never hear it off-world."

Phex, who grew up in space, had a sudden shocking realization. "You do not let your children leave the planet, do you?"

Jinyesun's crests fluttered back. "Of course not! Far too dangerous."

Phex wondered if there was a cave somewhere on that ringed world below that was full of the Dyesi version of crudrats, useless kids without ducts to clean or coffee to serve.

"What happens to Dyesi rejects?" he asked, before he could stop himself.

"Rejects?" Jinyesun was confused, crests drooped and wiggling like wilted greens in water. Probably because Phex had used the Galactic word *reject*, since he had no idea on a Dyesi word for it.

Phex reached for other words in Galactic. "Disabled? Deformed? Orphaned?"

No change in the crests.

Phex tried again, this time using the Dyesi term for *refugee*, which he had memorized, plus their word for *children* and then *trash*. Jinyesun remained confused. Phex checked his ident chip for a translation and finally came up with a different way of phrasing it.

"What do you do with *unwanted* children?"

Jinyesun reared back in horror, crests flattened all the way against its skull. "All children are wanted," it said, its tone low and crisp and precise.

Now it was Phex's turn to be confused. "But what about the broken ones? Or the malformed ones? The permanently injured? What about the ones who can't learn? Or don't grow properly? What about the ones whose brains are not the same as the others? The ones who don't fit or adapt? The ones that can't?" Of course he was thinking of his own childhood. Of his malformed immune system that had rejected the Wheel implant.

Jinyesun said firmly, crests back under control, "There is no such thing as an unwanted Dyesi child." It paused and then added, in a very formal register, "There is no such thing as an unwanted Dyesi." It was clear it would not abide further discussion on this topic. Even Jinyesun, apparently, had verbal limits.

Phex didn't want to hurt the Dyesi's faith in its own culture by challenging such a patently impossible statement. It was sweet that Jinyesun actually believed such ideology. But Phex knew without doubt that there were *always* unwanted people in the universe. No alien race was that *much* alien.

It was the first time he really considered the fact that

some of what he learned from the divinity might be simply wrong. Or, perhaps more aptly, a shared delusion. It made him wonder how much of the divinity was like that, less the dome itself than the images that moved across it – beautiful but without substance. It made him wonder if he would ever believe such a fallacy. Like the Dyesi language taking over his dreams, would he also become subsumed by faith in the aliens who spoke it? If that happened, would he have become good or stupid? Either way, he was scared of the possibility, and he wasn't sure why.

Conversation was tense among those gathered in the cantor dorm the night before eliminations. Phex, even more uncomfortable than usual, hadn't left the kitchen all evening.

"What do you think of training so far?" Yislofei asked him, tall and shimmery at the end of the counter. They'd never much interacted socially. Yislofei was usually surrounded by other cantors. It had escaped to the kitchen, which Phex could understand, but also it wanted to chat, which Phex could not understand.

Still, Phex was disposed to be nicer to the Dyesi potentials than to his fellow Sapiens. They never got overly emotional or erratic in their manners or address. They were predictable, more so than his own species. Also, after Jinye-sun's reveal, Phex thought of them as innocent and naive – as if they were, for all their alien height and beauty, collectively younger than himself.

So, Phex took Yislofei's question seriously. After a month, how did he feel about being a potential? It was better than school. Better than working at the cafe. Harder, too, but that was part of the appeal. He wasn't sure he trusted any of it, but did his trust matter?

"I like it," he replied.

Yislofei turned to its other side to politely include Kallow in the conversation. "And you?"

Kallow winced. "It is not what I expected."

"And what was that?"

"More performing. More creating new music. More congregations. More collaboration."

Phex filled in the rest in his own head. *More fame. More celebrity.* Kallow wanted to be a god and thought for some reason that it would happen quickly and easily simply because she had the talent for it.

"The divinity is not about music," said Phex.

Yislofei crested at him. Impressed or shocked? Phex still wasn't great at telling the difference. Still, he definitely had the Dyesi's attention.

Kallow scoffed. "Don't be ridiculous. We are here to be gods. As cantors, isn't that entirely vested in our singing?"

Phex put down the drink he was working on and gestured at Yislofei. "No. It's about skinsift. It isn't what we sing, or even that we sing well. It's that we sing *for them*. For the Dyesi."

"Is that your secret?" Kallow wondered.

Phex shrugged. He wasn't certain enough to defend his opinion. But he did know that watching the sounds he made shiver over alien skin was the best part of every day.

Yislofei cocked its head at Phex. "You enjoy skinsift?"

Phex nodded. "Don't you?"

Yislofei's face clouded in embarrassment. "More than is proper."

Phex thought that maybe that was why Yislofei was so popular.

Jinyesun joined them, explaining, "Ours is not to feel anything, just to manifest the beauty."

"That seems kind of sad," said Kallow.

"Why? Do your emotions negatively impact your sift?" asked Phex.

Both Dyesi gave soundless laughs.

"Can you imagine the chaos that would result?" said Yislofei to Jinyesun.

"And yet everyone seems to find Yislofei fun to work with." Phex let his curiosity get the better of him.

Jinyesun nodded. "Yislofei is popular."

Kallow looked embarrassed. "You can tell?"

"Sapiens are often mysterious to us, but cantors less so. Yislofei is good at skinsift, even while enjoying it a bit too much," said Jinyesun, as if that explained everything.

"Would you say Yislofei is the best of the sifter potentials?" Phex asked, wondering if the Dyesi talked in annoyance behind Yislofei's back about it having arrogant superiority and creepy behavior.

"Certainly not," said Yislofei and Jinyesun at the same time.

"There is no *better* or *worse* as a solo sifter. Until we find balance, we exist in limbo." Jinyesun gave a funny twitching movement that Phex thought might be a Dyesi shrug.

"Balance? You mean your sifter pairing?" Like dark and light grace, high and low cantor, there were two sifters in every pantheon. Phex had been unable to determine why there needed to be two when they did not have defined roles. "How do you figure it out? This balance?"

Jinyesun's crests lowered. "We do not know. The acolytes tell us even less than they tell you. The only advantage we sifters have is cultural. This is a competition for us as well. The divinity guards its secrets, even from sifter potentials."

"Especially from us," added Yislofei.

"Do you have preferences among the cantors?" Kallow

asked. "The way many of us like Yislofei? No offense, Jinyesun."

Jinyesun crested at Kallow. "None taken. We are here to be gods, after all. It is best never to be upset over popularity, since that is something gods compete for all their lives."

Phex thought that was a healthy attitude.

"So, is there one?" Kallow pressed. Because she was Sapien. Because she *did* care about popularity.

"Not really. Many of us like Phex, but not because we perceive him as a better cantor." One of Jinyesun's crests drooped.

Kallow looked hurt. "Of course *him*. Why, then?"

Phex turned to putter about the kitchen, embarrassed. The Dyesi were handing out another reason for his fellow cantors to hate him.

Yislofei answered. "Phex is gentle with us. Cautious."

"Phex is careful about everything." Berril nosed into the conversation, hoisting herself onto a stool. "It's like he is afraid any one of us might shatter. To him we are all fragile." She leaned her head on Kallow's shoulder. Which was good, as Kallow seemed to need affection. The chiropteran looked sleepy.

Phex thought they gave him too much credit. "You *are* fragile. Little bird bones."

"He is careful with his words, too." Kallow nodded at him, forgiving him a little for being chosen above her. Or maybe not. Maybe she was faking it. Phex had no idea anymore. It seemed he couldn't really read Sapiens. He wished they had crests.

"Is that why he uses so few?" asked Yislofei.

One of the other Dyesi, Fandina, joined in. "I agree with my compatriots. He is nicely careful with his cantor."

Fandina and Phex had practiced together for the first time

that afternoon. Phex thought the Dyesi had a lovely sift, bright and clean, almost too sharply patterned. He'd liked how responsive Fandina's skin was, even if there were other sifters he'd managed to sing into more saturated colors.

"And he's careful with his grace," added Berril. The graces had started doing partner work recently. Berril enjoyed working with Phex because she trusted him.

Since Phex was strong, he'd been doing lots of lifts and catches. He was constantly afraid he'd drop someone. In fact, he was afraid for many of the alien potentials most of the time. Afraid they would be hurt by him with song, or word, or deed. But more, he was afraid of making a mistake. That he might give the acolytes some excuse to eliminate him. And now the Dyesi potentials praised him for protecting them when, really, he was protecting himself. It made Phex feel ashamed.

"*Careful* is better than trying as hard as you can?" wondered Kallow.

It hadn't occurred to Phex that his own caution might be a reason for expulsion. Was he too tentative? Would the acolytes hate him for holding back? Gods were not meant to be wary. Gods were meant to be bold and glorious.

The three Dyesi looked at each other. "We do not know."

"I suppose we will find out soon," said Kallow.

Phex began to clean the kitchen, which, as usual, their visitors took as a sign that the gathering was winding down.

Elimination exams were conducted in front of everyone. All the other potentials and any curious acolyte who wanted to attend made up the congregation. Like with auditions, the potentials were judged by a panel of three highly ranked acolytes. They were instructed to perform their audition songs so their progress could be comparatively assessed. This time, however, audience members were encouraged to critique each performance too. That was nerve-racking. But Phex figured that was also the point. Gods could not have stage fright or fear of criticism.

The potential cantors were each paired with softskins. The sifters were paired with a resident set of cantor demigods from a minor pantheon. The graces performed solo pieces. With thirty-six auditions to get through, plus discussion after each, it was a very long day.

Phex's turn came about halfway through. He sang his Errata piece, and, because it was his voice alone and a soft-skin he'd worked with before, he had some fun switching to high cantor on occasion. He did it because he could and because he wanted a little variation to the dome – low cantor alone struck him as boring.

Afterwards, one of the judges commented in that neutral Dyesi way on Phex's range. "You can sing both high and low cantor? How is that possible?"

"Did you not read this one's file?" one of the other judges reprimanded mildly.

The confused Dyesi opened the divine infonet to, presumably, read up on Phex.

Meanwhile, one of the other cantors in the audience said sarcastically, "Phex, are you sure you're Sapien?"

Phex squinted to see who it was. Gemma, maybe?

"Isn't it impossible for one god to sing both high and low cantor?" asked one of the grace potentials.

"Just because something's never been done doesn't make it impossible," shot back Berril in Galactic Common.

Phex was startled. Were they arguing? About him?

"Oh, yeah? Why not ask an acolyte?" That was Kagee.

"No need," said Jinyesun. "Any sifter potential could confirm it. We have all worked with Phex at this juncture. We know his voice."

Kagee was in one of his moods. "What kind of Sapien are you then, Phex? We've been wondering that for a while. You're not actually from Attacon. That's obvious."

Phex tried not to think about the cantors talking about him behind his back.

"He must have surgical mods. If not cyborg, then at least carborg." Villi said this with a good deal of disgust in her tone.

Phex didn't know how to respond. He'd never understood why it was such a horrible thing to be augmented with tech, organic or otherwise, but Sapiens always viewed it negatively. Like it was cheating at life.

Fandina, surprisingly, came to Phex's defense. "Not that it matters to the divinity, but Phex obviously does not have mods."

Phex had no idea how Fandina would know such a thing with such confidence. They'd only practiced together once. And while Jinyesun was maybe a friend, Fandina had no reason to defend Phex. Flattered and a little confused, he gave the Dyesi a nod, wishing he could crest his ears in gratitude.

"He doesn't?" Villi asked, truly shocked.

"That ten-octave range is *natural*?" Kagee was floored, as if his whole worldview were under attack.

The Dyesi potentials all nodded in agreement. It was a very Sapien means of affirmation, and it looked funny, all those alien heads bobbing in unison, crests waving. But the point was made.

The acolytes had stopped arguing among themselves and were listening to the potentials with interest.

One of them said, "His medical records show no modifications of any kind." But that was all. They didn't seem inclined to defend Phex further.

"Is that true, Phex?" A direct question from Kallow.

Phex didn't want to dodge it. He kind of liked Kallow. "Not *exactly*."

Kagee blinked grey eyes at him. "You either have mods or you don't."

Well, if he put it like that...

"Don't." Phex wasn't going to lie.

Mods implied something done artificially to his body after birth. Technically, that had never happened to Phex. The one time the Wheel tried to give him an artificial implant, his brain had rejected it. Not only was he no cyborg, but it was physically impossible for him to become one. The medic said his body would also reject organic transplants, which meant he could never be a carborg, either. If anything, he was the opposite of a mod.

"I was genetically altered *before* birth. It's common practice in my home sector." Phex said this into the hostile silence. Phex had never seen or heard of the part of space that spat out sour, grey Sapiens like Kagee – why should he expect Kagee to know about the Wheel?

Gemma, holder of truths since she too came from Atta-con, said, "He's a Wheel refugee. We get them sometimes in our sector. Xenophobes, small population with relatively low tech, no expansion intentions, and enough intra-political conflict to make them uninteresting except to those of us unlucky enough to border them." Her tone was very superior.

Phex was used to it.

"You are a freak," said Kallow. She said it hard and grating. Like her mouth tasted foul.

Phex looked at her quickly and then away, tugged on one of his ugly ears. Felt his eyes burn. Kallow too?

The Dyesi crested at the obvious Sapien hostility.

Kagee projected like the singer he was to regain attention. "You were genetically perfected in utero?"

Phex considered this. "They *tried*."

Now all the Sapiens were clearly uncomfortable.

Phex added, because he was contrary by nature, "Including my vocal cords."

"You're *manufactured*, not born?" Villi sounded ill. "That's cheating!"

Phex imagined himself like a fetus version of a god statue, coming off an automated production line. He poked at the idea. Found it acceptable enough. Probably not accurate, but who cared?

"I was manufactured *and* born." He hoped that would settle matters.

"Is that why you grace, too?" asked Berril, genuinely curious.

Phex could not quite articulate how relieved he was that she, at least, didn't seem disgusted.

"Progenetor breeding prioritizes physical fitness, yes." He decided not to add that his actual tricks were learned as a child, not coded into him. Because crudrat work had upset the Dyesi before, he didn't want to alienate all the potential cantors *and* all the potential sifters, too.

"Either way, you have an unfair advantage," pointed out Gemma.

Phex wondered why, as she'd known about him all along, she'd not revealed his Wheel identity sooner. Had she waited specifically for this moment to expose him in front of everyone? Did she think it might get him eliminated?

It didn't work.

The Dyesi were clearly uncomfortable with the Sapiens' reactions to Phex's genetics, but they didn't punish him for it.

Phex was not one of those eliminated. Three were kicked out that first month – one high cantor, one dark grace, and Yislofei.

Yislofei didn't look as sad as the others, though. It packed its stuff only to move to a different dorm in the same building. Apparently, Yislofei was staying to train as an acolyte for a very specific divine role. Its dreams of becoming a god were over, but it was being given a new dream.

Berril explained to Phex, although he hadn't asked, "Apparently, Yislofei combines the best qualities of softskin and true sifter. But that means it doesn't have a distinctive-enough look for the dome, nothing to build a brand on. I think it's a bit like being a singer who can only mimic other people's voices."

No one gathered at Phex's kitchen counter that night. A few cantors talked quietly nested in the couch puffs, backs to Phex. The others were in their niches. They no longer needed to talk behind his back. They could dislike him outright now.

Phex wondered if his life on Divinity 36 would become like the cafe. If the others would come around eventually because he controlled the drinks. They hated him now for having been given a talent rather than achieving it. His beverage skills, which had been learned, were perhaps a poor reason to like someone when they might be disliked for something they had no power over.

He wondered if he should learn to cook, if food would help cantors like him where beverages had not been enough. Maybe it was too late with his fellow Sapiens. He couldn't fault them for disliking him – apparently, he was extremely unlikeable by birth, personality, and ability. But the hurt from hearing their words was warning him away. Had served to remind him that they shared very little beyond what they could do to Dyesi skin with their voices.

Things did not improve over the next week.

Kagee, of all people, was the only cantor who even talked to Phex. And then only once, in private, when he caught Phex alone. As if he didn't want to be seen doing so.

Phex hadn't thought Kagee the type to worry over the good opinion of others.

Kagee wanted to explain. Phex had no idea why. "They're prejudiced or jealous. Either way, they're threatened. You used to be just a bad cantor who could grace, then you became a great low cantor *and* a grace. Now it's high cantor, too. You're a triple threat."

"And you?"

Kagee didn't look any grumpier than normal. "Oh, I'm jealous, but not like them. I could have used a little genetic manipulation." He fluttered his ring-covered fingers in the air like he was playing notes on a forgotten instrument.

"Interesting," said Phex, wondering what sort of gene adjustments Kagee wanted. Was Kagee trying to apologize? For himself or the others or both? Surly not.

"Don't get me wrong. I also don't need a reason to dislike you."

"Fair." Phex figured Kagee didn't need a reason to dislike *anyone*, since he seemed to function entirely misanthropically.

"See? You're unbelievably annoying." Apparently, Phex had just proved Kagee's point.

"Why are you telling me this?" Phex asked.

"Because you look lost and confused, and that's annoying too."

Phex didn't understand Sapiens, and he *really* didn't understand Kagee.

Fortunately, Berril had decided to entirely adopt him and would not be swayed. She simply scooped him up and took him with her and Sharm to hang out in the Dyesi's dorm instead of with the cantors now.

Phex had to learn a new kitchen – one that wasn't his and made no attempt to accommodate Sapien taste. Also, one that already had a denizen. Its name was Seryloh and, like Phex, it wasn't talkative. Initially just as territorial over the Dyesi's kitchen, they reached a nonverbally negotiated peace where Seryloh ceded one corner to Phex because it was genuinely confused by grace taste and nutrition needs. And they had regular graces visiting now. Phex proceeded to stock that zone with drinks that he and the graces could ingest, plus sweeteners and snacks that everyone liked. During their evening gatherings, Phex took over making sure the graces had something to consume while Seryloh handled the Dyesi.

It's not that he thought helping in the kitchen would make them like him or anything stupid like that. It was just that Phex only knew how to relate to people from behind a counter. Somehow, all his social interactions had become folded and compressed into those years at the cafe. He'd been forged like a god under a dome, only a very small dome, and so he'd become very small god capable of only simple graces: tea and coffee and corrosive dark. Simply put, he had nothing else to offer. Which was why he decided he wanted to learn to cook.

Sharm turned out to be their pickiest eater. Apparently, Dorien were known for being snobbish about food. Sharm could eat most things safely but didn't like doing so. As a result, the Dorien had become too slender. Phex found Sharm fun to dance with and a passable dark grace, but if the Dorien wasted away into weakness, injury, or death before completing training, none of that mattered.

"You are worried about Sharm?" That was Seryloh's low, raspy voice. They were puttering about the kitchen together in that familiar cafe dance of two competent people sharing a well-known space.

"You as well?" Phex flicked a glance at Seryloh.

The Dyesi clicked informally. Most of the time, the sifters accommodated the other potentials by sticking to Dyesi formal speech, but clicks sneaked in. The Dyesi spoke casually among themselves, but Phex and the others were taught polite register, since that was used in godsong. Phex wondered if, as their refugee, he counted as Dyesi enough to learn how to be rude.

"Can you cook any Dorien dishes?" Phex asked.

"No. I understand they are quite complicated." Seryloh's cheeks went opaque in embarrassment.

That's what Phex had read, too. "I have been trying to get extra nutrients into Sharm in drinks, but they are so fussy."

"Noodles?" suggested Seryloh.

"Noodles?"

"Does not every species like noodles in some form or another?"

Phex had to agree. It was a truth universally acknowledged. "But we need to know which kind."

Seryloh clicked again.

Phex cleared his throat and turned toward the counter. "I have a question."

Everyone stopped talking and stared at him. Phex had never projected so loudly outside of the dome. And he never asked questions of the group.

"He speaks!" Berril clutched at her wings and pretended to stumble in shock.

Phex scowled at her. "What is everyone's favorite noodle dish?"

"Of course he wishes to know about food." Jinyesun's ears crested, big eyes squinting slightly in the expression Phex had come to understand meant both interest and mild amusement.

"I love ramen," said light grace Pommey, naming an ancient noodle soup that had been around forever and was still popular, particularly on space stations. Phex had actually eaten that before, so he knew the basics. Even a sad little moon like Attacon 7 boasted a ramen stall.

A few other graces chimed in that ramen was their favorite too, but not Sharm.

Some of the Dyesi named noodle dishes native to their planet, made with the high-protein spud that seemed to form the base starch of their diet. Spud was grown in massive quantities in the caves of Dyesid Prime. It was a major export, too, for it was highly nutritious even dehydrated, and extremely good as a flour for making, among other things, noodles.

Fandina said, surprising everyone, that it really liked an old hu-core noodle dish called naengmyeon it had once tried from a cuisine trader.

A few mentioned noodle dishes that Phex had never heard of, and, eventually, Sharm spoke up. Phex asked the Dorien to repeat the name of the dish and elaborate on the ingredients. He made careful mental note to research it up later. Exchanging looks with Seryloh, he was confident the Dyesi would do the same. They'd compare notes and see if they could come up with a facsimile tempting enough for Sharm's discerning palate.

Fandina seemed to be following their plot. While the others continued chatting about noodles, Fandina eyed them as they resumed puttering about the kitchen.

"Get what you needed, Phex?" Fandina leaned over the counter, crests interested.

Phex didn't answer.

Fandina huffed. "Worry is a pretty color on you."

Phex shook his head at the Dyesi's pertness. "Hush, you." But he decided to look up naengmyeon as well. It might be fun to cook something special for Fandina, too.

It worked. Between them, Phex and Seryloh came up with a few dishes that Sharm would eat. They at least managed to stop the Dorien from getting any skinnier. Fortunately, the things Sharm liked were things that most of the other graces thought were tasty, too. Dorien food came by its reputation honestly.

Phex was lucky to have Seryloh's help. The Dyesi knew local trade agents and had mysterious ways of getting supplies delivered to the dorm, even though they weren't supposed to have contact with the outside world. With Seryloh, Phex had access to a wider range of ingredients and someone who could teach him not just what things were but how to cook them and make substitutions. It wasn't difficult – cooking was mostly a matter of following instructions carefully and improvising when necessary, like gracing this was something Phex could learn to do so long as he concentrated.

So, in the end, being estranged from his fellow cantors wasn't so bad. True, he no longer spoke to anyone in his home language. True, the gaze of his fellow Sapiens slid off his face in discomfort. And true, he stayed up late in alien dorms because he no longer felt comfortable in his own.

But it wasn't so bad. At least he had Seryloh, a kindred spirit in the kitchen.

That's what Phex told himself.

Then he had to go and wreck that, too, by opening his mouth.

Almost two months into training, in a one-on-one cantor practice with Seryloh, an acolyte asked Phex to push the pattern, flexing from low cantor to high.

It was a Tillam piece, challenging and complicated. Phex was singing Fortew's role with no Missit to meld, blend, or modify his reverberations. Seryloh was strong, its skin elastic and tough. This made the Dyesi hard work for a cantor to sift. Even though Seryloh's patterns were stunning, its colors were challenging to fix to the dome. Phex flexed his voice and watched his godsong shimmer over Seryloh's skin. The Dyesi almost stumbled from it.

"You need to force that bright red to stay three beats longer, cantor," instructed the acolyte. "Shift the note slightly up, then down again, and put more power behind it. Your voice does not crack. This should be easy for you."

Phex puffed out a breath, looked at Seryloh. The Dyesi was stoic, but it couldn't control a slight shiver in its ear crests.

Phex sang the verse again, applying the inflection as ordered. The colors wavered, but the pattern stayed strong.

"Again. Harder. More."

Phex pushed with more resonance. It wasn't his max, but it was more than he'd ever blasted at skin before.

Seryloh seemed to brace against the wave of red that resulted. It was almost eye-searingly bright on the chamber around them, but the tone of that red still wasn't stable, wavering from orange to pink unpleasantly.

The acolyte hissed in frustration. "Again. Focus the color, pull back on the pattern."

Phex tried to modulate his voice, waver the note at exactly the right pitch to generate a true red without moving into pattern instead. It was really difficult, especially with someone like Seryloh who lacked an affinity for color – at least within the context of Phex's voice.

The acolyte slammed a six-fingered hand against the amplification chamber wall, disrupting the display. "You are limiting yourself, Phex."

"I am scared of hurting him."

"Have you hurt a Dyesi with your voice before?"

"Can't every cantor?"

"No. And it is rarer in low than high. Why should you be so special?"

Seryloh came to Phex's defense. "One does not have to cut flesh with a blade to know that it can cause injury."

The acolyte's crests flattened. "The softskins reported him very gentle. Seryloh, you are the toughest potential we have. You can take it." It turned back to Phex. "Push more."

Seryloh looked scared and very much like it didn't think it *could* take it.

Phex caught the sifter's gaze, searching for reassurance. Seryloh crested at him slightly, clicking encouragement.

Phex tightened his lips, took a breath, then sang the verse once more. Not at all how Fortew did but instead exactly how he would if he were alone in a dome somewhere, singing Tillam's song with no concern for how the noise affected those around him.

Seryloh's skin burst into jagged shards of bright red, a star nova over flesh and chamber walls simultaneously. Crimson dominated a bleeding pattern, feeding shapes into each other like they were living creatures rotating from one angle to the next – square to triangle to diamond to long rays of rosy light.

It was glorious and way too bright. Phex shaded his eyes

and cut the verse early. He blinked away spots, saw Seryloh folding slowly down, body oddly stiff.

Phex leapt to catch the Dyesi before its knees hit the floor.

The acolyte hissed. "How very tiresome."

The iridescence of Seryloh's skin was cracked in fine lines over the surface, like a glass that had been dropped but not shattered. No pattern to it, just a random web of opaque threads like scratches, pink-tinged and angry, etched into flesh. It was ugly-beautiful but looked painful.

"Songbruise," explained the acolyte.

Scared to touch that fractured skin, Phex nevertheless picked Seryloh up in a dancer's lift and made for the doorway.

"Where are you going?" asked the acolyte.

"To the medics, of course!"

The acolyte crested at him. "Not your responsibility. Put it down. A medic has already been summoned."

Phex set Seryloh carefully on the floor, wanting to give comfort but not knowing how.

"Why did you push me?" Phex let rage enter his tone, wishing he knew a low-register insult in Dyesi. But he was more upset with himself for letting go and not listening to his instincts than he was at the acolyte.

"We needed to see if you could. Now we know you can," said the acolyte, as if that were an excuse.

"You did this on purpose? Seryloh is a friend!"

"What has that to do with anything?" wondered the acolyte.

"I do not want to do this again."

"What, low cantor?"

"Hurt someone with my voice."

"So, do not do it. Learn control without limiting yourself."

"How?" Phex was frustrated.

The acolyte regarded him. "You cook, do you not?"

"Sort of." Phex wondered what that had to do with anything.

"You use a knife to prepare food. A knife that in other hands could kill. Your voice is that knife. It is up to you to use it as a tool instead of a weapon."

Dangerous voice indeed. Phex stepped back while the medics came in and carried poor Seryloh away.

The acolyte's big blue eyes stayed focused on Phex. "You have been keeping it sheathed. That is no longer an option."

Only Berril was brave enough to ask Phex about it later that night. "That thing you feared – it occurred today with Seryloh, didn't it?"

"Songbruise," explained Phex, who was hanging out in the grace's dorm for a change. It's not like he could seek refuge in Seryloh's empty kitchen. The idea made him feel queasy.

"Was it as bad as you thought?"

"Do all the potentials know Seryloh ended up in medical because of me?" Phex countered.

"Yes." Berril looked sad.

Phex felt his face freeze. Of course they did.

"Will the Dyesi potentials be scared of me now?" Stupid question when he was scared of himself.

"Can you stop yourself from doing it again?" Berril's tone was sympathetic. But how could Berril understand? She would never, could never, hurt anyone.

"I don't know."

"Then yeah, they'll be scared of you."

And they were.

Training became a new kind of torture for Phex in the weeks that followed.

The Sapiens already hated and avoided him for what he was. Now the Dyesi feared and avoided him for what he could do. Or at least they should. This thing he had done was worthy of fear. Only the graces were still available to Phex, and of them, only Berril and Sharm really tried to be friendly. He was becoming an anathema on Divinity 36 – once again the unstable outsider. Once more a blue-haired crudrat who ran the blades but had outlived his usefulness. Instead of dying on a blade, he had become that blade. His voice was a knife he'd lashed out with indiscriminately, and instead of hurting himself, he'd hurt others.

Phex resented himself for its power – this weapon he had been handed and did not know how to use.

9

REPUDIATED BY CANTOR

The second round of eliminations was much the same as the first.
Phex, Berril, Sharm, Jinyesun, and Fandina all came though
okay. Phex now spent as little time as he could with his fellow
cantors, but he could still understand how everyone was improv-
ing. His own voice was going from strong to educated, his
dancing becoming more like grace and less like running blades.

And then, three months in, came the third round of eliminations.

Sharm came out of the testing dome and walked straight
to Phex, of all people, and hugged him.

Phex wondered why graces were always hugging him.

"I finally get to go home," they said.

"To a world covered by oceans?" replied Phex, wondering
what that was like.

"And food that is always delicious." Sharm's smile was
twisted and wobbly.

"Must be nice there."

"It is. Come visit me sometime, when you're a god."

"Travel safely, Sharm," said Phex, because he couldn't

make that promise. Even if he became a god, his time wouldn't be his own. He'd go where the divinity sent him. Gods never belonged to themselves – they belonged to their believers.

But Sharm? Sharm was indeed free.

They were testing separately this time. Which meant the potentials were all waiting outside of the dome in nervous huddles, and everyone had seen Sharm hug Phex and say goodbye. Weird sensation, observed affection. Parting with a person and not a place.

After testing the graces, the divinity started evaluating the cantors.

When his name was called, Phex entered, greeting the space out of habit. He was somehow not surprised to find five minor gods waiting on the dais.

Real, actual, living gods.

He recognized the members of Orrow, although he didn't know any of them by name. They were a newer pantheon, recently made manifest, with only a few famous godsongs. They had a small collection of maybe a billion devoted worshipers, and a solid, upbeat brand.

Orrow's low cantor sat below the dais next to the three acolyte judges. She waved at Phex in a friendly way.

Phex climbed onto the dais and assumed low-cantor position. They had sung one of Orrow's godsongs in practice that week. Now he knew why. He'd found the low cantor part not particularly challenging, although he didn't know any of the pantheon's choreography.

"Run him through three rounds of basic training for the first verse and chorus."

Phex assumed the instructions were for his benefit, since presumably all of the low cantors who'd tested before him had performed the same song, and the same part in the same way.

Orrow coached him efficiently. The steps for low cantor were simple. Phex had enough grace training now to pick them up easily.

"Start whenever you are ready," said an acolyte.

Phex held up a hand, saying "Wait," so the aliens understood the gesture.

He approached Orrow's two sifters.

Orrow's Dyesi looked very similar – of a height, same eye, nose, and mouth shape, both leaning toward purple skin. Phex thought they might be siblings or even twins.

He touched his lips with three fingers and then flicked a Dyesi formal greeting. "I will try to sing for you softly." The idea that he might songbruise an actual god was terrifying. He wondered if, since there were two sifters, the risk was diminished or amplified.

Orrow's high cantor gave him a tolerant look. "Coil to my lead and you'll be fine."

One of the judges said, "You have not heard his voice, Chaymay. The caution is warranted."

She was cantor enough to push anger into her tone. "You risk my sifters on a mere potential?"

Orrow's Dyesi gods moved to flank her. They touched her arms, though whether to comfort or caution, Phex couldn't tell.

Chaymay turned to Phex with much less warmth in her eyes. Another Sapien to dislike him. Yet he understood her protective instinct. How would he feel if this were some strange grace told to catch Berril on a toss?

"Have you caused damage with your voice before?" she asked.

Phex nodded, ashamed.

Chaymay glared down at the judges, not moving.

"Sing the song, minor god. This is not a debate." The acolytes were firm with her.

Phex gave an apologetic grimace.

Chaymay pursed her lips, but she took position and began the song.

It was only one verse and one chorus, but it was still Phex's first experience with a full pantheon, and it was exhilarating. Limited though it may be. Careful as he was being. It was still glorious.

There were so many aspects to keep track off. The way Chaymay's voice blended with his, how that made for an entirely different wealth of color and pattern on the Dyesi skin and the dome overhead. How the rhythm of light and dark grace formed and interrupted their collective sound, breaking patterns and pausing them, shading, focusing. The fact that it all worked together to produce an insane beauty made Phex proud. He hardly knew where to look – the dome or the skin, the dais to make safe his own movements, or the fluidity of the graces as they danced around him.

And this had been *simplified* for the exam.

All too soon, it was over.

Phex held his last note, even though he wasn't supposed too, just to see his color and pattern without Chaymay's higher voice to mitigate it. It turned out to be a sort of dark blue with low speckles of deep purple and a sunburst pattern.

"Stop fooling around. This is an evaluation, not playtime," interrupted one of the acolytes.

Phex dipped his head and ended the note.

However, none of the Dyesi, acolytes or gods, seemed *actually* annoyed with him.

"Can we do it again?" Phex asked. "I missed that one

harmony at the end of the verse, and I forgot to step away for the light grace during the chorus."

"No." The acolytes were firm. "At least not that way. We want to experiment with you."

They were testing him more? Phex had already taken longer than any of the previous potentials.

He looked covertly around. The gods on the dais with him were confused too. Phex found that reassuring.

"This is to take advantage of Orrow being here," explained one of the acolytes unhelpfully. "Wyn, show him your part, please."

The dark grace stepped forward, confused but willing.

Wyn was an alien species that Phex didn't know. He was big, about the same size as Phex, and seemed to have more looseness to his joints than a Sapien. Phex followed Wyn's moves, but there were a few he couldn't execute, as his body simply didn't bend that direction. He had to modify the choreography, so it wouldn't look as spectacular.

One of Wyn's knee-lands after the first verse left enough lead time for Phex to execute a wall flip instead. He figured he might as well show off what they'd made him learn. He bet he could land it in the same spot, with about the same force, and on the right beat, too.

Phex looked down at the judges with a challenging tilt to his head. "You sending Orrow's low cantor back up here, or do you want me to sing *while* I grace?"

"Can you do both?" All three acolytes crested at him.

"I suspect I would do neither well, and my breathing would be impacted, but I am willing to try."

The acolytes consulted with each other, then one of them said, "Wyn, leave the dais."

"A pantheon of five is ugly," objected one of the sifter gods.

"And unbalanced," said the other.

"This is for science, not forever," replied an acolyte.

"Is the divinity getting messy these days, or is it just me?" asked Chaymay.

Phex arched his brows at her. "You talk like someone who has never met Missit."

She laughed. "Quite right. Very messy. And he has been around forever."

The acolytes were getting increasingly impatient. "Begin, please."

Phex sang the song again, trying not to mess up the notes as he performed dark grace at the same time. It wasn't easy, since the beats and pauses he danced intentionally didn't match the cadence of his cantor. He messed up more than once, both the movement and the song. And every failure was depicted full and bright all around him. The patterns were ugly enough to make a Dyesi cry – a species that had no tears. But his colors stayed true. He thought it might be possible to perform an adequate version of both positions at once, but the pattern and the tune would need to be simplified, which would result in a suboptimal skinsift and an immature-looking dome. Like the visual version of a nursery rhyme.

Phex ended everything with his running wall flip instead of Wyn's doubled-jointed jump slide. He managed to land it on beat, if a little too deep and reverberating. It was supposed to be the thing that interrupted his own final note, so instead, he had to cut the godsong at his landing, which was no doubt jarring. But he couldn't very well use his own grace to fade his own voice. At least, he didn't *think* he could.

He landed kneeling, head down. It wasn't until he stood back up that he noticed one of the sifter gods was kneeling as well. The Dyesi was bent over hugging both arms, and it looked like it was in pain.

Chaymay, the other sifter god, and Orrow's light grace surrounded it protectively.

Phex ran to the fallen god. "Did I hurt you?"

The crumpled Dyesi was clearly suffering, but its iridescent skin wasn't showing the fracturing of songbruise. Instead, its all-over base color was now a blotchy orange.

Chaymay looked at Phex like she wanted him dead.

Phex moved quickly out of striking distance. He could fight – any kid with his background could fight – but he thought it would be a really bad idea to get into a physical altercation with a god.

He took three fast steps, then executed a staggered leap down the side of the dome to get off the dais the quickest way he could. No need to use the lift or the stairs – this was faster, and it put him right in front of the judges. At least, they might be disposed to protect him from the wrath of the gods.

Chaymay watched him do this, mouth pinched. "What exactly *are* you?"

"Sapien, I assure you." Phex would never again, voluntarily, reveal more than that.

She turned back to her fallen sifter. "Potentials these days," she said, as if Orrow weren't barely out of the practice domes themselves.

"That was interesting," said one of the acolytes, not concerned over the health of Orrow's sifter.

"A good illustration as to why the roles cannot be combined," said one of the others. "Or the number of gods on the dais altered."

"We should have known a cantor cannot pause themselves. That such an abrupt stop would injure."

"But we did not, because it has never been tried."

"Now we will not allow it again."

Phex interrupted their discussion. "Is the god going to be all right? Was that songbruise again? Did I damage it permanently?"

"Songburn," said an acolyte, clearly annoyed.

"I can *burn* them, too?" Phex was absolutely disgusted with this idea.

"It is extremely rare. Only happens with low cantor because it is tied to pattern and not color." The acolyte was dismissive. "It will heal. We appreciate your performing two roles at once. It was, in a primitive way, interesting. Even as it damaged. That flip you did at the end was lovely. This trick comes from your past?"

Phex supposed they would have researched his crudrat history and included everything they could in his file by now. Gods did not keep secrets from the divinity.

"Yes."

The acolytes exchanged rapid crest-wiggles.

Phex didn't know what to do, so he just stood there, feeling guilty and foolish.

Finally, one of the judges said, "Unfortunately, grace is not what we want of you. Your voice is remarkable but proving too dangerous to be of use to us. You are dissociative and antisocial as well, failing to bond with other Sapiens. Do not take offense. This is our mistake. We have made a note not to accept Wheel refugees again. You can rest assured the divinity has learned from you. Sad. For you had such…" It paused and then added, amused with itself, "Potential."

Phex felt the bottom fall out of his stomach. Rejection. The horror of being once more unwanted. Had he, at some point, lost his much-prized indifference?

One of the other acolytes said, "We should have tested

this one at the end of the day. We needed to examine the others with Orrow, but now the pantheon is down a sifter."

"Just use a softskin."

"Would that be a fair test, a weak pantheon?"

"What is fair? It should be sufficient."

"Acolytes?" Phex's voice sounded broken and cracked. His skin was clammy and cooling too fast. His throat was hot with acid fear.

"Oh, right, yes. Phex. You are dismissed as both a low cantor and grace candidate. One of the acolytes outside will see to your resettlement paperwork."

"I am eliminated?"

"You are no longer a potential god."

Phex felt like throwing up. Not allowed to sing the colors anymore? No kitchen to hide in. No Berril to hug? No Jinyesun to chat with? Where would he go now? What would be done with him? His shoulders folded, physically manifesting defeat. What a graceful reaction.

He turned back to the dais, numb and stunned but still compelled to try to right the wrong that caused it all. "Sorry about the burn." He owed Orrow an apology. He'd hurt one of them with his voice. Really hurt. He deserved to be dismissed. It should have been done months ago when he bruised Seryloh in the practice booth. Why had they let him stay and hope?

Chaymay pointed a finger at him. "Get out."

Phex got out.

Oddly, his first thought after the leaving the dome was that he'd never see Missit again. Not in person. He hadn't even realized he wanted to. He hadn't realized he *wanted* any of it.

And now it was gone.

In addition to Phex and Sharm, Kallow, one other grace,

and two sifters were eliminated that third month. Six of them in total.

Berril cried. Her small, sharp face wet, her hands clinging to Phex. Jinyesun, Fandina, even Seryloh made the time to run after Phex before he climbed into the transport. The aliens were all Dyesi-elegant and Dyesi-stiff with formal goodbyes and wilted crests. From Seryloh, it hurt. That someone he'd injured forgave him enough to lament his leaving. It felt like the fracturing of Dyesi songbruise had been transferred into Phex's own stomach – cracked and pink-tinged injuries inside his body. The burn of orange that Phex would never sing again was lodged in his throat. A hot brand of failure to swallow around.

Phex wondered if a person healed from invisible wounds or if they too scarred like flesh did. Then he shouldered his tiny pack and his infinite regrets and left Divinity 36.

The six rejects were put onto a fast-moving transport ship and reminded that their divine contracts included a gag order. They couldn't discuss their experience as potentials in private, public, or on the infonet. They were not allowed to indicate by word or deed that they'd once nearly become gods. They were, however, encouraged to work for the divinity in some capacity – at local domes or as divine disciples. Phex figured the Dyesi wanted keep an eye on them.

They were each transported right back to wherever they'd started from. Even Phex, the Dyesi refugee, went back to Attacon 7. The Dyesi paid his resettlement fee. He was, after all, their refugee. Their responsibility. Their burden. But he wouldn't be resettled on one of their moons or their planet. They didn't actually want to keep him if he couldn't be a god.

Attacon 7 looked small and sad. Galactic Common sounded harsh and unfriendly in Phex's ears. Everyone's movements were jerky and abrupt. No one greeted unfamiliar spaces in lyrical Dyesi phrases of acceptance. But otherwise, nothing had changed.

Attacon 7 allowed him to return, doing their duty by a refugee no longer their own. Phex did not know how much the Dyesi paid for his retainer, but Attacon demanded his presence be accounted for with contribution once again. Quite rightly. The divinity probably pressured them to connect him with a dome, so Phex got his old job back at the cafe. No doubt Attacon was content to have him tucked away in service to social capital, and the divinity was content to see him safely inside a cupola.

At least Del was pleased to have him back, so much so she almost cracked a smile.

"Oh, good. You're home. Are you willing to go full-time? I've started a new cafe two bubbles over. How do you feel about becoming the manager of this one?" She didn't even ask him where he'd been. Apparently, that didn't matter.

Phex had been gone almost five months by Attacon standards, and now there he was – same boss, same cafe, same customers, same beverages as before. He had a new pod to sleep in, but it was the same design. The cafe had grown more popular, but apart from that, little had altered on Attacon 7 except him.

The moon seemed shabby and tight, ill-fitting. Like clothing once comfortable but now outgrown. Except he was the one who'd been stretched out of proportion. He ached from the constriction of it. He wasn't sure if it was shame or grief or some other emotion he couldn't name.

Phex found himself doing crudrat tricks more than he ever had before. He missed gracing a lot, and running the neighborhood was his best alternative. It cleared his mind. It didn't loosen that tight ache, though. His stomach never really seemed entirely happy with him.

He never sang.

Godsong on the cupola still marked out the refrain of his cafe workday, but now it also beat on the tattoo of memories in his brain. He no longer hummed along. Lyrics he knew all too well bruised him with disappointment. He missed singing skinsift so much, sometimes he became dizzy with it.

Occasionally, the ache faded to numbing acceptance and he stopped being constantly distracted by the churning in his belly. There was something safe about the cafe then, about Del's grumpiness, about the ritual of it all. His heart took reassurance in the recognizable patterns of making drinks, changing the heavy casks, and cleaning the counters – patterns that were not grace nor sifted skin but were at least something he could create. Not beautiful, just safe.

The cafe's cupola made him feel grey and hard and cold, like a dormant dome. Colorlessly waiting to become something that was no longer an option – unsure and incomplete, but permanent. He was stuck in a stasis of dissatisfaction, lodged between the nameless ache and the numbness. But at least it didn't hurt there.

Then one morning when he was covering someone else's shift, a song they'd been practicing right before he left swept over the dome overhead. A song he hadn't heard since Divinity 36.

Suddenly, he was automatically making corrosive dark for Jinyesun instead of the bubble tea on order. He found himself staring dumbly at his own hands, that they were doing a thing he had not willed, his muscles remembering a person that his brain had tried to forget. His fingers were curved around a beverage that no one there wanted to drink – liquid loss. He threw the toxic stuff away and willed his face to stay impassive.

"What's taking you so long?" wondered the regular, quite rightly wanting her tea.

"Sorry," said Phex. "I'm moving slow this morning."

The customer was sympathetic. "Aren't we all, dear?"

Phex would have to be on his guard. If a song could transport him vast distances to an alien moon around a ringed planet and his past self – it had become a kind of time travel. The divinity already defied space – why should it not defeat time? All the songs on the dome were now part of Phex's history, so this could happen again.

And it did.

And then again.

Phex, frozen by song, lost and regretful, in a cafe. His customers increasingly annoyed with him.

Phex began to pray to the divine, like a proper worshiper, for new godsongs to be created. Songs with which he had no connection. No memories.

Because he was in the cafe all the time now, surrounded by people, he thought it was the songs doing it to him. He thought it was the dome. He thought that, maybe, he actually missed the divinity.

Then the divinity *did* release a new godsong.

And it was Tillam.

Missit's golden voice gilded the dome with all the warmth and promise that Phex had left behind.

At the revival, even though it was an entirely new song, Phex found himself standing frozen, alone in a way he'd never been before. As if he himself were a song that had ended mid-chorus, prematurely cut off from whatever it was destined to become.

Missit's voice hurt him in pricks all over his skin. As if

his dumb blank human flesh was trying to sift. It was a new song, but it still reminded Phex of gracing with Berril. Missit's familiar notes and rifts reminded him of the ones Jinyesun colored so beautifully. It reminded Phex of Missit, too, of course – a roll of bright gold in his bed. Smile quirked and cheeky, flecked eyes focused on Phex, curious and alive and *real*.

"Hey! Where's my coffee? Why are you just standing there? So annoying." Some customer was being sharp in exactly the way Kagee was sharp, like it was habit and not cruelty.

Phex looked over at the counter, and Missit's statue winked gold at him. He hated that statue. He dug his nails into his palms to stop himself from crying or throwing up and went to make the coffee.

Late that night, his pod seemed unnaturally quiet, with no other potentials in niches around him, no heavy curtain flapping or greetings being called to the space. He found himself with eyes sandy and wide, looking into the darkness as if it held all the answers the colorful dome never could.

It took him three weeks to figure out what that ache was about.

He didn't miss the divinity.

He didn't miss godsong or singing it.

He didn't miss being good at something glorious.

He missed his friends. He'd actually had friends. That's what they'd been. Berril and the graces, Jinyesun and the sifters. Missit.

Phex had been alone his whole life, but now, for the very first time, he was lonely.

It was another ordinary evening at the cafe.

There was a revival being beamed the next night, but it was Orrow's, not Tillam's. Phex had assigned extra shifts and ordered additional stock in anticipation. The cupola would be packed, and he was concerned they'd run out of boba. But no one rioted over lack of boba – at least, he didn't *think* they did, so he didn't know why he was so fretful about the whole thing. Two months back on Attacon 7, and Phex should be accustomed to his managerial role. He even had employees under his charge, as if he were an actual adult.

Teenage malcontents still tried to steal Missit's statue, but these days, the older generation also showed up, and even families frequented the cupola. The cafe was no longer the territory of youth.

Missit's statue was flirting with a customer at the retail port. Phex kept the horrible gold thing at the counter with him most days and chose not to explain that decision to himself or anyone else.

"Tillam's Lament" was playing when the alien entered Phex's cafe.

His cafe in truth this time, and almost *his* alien too – a not-quite stranger with familiar purple eyes. Perhaps not *alien* at all. Could he call them aliens when he still dreamed in their language instead of his own?

The cafe hushed in the presence of greatness.

The Dyesi approached Phex, liquid elegance no longer seeming predatory just habitual.

Phex gave it the three-finger flick of respect.

"Beautiful greetings," it said to him in Dyesi.

"What, no acknowledgment of a spatial relationship? You have been in my cafe before," Phex replied, also in Dyesi. The language relaxed his mouth, easy on his tongue like sugar crystals.

The alien flicked a crest at him in amusement.

Everyone was staring at them.

The Dyesi said, "The divine compels me. This is a matter of business, not protocol."

The ritual words of an acolyte under pilgrimage. "You are here on missionary work?"

The alien clicked.

Phex tapped his com unit.

"Yes, boss?" a slightly breathless voice answered him.

"Break is over, kid."

"But you always let me take extra time when my girl-friend visits!" Lhar's voice was whiny.

"Something has come up. I need to step out for a minute."

"You want to leave the cafe mid-shift? *You*, boss?"

Silence.

"Okay. I'll be right up."

Lhar appeared from the basement, girlfriend in tow, both a little mussed.

Phex coded the port over. "Keep an eye on that one – he has been extra flirty today." He pointed at Missit's statue.

The statue blew him a kiss.

"Follow me," Phex said to the Dyesi, leading it beneath the dome. Ignoring Lhar's shock at both the presence of the alien and Phex's mastery of its language.

The lower level was tiny. Cupolas were already the smallest domes, and they were not designed explicitly to be cafes – just entertainment units – so the arrangement was awkward. The underground area, carved out of hard moon rock, was cramped and crammed with stock.

Phex was big and the Dyesi bigger. They took up most of the free space, standing too close for either one's comfort and breathing each other's air. The dimness made it difficult for

Phex to read the Dyesi's skin opacity. All he had to go on were crest-wiggles.

"How can I help the divinity, *friend*?" Phex asked.

"It is good that you retain our language."

Phex waited.

"I have been tasked with…" Its crests trembled in an unfamiliar way. "That is to say, the divinity would like you to consider…"

Phex had never known an acolyte to be hesitant with its divine duty before. Did the Dyesi want him to do something illegal? Surely, his obligations as their refugee and former potential didn't include that.

Finally, it said, "You are aware you remain under divine contract?"

"I am." *The gag order, among other things.*

"You are. Wait. You *are*?"

"The contract was for a full Dyesi year, not just the duration of my time as a potential. It did not terminate just because I got expelled."

"Oh, you *do* know. That is not the usual response."

"Acolyte, what can I do for you?"

"Divinity 36 changed you, Wheel-child."

"I cannot leave Lhar unsupervised for much longer. Say your piece, please, so I can get back to the cafe." Phex used formal Dyesi, but he let his tone go curt.

"We wish to recall you."

"What?"

"Back to Divinity 36."

"*What?*" Phex reached back with both hands, bracing himself against a stack of milk powder.

"It has come to our attention that we may have miscalculated."

"Has something happened since I left? Is Berril okay?

Jinyesun?" *Fandina, Seryloh, Kagee? Missit? Oh, gods, was*
something wrong with Missit?

"I am unfamiliar with the particulars. Your expulsion was
a shock to me and a stain on my recruitment record. I had
high hopes for you. To me, this recall is a good thing."

Phex's skin prickled. He felt so nauseous, he thought he
might actually vomit, for a change. Panicked because he'd
make a mess and have to clean it up.

He breathed shallowly around the churning and held
himself completely still.

"Sapien?" questioned the Dyesi. Crests pointed at him
and his odd immobility. "Potential?" A plea and an offer.

"Can I say no?" Phex asked, voice thinned by the acid
burn bubbling up inside him, wondering if, after all this, he
was actually a coward. There in his cafe domain with his
aching loneliness, at least he knew exactly what to expect.
The divinity had proved itself unpredictable.

"What possible reason could you have to refuse us?"

"I need to sit down." Phex said, and did, dropping fast to
the cold stone floor. He folded long legs and looked at his
hands, as if something so plain as human flesh held any
answers.

Going back would fix the loneliness – at least in the most
immediate sense. But what happened if he made more
friends? What happened when he burned or bruised them?
What happened if they got expelled? What happened if he
started to believe again? If he proved good enough to be
hated by others? If he started to hope? What happened if the
divinity expelled him a second time? Could he dwell in aches
and numbness all over, or would it be even worse? Was there
worse? What came after disappointment and loneliness?
Despair?

"We would prefer it if you did not decline. We could

make it very difficult for you, here on this little moon. But we do not wish to be cruel."

Phex pressed his palms to his hot forehead, thought about where he wanted to be, what he wanted to become, wondered about purpose and desire. Hated the divinity for jerking him around like a toy. Like a statue in the making.

He found a square of packaging discarded between stacks, pulled it out, so grateful he almost cried. Threw up the entire contents of his stomach into it. Didn't feel much better, just shaken and weak, empty but still queasy with fear.

The Dyesi watched all this with interested crests. "It would be *a second chance,* as you Sapiens say." It switched to Galactic Formal for the phrase. The human words sounded odd coming out of its pretty mouth.

But the Dyesi dwelled in threes. By insisting on a second chance, would there also be a third?

"Despite my dangerous voice?" Phex asked, shaken. That voice was scraped and husky. He did not know what to do with his improvised bag of vomit. His only option was to force trembling hands to hold it closed, trying not to look at it. Trying not to smell it. Looking up at purple eyes and cruel crests instead.

His only option.

"It is in your contract," reiterated the Dyesi.

Phex knew the section because it had jumped out at him at the time. *All potentials are subject to recall. It should be known that this clause is activated less than 1% of the time and only when there is no other possible recourse.* Phex had somehow become the divinity's last resort.

"I do not have a choice, do I?" Phex stared desperately at the alien, an elongated silhouette of terrible possibilities.

"You have no choice," the Dyesi agreed, seeming neither regretful nor sympathetic.

Phex thought about Berril's face when she saw him again. She would be so happy. Someone out there in the universe would be genuinely happy to see him again.

He stood. "As the divinity commands. But I am finishing my shift first."

And he did.

Del's face was sullen and very annoyed when he told her. "Really? Again? I won't hire you back next time."

"I figured." What would Phex do then? No cafe to catch him. And there went his stomach again. Phex had been throwing up a lot lately.

She snorted. "What a bother. Ah, well, I always thought you had a nice voice."

Phex stared at his boss. Well, former boss.

She frowned fiercely. "I'm not an idiot, you know? Don't worry. I won't tell anyone. They wouldn't believe me even if I did." She snorted. "Blue-haired refugee from Attacon's saddest little moon becoming a god? Don't make me laugh. It'll be fun, though, to see you on my cupola someday. I will be able to say, *I knew him when*."

Phex wondered who she'd say that to. "They booted me once already."

"So, don't let it happen as second time. You're tougher than that. Tougher than they are."

Phex didn't think it was a matter of toughness, but it was oddly reassuring to know that one person from his past thought he could actually succeed.

Still, Phex checked his accounts. The divinity had paid him for his time as a potential. The cafe had paid him for his work. He wasn't rich, but he had more money than he'd ever had before. Maybe enough to start a new life somewhere? What kind of life could he have, if he couldn't come back to this cafe? Was it enough to open his own cafe? As a refugee, he doubted it. But it should have been enough to quiet his unruly stomach. It wasn't.

Then, in no time at all, blessed by a fast spaceship and divine mandate, Phex was back on Divinity 36.

A disinterested acolyte ushered him off the transport, escorted him to the cantor dorm to dump his bag (someone else was in his niche – very annoying), and then led him directly to a practice dome. For some reason, everyone was there, in the same dome. Well, all the potentials who were now left on Divinity 36.

Berril's face was a picture. Phex thought he'd always remember the way she looked in that moment. As much as he'd missed her, she'd missed him more – or was better at showing it. She, who liked everyone and whom everyone liked, thought he was special.

The moment he greeted the space, Berril flew at him, literally. Just unfurled her wings and dove off the dais.

He caught her easily. "Hi, birdie."

"You! You you you!" She buried her head in his neck and hugged him as tight as she could with arms and wings. "Phex, my Phex."

She pushed back a bit, so he set her down on her feet. She cupped the side of his face. "You lost weight."

"It's muscle. I haven't been gracing enough."

"Well, that will change soon." She threw her arms around him again, shrouding him in unfurled wings. Bumped her forehead against this chest.

Many of the sifters and all of the graces followed Berril, though at a much more sedate pace.

"You're back, then." That was Kagee, looking as annoyed

as ever, but he was also the only cantor to come over. "I thought it was strange. We've been an odd number since the last round of eliminations."

"Recalled," said Phex. If they wanted to know more, they could read their own damn contracts. "Why are you here all together?" he asked.

"Selection. Each week, we divide up into groups of six," explained Jinyesun, crests puffy, clearly pleased to see Phex.

Fandina and Seryloh were puffed too. Phex was flattered.

"It's pantheon work all day every day now," said Berril. She shoulder-checked Phex gently. "You have some catching up to do."

Phex was travel-weary and sore from stasis, weak and out of practice, but none of that mattered. "So, what are you all standing around me for?"

From that second on, Phex tried to climb back into the routine, but it was awkward.

His friends were happy to have him back, but the memory of why he'd been expelled, and that he *had* been, remained fresh. Since he didn't know exactly why he'd been brought back, everything was more risky now. He had to figure out how to become not just a good cantor but *invaluable* to the Dyesi. How could he use his dangerous voice but not be kicked out for it?

The sifters probably feared working with him because of songbruise *and* songburn. None of the cantors wanted to partner with him either, because they still thought he was a genetic freak. And no doubt now *everyone* was leery of him because he'd failed once already.

He spent too much time wondering why the acolytes bothered recalling him. They treated him mainly with an indifference he could not fathom. As a result, he spent too much time afraid. He could no longer get by on being the best, being *special*, as the Sapiens had called him. His specialness was a hazard – instead, he needed to be just *good enough*.

The only way to make it through was to form a pantheon, but most of the cantors had paired up while he was away. There seemed no one left for Phex, or at least no one left who would tolerate him.

The sifters had also begun to form pairings, although they seemed more fluid in their preferences. Jinyesun and Fandina enjoyed working together, but Seryloh also balanced with Fandina well. *Balance* was the way the Dyesi put it, since it had to do with how their style of color and pattern commingled.

The graces, too, had developed partnerships between light and dark. If anything, they were the most egalitarian. Some-thing about dancing brought with it flexibility. Phex under-stood that. The act of constant physical touch, the need to depend on each other for lifts and catches – it made differ-ences in personality less important. But also, occasionally, more profound.

For example, while Berril genuinely got along with every-one, she did not like working with Monji. Monji had dropped her during one of their lifts. She had to deploy her wings to keep from tumbling off the dais, which had cut off a high cantor mid-note. That, in turn, had songbruised Fandina. It was a total mess. Serious bruising resulted, too. Fandina had been in medical for two whole days. Berril and Monji felt awful about the whole incident and were now too careful around each other. Any partnership between them seemed unlikely. Phex empathized.

The incident actually worked in Phex's favor, though.

Suddenly, he wasn't the only one who could songbruise. Suddenly, it was a risk they all took. He was simply the first.

The sifter potentials started relaxing around him a bit more as a result, as much as any Dyesi relaxed. Or perhaps it was Phex who relaxed more around them.

They practiced in groups of six and worked on existing godsongs – popular hits. But they were encouraged to experiment, forming their own patterns and colors for the dome. Not that Phex did that much – too afraid of the damage he'd done when he took liberties with his voice. But he could play with the moves on the dais, dip his toe back into gracing.

Phex liked it best when Berril was part of his group. He'd learned to trust her grace despite her delicacy and could toss her increasingly high into the air. She knew without a doubt he would always catch her. And he always did. He would risk himself to do so.

His favorite trick was a wall run into a full straight-body flip during which he would reach down, grab Berril by the shoulders while upside-down over her head, and use the momentum of his own tumble to throw her off the dais. She would hit the height of his toss and allow her wings burst forth like a star exploding. It looked spectacular. Also, it felt like Phex had done that – caused her to take flight.

It was possible that they had too much fun together. But when he was dancing, Phex didn't feel pressure like when he sang. It was freeing.

The rest of the time, Phex remained tense in a way he'd never been before. Scared of losing – pathetic. He wanted to stay now. To win. He cared, and this was a new sensation.

He stayed awake long after everyone else now, not because he wanted the dorm to himself but because he could not sleep. He played the day over in his head, relieved to have made it through but still examining it for flaws. Occasionally, he turned those flaws into bile and threw them up late at night, grateful for the empty hygiene chamber and sleeping cantors.

His only respite was that, despite their general animosity, the cantors didn't stop Phex from taking over their dorm kitchen once more. They even, reluctantly, came to his counter in the evenings. He resumed serving them beverages and keeping things tidy. He tried to learn to cook a few Sapien dishes that they liked. It was the only trick he had left. A few cantors even started talking to him again. Well, Kagee, but that was something.

"This is actually good." Kagee crunched on some pickled tubers Phex was experimenting with. "Ironic that you're into cooking now." His grey gaze slid to the hygiene chamber, then back to Phex, then focused on his snack.

Phex said nothing. Not sure how he felt about having his weakness noticed.

Kagee ate another tuber. "We all have secrets."

Phex wondered what was keeping Kagee up late at night. Kagee who talked to Phex but didn't really like him.

Phex thought that even if he made it through to godhood, he'd never be a particularly popular god. He couldn't go around serving drinks to the entire divinity, even if it was the only social skill he had. To be a god, he needed to be *liked* by more than just Berril. Something else to worry about.

He was wrong, though.

The divinity started beaming the potentials' feed out into the galaxy – various practice sessions in the big performance domes and even the occasional dorm gathering. Rumor was that some potentials were already getting worshiped. Phex was one of the names that kept coming up. No one knew for certain, since their ident chips had been blocked from anything but basic infonet. No outside communication allowed and certainly no access to the divine forums.

The acolytes began treating Phex differently, not just indifferent anymore. There was, almost, respect to their crests. Apparently, he was getting votive offerings, too. The acolytes began delivering cookware from his believers. Ladles were particularly popular. Phex was confused but flattered.

At six months, halfway through, they tested in pantheons for all the galaxy to see.

Anyone who wanted to tune in to the divine beam could watch the entire process, judging and everything. More potentials were cut. But they would go back to their homes known faces and known failures now. That had to be worse than what Phex suffered through. He couldn't imagine going back to his cafe when everyone *knew* he'd nearly been a god. The questions, the attention would be overwhelming. He never thought he'd be grateful to be kicked out when he was.

This exam, Phex passed easily, though.

And then the divinity changed everything on him, all over again.

10

TYVE BE THE GLORY

Two weeks after their six-month exams, the potentials awoke to start their regular routine, but instead, they were told to pack.

All of them.

For one horrible moment, Phex thought they were being expelled en masse. Instead, they trundled together to the second column of the building and up two levels.

Apparently, they were just being relocated.

Phex had a lot of stuff to carry this time, mostly cookware. So much, Kagee had to begrudgingly shoulder three of Phex's beloved pots. He was wearing one of his elegant painted robes, but the swirls of the pattern sort of went with the shape of the pots, if one coordinated one's cookware with one's formalwear. Which Phex suspected one did not, certainly not if one was Kagee.

"Why are you being so nice?" Villi asked.

"Phex rules the kitchen. I'm always nice to him," replied Kagee. Which everyone found absolutely hilarious. Kagee wasn't nice to anyone.

Even Phex had to work not to crack a smile.

Kagee looked surprised, like he didn't realize he was making a joke.

Phex had cooking equipment, spices, and other foodstuffs he'd acquired since his return, mostly from the graces. After Sharm's noodles, several grace potentials had started coming to Phex with hopeful requests for home-planet favorite meals. Phex was willing to try, so long as they could get him the necessary ingredients, instructions, and, occasionally, utensils. He never asked after their sources for such things, but in his absence, it seemed many of the potentials had established contraband pipelines off-moon. He didn't always get the dish right – he wasn't a trained chef, after all – but he usually managed something edible.

The result was that Phex clanged as he walked from their old dorm to their new one, he was so laden with pots and pans, spatulas and rasps, and all manner of other objects he'd learned to use – probably not as originally intended. He'd also developed a real affection for a nicely shaped ladle.

Their new dorm had a similar layout to the previous, only instead of twelve bed niches, there were six. Phex and Gemma were left together in the first one, while the other cantors continued on. Phex claimed his preferred bed nearest the entrance, and then went to set up the kitchen. He left his pack of meager clothing in his niche.

"You're the only person I know who has more ladles than he does clothes," said Gemma, sounding like this was a character flaw.

Phex ignored her.

She followed him to the kitchen, choosing not to unpack her own large case full of pretty outfits. "How come you only have old moon-issue jumpsuits, Phex? You left and then came

back in exactly the same rags. The divinity pays you. Rather
well by your standards, I'm sure. Why didn't you buy new
clothes?"

Phex thought that what he had was perfectly sufficient to
meet his needs. He could run the auto-cleaner each night, so
technically he only really required one set of practice clothing. Three was a luxury. He did have a small, private desire
for silky pajamas like the ones Missit wore. Not gold –
maybe dark blue or black. But he wouldn't even know how to
acquire something so frivolous. Besides, Missit's set had
looked expensive, and Phex wouldn't waste money on something so silly as clothing. If he got expelled again, he'd need
his savings – one couldn't live off of silky pajamas. Although
one might be tempted to live *in* them.

They were joined at that point by two graces, one of
whom was Monji, and two Dyesi, one of whom was Fandina.
Thank goodness, because this distracted Gemma.

The six of them roomed together for one week, but then
everyone but Phex was kicked out and a whole new set
came in.

Phex could guess, of course, that the Dyesi were assessing
pantheon chemistry. Pantheons not only performed, toured,
and composed new godsongs as a group, they also lived
together.

Gods *must* form cohesive pantheons. And it was the
hardest thing to build – a marriage of six, where sifters
balanced, cantors harmonized, and graces formed the backbone of godsong. Really, it was a wonder the divinity
managed to form any pantheons at all.

Phex found it odd that he was never moved. Others were
moved in and out and sometimes back in again, but never
him. He began to think of the entire dorm room – not just the

kitchen – as *his*. At some point, he no longer bothered to formally honor the room when he entered. Dyesi custom dictated that once the space became yours, so did its honor.

His kitchen got cluttered, a testament to the fact that Phex was indeed one of those potentials who already had believers. Apparently, his interest in cooking was thought particularly *cute*. worshipers began to send him more and more tribute. But Phex's tribute was not the usual votive offerings of lovely objects or decorative apparel. No, Phex's believers sent him food, clay pots, and pretty spoons. Anything edible was taken away by the acolytes – they couldn't risk poisoning – but Phex was allowed to keep the utensils, cutlery, and serving ware.

No matter who lived in Phex's dorm at any one time, there were always potential grace and sifter visitors at his counter, drinking his tea and partaking of his latest noodle experiment.

Berril moved in on the third rotation and was never reassigned.

"Why do you think that is?" she asked one evening.

Phex was preparing dinner. He'd entirely assumed that task. The others always got it wrong or forgot stuff or didn't take alter-species tastes into account. It wasn't a hardship – six was a lot more manageable than twelve. Mostly, Phex just shoved cartons into machines and pressed buttons. He only had time to actually cook once a week. Sometimes, Seryloh joined him to experiment on those evenings. They would never again work together under the dome, but Seryloh had completely forgiven him for songbruise. The Dyesi had ended up in the dorm opposite Phex's. And since the second week, Seryloh, too, stopped being moved. Phex was delighted. They would not be in a pantheon together, but at least they were close enough to share recipes regularly. He had a Dyesi friend.

This evening, however, it was just the six assigned to Phex's dorm, exhausted after a *very* long day.

Berril and Fandina were sitting at the counter, watching Phex heat things up. Fandina seemed to find Phex's nightly rituals particularly fascinating.

Fandina was the third longest in his dorm. The Dyesi had come in for one week at the beginning, been moved out, and then back in on the fourth rotation. Now it was happily settled in the niche nearest the kitchen and wasn't going anywhere.

The three of them – Fandina, Berril, and Phex – had become, for lack of a better term, a set.

"Why do I think *what* is?" asked Fandina, who now used Dyesi informal language with them when there were no acolytes present.

"Phex is the only one who hasn't been moved. Why?" Berril rephrased her question.

Fandina pointed at Phex with three elegant purple fingers. "He is sun."

Phex took mild offense. No aspect of his appearance or personality could be, in any way, described as *sunny*. He didn't let his offense show, though.

"Don't be ridiculous. Phex isn't remotely *sunny*." Luckily, Berril protested for him.

"Thank you." Phex put her favorite fermented-vegetable condiment down in front of her so she could nibble while waiting. Chiropterans never ate much in one sitting, but they snacked an awful lot.

She poked at it in delight and then selected and waved a limp leaf at Fandina like a confused crest-wiggle.

The Dyesi puffed a silent laugh. "No, I mean he's the sun of this pantheon, or he will be."

"Like Missit is for Tillam? The most famous?" Berril chewed her leaf happily.

"No, Missit isn't Tillam's sun."

"He's not?"

"Of course not! Can you imagine relying on him for anything? He is glorious, of course. Don't take insult," Fandina added quickly because Berril rather liked Tillam. "I mean, Missit doesn't hold his pantheon together. The sun is the one the others orbit around, the force of cohesion. It is an identity that exists not for the dome but for the gods themselves. For the pantheon."

"Like the leader?" Berril asked. "Phex, do you feel like you're *leadership* material?"

Phex was horrified. "No."

Fandina's crests lowered. "You aliens and your preconceived individualistic notions of dominance. That is not what *sun* means. If I had meant *leader,* I would have said *leader*. He is *sun*."

Berril shook her head. "I don't get it."

"He's cooking and what are you and I doing?"

"Sitting here, talking to him."

"No, we are sitting here talking to each other. We just happen to want to do it near Phex. We happen to want to talk *about* him. What did you do when you first met Phex?"

"Talk to him," said Berril cheerfully.

"No, you didn't," said Phex.

"I didn't? What'd I do?"

"You hugged me."

"Yeah, but I do that to everyone."

Phex cocked a brow. "Before even saying hello?"

"Well, no. I'm not usually *that* bad. Even us Shawalee have learned we should probably introduce ourselves first."

"Why was he different?" pressed Fandina.

"He looked solid and dependable. Sort of safe or some-thing. And like he needed a hug. I don't know. I was just drawn to him."

"See. Sun."

"But he's not a warm person."

So, I'm a black hole, thought Phex.

"Yet he is the one who has made this place homey." The Dyesi pointed to the way Phex was moving around the kitchen efficiently. His ladles hung in a neat row. The whole space entirely arranged to his taste.

Phex glanced at Fandina and then took in the rest of the dorm. It was tidy, and everyone who came in seemed to sense that it should stay that way. Phex liked tidy spaces. But not overly so. There were warm, fuzzy blankets strewn about because Berril got cold easily. And long, thick drapes on the wall because the Dyesi were sound-sensitive. Phex had been the one to ask the acolytes for extra drapes and throws, even specifying colors and textures (mostly blues and creams, soft chunky knits) because he considered them comforting. He found it easy to request things for other people – it was like ordering stock for the cafe.

"He's grumpy but honest," suggested Berril.

"More importantly, you always know what to expect from him. He's never erratic or unpredictable."

Phex wondered if that made him boring.

Fandina's crests pointed at Phex. "The sun of a pantheon is difficult to find. We gods are a bunch of musicians and artists and performers. Being the center of attention is in the job description, but not being the center of gravity. The divinity needs someone like Phex to hold a pantheon together."

Apparently, Fandina had really been studying him. Phex was a little disconcerted.

"Like Phex *how*?"

"Someone who doesn't want it as badly as the rest of us but somehow is good enough to do it anyway."

Berril looked at Phex with wounded eyes. "You don't actually want to be here?"

But what she was really saying was: *You don't want a pantheon? You don't want me in it? You don't want godhood?*

That wasn't true anymore. After being kicked out, Phex did want to stay this time. Or, to be precise, he *needed* to stay. But not for the same reasons they did. He needed it mostly *because* of them, because he feared losing them. Because he feared losing everything. He'd grown into ambition because of friendship and fear. And now kitchens and ladles and hope. But that seemed too exposing to admit. As if he would be placing too heavy a burden on them. Even though this was *his* dorm with *his* people in it, sometimes he was convinced he wouldn't make it to godhood. And sometimes late at night, his stomach was nothing but nauseous. Occasionally, he even threw up. Quieter, stealthier, and not as often as he had back on Attacon 7 but still losing what he had eaten for fear of loss. After all, it had once been *his* cafe, *his* dome, *his* voice, *his* grace, and the Dyesi had taken those away. The Dyesi could take all of it away at any time.

Instead, he said, "They wanted me." Phex gestured with his thumb at Fandina but meant the Dyesi. *When has what I wanted mattered? Do I even know what I want? Am I allowed to want anything?*

"Then why put yourself through all this? Why bother to come back?" Berril was clearly hurt.

Phex winced. "The divinity insisted." He plopped food in front of them. "And I missed you."

Berril grinned at him then. *Thank goodness.*

"Eat. Stop talking nonsense," he grumped.

Still grinning, she turned and called the rest of the group over, because she knew Phex didn't like to shout and he preferred it when they all ate together. This was because Phex liked to clean up all at once. It was certainly *not* because he actually enjoyed their company.

The others joined them at the counter. Phex poured himself a cup of milk, the Dyesi kind that came from a legume. Berril and Jutte got spiced tea. Fandina and Lenqihe got corrosive dark. Phex gave Kagee water. The grey boy was currently back in rotation as Phex's high cantor. Phex didn't think Kagee would last any longer this time than last. They warred with each other vocally rather than harmonize.

Berril said, during a short silence while everyone chewed, "Apparently, Phex is a sun."

Lenqihe, crests unsurprised, said, "Of course he is. He anchors this space."

"What does room occupation have to do with habitable star systems?" asked Jutte.

Berril explained for the benefit of both Jutte and Kagee. "The sun is like the core of a pantheon. It holds the others together."

Jutte nodded, understanding. "Like Fortew is for Tillam."

"Not Missit?" Kagee asked.

"Of course *not* Missit. That boy is practically a dust mote, he is so erratic," grumbled Phex, then glowered when he realized the others were staring at him.

Kagee looked shocked.

"See, Phex gets it." Fandina was as proud as any acolyte who had taught a new skill.

"You're certainly my sun, big boy," declared Berril, grinning at Phex. Cheeky.

Phex was done with the whole conversation. "Shouldn't it be *barycenter*?" he asked the Dyesi.

"*Sun* sounds cooler," replied Fandina.

Phex rolled his eyes and pushed over a shaker of seeds. "More koriemin?"

"Please."

On the next rotation, Lenqihe left and Jinyesun joined them as their second Dyesi. Fandina, Berril, and Phex were all delighted. Jinyesun was a dear friend and also a lot of fun to sift with.

Jinyesun never left.

When told that Phex was their sun, Jinyesun was entirely unsurprised.

"Of course he is. It is why the Dyesi recalled him. They expelled him for not getting along with the Sapiens but neglected to realize he was tethering the rest of us. Don't you remember how bad it was when he was away? Nowhere to gather, everyone sad or angry or scared all the time."

"Oh, I remember," said Berril.

"The drinks were terrible," griped Kagee.

"They brought me back for this?" Phex, shocked, gestured around his kitchen. His hanging ladles. The dorm room.

"Of course. Can you think of a better reason?"

"My voice?" Dangerous though it might be.

"There are many good voices in the galaxy that can color a dome, but far fewer suns who can hold together a pantheon," replied Jinyesun, using informal Dyesi, crests relaxed, seeming smug and content.

Soon enough, Berril, Fandina, and Jinyesun no longer honored the room as they entered in. It belonged to all of them now. Even the ladles.

Phex knew what was happening. He wasn't stupid. They were building a pantheon, or trying to – he and Berril, Fandina and Jinyesun. But he also couldn't see how they were going to complete the six. None of the remaining high cantors fit with him, and none of the remaining dark graces fit with Berril. Even if they did, none of those worked well with Fandina or Jinyesun.

They couldn't be a pantheon of four, so how were they were going to make it through the final months of training? They would probably be expelled as a group in the next eliminations. Phex wondered if he should ask to switch to high cantor. He had the range, and there were a few low cantors who might fit better with his pantheon, like Villi. He wondered if he could dance dark grace as well as sing. If he was *very* careful, they might still pass and get to stay a little longer.

But at the end of their eighth month, only two were cut – Gemma from the cantors and Jutte from the graces.

Phex had underestimated the acolytes. He had been recalled. Why not others? Because after that, two new potentials were brought in. Potentials who came directly through the building to stay in Phex's dorm.

It was odd, because these two hadn't been there from the start. They were complete unknowns. Phex hadn't liked Gemma, but at least he knew her skill under the dome and her basic personality. Now, suddenly, he had to contend with complete strangers living in their midst.

But Berril, being Berril, was excited to meet new people no matter what. "Beautiful greetings. Come in, please!" She pointed to the two vacant niches. "Those are the empty beds. You can decide who gets which."

An alien and a Sapien entered the room.

"I'm coming in," they said in unison. Both used phrasing that meant familiarity with the space but not the current occupants, identifying themselves as female and male respectively.

The first one looked a lot like Tillam's dark grace, Zil. Which meant she was from a species called Jakaa Nova. They had the reputation for being tough. Members of the Kill'ki Coalition, Jakaa Nova were generally more concerned with fighting enemies, hunting game, and being the galaxy's resident badasses than musical performances. Zil was the only Jakaa Nova god. And while Tillam was a big deal everywhere, the divinity wasn't particularly popular with *any* members of the Kill'ki Coalition. Domes and their associated trappings were considered more frivolous than divine.

Phex stood in his kitchen and watched the Jakaa Nova throw a practical-looking pack into the nearest vacant niche, apparently not caring which one she got. She looked around, nodded politely at Berril, and greeted Jinyesun and Fandina with the Dyesi formal lip-touch and flick before finally meeting Phex's eyes. She was bigger and tougher-looking than Phex but didn't seem like she wanted to play a dominance game with him. At least, not right away.

Berril, being Berril, made introductions. "I'm Berril, light grace. That's Jinyesun and Fandina, our sifters, obviously, and that's Phex in the kitchen, low cantor."

The Jakaa Nova smiled, showing sharp teeth, then moved toward the counter. "I'm Tyve, dark grace."

Up close, she looked even more like Zil, and not just because she was from the same species. Phex wondered if they were biologically related to each other.

Jinyesun crested at her. "We don't get many Jakaa Nova in the divinity."

"Just my brother."

Phex was pleased to have his hypothesis so quickly confirmed.

"Zil of *Tillam*? That Zil! He is your *brother*?" Jinyesun's crests went very puffy.

"Genetic?" Fandina was also impressed, although not quite so puffy about it. "No wonder you were recruited."

Tyve took a stool. She had a big-boned, easy way of moving, like she was comfortable with every muscle in her body and accustomed to pushing them to their limits. An athlete, probably. Phex admired that a lot. "This is my second time through training."

"You are a recall?" That was Jinyesun, still cautiously formal with his language.

The Jakaa Nova dipped her head. She had the same long red hair as her brother, and the same dark-red skin and bright-red eyes. But it wasn't, Phex thought, quite the same shade of red. Tyve was a bit more magenta than Zil. She also wasn't quite as big.

"I wasn't trained in the same way as Zil – as a child, I mean, before the divinity got us. My first time through training, the acolytes couldn't find me a pantheon that fit my style. I got recalled because of you." She pointed two aggressive fat-tipped fingers at Berril.

Berril looked comically surprised. "Me?"

"Yeah. They said you were good working with a runner. Whatever *that* means."

Phex knew that it meant him.

"You are a *runner*, then?" asked Jinyesun.

"More of a chaser, but you know the acolytes. Throw whatever they can at a problem and see if they get a pantheon to come out the other side."

"I'm a *problem*? How exciting." Berril moved to stand next to Tyve. Even she wasn't brave enough to hug a Jakaa Nova, so instead she bumped the newcomer with one small shoulder. "Happy to have you as a partner. This could be fun."

"Could it?" asked Tyve, giving her a funny look. "You chiropteran?"

Berril nodded.

"Ugly little thing."

"Hey, now," said Phex, without raising his voice.

The Jakaa Nova's head moved sharp and predator-like in Phex's direction.

"By their standards." Tyve gestured at the two Dyesi.

Berril wasn't offended. "And theirs are the only standards that matter. I suspect they're going to dye me. If we make it through, I mean."

Among other alterations, thought Phex, considering his own misshapen ears.

The Jakaa Nova stared at Berril, head tilted. "Okay, then." She tuned back to Phex. "You gonna offer me a drink, kitchen Sapien?"

"Not sure yet," said Phex, because he wasn't.

Berril turned to the other newcomer, who had put his small, hard case down on the last vacant bed and was standing there, on the other side of the room, watching them. His expression was passive, his demeanor standoffish, but Phex thought he was probably just shy.

Their new high cantor was small and slender, about Missit's shape. He had long brown hair, smooth brown skin, and symmetrical features – pretty but not remarkable. Phex paused to marvel that his own judgment had already been so influenced by Dyesi aesthetics.

"Are you a recall too?" Berril asked, bouncing hopefully over to him. She grabbed at his wrist and tugged him toward the kitchen.

Phex tensed, wondering if he was going to have to intervene. But the Sapien responded with bemused acquiescence, allowing Berril to pull him over and push him gently onto one of the vacant stools.

"Yes." He had a soft, sweet voice, lyrical and high enough to indicate cantor even without singing. Phex was excited to work with him.

Tyve said, tone gentling slightly, "Cassin was a potential with me. We were asked to stay, even though we couldn't make a pantheon. They've kept us training and practicing, presumably for just this kind of thing."

"Here on Divinity 36?" asked Berril.

Cassin and Tyve both clicked.

"Where are you from originally?" asked Berril.

Cassin looked resigned to being the focus of questioning. "Attacon."

"Oh! Like Phex."

Cassin was visibly relieved. "Really?"

Phex hastened to add, "Attacon 7, not Prime. And I wasn't born there."

"Oh." Cassin seemed sad, like he'd wanted to reminisce.

"Sorry," said Phex. Not sure what he was sorry for.

"Not your fault." Cassin tucked a lock of hair behind one shapely ear. He'd obviously been growing those long locks all his life, raised with godhood in mind.

Berril suddenly launched herself at Cassin and gave him a hug. "Welcome."

Cassin looked around at all of them with desperate eyes. Obviously, he had no idea what to do with Berril's enthusiastic brand of casual affection.

"You'll get used to it," said Phex. He placed a cup of the green tea he'd invented in front of Cassin. It was a beverage that mostly only Sapiens liked, and he thought it was the right choice. He placed some sweetener next to it.

"Berril, let him drink in peace," said Fandina gently.

"What about me?" said Tyve plaintively to Phex.

Berril mistook this remark to be addressed at her. She trotted over to the Jakaa Nova and hugged as much as she could of the alien. "Welcome, too!"

Tyve looked surprised, then amused, then confused when Berril kept hugging her.

"Like I said, you get used to it." Phex considered the Jakaa Nova. She'd been living among the Dyesi for a while, and she seemed like the kind of person who enjoyed pretending to be tough. "You drink corrosive dark, don't you?"

"How'd you guess?"

Berril explained. "It's what he does. He's like a beverage psychic."

Phex looked at Jinyesun and Fandina. "You want?"

"Why not?" said Jinyesun, "We are clearly going to be awake getting to know each other for a while."

Phex made a pot of the toxic stuff, and then poured it out for his sifters and their new dark grace.

"What's his deal, then?" asked Tyve, sipping her disgusting drink with evident bliss. She threw a casual arm around Berril's boney little shoulders, which delighted Berril. Phex was pleased too. It was like the Jakaa Nova had passed some test Phex didn't even realize they'd been running on her.

"Who? Phex? He's a recall too. Sooner than you, though." Berril grinned. "Just you wait until you see him on a dais."

"Shouldn't have much to do with me at first, should it?" Tyve gestured with her head at Cassin. "More his problem."

Berril bounced. "I think Phex might surprise you."

Phex put a fresh drink down in front of her, extra sweet this time, as she looked a little low on energy. "Let them find out for themselves, birdie."

"Spoilsport," said Berril, sipping the spiced tea eagerly.

"Are we permitted to ask about your godly brother?" Jinyesun asked Tyve, carefully polite.

Jinyesun wasn't a huge Tillam worshiper – certainly nothing like Gemma – but it admired Tillam above the other pantheons and was always curious about aliens. The four of them enjoyed performing Tillam's songs more than most potentials, and Phex suspected that was due in part to Jinyesun's affection for the galaxy's most famous pantheon. Phex would always consider Errata's songs and Orlol's voice more suited to his own abilities and taste, but since both Jinyesun and Fandina loved sifting to Tillam, and Berril enjoyed Tern's gracing style, he'd been singing *a lot* of Tillam lately. And while Phex couldn't imitate Fortew's low cantor perfectly, he could bring his own take to the role that, so far, no one found objectionable. Or dangerous.

"We have been doing a lot of Tillam as part of training recently," explained Fandina. "Naturally, we are interested in the fact that you are related to Zil."

"Are you any good at Missit's parts?" Berril asked Cassin.

"Is anyone?" Cassin replied. It wasn't a fair question.

"Kagee," answered Fandina and Jinyesun at the same time. Which was true. Although he was by no means the same as Missit, Kagee could push a beautiful sift on most of Missit's vocals. No one really liked Kagee very much, but they couldn't deny his talent.

"Is he any good at Fortew's?" Tyve stuck her thumb toward Phex.

"No," said Phex cheerfully. "So, I don't try." He looked at Cassin. "I recommend you do the same."

"Because no one is as good as Missit? Not even this Kagee person?" Cassin's face was carefully blank, but there was anger there, or hurt.

"More that no one can beat Missit at his own game, so why bother? Pick a different game," replied Phex.

"Oh, I see. You like to play with the dome." For the first time since he entered the room, Cassin looked lighter, actually interested in them.

Phex inclined his head, sipped his own drink, leaned back against a kitchen cabinet.

"Phex isn't really like the rest of us," explained Berril.

"In what way?" asked Tyve.

"He's doing all this for fun."

Phex might have protested. But if Berril wanted to think of him as doing this for a lark rather than for survival and affection, that was probably better for her mental health.

"He's becoming a god for the *fun* of it?" Tyve let the shock show in her voice. She looked around at the others. None of them protested. "Is everyone in this dorm a little bit mad?"

Fandina wiggled its crests. "Welcome to the oddball club."

"What does it say about you two that they stuck you in with us?" wondered Berril, cheeky as ever.

Jinyesun said, "Zil is also a dark grace. Do you dance like him, Tyve?"

Tyve gave that sharp-tooth smile. "Not *exactly*."

"See?" said Fandina to Cassin, even though he hadn't said anything. "Oddball."

Phex settled back to watch his light grace and his two sifters charm the pants off their new cantor and dark grace. He thought that tomorrow, under the dome, it was going to be fantastic.

It was, instead, a total disaster.

GO, SING IT ON THE DAIS

It shouldn't have been a surprise. They'd had no practice with each other. To be plunked into a dome and told to perform was insane. The result was a chaotic mess – and not in an artistic sense.

Tyve didn't know the steps. Why should she? Berril quite rightly didn't trust her to catch or lift. Phex split his attention, half watching the graces because he worried about injury, half trying to figure out Cassin's voice.

Cassin had a good voice. Phex could tell exactly why he'd been recruited, but they still struggled to match each other. For lack of a better word, Cassin's voice was *weak* and too easy for Phex to overpower. Phex had to hold himself back even more than normal. He was deeply worried about song-bruising Jinyesun or, more likely, Fandina, without a high cantor to mitigate his power.

Without cantor harmony, skinsift didn't work properly. With misstepping graces, the melody couldn't develop into godsong. The colors were muddy, the patterns didn't hold, it was as close to ugly as Phex had ever wrought on a dome. He felt sorry for the other potentials who had to sit through it, the acolytes who had to judge, and even the poor old dome itself.

The acolytes stopped them before they'd even made it through the first half. Thank the gods.

"That was a cataclysm," said Tyve cheerfully. They stood still in the center of the dais while the three acolyte judges below them engaged in a fiercely whispered argument.

"Ridiculous," said Jinyesun, looking as grumpy as Phex had ever seen a Dyesi, let alone Jinyesun – who was notoriously easygoing. "We do not trust each other *at all*. How can they expect us to make the dome do anything?"

Fandina didn't seem as upset. "It is to be expected. Phex, you are going to have to teach Tyve grace."

Phex nodded. He'd noticed that Tyve moved a little like he did. Not flipping over invisible blades or anything, but the Jakaa Nova danced grace as if she were a runner. She threw herself into movements via speed first and dexterity second, the way Phex did. Whatever she'd done originally to earn grace, it was a physical sport or the like, not formal acrobatic or dance training. Like Phex, Tyve had been an athlete by necessity.

Phex found himself staring at the Jakaa Nova and remembering something she'd said last night. "Wait. *Chaser*. Did you literally run after other people? Or hunt wildlife?"

Tyve was looking between him and Fandina. "Chasers run, yes. But what can a low cantor possibly teach me about grace?"

Fandina dismissed her with a flattened ear crest. "Later. Phex, you are being overly careful with cantor because you do not trust Cassin. Cassin, do you have any more power?"

Cassin shook his head.

"Phex, did you notice his patterns?"

Phex hadn't. He'd been too worried about controlling his

own while simultaneously saturating most of the color because that was what he was best at. He glanced at Cassin apologetically.

Cassin gave a self-deprecating smirk.

"His patterns are amazing. Much better than yours. Almost as good as Kagee's, and that is saying something. But they are soft." It would be Fandina who noticed this. Of all the sifter potentials, Fandina was the best at proving pattern. Phex was weirdly proud of this.

Cassin looked at Fandina as if this was the nicest thing anyone had ever said to him.

"The colors love Phex," explained Jinyesun to Cassin, "but the patterns not as much. They are harder for him to control. That is why he causes songbruise – he pushes pattern when he gets frustrated or distracted."

That was a revelation to Phex. He wished someone had told him that before now. If a failure in the complexity of pattern caused bruising, did a failure in color saturation cause burning?

Jinyesun continued explaining things about Phex to Cassin and Tyve that, frankly, Phex wished someone had explained to *him* at some point before now. "Phex is scared of forcing his voice into patterns because he has bruised us in the past. Well, not us *exactly*, but other Dyesi."

Cassin winced.

Fandina added, "Burned once, too." As if Phex had won acclaim with this.

"He's quite dangerous, actually, our low cantor." Jinyesun also sounded like it admired the damage Phex could do.

Phex dipped his head, ashamed.

Tyve looked at Phex with something like respect. "Weaponized voice, huh, pretty boy?"

Cassin was suspicious. "How can he have the range? If he can burn, that means he could sing high cantor, doesn't it?"

Jinyesun clicked. "Yes, he could."

Kagee spoke up from the audience, snide as ever. "We got us a genetically manipulated freak in this batch of potentials. Does that upset you?"

Phex couldn't figure out if that barb was directed at him or Cassin. Maybe both? Why? Kagee hadn't been that cruel in ages. Since Gemma left.

Jinyesun was obviously annoyed by the interruption. Its crest went back, and its large eyes focused hard on Kagee.

They'd totally forgotten they were being observed by judges. Which Phex supposed showed how comfortable they were on a dais now, even if they weren't comfortable as a pantheon.

Kagee was staring at Cassin, challenge written all over his grey face.

Phex hissed at everyone. "Leave it. It's just Kagee being Kagee."

Unfortunately, Kagee continued being himself, loudly. "Are you dismissing me, Phex? Cute." His pretty mouth twisted.

Phex tilted his head, seriously confused by the vitriol. "Are you... jealous?" He hazarded a guess. *Surely not.*

Kagee sputtered.

The acolytes generally did not like to intervene in the socialization of potentials. They preferred their nascent gods to work these things out for themselves. Now that the potentials were loosely arranged in pantheons, the acolytes tended to treat them as units – and observe with interest how those units operated in contrast to each other. Like now, they were watching closely. Big eyes flashing, mostly between Cassin, Kagee, and Phex.

Phex wished he could read Dyesi minds. Or Kagee's mind, for that matter – though it was probably dark in there. He switched his attention from the high cantor in the congregation to the one sharing the dais with him.

What was that on Cassin's face? Disgust? Horror? Hatred? His eyes were fixed on Phex, running over his body, assessing, and not in a nice way. Not even in a Dyesi way. Overly critical.

"Are you *altered*, Phex?" he asked, tone flat.

"I came here from Attacon 7 but I was born to the Wheel." Phex glanced at Kagee to see if he intended to keep pushing. No reaction from the grey cantor, just continued frowning.

"What's *Wheel*?" asked Cassin.

"Wheel mucks around with Sapien genetics before birth, in the fetal state, just for fun." It was, of all people, Tyve who explained. Their new dark grace had guts and apparently knew about the Wheel.

"Oh, it's not *fun*," said Phex.

"I mean, they don't do mods for survival or somaform or planetfall or abnormal gravity but for status and *appearance*." Tyve gave him a nod.

Phex figured that was basically true.

The Jakaa Nova moved closer, angled her body away from the audience. Her red eyes were oddly soft on Phex's face. She lowered her voice, gentle and gruff. "Blue hair. You're a crudrat?"

Phex felt sick at this naming, a now-familiar churning in his stomach – but this was relief and fear at the same time. Here was someone who knew his past without need for explanation. He wouldn't have to talk about it – she would simply understand. But if Tyve knew all about his crudrat childhood, she would also judge him for it.

Suddenly, Phex remembered his medical exam. What had they said about the Kill'ki Coalition? Something about them starting an extraction program to rescue crudrats. And the Jakaa Nova were members of the Coalition.

They had no time to talk now, but Phex realized they would need to discuss this later. He had questions. He, Phex, had *lots* of questions. But for now he merely said, "Yes."

Tyve gave him a curt little bow. "Congratulations on getting out." Then she blinked, red eyes flashing. "Running. Ah. I see. Crudrat would make for an interesting grace, wouldn't it?"

She paused, got excited and pivoted to face the others. "Does he do those crazy wall flips?"

"Oh, my god, yes," squealed Berril, "Just runs up the side of the dome, then bounces off. It's *so cool*-looking."

Fandina joined them. "He and Berril do this somersault-toss thing into wing deployment that is spectacular. We will show you sometime."

"Oh, *we* will, will *we*?" Phex pretended affront, although he was flattered by their enthusiasm. It *was* a really cool trick.

"So, why am I here? Why isn't he your dark grace?" Tyve didn't seem threatened or upset, just curious.

"Oh, because he can sing the colors like they are going extinct. When he is not scared of his own voice." Jinyesun was puffy-crested.

That made Phex self-conscious. "Let's go find a practice dome. We need to talk and figure this all out."

"Talk, Phex?" Berril pretended shock.

"You want to *talk*?" parroted Jinyesun.

"Are you feeling all right?" added Fandina.

Oh, his pantheon thought they were *hilarious*.

"Hush, you lot." Phex flapped a hand at them, including

Tyve, who probably would also tease him if she were in on the joke.

Cassin, however, was now standing at the farthest edge of the dais as if physically repulsed. He flinched when Phex moved.

"I cannot sing with him." He addressed the acolytes. Then he made a kind of bow to the rest of the pantheon. Not to Phex, though. He seemed unable to even look at Phex.

One of the acolytes said, "You object to the pantheon?"

"I was raised Post-Darwinist. No offense, but that *thing* is an anathema."

The acolytes exchanged crest-wiggles. "This has happened with you before."

"Apologies. I cannot escape my upbringing." Cassin didn't seem actually apologetic.

The acolytes added, "This keeps happening with our Phex. Never before have we had a cantor so universally disliked by other cantors. How do you do it, Phex?"

"It's a gift," answered Kagee for him.

The Dyesi crested at Kagee, curious. "You seem very invested."

"Do I?" Kagee pretended indifference. His pointed little chin up-tilted slightly.

The acolytes consulted briefly with each other. "Cassin and Phex, your voices are incompatible regardless. We thought you could balance. We were wrong."

Phex was surprised to hear acolytes admit to a mistake.

"It is for a high cantor to match *him*?" Cassin asked, sounding bitter.

The acolytes were unrelenting. "It is now. He is a sun. You know how pantheons work."

Cassin sighed. "All too well. Is there anyone left who might switch? Or was I brought back only for this pantheon?"

The acolytes consulted again.

"There is one, but the personalities conflict."

"That is easier to overcome than cultural taboo."

"Agreed." The acolytes turned to the audience of potentials.

"Kagee, switch with Cassin," one of them ordered.

Kagee started. His grey face paled. "Me? But we've tried already. Several times."

Tyve said, from the dais, "Not with me as part of this pantheon, you haven't."

Phex thought, *Also not with me knowing what the problems are with my own voice.* Not that Phex really *wanted* Kagee to be their high cantor, but still.

Cassin quickly climbed off the dais. Too quickly. Like he wanted to run.

Less reluctantly than Phex would have predicted, Kagee climbed up.

He glared at Phex.

Phex glared back.

When they'd sung together previously, it hadn't worked because both their voices were strong and they'd fought each other with them. But now Phex knew something he hadn't known before. It was too easy for him to overpower others, so Kagee's ability to stand up to him vocally was actually an asset. He'd thought his strength put his sifters in danger, but it was his own fear and lack of dexterity with patterns that did that.

Phex glared at Kagee. "Can you really shield them?" He gestured at Fandina and Jinyesun.

"From what?"

"From my voice."

"With *my* voice?" Kagee gave a disgusted snort. "Of course I can."

"Why didn't you *say* so?" Phex was absolutely delighted. "Then let's try it for real this time."

"You won't fight me?"

"I won't."

"You thought I was a risk to them?"

"I thought our harmony would be too much because I don't know how to limit myself."

Kagee actually laughed at him. "You're an idiot. It's not about power."

Phex thought that was false, but he didn't want to argue. "Show me, then."

"If you don't mess with me, then this will be easy," replied Kagee, cocky.

Phex looked at Fandina. The Dyesi seemed excited, not scared, as if it had been hoping for this for a while.

Why had no one told Phex that he was sabotaging them all because he didn't trust high cantor to help him hold the pattern? *Balance* – of course. There was that word. He knew Kagee was great at patterns. He'd seen it. This time, he needed to trust that the high cantor's ability to hold a pattern would protect their sifters from being bruised.

So, the six of them sang the dome together.

It wasn't spectacular, not by a long shot.

But it was safe.

Kagee's voice was stunning, always had been. It had character to it – a gentle burr that was very different from Phex's own excruciatingly clean tones. Phex found Kagee challenging to harmonize with but easy to match, note for note. True, Kagee seemed to be missing something, some secondary visual quality beyond the music. His cantor was lovely but somehow also as grey as he was. Did Phex contain enough multitudes of color to fix that? He wasn't sure. But he was optimistic that it might be possible.

This time, Phex ignored the greyness. Instead, he allowed himself to enjoy the fact that Kagee was powerful, noticeably stronger than Cassin, and that his patterning was deft and sure. Fandina and Jinyesun were confident and untroubled by pain, never once wincing, never cowering back. Phex could just cantor, and Kagee with him, and perhaps they weren't perfectly harmonized, but it *worked*. For the first time, it worked seamlessly with the dome. On the dome.

When they finished, the acolytes exchanged crest-wiggles. No words spoken.

Fandina addressed them. "Permission to exit the dome?"

"Granted," said the acolytes, in unison, looking rather pleased with themselves.

They went to a practice dome together. It was possible an acolyte followed them to keep an eye on things, but if it did, it lurked outside the entrance and only stuck its head in when no one noticed.

The six of them took to the dais but didn't immediately start practicing. Instead, everyone but Phex and Kagee started talking excitedly.

Phex took some time to get things straight in his head. He let them talk themselves in circles for a while until there was a lull. Then he decided it was time to risk offending the Dyesi to get necessary information.

"I need to ask intrusive questions," he said.

"Oh, you really did mean *talk*." Berril was genuinely startled.

"Sit first?" Phex suggested.

They all sat in a circle. Berril and Tyve stretching like the dancers they were.

"Please do not take offense." Phex glanced at the Dyesi, but he included the rest of the pantheon, because in the end, they were all aliens from different backgrounds. "What I do not know is becoming a problem for all of us."

"We have been waiting for you to say something, Phex. Anything, really. We will not get mad." Jinyesun crested at him, hopeful and encouraging.

Phex nodded. "Fandina, you are really good at patterns, but your colors are not great. That patterning – is it an innate skill or a creative ability that has been cultivated? Is it physically to do with your skin type? Or did you train focusing on it? Or is it just that you are more responsive to one kind of cantor over another?"

Fandina considered. "Some of all of that. Ability to sift is like the ability to sing or to dance. It can be practiced and learned, but to be a god, you need to be born better at it than most. However, just like the way some Sapiens are better at low cantor and others at high, some sifters are better at pattern and others at color. Generally speaking, pattern responds more to low cantor and color to high cantor, but not always. I can pattern to a range, but I also tend to brighten the whole dome with overexposure. That is why Jinyesun and I work well together."

Jinyesun added, "I lean dark, and I am way more responsive to high cantor and generating color."

"There's the shape, too," Phex said. "You are more round and swirly. Fandina is sharper and spiky."

Jinyesun looked pleased that he'd noticed. "That is birth location – like a regional accent. I am from the far south caves. Fandina is from the northeast. Also, it has to do with the song and the singer and, more importantly, how the two cantors harmonize. How you two sing together is also how the patterns and colors are made to work together and match on our skins."

"So, because I cause songbruise easily, and Fandina is more sensitive to patterns, does that mean Fandina is more at risk than you, Jinyesun, when I sing?"

"Not exactly." Fandina shook its head. "At any point in the godsong, either of our skin could be carrying the weight of the dome while the other one sifts a transition or a burst. Or if the flow has been interrupted and redirected by a grace, the balance can be intentionally off. A bruise or a burn is the result of both a vocal strike and an imbalance occurring at the same time."

Phex nodded. "So, how do I stop it from happening?"

"You don't, dumbass, we do." Kagee gestured at the rest of the pantheon. "I mean it will mostly be me, but part of how we structure every performance is to make sure neither sifter takes on the burden of the dome. Songbruise I can definitely help with. I'm really good at patterns for a high cantor. Better than most low cantors, actually."

Phex frowned. "That is probably why the acolytes kept trying to pair us up – because I am better than I should be at color for a low cantor."

Kagee grimaced. Nodded. "I'm also actually pretty decent at balancing a song. I was trained in three-part harmony back home. Two is child's play. If you'd just give me a chance. Stop trying to fight me for breath every time."

That annoyed Phex. He objected to being told to do something he was already trying to do anyway. Now it felt like compliance and not personal choice. But this was Kagee, abrasive and all sharp edges like unweathered quarry stone. Phex would have to learn to be the one who softened.

"I will stop," said Phex.

Kagee's pert nose twitched at the abrupt capitulation.

"You will? Oh. Well, then. I should say that I am, uh, not great at pulling back from leading a song, but balance is different."

Was he trying to be accommodating? Phex hid his surprise and nodded. He would have to learn to trust Kagee and push his own parts to the fore when necessary in a way that would not give offense. This was going to be difficult. Phex neither trusted nor coaxed well.

"See, you two *can* get along," said Fandina cheerfully.

"Any other questions?" Berril was grinning.

Phex considered. The others waited patiently. He looked at Tyve. "Your people are pulling crudrats out of the Wheel, in truth?"

Tyve nodded.

"How come you never came for me?" It wasn't the right question, but it was the one he needed to ask. It was born from a deeply childish place – the pain of knowing there had been salvation but that he had not been deemed worthy of it.

Tyve shook her head, eyes gentle. "We only started a few years ago. You were out before our extraction efforts began."

Phex nodded, relieved. It wasn't him. It was timing and bad luck. "Why did you start?"

Tyve winced. "I don't know for certain. My family isn't exactly on good terms with Coalition politicians. But the Kill'ki are really into it. Apparently, crudrats run Kill'ki challenge courts like it's a game. Like it's *fun*. And it's weird because it's not like crudrats can fight, but the skills you learn make for near-perfect Kill'ki countervails. And countervails are really difficult to recruit. So, the Kill'ki decided they want crudrats. They started up a program to steal them from the Wheel. Kill'ki are like that."

Phex shook his head. "That is insane."

He didn't know what *countervail* was, but the idea that

anyone would actually want a crudrat for anything that wasn't dodging blades and scooping crud was weird. Then again, he supposed being a crudrat had given him gracing skills of a kind. Maybe it developed skills for other things that aliens desired.

Tyve's words brought Phex some comfort. Not that he felt any great loyalty to other crudrats, and who knew if these Kill'ki used them just as badly as the Wheel did. But it was nice to know that others like him might escape. They'd not be spaced. They'd maybe get a chance to grow up. It was oddly gratifying to know he wasn't alone in the universe anymore.

"Thank you," he said to Tyve, meaning it.

"What for? It's not me getting them out."

"The knowledge that someone tries is invaluable."

Berril plucked at his sleeve. "Phex? What's *crudrat*?"

Phex looked at Tyve pleadingly.

"The Wheel uses kids, little ones, to clean their scythers, these blades that harvest dark matter for spaceport functions. We have the same tech, but we use it on a micro scale. We clean with liquid flush, not children." It was pretty clear the Jakaa Nova was disgusted by the Wheel.

"Child labor?" Fandina's crests flattened, horror tingeing its skin dark about the mouth. Phex hadn't seen such an extreme reaction from a Dyesi before.

Tyve nodded. "And it's high-risk. Crudrats run through these tunnel-tube things, and the scythers are these sharp, rotating blades that never stop moving. The kids have to be small enough to fit in the tubes and nimble enough to run while dodging the blades, and strong enough to scoop up the crud. That's it, right?" She looked at Phex.

Phex clicked a Dyesi affirmative. It was good enough for understanding.

Jinyesun also looked upset. If it weren't a Dyesi, Phex

would have said Jinyesun wanted to hug Phex. Not just to comfort him but to comfort itself. The Dyesi really reacted badly to the idea of children working dangerous jobs. It seemed almost taboo to them.

Weirdly, Kagee scooted closer to Phex, as close as Berril was to his other side. Berril was doing it for her own reassurance, but Kagee seemed to be trying to soothe Phex. Like he sympathized or understood some part of being outcast.

Phex glanced down at him. "You okay?"

"Am *I* okay?" Kagee shook his head. "So damn annoying."

Funny, crudrats were such a normal thing to Phex, and it had been such a long time since he was one. They all seemed so sad for him, yet it had simply been his reality.

Phex figured if they were going to pity him, he'd better get it all out and over with at once. He unzipped the top part of his jumpsuit and pulled it down off his arms and torso so they could see the scars. Some of them may have heard about his scars from the Sapiens at some point, but it was easiest to show the truth. He lifted his arm to display the big scar under it, then twisted to show the massive one on his shoulder and back.

"What are you doing?" Kagee's eyes bugged out of his head.

"Blade scars," Phex explained. "I was not a very good crudrat."

Tyve suddenly laughed – a funny barking sound. She wore a tightly belted short robe over trousers, which she untied to show off her own torso.

Phex had three deep scars and several smaller ones. Tyve had hundreds of scars – mostly shorter and shallower than Phex's but clearly also the result of blades of some kind.

"Impressive," said Phex.

"The marks of a person who can't dodge."

Phex found himself amused. He'd said something similar to the medic back at the beginning of all of this. "So, what were *you* not particularly good at?"

"Fighting," said Tyve, sounding not at all pleased.

Phex nodded. Jakaa Nova were a warrior people, by reputation at least. If Tyve couldn't fight, her social status probably suffered.

Which she confirmed when she added, "I don't have a kill instinct. It's considered a major character flaw." She paused. "Well, it was when I was a kid. Last I heard, things seem to be changing a bit. But it's been a while since I went home."

"That is why you chased?"

Tyve tilted her head. "That's why I chased."

"And were you any good at that?"

The Jakaa Nova inclined her chin, the straight pupils of her red eyes widened into circles. "Better than I was at fighting."

They both pulled their clothing back into place.

"You think we can figure out how to make your chasing more like my running, and both into a dark grace this little one can trust?" Phex wrapped an arm around Berril's shoulders so he could pull her close like she needed right then.

Tyve belted her robe. "Not only do I think I can. I think we're going to be good at it."

Fandina said, "You three work on gracing first. Jinyesun and I will work with Kagee to figure out his voice and how it affects our sift balance. Then, Phex, you can join us after that?"

Phex clicked his agreement. That sounded like a plan.

They split into groups of three and went to work.

PRACTICE MAKES PRETTY

Tyve was a quick study, and they did have a similar approach
to dark grace if not exactly the same style. Phex's tricks were
all about avoiding a blade, learned as act of nimble fear.
Tyve's style was designed to chase after something. She ran
with an eye to a target, constantly pursuing a goal. This actually made her a better grace partner. She focused entirely on
Berril in a slightly predatory way. Phex was confident that it
meant Tyve would never drop her. After all, the whole point
of Tyve's run was to catch and hold. Also, she was much
better at actual grace work than Phex. Simply put, she was a
superior dancer. It was clear she'd trained for the role, while
Phex only picked up what he could on the side. Thus, relatively quickly, they were able to get to a place where Berril
trusted Tyve, if not fully, at least enough to work toward a
time when she might.

Phex had fun teaching Tyve. Perhaps too much fun. It was
less about the gracing than it was about the tricks and the
leaps. Tyve got excited to see him wall-walk or flip and
wanted instantly to try it herself. Phex liked Tyve's blunt
personality and direct approach to everything. He would

never have to guess where he stood with her. Not that they *stood* all that much.

During a hydration and stretching break, Tyve turned to him and said, "You don't have to do this, you know? Be a god, I mean. You could be a countervail. The Kill'ki would take you in a heartbeat."

Phex shook his head. "I don't want to be a warrior. Not even the stealthy kind. That's what countervail is, right?"

"Yeah. And I understand. Neither do I." Tyve seemed sad about this, as if her lack of passion for dealing out death was a personal failure. "Funny how becoming a god is basically the last best option for both of us, isn't it?"

"It means we should try harder."

"Fair enough. Come on, show me that backspin somersault again."

"Catches first." Phex wanted Tyve to focus on becoming a dark-grace partner, not learning his dumb crudrat flips.

Tyve made a face but acquiesced. "Someday?"

"Let's get to gracing. Tricks later."

Tyve pretended a reluctant slumping walk to Berril at the center of the dais. "You sure treat the dome like it's a job, Phex."

"Because it is."

Several hours in, Phex sat back and watched Tyve and Berril. They looked good together. Tyve was so big and dark, all red-tinged and softly solid. Berril was a perfect contrast of light and bright, all yellow fuzz, slender bones, and sharp movements. He could see what they might become, and it would be beautiful in its way, even possibly by Dyesi standards.

He left them to it and turned his attention to the dome.

Kagee and the two Dyesi were producing some pretty pattern work, but their colors were dull. Which was to be expected with only one cantor, especially one who'd already admitted that color wasn't where his ability lay. Of course, it was also the song's fault. They were singing an Errata piece, but without Orlol's low cantor, it wasn't going to go anywhere worthy of a dome.

Still, Phex was pleased they'd chosen that song, because it was one of his favorites. It was also relatively slow and simplistic, so it would be easy to perfect and then fun to experiment with. Harder to hurt anyone with it, too, since it wasn't very challenging.

"I love this song," he said, interrupting them.

Kagee cycled off the verse and turned. "You a worshiper?"

"Of Errata? No, but I like Orlol's voice a lot. Always have. It was my audition piece."

"I can see that," said Fandina. "You two have certain similarities in precision."

"Is that a compliment?" wondered Phex.

"It is a fact." Jinyesun's tone implied that was sufficient explanation.

"Shall we try it with all four of us, then?" suggested Fandina.

They did, working over the chorus, bridge, verse, and pulse points until they had a serviceable version.

Except that Kagee kept getting the ending chorus note wrong. Phex was looking at the dome, not his pantheon, so he caught the issue there first. The pattern stayed beautiful, and the colors were okay, but the introduction of the final note melded poorly, resulting in a runny muddiness. Phex finished out his own balancing note and then stopped. The others followed him into silence.

"That bit just there, Kagee, on your high note – can you round over the aggressive pink to resonate better with my purple? I know a grace is required for the transition, but it is your introduction of the new color in the final line that is not working. Did you see?"

Kagee shook his head, clearly annoyed.

Phex thought maybe he was more annoyed with himself than anyone else. For a change.

"Could we try just the chorus over?" Phex asked the two Dyesi. Both crested with eager interest.

They sang it again, and as they did, Phex pointed to the part of the dome that Kagee needed to focus on. "There, see? That muddy bit around the edge of the pink. That is the false note."

They stopped.

Kagee tried again.

It happened a third time.

Frustrated, Phex asked Kagee to stay silent for their next attempt. This time, Phex dropped his own part early and did the high cantor note correctly to show Kagee what was required. He had to adjust into the much-higher range, but he managed to remain true to the song.

"Did you see? Better color introduction and no interruption of the pattern."

"Not really, but I think I *heard* the difference." Kagee tried again, and this time, he hit the note perfectly. His ear was clearly a lot better than his eye.

All three grinned at him. Berril paused in her latest tumble to clap. "That was lovely!"

"It is so weird to hear a low cantor sing a high note like that." Kagee deflected the praise by attacking Phex. But then he added, "Your voice is so pristine."

"Yes, Phex sings clean. Too clean sometimes," Jinyesun agreed.

"Whereas I'm a bit too rough and terrible at mixing colors." Kagee was ashamed.

Phex wondered how much of Kagee's general bitterness came from frustration with himself, not others.

Phex tried a mitigating tactic. "So, we compensate for each other. It is not unprecedented, especially in graces. After all, very few light graces are actually chiropteran. They cannot fly, and they do not have a wingspan, yet they still do the aerial maneuvers necessary for the dome. Let's try it again. You focus on that note. I will watch."

They did it yet again.

Kagee was back to not pushing into the right visuals.

Phex dropped his low-cantor part to correct for the flaws in Kagee's colors with high cantor. He sang, pressing into it, supporting Kagee rather than harmonizing. It edged toward the buzz that could happen when two slightly different voices hit the same note in subtly different ways.

They stopped again.

"Jin, how did it feel?" Phex asked, worried.

"That was intense," said the Dyesi, but it looked unharmed. Then its crests puffed. "*Jin*? Is that Sapien affection?"

"Sorry, is it inappropriate to shorten a Dyesi name?"

"No. Just odd. You wish to use a grace name with me?" Jinyesun's crest wiggled in confusion.

"I will not do it again." Phex instantly backed off. It was an old habit from the cafe. Everyone got a shorter name. More efficient that way.

Jinyesun considered a long moment and then said, "No, I like it. But only in private. Now back to the song. I think if you actually emphasized meshing two high cantors in that one moment, leaned into it as if it were intentional, it might work better, visually."

Kagee said, "Highlight the flaw?"

"Make art out of a mistake?" Phex tested the idea.

Kagee actually smiled. "I like it."

Phex said to Jin, "So long as you are safe. And Fandina?"

"Actually, I think that sounds fun." Fandina wiggled its ear crests in a manner Phex had never seen before. It was completely adorable.

They tried again.

This time, Phex faded out his low cantor a beat early – in the performance, they'd use the graces for that. Then he joined with Kagee to push his high-cantor note hard onto skin and onto the dome. This resulted in a spectacular starburst pattern of brilliant magenta.

"Ooooo," said Berril. She and Tyve paused grace practice to admire what the other four were doing to the dome.

Phex and Kagee shared an approving look and tailed off the final note together.

"It looks *nothing* like the Errata original." Jinyesun sounded more thoughtful than critical.

"No, but it's really cool." Tyve was grinning hugely.

"We should work it this way. They never told us we couldn't put our own spin on things." Fandina was firm. It liked what they were doing. Liked the difference and the uniqueness. Phex wondered if this Dyesi of theirs was a bit of a rebel. Jinyesun liked to play by the rules and discuss the reasoning and art of it. But Fandina liked to push boundaries and was often irreverent, for a Dyesi.

Kagee was looking less sour and more thoughtful. Relaxed, his face was as pretty as his voice. "We could do minor variations on that kind of high-cantor note combo throughout the verse, since Phex can jump cantors. That way, when it happens so strongly in the chorus, it's not as much of a surprise."

"Tease it ahead of time with smaller starbursts?" Jinyesun crested with interest. "That is a great idea. Can you do it, Phex?"

Phex nodded. "Why not?"

They tried it through a few times with Phex dropping out of low cantor for high to emphasize Kagee's notes here and there, each time causing small versions of the starburst over different parts of the dome. Phex experimented until these small bursts were color-coordinated with the dominant themes, so that the big magenta one, when it finally appeared, was both a contrast and a spectacle. Like a reverse echo in visual form. The entire dome pattern became a bit oversimplified each time Phex dropped his low cantor, but since the starbursts drew focus, Phex thought it wasn't that noticeable to an untrained eye.

It was fun to play with the godsong in this way. Phex experienced a strange kind of joy in the challenge of taking what was flawed and turning it into something to be honored.

Once the sifters and cantors felt like they had the song down, they added in the graces.

They couldn't do a full performance with all of them impacting the complexities of the dance as well as the song. Not yet, anyway. That would have to wait. This was only their first day as a group together. But they did manage to execute the song well by evening. There was a certain aura of shared jubilation as they left the practice dome together – exhausted but happy. Phex had never experienced communal pride like that before.

Together, they had done something beautiful. *Together*. Not just because they'd each fulfilled their roles and done their best but because they'd compensated for each other. It was a heady sensation. Phex wanted to feel it again. He was already looking forward to tomorrow and was entirely startled by the unexpected sensation of reveling in the abilities of others.

Kagee moved his stuff back into their dorm that night and never left it again.

Phex went to bed early.

―――――――

That was their first breakthrough as a pantheon. And that Errata song helped them survive the next round of eliminations. It also gained them worshipers. Not that they witnessed this themselves, but the acolytes informed them of it. They were the first potential pantheon in divinity history to trend under an aesthetic keyword – *starburst.*

Their second breakthrough came not in the dome but in the dorm about a month later.

It was late. They were tired. Phex was cleaning the kitchen before lights-down, humming softly, an old habit from his cafe days. He was singing Xillon's debut piece. Old but still popular. Tyve was tidying up the sitting area at the same time. She'd taken it on as one of her duties, partly because she liked chucking discarded clothing at the other pantheon members, partly because she was a bit of a neat freak.

Tyve was dancing to Phex's humming, so he increased volume and started actually signing – not cantor, no direction or intent to it, just plain old-fashioned Sapien singing. Tyve wasn't gracing, either, just swaying and twirling as she cleaned. The others continued about their nighttime routines. It was common for someone to be singing or dancing in a pantheon, off hours or not.

Phex reached the chorus. Kagee joined in from where he was lying in his nook, reading something. He clearly didn't know the words, so he just hummed out a harmony. Tyve, however, knew them and belted along. Phex dropped back to humming so he could listen. She wasn't great, no real cantor strength or focus, but she wasn't out of tune, either.

He stopped cleaning and leaned on the counter to stare at her.

"What?" She was immediately defensive. "Did I mess up?"

"No." Phex left the kitchen and walked in a measured manner around Tyve.

She made a very funny face at his pointed examination.

Kagee hopped out of his niche and took a seat at the end of Phex's counter, then swiveled to focus on Tyve too. He cupped one hand behind the other and tapped his silver rings against each other in a measured way, thoughtful metallic clicks.

"You're not half-bad, actually." He looked over at Phex. "Low cantor?"

Phex up-tilted his chin in agreement.

Kagee frowned fiercely. "Tyve, you think you could sing? Like properly belt out a note or two of cantor under the dome?"

"No. Why? Are you crazy?"

"Phex sings high cantor and he can dance grace."

"Yeah, but he's a freak of genetic engineering." Tyve wasn't being cruel. Just blunt.

Jinyesun emerged from the hygiene chamber, robe on, interested ears crested. "Who is a freak?"

"Phex."

"But he is *our* adorable Sapien nugget of a freak," pointed out the Dyesi.

Phex gave everyone a dour look.

"Doesn't mean I can sing low cantor," protested Tyve.

Kagee emitted a protesting rumble. "We don't want you to sing a whole part – just a note or two when Phex jumps into my role or maybe does a trick for grace. If you could compensate for his absence, that would make our pantheon even more flexible."

"Are we messing with established roles and protocols again?" Jinyesun was understandably suspicious. After all, the divinity had spent years putting their one highly specialized system into practice – six roles, two of each type, everyone sticking to their positions, little deviation, and less damage. That tactic had built the Dyesi an entertainment empire, a galaxy-wide religion. But it was basically the same thing over and over again.

It was risky to mess with patterns, on the dome or off it. Risky to the gods, risky to the pantheon, and risky to the acolytes. No one knew that more than the Dyesi.

Except apparently Fandina, who said, "I like it."

Jinyesun made a Dyesi clicking, sounding not unlike Kagee's jewelry-tapping. "Of course you do. Next, *you* are going to want to sing."

Fandina gave the Dyesi soundless laugh. "Not possible, but we could maybe do a grace or two, especially at the end."

"This is madness." Jinyesun's ear crests flattened, but the Dyesi's iridescence remained normal. It wasn't actually disgusted – more pretending shock.

Berril joined them, throwing both arms around Tyve. "I think you'd make a great low cantor."

"Thanks, birdie, but let's just try a note or two first." Tyve appeared to be folding under pantheon pressure. She looked at Phex. "Well, wall-walker?"

Phex let himself feel a tiny bit smug.

Tyve's lips twitched. "Okay. Fine. I'm game." She looked at Kagee. "You don't feel challenged?"

"It's not my position you'll sing."

"No, but Phex is usurping yours."

Kagee, for some reason, laughed. "*That* I'm getting used to. He doesn't do it by intent but by default." Which was a confusing thing to say. The grey boy waved a hand at their mystified expressions. "Phex is growing on me."

"Like a very large mushroom?" suggested Fandina.

"Exactly. I thought he thought he was perfect."

Phex snorted.

"Now I realize he's just stressed and odd and shy and grumpy."

Phex said, "I could have told you that."

"Because you speak so often?" snapped Kagee.

"Now, now," said Berril.

"At least you're not throwing up half of what you eat anymore," Kagee muttered.

"He *what* now?" That was Tyve.

Phex realized he hadn't thrown up in a while, since Kagee moved in permanently. Why?

"He doesn't even bother to defend himself," grumbled Kagee.

"You still stay awake late?" Phex asked instead. Kagee must have had worries of his own, since he'd been awake long enough to hear Phex.

Kagee gave an exaggerated sigh. "I don't need to anymore."

Phex clicked. "Same."

"Are they having a conversation or is this some kind of grumpy code?" asked Tyve.

"It's not like Phex is the only one who's closed off." Berril squinted her whole pointed little face at Kagee, but her eyes darted back to Phex, worried.

"What did I do?" Kagee was shocked to be targeted by their nicest member. "I talk all the time."

Berril looked cheeky. "Yet it has not escaped my notice that you still haven't told anyone where you're from."

Tyve was surprised. "He hasn't? But I know that."

Kagee glared. "Of course you do, Jakaa Nova."

Berril turned excitedly on their dark grace. "You do?"

"It's not like there are a ton of grey folk wandering around the galaxy, Sapien or alien." Tyve made a funny face.

"It's not a popular color," agreed Jinyesun.

"My people rarely leave planet," admitted Kagee. Phex wondered if they were similar to the Wheel. "But we are open for trade. Especially for medical supplies, weaponry, and associated technology." *Ah, so,* not *like the Wheel, then.*

"Where's this planet, that very few leave but some people visit?" pressed Berril.

Phex wondered if he should curtail her. If Kagee didn't want to talk about it, then he probably had good reason.

Kagee stayed silent.

Tyve was not so reticent and was already vested in making Berril happy. "He's from Agatay."

Berril frowned. "I've not heard of it."

Neither had Phex. And he'd had to memorize all the major Sapien colonies – moon, space station, conglomerate, and planetfall – as part of his education on Attacon 7.

"Agatay." Fandina's crests flicked in thought. "Why do I know that name?"

Jinyesun looked down at its ident ring and pinged a query. "Agatay. Minor planet with a population of less than a billion. Near the quarantine zone. Earth compatible. Small yellow star. Xenophobic. Oh! Classification S3. Nice."

Phex had never heard of a colony carrying an S3 classification, although he did know about the quarantine zone. Even the Wheel knew of that. *Everyone* knew about it. But if Agatay was xenophobic, perhaps Kagee was another refugee. No. The acolytes had said Phex was their first, and Kagee had said his people engaged in trade. But perhaps they shared some other similarities in background.

"Are you triggered, then?" Phex asked.

Kagee looked at him, brow arched. "Triggered?"

"To be all grey," Phex explained.

"No."

Tyve, clearly impatient with the whole thing and knowing all the answers, said, "He's ex-core, not somaformed but evolutionarily diverged from the original genetics so much, he no longer qualifies as strictly S1. Can't you see? That's the only possible explanation."

Kagee rolled his eyes at the Jakaa Nova. "I take it you've traveled to my world in the past, star sailor?"

"Weird place. Were you born affiliated?"

"Of course."

"From one of the elite families?"

"Oh, *very* elite, especially according to them."

"Delineated?"

"How else would they let me go?"

Now they were speaking in some kind of code Phex couldn't follow, but he suspected Kagee was from the Agatay equivalent of high stock – elite status and moneyed. It explained his attitude, his jewelry, and his pretty clothing. Spoiled.

Berril interrupted. "S3? Oh, my gods, that's so cool." She bounced up and down with excitement. "You're *naturally* evolved? That's awesome."

Kagee clearly didn't agree, so he only said, "Got a nice voice out of it."

Jinyesun suddenly gave the Dyesi laugh.

"What?" asked Berril.

"He is basically the opposite of Phex."

"Oh," said Berril. "That's true. How cute!"

"Cute!" said Phex and Kagee, horrified, at the same time.

Time flew by after that. Tyve couldn't manage more of low cantor than a note or two, but if she practiced hard on the few she was given, she could hit them well enough to push skinsift.

Their performance for the judges at the end of the next month was more startling than spectacular. Some of their choices had already been noted by acolytes during practices, but not all of them. Phex and his pantheon stuck in some of their favorite new elements, like the magenta starburst, and a few moments when they swapped Tyve for Phex so Phex could walk up a wall, flip, and throw Berril into taking wing. Phex wished they could do both those at the same time – now, *that* would be truly impressive. But he couldn't hold a steady note and perform a major grace simultaneously.

The acolytes seemed, if not impressed, at least not upset by how experimental they were becoming with their different roles.

It was Jinyesun who reined them in, reminding them that they needed to master their actual assigned positions before they could really afford to push each other out of comfort zones. They must establish those comfort zones first, both within themselves and with each other as a group.

Phex and Kagee agreed immediately. So, Berril, Fandina, and Tyve reluctantly did as well.

Thus, Phex focused on the low cantor work he needed to

do to compensate for Kagee, and how Tyve might help with that, and left grace play for later.

Still, they had impressed the acolytes enough to stay. They were officially no longer just potential gods but a potential pantheon. There would be no more moving dorms. They were stuck with each other.

Other things changed then too.

There were no more language or enculturation lessons. If they had questions about the Dyesi, they were expected to ask their sifters for help. Instead, they spent the mornings watching the live performances of true pantheons, training their eyes and ears for teamwork and technique, figuring out what worked for which groups and why, and what might work for them.

One of the groups they studied the most was Tillam.

Phex started to notice things about the gods as artists. The more he understood the nature of the interrelationship between cantor, skinsift, and grace, the more he admired different aspects of what the great pantheons could do. Tillam was revered because they were popular, but they were popular because their colors were unmatched in brilliance. That was mostly Missit's doing. Hard not to admire the brat a little bit because of it.

But mostly?

Mostly, Phex and his new pantheon just practiced together *all the time*.

They started doing more and more movements as a group. Syncopations so that the graces were not the only ones on the dais in motion, dance steps that visually supported grace-work. Phex only seriously graced once in a while, but he was still sore at the end of each day. He had no idea how Tyve and Berril, who were dancing constantly, did it. He started making more and more specialized evening drinks, soothing herbal infusions for himself and Kagee and their taxed throats, wholesome broth to add protein to the graces' diets.

Kagee tentatively offered to massage the graces' sore muscles one evening. Sarcastic about it, of course. Waiting to be rejected. Self-satisfied when the graces were pathetically grateful. He was small but remarkably strong. Fandina, intrigued, learned how to do it too. So, the two of them helped soothe Berril and Tyve's sore feet, legs, arms, and backs on the worst nights.

Jinyesun would seek Phex out on those evenings. Not for chitchat but to solicit questions of culture or philosophy. Phex understood what puzzled many, and was confused on things others just accepted, but he had to be prodded into actually asking about it. Apparently, Jinyesun thought this worth the effort. The Dyesi would sit next to him but never too close, as if afraid of contact with a Sapien. This made Phex sad. Not because he desired the Dyesi, or because he did not get enough physical affection – Berril saw to that – but because sometimes he sensed that Jin would have liked to rest its head on Phex's shoulder or lean against him. But for some reason, the Dyesi felt that wasn't permitted, and Phex lacked the ability to make himself any less threatening.

During one of these quiet evenings, Phex asked something that a month before, he never would have – out of fear of offense. Now he thought they were close enough for Jin to forgive him, even if it was an inappropriate question.

"Does it hurt you?"

"Does what hurt, Phex?"

"Kagee and I get sore throats. The graces get sore muscles. With you and Fandina, does your skin get sore?"

"From sifting all the time? Kind of. It can feel stretched tight, like after being submerged in very hot water."

Phex must have looked entirely confused. He'd never

been inside hot water. What a weird idea – as if he were a tea leaf. He wondered if water felt heavy.

Jin grappled for a different metaphor. "It can feel contracted and achy, like after being cold for too long without realizing it."

That Phex understood. He'd been cold a lot as a child. "Is there something we can do to help with that? Some food I could prepare?"

Jinyesun clicked happily. "Very kind of you to ask."

Phex felt himself relax, glad it hadn't been a rude question. "Drink? Moisturizer?" He suggested.

Jinyesun soundlessly laughed. "It's mostly sleep that helps. But also, perversely, more training. The more we sift correctly, the stronger we get. Like your voice and their muscles. But if we push too far, then only rest really helps. Maybe moisturizer. I should ask."

Phex nodded. "It'd be a good question, next time we get visited by a great god."

Jin nodded. "We're about due for another dose of godly mentoring, I think."

"They're all away on tour or retreat," said Tyve, groaning as Kagee hit a particularly sore part of her lower back.

"No sector conflicts at the moment," added Jinyesun.

Fandina looked up from Berril's leg muscles. "Good." It sounded almost self-satisfied about this.

Jin added, "Gods are taking advantage of peace. The divinity is expanding."

"Off to the far reaches of space to entertain the masses," agreed Tyve. "I got a beam from Zil saying Tillam were all the way out near the quarantine zone. Although that was weeks ago. Near your planet, Kagee."

Kagee made a face. "Never thought I'd feel sorry for Tillam."

Phex said to Jinyesun, "You'll try to remember to ask? About moisturizer, I mean."

"You do like to worry."

That made Phex feel self-conscious, so he went back to prepping corrosive dark for tomorrow morning and tried not to worry about Missit being close to the quarantine zone. If the golden god went up against the singularity, it was a genuine mystery as to who might come out on top and who might be destroyed in the process.

13

GODLY VISITATION

Nine months into the whole process, and the potentials no longer gathered in large groups at all. Each pantheon kept to its own dorm. For one thing, they'd been cut down to only eighteen potentials. Three groups of six. Three pantheons. That was it.

For another, their training felt more and more like a competition. They were being recorded and pitted against each other constantly. On the divine forums, polls and surveys and ranking systems popped up. All their end-of-month exams were beamed out into the galaxy for public voting. They were still only doing covers of other pantheons' godsongs, but unique twists on old classics were almost as welcome under the dome as new releases. Worshipers were happy to get anything unique, and fresh-faced gods-in-waiting made for an appealing novelty. Everyone wanted to be the first to believe in a new god. The acolytes were thrilled.

In the privacy of the practice domes, they worked on original songs. Phex thought it was probably paranoia, but he didn't want anyone listening in and stealing their ideas. So, now they barely even spoke to the other two pantheons.

One evening, his pantheon was eating together in companionable exhaustion when true gods lowered themselves to grace them in truth. Phex was in the kitchen with a view of the entrance, so he saw them first. Two heads peeking in between the skins over the doorway – one of them golden and the other vibrant metallic red.

"We appear to be experiencing a divine visitation," Phex informed his pantheon.

The five turned in their stools to take in their august visitors.

"I'm coming inside." Zil and Missit greeted the room in unison – and harmonized, of course.

Jinyesun and Fandina both crested sharp and high. Jin also blushed opaque in embarrassed excitement. Berril let out a little squeak. Kagee seemed unruffled. He ignored the two gods in a way that would indicate intentional rudeness in anyone but Kagee. Kagee was unintentionally rude most of the time. He was only *intentionally* rude when wit or extreme stupidity demanded it of him.

Tyve hopped off her stool and went to greet their visitors.

The two gods moved easily toward the small kitchen as if they were regulars. Their ritual greeting revealed they were former residents of this space. This must have been their dorm back when they first formed Tillam. Phex wondered which bed had been Missit's.

In the same room together, Zil and Tyve looked even more alike, although Phex could see the subtle differences in muscle and frame that demonstrated Zil's training as a fighter as opposed to Tyve's as a hunter. Zil was bulkier than his sister, although Tyve was almost as tall.

Of course, Phex's attention was drawn to Missit. This was

Missit, after all – hard not to stare. The god was tinted differently from last time, still all-over shimmery golden but sort of shiny metallic pink as well. *Rose gold*, Phex thought it was called. He looked less like his statue that way.

"Finally got yourself a pantheon, sister dear?" Zil slapped Tyve on the back, hard. "It's not as pretty as mine."

"To be fair, is there a pantheon as pretty as Tillam?" Tyve replied.

"Xillon," said Missit, Berril, and Fandina all at the same time.

Xillon was a second-generation pantheon widely regarded as the prettiest in all divinity.

Phex gestured with his chin at the pot of corrosive dark and looked pointedly at Tyve.

"He doesn't drink it," replied the dark grace.

Phex raised both eyebrows in silent query.

Tyve understood. "Zil will have milk to drink. I know, right? Big tough boy. Missit, what do you want?"

Missit grinned, bright and cheeky and lopsided, eyes on Phex. "Got anything stronger? Wine? Beer? Rubbing alcohol?"

"Been a long tour, has it?" said Tyve sympathetically.

Phex poured three cups of milk, including one for himself, as he'd grown to enjoy the nutty, creamy flavor. He passed the other two to the visiting gods.

Missit grimaced but drank. "Spoilsport." He pouted at Phex.

"Does your friend want something?" Phex asked.

"Friend?" said Missit, looking around.

"In the hallway."

"Oh, that's just a bodyguard," said Zil.

Phex thought that bodyguards probably got thirsty. He tilted his chin at Kagee.

The high cantor rolled his eyes but hopped off his stool went to stick his head out the door and ask.

He came back. "She says no thanks."

Phex handed him a flask of water anyway. Kagee gave a put-upon sigh and took it back into the hallway, returning empty-handed.

Missit watched this whole exchange with interest.

"How's the new crop?" Zil asked his sister.

"Pretty good. We're the best of the three groups, though."

"You're certainly the most unique." Zil was looking at them with interest. "What does the divinity think it's doing? Agatay? Seriously?" He pointed a fat-tipped finger at Kagee.

Kagee only raised his own cup at Zil. "They should be so lucky."

Zil said, "See? Classic Agatay."

Kagee didn't take offense. In fact, he looked kind of proud. Phex supposed that they were all used to Tyve by now. They knew that any kind of insult from a Jakaa Nova meant interest and that bluntness meant affection. It was when a Jakaa Nova got *polite* that everyone was in trouble.

"This is a brave new galaxy, brother dear. You're out of touch." Tyve threw an arm around Kagee's shoulder. "He sings like he was bred for it."

"Naturally?" Zil was impressed.

"And my little foil here is a chiropteran." Tyve gave Berril a flash of sharp teeth.

Berril made a smooching face. "Love you too, T."

Missit was looking at Phex.

Phex met gold-flecked eyes and stared back.

Kagee made an annoyed noise.

Missit pointed at Phex. "And what's he, exactly?"

"Grumpy," said Tyve. "Don't poke at Phex. He won't tolerate your brand of brat."

"No? But I'm adorable. Everybody loves me." Missit smiled sweetly.

Kagee got up and walked to the hygiene chamber.

Phex looked over at Jinyesun. The Dyesi didn't look like it was freaking out, but it did get overwhelmed easily, and there were two major gods in their midst. Phex shifted toward that end of the counter and made eye contact.

Jinyesun had recovered some of its cheek iridescence, and its crests were now neutral. It clicked softly at Phex. It was fine.

Fandina merely sat, crests perked, taking it all in like a giddy child.

"How long have you been together?" asked Missit, still watching Phex like he was a fascinating new food product.

"Two and a half months," said Tyve.

"Tight," said her brother.

"How's your dome looking?" Missit reached over to pick up a handful of nuts. Phex went to the pantry, found another bag with different flavors, and set it out, too.

"Getting there," replied Tyve. There was a brief pause while she opened the nuts and offered them to their guests. "Is Tillam back for a while? Is it because of—" She cut herself off.

Phex was watching Missit close enough to see the shadow behind his flecked eyes before the god remembered to keep his impish mask in place. "We're here to help you poor little lost potentials with our vast wisdom."

"Don't you mean *vast age and experience*?" teased Tyve, quickly recovering herself.

"New songs to work on, too," added Missit, grinning a bit too brightly.

"And you'll rest?" suggested Phex because both the gods

looked tired. Beautiful and godlike and amazing, of course, but also exhausted and stressed.

"Bossy bit of sun you got there, kid," said Zil to his sister.

"No one is safe," Tyve agreed.

Phex shook his head. "Give the gods seats, if they're staying, before they fall over."

Fandina hopped up, vacating a stool. Kagee returned just in time to gesture at his still-empty one with a sour-faced flourish.

"*Very* bossy," said Missit, not sitting but somehow sounding like he approved.

Phex scowled at him. Did he want to fall over? What the hell were they doing visiting potentials as soon as they got home, not just going to bed? He supposed maybe Zil was excited to see his sister, but Missit looked dim and wan underneath the gilt. He also seemed thinner than last time.

"You look like you haven't slept in a week. Mine's the same bed if you wanna go make a roll of yourself." Phex gestured toward his niche.

"What's he talking about?" Zil asked Missit.

"It's nothing. I might have been avoiding my responsibilities and ended up in the potential cantor dorm last time we were here."

"Oh. The usual." Zil could be snide, apparently.

Phex filed that information away. Missit did that kind of thing a lot, did he? Good to know. *Irresponsible flirt. Don't take this god too seriously*.

Phex went hunting for a sweet snack for Berril.

"Your sun is so caring, he extends his light to other pantheons," said Zil, sounding odd.

Phex turned back, handed Berril a little cup of dried fruit. She took it gladly, offered some to Kagee, who turned up his nose. Tyve took a few pieces, though.

When Phex returned his attention to Missit, the god wore a funny expression, but as soon as he noticed Phex was looking at him, he lost it.

"You are good with them," Missit said, poking through the nuts, voice flat.

"They are my pantheon," replied Phex, because that was the entirety of the explanation needed, so far as he was concerned. "You don't feel the same about yours?" He glanced at Zil, who was looking more amused than offended.

Missit gave an exaggerated sniff. "We've been together a very long time, and I am the youngest."

"Ah, so they look after you. Did you want something proper to eat?" Phex presented the question carefully.

Missit gave a funny, half-pained grimace. "I'm the great god Missit. I do not need looking after."

There were cracks in that capriciousness. It was definitely a defensive mechanism. "Yes, yes, you're very special and superior. Drink your damn milk." At least it had some protein and nutritional value.

Missit made a face but raised the cup to his lips and drained the last of it. The muscles of his neck made Phex feel hot and annoyed. Why should he care for a childish god not of his pantheon? And why wasn't Missit eating or sleeping properly?

If he wasn't hungry, he should go to bed. There was only one way to get the two gods to leave, though, and that was to shut things down. So, Phex took away Missit's empty cup and started cleaning the kitchen.

Fandina gave that soundless Dyesi laugh.

"What's funny?" asked Missit.

Kagee's mouth twitched like he was suppressing a smile. "You've been dismissed."

"What?" Missit said. "We just got here."

Berril bounced off her stool. She too looked tired. The dried fruit hadn't helped enough. They'd had a long grace practice that day. Tyve was trying to perfect a throw that deployed Berril's wings in a way as cool as Phex's flip. It was proving a difficult trick to develop.

"Phex is cleaning the kitchen," Berril explained cheerfully. "That means it's bedtime."

Zil looked genuinely flummoxed. "You're kicking us out? You?" He turned to his younger sister. "You infants?"

Tyve was also grinning. "Not us. Phex."

"Gods' breath, really? He's *that* bossy?"

Phex finished loading the washer with their used cups and checked the kitchen to make sure everything was back in its proper place.

Missit was leaning on the counter now, watching him with bright, tired eyes, red-rimmed under blush gold.

Zil looked back and forth between them. "What is *with* you?" Then he returned his attention to his sister as if for further explanation.

Tyve tapped her temple with one fat-tipped pinky finger.

Zil nodded. "It's like that, is it?"

"If you're here for a while, we'll catch up later." His sister was firm.

"We had better. You've clearly got stories to tell. Come on, Sparklepants, let's leave them to their beauty rest. They need it." Zil swooped in and slid his shoulder under Missit's waist, lifted him up, and carried him out.

Missit didn't react, just kept staring at Phex from upside-down, like Phex was the most fascinating thing in the room. Or the most offensive and presumptuous, daring to dismiss gods from his presence like that.

He looked completely ridiculous. Phex hid a smile.

"What's it mean?" Jinyesun asked Tyve, finding its voice

again as soon as the two gods were gone. It tapped its temple
with its pinky finger like Tyve had done.

"It's a Jakaa Nova thing," she replied.

Everyone waited for further explanation, since that part
was obvious.

Tyve pursed her lips. "The pinky is the weakest finger, so
the gesture implies the power of persuasion or charisma over
physical strength. It's both a compliment and an insult."

"Well, that's Phex for you. A big old complimentary
insult to the universe," said Kagee.

Phex shut off the kitchen lights and made his way toward
the hygiene room. Normally, he waited to go last, but no one
else seemed to be taking the hint. He supposed they were in a
little bit of shock. After all, they'd just been visited by the
gods.

Thus Tillam burst back into Phex's life.

They weren't around all the time, but their presence was
definitely *felt*. When gods walked among mortals, it always
had a ripple effect. Occasionally, a member of Tillam would
sit in on a practice session, offering advice or criticism or
both. It was nerve-racking. But Phex found it oddly comforting, a warmth in his belly. Like having Missit around settled
his stomach a little more than not having him.

Still, they weren't around often. They clearly had other
things to do. And it was usually only Missit, Yorunlee, or Zil
who bothered with the potentials. Or maybe the other half of
Tillam visited the other groups. Phex saw Tern once, Tillam's
light grace, but never Melalan or Fortew. He supposed that
mentoring wasn't for everyone – some gods didn't have the
right personality to teach with gentleness. He thought, should

he ever get to that point in this career, that he would make a terrible mentor. Berril would be great, though.

Phex and his pantheon were having fun with a Tillam piece. They'd put that spin on it where Phex jumped from low cantor to high and joined Kagee to master some complicated note that normally only Missit could push to the dome. With two voices, they could make it into something pretty – different-looking but still pretty.

At the end of one focused session, they were sitting on the dais, chatting about how it had gone and what might be rearranged, when a voice spoke from the doorway.

"Why would you drop Fortew's part like that?" Yorunlee walked in without announcing itself. One of Tillam's sifters, it was tall and impossibly elegant with vibrant blue resting skin.

Phex couldn't say what made a Dyesi attractive to other Dyesi, but in his opinion, Yorunlee was one of the most beautiful he'd ever seen. Yorunlee was also cool and reserved, poised even among a species known for being so.

Something about what they'd just done to Tillam's song seemed to have upset the Dyesi, though. Hard to tell for certain, because Yorunlee had excellent control over its crests and skin opacification.

Fandina came to their defense. "Kagee isn't Missit. We make adjustments to sift a better dome using our pantheons' abilities. You know how it is played. Modification is not mockery."

"But parody is," replied the Dyesi god, coming closer to the dais. Yorunlee's bodyguard followed it inside, taking an aggressive stance near the doorway. That was interesting. Usually, the bodyguards stayed outside of the dome. Phex thought it was a better defensive position to be outside, where the dome could not distract, impact, or influence. After all, even bodyguards could experience godfix. It wasn't something the brain could be trained to resist. Presumably, there were some species in the Galaxy immune to the dome, but Phex had yet to meet one.

"We meant no insult," apologized Jinyesun, formal Dyesi, crests flat back and body posture that of a cowed youngster.

Phex didn't like to see that. It felt as if Yorunlee were bullying his friends. He jumped off the dais so he was on the same level as Tillam's sifter but between it and the others.

Yorunlee focused on him. "You drop Fortew's part to sing Missit's as if low cantor were unimportant."

Oh, Yorunlee was *actually* angry. As if Phex had personally diminished Fortew's godhood.

"We were messing around with the song, not the singer," Phex said carefully.

"The singer *is* the song."

Kagee jumped down, interposed himself between them.

Phex scowled at him. What was he doing? He was smaller than both of them – a delicate, grey wraith. But something about the way he stood seemed dangerous. Phex would have said, until that moment, that, physically, Kagee was one of their weakest members. Even the Dyesi seemed tougher than him. But now Phex wondered about the past their high cantor never talked about. Perhaps ex-core life was harder than anyone thought, even for the planetary elite.

Kagee's voice was melodic but cool. "It is I who am unable to sing Missit's dome. Don't get angry at Phex for compensating for me. I can't push the right colors without Phex's help. Since high cantor is required during that section and low cantor is not, he switches. Were you watching the dome? Or were you only listening to find flaws in the singing of it?"

Yorunlee's posture relaxed slightly.

Kagee pressed his advantage. "You cannot blame my pantheon for a desire to correct for my deficiencies."

Phex was weirdly delighted by Kagee publicly claiming them. As though his cold, grey, angsty little heart had warmed enough to accept them all, even Phex. He was also annoyed that Kagee thought of himself as defective. Kagee wasn't lesser. He was just less than Missit. And wasn't everyone?

"Actually," said Tyve, still on the dais, "we turned it into something spectacular. Did you not see the starburst?"

Phex was carefully formal but not subservient when he said, "I did not mean to imply erasure or replacement of Fortew."

Yorunlee closed its massive eyes for a long moment. Then it turned and walked out of the dome, bodyguard close behind. That bodyguard was obviously concerned, and not just about Yorunlee's safety but about the Dyesi's emotional stability.

Phex and Kagee returned to the dais.

Phex looked hard at Tyve but decided he would wait until they were in private to ask about Yorunlee's odd behavior. No use worrying the others with his suspicions about Tillam.

Instead, he turned to Kagee. "You have defensive training?"

Kagee looked startled. "What?"

Tyve followed what Phex was asking about. She explained, "Just now, you acted like a warrior."

Phex added, "I can fight because I had to survive, but I was never trained. Tyve moves deadly, for all she talks about chasing. She was raised to fight. You're like her. What happened?"

Kagee stayed quiet, processing.

Phex was prepared to wait him out, but Tyve got impatient.

"Jakaa Nova say there are only two types of people in the universe – those who can kill and those who cannot. I never noticed before Kagee, but you can kill."

Kagee winced. "I was raised a proxy. It's hard to translate the meaning to aliens."

"Try," ordered Tyve.

Kagee made a face. "It's a little like a body double, only in life rather than performance. Protection is part of the service."

"Because you delineated?"

"Exactly. What else is there to do with us elites who cannot participate in politics?"

Phex wondered if that meant Kagee had been raised to die defending someone else and if that was why he left Agatay. If Kagee was something like a crudrat for his people. If the two of them really did have more similarities than differences.

"What's the practical application of proxy?" Tyve asked. "I mean, I can only really do damage with blades, because that's my training. Phex comes from the rough" —she glanced at Phex, red eyes narrowed— "so you... what? Punch when you fight?"

Phex shook his head. Most of his strength and reach was in his long legs, not his arms. "Kick."

Those few times he'd had to fight his corner as a crudrat, and later on Attacon 7, he'd kicked, and it had worked. If someone around him was under threat, he'd probably instinctively do the same. Then he'd run. He wasn't an idiot.

Tyve tilted her head at Kagee in inquiry.

Kagee suddenly looked very small – still truculent but also scared.

Jinyesun said, "We will not look down on you for whatever you were made to do before you came to us, Kagee. You should know that by now."

"We'll look down on you because you're a jerk," said Phex.

Kagee laughed. "Takes one to know one."

Phex made a rude gesture at him. It was old, from his crudrat days, but Kagee understood the concept.

"Your past is not your fault," said Berril kindly.

"I don't put any effort into being antisocial." Kagee sounded almost smug.

"No, I'm sure that being ex-core, you come by it naturally," shot back Phex, feeling rather proud of himself.

Kagee looked impressed. "Where did this snarky Phex come from? Did they roll out a new, improved, sexy version when we weren't looking?"

Phex was confused. "I'm sexy when I snap at you?"

"No, you're sexy when you're an asshole."

"Boys! Stop now," Tyve said. "So, Kagee, *proxy*?"

"It's not a nice kind of protection," hedged Kagee.

Phex said, "You know how I met Missit?"

"He crawled into your bed?"

"No. Before that. When we arrived. I had to protect him from a fixed. Brat gave his bodyguard the slip. This fixed was bigger than me, but I was all that stood between them. I'm more imposing than Missit. And I can kick. But it was still a close call."

"So?" Kagee was confused.

Phex was annoyed he'd wasted words on a story that hadn't made his position clear. "It'd be nice to know which of us can protect the others and under what circumstances. If we become gods, we will be under constant threat." He looked around.

Everyone seemed surprised, even Tyve.

Phex blinked at them. "You think Tillam is trailed everywhere by bodyguards for fun?"

"But they're *Tillam*!" said Berril.

Phex shrugged. "And maybe someday we become major gods too. We already get tribute. We already have worshipers. You think those who fixate on us will be saner than others? Godfix defeats reason." He didn't say he thought that was the point. The Dyesi didn't call it *divinity* for nothing. The divine system encouraged unadulterated devotion. Phex only knew the galactic history he'd been taught on Attacon 7, but there had been one constant throughout time and space – belief tipped easily into obsession and from there into madness. Alien or human, it didn't matter. After love and worship came possessive need, and need ate away at logic like a parasite.

Phex was annoyed by his pantheon's shock. "Surely, you knew this is dangerous." He gestured at the dais and then all around them.

Berril's eyes were very big and very yellow in the dimness of an unsifted dome. "I never seriously thought about it before."

Kagee was frowning. "You're wondering about whether you have to worry about me in a physical altercation?"

Phex didn't say he'd read studies on the fixed. On how their brains worked or, more precisely, ceased to work. On how the need for a god's attention could warp into owner-ship and violence. For some reason, the acolytes allowed potentials full access to information on clinical fixation. There were fixed who wanted to kidnap and lock gods away, keep them forever like pets. The corruption of care into possession. There were fixed who wanted to tear gods open with their bare hands, to properly release all that talent into the universe. The corruption of generosity into excess. There were fixed who wanted to eat gods alive because then the god would be part of them forever. The corruption of desire into consumption. Fixed would do anything to be noticed, to be remembered, to have an effect on their god's existence.

"You don't have to worry about any of us, Phex," said Fandina.

Phex exchanged a look with Tyve. That was a ridiculous thing to say, since all he ever did was worry about them. His pantheon. He'd never had family or friends to worry about before, and it seemed his brain was getting in eighteen years or so of the stuff all at once. It was not the same as the fear of failure that had driven him into the hygiene chamber late at night, but it was still fear. And it still lurked in his gut, making him queasy sometimes. He thought this was what he did now, processed stress into bile. Worried about his pantheon.

"Even me?" said Kagee in a small voice, as if he couldn't believe himself worthy of concern.

Phex scowled at him.

Kagee grinned, the expression lighting up his grey face. Mercurial, he rolled his eyes and sighed. "Fine, then. These." He raised up his hand and wiggled his fingers, indicating the chunky silver jewelry he always wore.

"You never take them off, not even in the hygiene chamber," said Jinyesun.

"Spur rings. They can deploy to inject a neurotoxin."

"It's deadly?" Tyve asked, not disgusted, just curious.

"Not to all species, but it is fast-acting. Paralyzing. For most."

Phex raised his chin in approval. "Good."

"Sapiens are scary," said Fandina to Jinyesun.

"At least they're on our side." Berril always saw the good in everything.

Phex looked at Tyve. "And you need a blade to be effective?"

"Yes, but I always carry several."

"Even under the dome?" Phex was dubious. In performances, Tyve would be made to wear outfits that were very tight or very sparse or both. Even a small knife would be difficult to stash on a grace. After all, part of the point of grace was to display perfect physique.

"I'm Jakaa Nova. We are always bladed." She arched her brows at the two Dyesi. "You think Sapiens are scary?"

She raised her hands, wiggled her fingers like Kagee had moments before. Then she flexed tendons, and five very sharp claws emerged, wickedly curved.

Jinyesun and Fandina both went puffy-crested, surprised. Berril pretended to swoon. Kagee acted like he'd seen it all before. Phex suspected he probably had. The Jakaa Nova and the Agatay clearly had regular diplomatic relations.

Phex narrowed his eyes at Tyve. "You've been holding out on me. I bet you can chop veggies really fast with those things. Should I have you help with meal prep?"

Tyve sheathed her claws hurriedly. "Nothing to see here."

"Shall we get back to work?" said Fandina, huffy with amusement.

Phex managed to catch Tyve alone later that night. They were doing their usual quick tidy while the others prepared for bed. Phex enjoyed this time every evening – the quiet, mellow hour. Organizing the kitchen brought him a strange kind of peace.

He hated to break the meditation of it all, but he needed to ask. So, he left the sanctity of his kitchen and caught Tyve's hand, tugging her to crouch behind one of the couch puffs.

"Is something seriously wrong with Fortew?"

Tyve looked away, nibbled at the corner of her full lower lips. "I shouldn't even ask how you figured that out. Was it Yorunlee?"

"And Missit." Phex dropped Tyve's hand, self-conscious.

"Missit?"

"He's scared."

"How could you tell?"

Phex had no idea – he just could. It wasn't like he'd made a study of the golden god, but Missit's obvious weight loss and clear stress weren't normal. Plus, there was that lost look in his eyes. And the acting out. Certainly, Missit was capricious by nature, but to hide from bodyguards and climb into a stranger's bed? This fear of his had been around since they met.

"They'd recently found out, back when I first started here. Hadn't they? That's why they were back on Divinity 36. That's why Tillam cut their tour short." It was the only thing that made sense.

"Yeah." Tyve looked at her hands.

"He's sick or irreparably damaged?"

"Zil won't talk about it. But I think Fortew is quite ill."

"Neuro Blue?" Phex guessed. It was one of the few incurable diseases still rampant in the galaxy. Only the Wheel had eradicated it, but no other civilization was willing to put the Wheel's particular methods into practice.

Tyve's lack of agreement was agreement enough. "He's been taken into restrictive care by the medics," she said. "Zil hasn't seen him since they got back."

Phex thought about that sad godsong back at the cafe before he was recruited, Missit's, all about loss. He tried to remember what it was called. "Tillam is in danger of losing their sun. Can they survive that?"

"Can any pantheon survive any loss, let alone a sun? Five

doesn't work under the dome." Tyve shook herself, part shiver, part desperate rejection of that future. Then she moved away from Phex and continued folding throws and placing them with great care on the couch.

Phex sat back on his heels and scrubbed at his face. The Yorunlee of earlier no longer felt angry. Missit no longer felt flighty, either. They both just seemed fragile and scared.

"Don't tell anyone, Phex." Tyve pressed down on the folded stack of blankets, glanced at him covertly.

Phex arched one silent, condemning brow.

"Of course you won't. What am I saying? Sorry. It's just, you know, my brother's whole world is crumbling. I'm worried about him."

Phex understood worry. He hadn't had his own pantheon for very long, but the idea of losing any one of them caused a near-physical ache – like sore muscles, or sore throat, or sore skin.

What kind of sore would occur if they were five instead of six?

What kind of scar did absence leave behind?

Missit didn't show up to watch them as much as Phex wanted him to. This was really annoying. Annoying that Phex wanted it. Annoying that Missit didn't. Annoying that Phex now had someone else to worry about. Annoying that it wasn't something Phex could fix or scowl his way out of. Annoying to care about anything, really, let alone other people.

When Missit did come, he rarely stayed for long. Maybe this was because they were workshopping a Tillam song. Maybe listening to it without Fortew hurt too much, or maybe, like with Yorunlee, hearing Phex drop Fortew's part with such ease hurt even more. All too often, Phex would look up to see Missit walking away, fast and smooth, the

Dyesi upbringing making liquid of his bones. Missit could wear a cloak of feathers and Phex would still recognize that walk.

After hours, Zil sometimes came to visit, but it wasn't the same kind of visit as before. Zil and Tyve would draw the curtain to her niche and talk quietly together in their native language.

The rest of the pantheon respected their privacy.

Phex took to going out into the hallway to talk to Zil's bodyguard. Not to ask about Fortew or Missit, but to ask about being a bodyguard. The conversation with Tyve and Kagee about protecting a pantheon made Phex worry – most things did these days. He thought maybe he should go to the source. Kagee and Tyve had actual training as warriors. Phex only had a rough childhood and not much memory of that anymore. He'd been so young – malnourished and intentionally small. He was grown and stronger now, big-boned and tough. Ten months of training and Phex was starting to look like a god. He'd put on layers of muscle – the consequence of rigorous physical activity and a diet the Dyesi tailored to maximize aesthetics. Phex's body was different now. He needed to learn how to use it defensively.

"I was wondering, as you are here, if you could teach me a few moves," he asked politely, using his best formal Dyesi.

Zil's bodyguard was a tough-looking alien of a species Phex had never met before. He wore close-fitting scaled green armor over most of his body. The result was somewhat reptilian-looking. Not human, he was well outside of the normal Sapien range and unnaturally slender – H6 class at the very least.

"You want *what*?" The bodyguard was so startled by Phex's request, he used the Dyesi particle for command and question.

Phex backed off quickly. "Are gods not allowed to defend themselves?"

"My Zil comes with blades attached and is better with a knife than I. That is not an issue. I have simply never been asked before, Sapien. There is no divine mandate against it that I know of." The bodyguard carefully evaluated Phex in turn, then resumed guard position, scanning the hallway for possible threat. "I cannot when I am on duty."

"When are you off duty?"

The alien raised a sharp, long, four-fingered hand. "It cannot be me. One of the Sapien guards would be better. I shall ask Itrio. She has nothing to do these days."

"I would take it as a kindness," replied Phex, using Dyesi extreme politeness.

"You will have the energy for it?" The alien was justifiably skeptical.

Phex was not. He'd already noticed that he seemed to recover quickly from the soreness, in both muscles and throat, faster than other graces or cantors. He was less tired in the evenings these days. His body had acclimatized to the rigorous practice regime. A medic had confirmed this at his last checkup – another consequence of his triggered genetics.

"I am Phex." Phex introduced himself, even though he knew the bodyguard would already have access to all of his information.

"Elder K," replied the alien. "Now go to bed, little Phex. Itrio will not go easy on you tomorrow."

Phex did as he was told.

Accordingly, Itrio showed up in the hallway the next night after dinner.

She was Sapien but from a heavy-gravity planet, so S2-class. She was shortish with the muscles common for that somaform type and the light, high-stepping walk of a body accustomed to much higher *g*. The Galactic Common slang term for them was *bouncers*. She was the first bouncer Phex had ever met in person. Now he understood the moniker. Her walk was a bit funny-looking but not her scowl.

Itrio introduced herself in Galactic Common. Phex fell back into that language with only a little awkwardness. It had been months since he'd spoken anything other than Dyesi formal. She also introduced herself as Fortew's bodyguard. Of course she was. Because that wasn't going to turn into a problem. Phex had stolen Fortew's cantor parts and now his guard?

What Itrio initially taught him was mostly self-defense. Phex took to it easily. It was not that different from throwing a light grace around, although the ultimate intent was to cause injury rather than prevent it.

After that first night, Phex and Itrio moved from the hallway into one of the grace practice rooms and arranged to meet regularly each week.

Phex told his pantheon what he was doing and where he went those evenings. They worried he was pushing himself, but they were too tired to protest. It's not like Phex would debate his decision with them. He would do whatever he thought was best, silently and without excuses. They all knew that about him by now. Kagee called him an idiot, but that was Kagee.

The acolytes might have put a stop to it, but Phex thought maybe Elder K had explained. Or maybe the Dyesi wanted him to push his own limits. Or maybe they were intrigued by the idea of a god who could protect himself. And protect his pantheon. Because Phex convinced Itrio to progress quickly from self-defense to defending others, especially in a crowd. He figured that was when gods were most vulnerable. He would never forget the shock of that fixed lunging at Missit.

Itrio was game. She proved easygoing and maybe a bit too gentle with Phex, but at least he was learning something useful.

So, Phex had a new schedule that included fighting in the evenings. Perhaps he got slightly less sleep than he should, but he felt a lot better about his ability as a sun and his responsibilities to his pantheon. And if that wasn't worth a little less sleep, he didn't know what was.

14

GODLY FRATERNIZATION

Itrio was showing Phex how to combine basic combat moves with defensive tactics when Missit discovered them. Phex had explained his natural tendency to kick. Itrio was modeling how to huddle over someone and use a back kick to get an attacker off. Phex thought this would be particularly useful if he needed to guard someone significantly smaller than him – like Kagee, Berril, or Missit.

"This is where you hide now," said a smooth, golden voice from the entranceway. "I'm coming in." Missit announced himself and his relationship to the space.

Missit's bodyguard was an unknown entity – fully modified, covered in high-tech armor, and disinclined to speak, but originally Sapien from general body shape and movement. The cyborg stuck their head in behind their god, nodded at Itrio, and then took a defensive position outside the practice chamber.

Missit crossed his arms. "Phex, what are you doing with Itrio?" There was a lot of emotion wrapped up in his tone. Phex wasn't sure if it was anger, disappointment, or jealousy.

"Learning how to be a bodyguard." Phex thought that was perfectly obvious.

"Of course you are. After practicing all day during the hardest final stages of potential training. When you have pantheon assessments coming up and the possibility of godhood. You thought, *I'll learn to fight as well.* On a lark?" He sounded angry.

Why should Missit care what Phex did?

Phex was genuinely confused. Perhaps it had something to do with Itrio being Fortew's bodyguard, working with Phex when Fortew was sick.

"Should I not be taking up Itrio's time?" he hedged, cautiously.

Missit winced. "Yorunlee would say you are stealing Fortew's voice and now his bodyguard."

Itrio came to Phex's defense. "You know I'm not needed. Fortew is entirely secure right now. There's nothing I can do for him."

Missit's face fell. "And you still want to be useful? Of course you do. I'm not mad at you, Itrio. It's Phex. Don't you think this is too much for him? He's only a potential. You know he does grace work as well as cantor all day, then he cooks for his pantheon, then he cleans, and then he comes here." Missit glared at Phex. "When do you sleep?"

Phex wondered if Fortew's illness had made Missit particularly worried about suns. If now he spotted potential disaster everywhere.

"You think I'm overreaching my capacities?" Phex asked, a little curt. He didn't want Missit thinking he was weak or incapable.

"You are only a Sapien, Phex!"

"I'm triggered, Missit." Weird that, for some reason, he'd expected Missit to know that already. As if Missit would have looked up Phex's medical records. As if gods had access to acolyte data, which he doubted. And even if they did, why would Missit bother with his?

Itrio was looking back and forth between them. "Should I step out while you two settle this?"

"No. We need to get back to training," said Phex.

"Yes, please," said Missit at the same time.

Itrio was not stupid. She did as the god requested.

Missit approached Phex as soon as the flap fell, pretty face bullish. "Explain *triggered*."

"I'm Wheel-born. I've been genetically altered for enhanced physical capacity." Phex didn't mind revealing this to Missit, for some reason. Missit wouldn't care like other Sapiens did. Missit was mostly raised by the divinity – he'd act more like a Dyesi about it. Or so Phex hoped.

"Go on."

Phex sighed and smoothed back flyaway hairs with both hands. "It's why I look the way I look. It's why I sing the range I sing. It makes me less tired than the others. And I need less sleep."

"Oh, really? You look tired. Gorgeous, of course, but there are dark circles under your eyes."

Phex was going to say the same thing about Missit, but he suspected the boy wouldn't thank him for it. He didn't want to argue, especially with a major god. One wasn't supposed to argue with gods.

"I'm fine. I know my limits." Or he thought he did. "I can still be sun for my pantheon." Phex said that cautiously, concerned about opening a fresh wound.

"You think that's why I'm—" Missit threw his arms up in annoyance.

Phex was always startled when Missit displayed mannerisms that seemed innately Sapien. But he supposed Missit's parents were human, as was his low-cantor partner of over a decade, and at least two of Tillam's bodyguards. Maybe Missit had not been so isolated from Sapien culture as Phex first imagined. Maybe he would be disgusted if he knew Phex's past.

He spoke carefully, stomach knotted, "They tinkered with my genetics before I was born."

Missit narrowed his eyes. "Triggered or sun, cantor or grace, you're still Sapien. You bleed and bruise like the rest of us, I'm sure."

Phex took a chance and moved closer. "That godsong you released at the beginning of the year. The new one. The really sad one. What did you name it?"

"Tillam's Lament." Missit let him change the topic.

"No, not the divinity's title for it. What did *you* call it when you wrote it?"

"Of course you'd ask that."

Phex waited him out.

Finally, Missit said, "Five."

Phex absorbed the horrible number. "He's not doing well, is he? Your sun?"

Missit sort of crumpled in on himself.

Phex took two big strides and pulled the god close. Hugged him the way Berril had taught him to hug. But also protectively, guarding the way Itrio had taught him to guard. Curled around and over, lower body free and loose to kick back if needed. Missit felt lean and fine-boned against him. He was so much smaller than his personality. The lights of the room reflected off the rose gold of Missit's neck, blinding enough for Phex to shut his eyes. Or maybe it was just Missit in his arms.

But Missit was also stiff, so much so that Phex jerked

away, retracted his offer of physical comfort. Perhaps hugging was not something Missit enjoyed.

But the god gave a little wet noise and said, "No, this is good. It's not exactly what I want from you, but it's necessary right now."

Phex wasn't sure what to make of that, but he pulled Missit close again.

Right now, all of Missit's pantheon was hurting. Those whom Missit could normally go to, those he leaned on, were all suffering the same loss. Phex understood a little of it from listening to "Five." Missit and his pantheon could share grief, but they could not lift the burden of it off each other. They were all in it together with no sun to keep them from spinning out of control. Phex was not Missit's sun, but he was a sun.

"Lean on me for a bit," said Phex. Because he couldn't say that it was *all going to be okay*. That would be a lie. He had no words of comfort. He never had the right words. All he had to give was the kind of love Berril taught him and the need to protect that Itrio was cultivating.

Missit relaxed against him, warming slowly. Became boneless Dyesi elegance, too liquid to contain Sapien pain.

Phex took Missit's weight. He curled one arm about the god's waist, pressed the other up against his back. He sank that hand into the silken fall of gold-tinged hair to cradle Missit's head and tuck him close. The god's cheek pressed on his chest, and Missit trembled, all that greatness no burden at all. As if Phex's muscles had been triggered with only this in mind – to support a god.

Phex held melted gold, hot and difficult to contain, burning as it dripped through his fingers, dangerous but still impossibly precious. He tried to do nothing but be there, solid and treasuring, even as he knew that stability could only go so far when faced with hopelessness.

Something changed after that.

Missit started showing up a lot more often. When Zil visited Tyve, Missit came too. While the siblings talked, Missit sat at Phex's kitchen counter and drank tea, chatting about inconsequential things. Eventually, the others forgot their awe and joined him – asked questions about godhood, listened to his stories of a decade-long career.

Missit turned up a couple times a week at Phex's evening bodyguard training, too. Sometimes, he just stuck his head in, as if gaining reassurance from Phex's kicking. More often, he came inside and curled in a corner to watch. After a few weeks of that, Itrio put Missit to work so Phex could practice with an actual body to protect.

Most of the time, and always around others, Phex got the public version of Missit. Flirtatious and easygoing, cheerful and sensual – Missit the great deity, god of gods. The personality chip in the golden statue.

But once in a while, that great god would order Itrio to leave them alone in the practice room. Phex would hold liquid gold in his arms in a desperate attempt to keep it from melting entirely away. He was pretty certain they weren't supposed to be left alone like that. It edged into fraternization, and Phex was still only a potential. In no corner of the galaxy was Phex worthy of being anything to Missit, not even a surrogate sun. But it never lasted very long, and Missit usually looked slightly improved afterwards. Phex, at least, slept better as a result.

———

Phex and his pantheon were busy butchering a Tillam song into starburst and spectacle when Missit, in godly frustration, took to the dais and ordered Kagee to sit out for a bit.

"Try it properly," he said, glaring at Phex and the rest of the potential pantheon.

Typical Missit – thoughtless action out of capricious interest. What did it say about Phex that he found it charming? He exchanged glances with Kagee. The grey boy shrugged. He didn't look any more annoyed than normal.

Kagee did as Missit instructed, hopping off the dais to sit in the audience with his arms crossed, glaring.

Phex looked at the rest of his pantheon. He wasn't scared to partner with the best-known voice in the galaxy, but he could tell the other four were going quietly bonkers with nerves.

Tyve was probably the calmest of the bunch, but even she would feel pressure, trying to muffle and control Missit, of all gods. Berril was wide-eyed with panic. She was going to have to beat out the pace for a major god she admired, and that was a lot of responsibility to put on a light grace of her temperament. The two sifters were beyond nervous. Sifting for Missit was probably one of the greatest honors of their lives. Both Fandina and Jinyesun were almost entirely opaque in shock, terror, and embarrassment. Their crests were flattened back to their skulls.

Missit grinned at them. "It'll be fun."

Phex said, "I don't think that's the word they'd use. Why are you being so mean to my pantheon?"

Missit lost his smile instantly and gave Phex a fierce stare through gold-flecked eyes. "Let's see what beauty we can inflict on a dome together."

Phex nodded. "For fun?"

"Fun."

An acolyte observer sat in the audience, most likely recording them for beaming later. The acolyte didn't try to stop Missit. Instead, it left the dome while the six of them arranged themselves on the dais.

Phex looked down at Kagee, sitting like a king, a congregation of one. "You okay?"

"Oh, I'm glad to be well out of this," said the high cantor. He looked smug. They were about to learn how genuinely difficult this role was to sing and, when sung well, how hard it was to work with.

"You're enjoying this," accused Phex.

"Oh, yeah. Suffer, you lot."

Phex pointed two fingers at him. "Is that a challenge?"

Missit did not like the focus to be off him. "When you're ready, low cantor."

Phex twirled to look at him. "Our choreography or Tillam's?"

Missit quirked one side of his mouth sarcastically. "Yours, of course. It's your gracing, isn't it? Why do you think I've been watching you?"

"This could get ugly fast," said Tyve. Because it could. Their gracing set to Phex and Missit's godsong? That's not how sifting a dome worked. It was a mismatch of beat and cadence.

"You scared?" asked Missit.

Tyve took that as a challenge. "It's you I worry about, old god. You sure you can keep up?"

Berril's eyes were huge. She plucked at Tyve's arm. "Tyve!"

But Missit found that very funny. "Let's dance, then, *children*."

Phex was accustomed to Kagee's voice now, especially with this particular song. Kagee's tone had developed even more rustic warmth when partnering with Phex, leaning into his natural burr. Phex smoothed it out sometimes, enhanced it

in others. There were also those moments Phex needed to
jump to high cantor. Missit required none of those things
from Phex, but he did still *need* low cantor.

Missit was bent on showing off. Phex had no idea why.
But Phex wasn't scared of Missit's voice. He had the power
to match him. He'd been designed that way. Maybe not *match*
in skill exactly, but balance him out. And Kagee had trained
Phex into figuring out the best approach. Phex's voice didn't
have Missit's smooth character, none of the golden syrup that
made Missit a great god. But Missit didn't require Phex to
execute vocally the way Kagee did, either. Low cantor was
simply meant to mold and contain a high cantor like Missit's
– stretch and compensate. Phex needed only to trust and
follow Missit into places few other cantors ever went. Not to
push but to rein him in. Missit needed to be controlled, and
Phex could do that easily.

It was, indeed, *fun*. Missit led him a wild run, like a blade
to dodge around – sharp notes to clean and smooth. A vocal
sparring match.

The sifters and the graces just had to keep up. They struggled but managed it. The dome was much more intense than
Phex and Kagee ever produced. It was also entirely different
from Tillam's original version.

Both Missit and Phex were best at color and saturation.
Under them, the sifters and their dome exploded with almost
blinding vibrancy. Tyve did her best as dark grace, and Berril
deployed her wings almost constantly to center and muffle
what she could, but in the end, the graces were overpowered.
It was visual volume turned all the way up. Dazzling.

It was insanely beautiful. But that was a problem, Phex
realized about halfway through. This kind of performance
might actually cause insanity. It was too much. Sensory overload. Certainly too much for the Sapien mind, possibly too

much for even the Dyesi. Godfix for everyone – not merely encouraged but *forced* upon them.

When Phex could finally drag his eyes away from Missit and their harmony, he noticed they'd collected a congregation of acolytes below. About half of them were covering their ear crests, the other half their eyes. All of them were skinsifting to match the dome. Only Kagee sat, apparently unaffected, with a tight smile on his face that spoke of pride and a slightly evil delight in the effect this was having on the aliens around him. He was enjoying the destructive nature of the art being wrought – a smug grey dot in a storm of color.

What Phex liked the most about singing with Missit was that he didn't have to care about limiting his own power. Somehow, he just knew Missit would protect the two sifters. Phex could finally let himself sing at full capacity – because for all that Missit was limitless himself, he easily caught Phex's power and redirected it, preventing it from damaging Jinyesun or Fandina. It was like using a controlled burn to contain a wildfire. There was no way Phex's sifters could be hurt with Missit's voice there to guard them. The earth around them had already been scorched.

The dome practically shook with godsong. After the last note and the last burst when the dome faded back to pearlescent grey, there was complete silence.

Phex and Missit simply stood grinning at each other in stupid delight. Phex's face hurt from the unfamiliar sensation. Berril and Tyve were panting and slumped behind them, exhausted. Fandina and Jinyesun both sat down, as if their legs had given up.

Phex lost his smile in worry and ran over to them. "You okay?"

"You know when you asked us about getting sore skin the way you get sore throats?" said Fandina.

"Now we have got it," added Jinyesun.

They looked uninjured. Still, Phex was compelled to check. "No burning or bruising?"

"None at all," Jin did not hesitate to reassure him.

"That was just *a lot*," explained Fandina.

Phex exhaled and nodded. Then he remembered himself and clicked reassuringly.

Missit came over and crouched down on the sifters' other side, also checking in with them. As exhausted and taxed as they looked to Phex, Missit seemed to think they were fine. But then, he might do this often when he sang with sifters not his own.

He turned to Phex. "*You* are a lot of work to sing with. Pushy."

"Me?" objected Phex, even knowing he hadn't held himself back. Hadn't tried to be gentle. That was only because, for the first time, it hadn't felt like he needed to. He looked at Jinyesun's slumped body, still elegant but wilted. Maybe he should have. "Sorry."

"Don't apologize. I enjoyed the challenge," said Missit.

"We did too!" reassured Fandina.

"Do not blame yourself, Phex." Jin crested at him, its ears only a little floppy. "You know how sometimes you push yourself to grace just for the pleasure of bouncing off walls? That is what we just did. This is an ache of accomplishment. There is joy in being challenged and meeting that challenge."

"I'm a challenge?" said Phex.

Missit gave him that signature crooked smile, the one he mostly seemed to reserve for Phex, as if they were in some conspiracy together.

"Is Fortew challenging to work with?" Phex asked, unguarded in his curiosity.

"Not at all. But he'll never be as vibrant as you, either.

Which is fine, I'm more than capable of taking all that on for both of us. Brightness and saturation are usually high cantor's responsibility, anyway. It's crazy how hard you can push the colors from low. I got to play with pattern a lot more than normal. Told you it would be fun. Someday, you and I should grace together."

"If you say so."

"God?" One of the acolytes approached the dais, recovered from its stunned amazement.

"Yes, acolyte?" Missit's godly mask was back in place in a heartbeat. He stood and turned, looking cold and regal.

Phex stood as well, a little behind him, protective, like a bodyguard. Was Missit in trouble?

He scanned the crowd. Kagee was still a smug speck of dull grey among collected iridescence. Untroubled by the shock his pantheon had wrought. Nearly two dozen or so Dyesi acolytes surrounded him. All sitting frighteningly still, wide-eyed and high-crested.

"Perhaps warn us next time," said the acolyte, showing submissive body language and using very formal speech.

"Too much?" said Missit, self-satisfied.

"Far too much."

"Did you record it?" Missit asked.

"Oh, yes."

"And you'll have to destroy it, won't you?"

"After analysis."

"Pity."

"It could damage domes less resilient than this one."

Phex suspected that the acolyte was more worried about what their performance had done to the other acolytes, but the dome made for a good excuse. Dome tech was extremely rare and expensive.

"Phex and I can always do it again," said Missit

cheerfully.

All the Dyesi present went opaque in shock, even Jinyesun and Fandina.

"You are a merciless god," said the acolyte reverently.

"I am only what you have made me. You knew Phex could push the dome that far, didn't you?"

"With someone like you, we suspected."

Missit looked out into the audience. "Which is why you matched him with Kagee. I understand entirely."

"Gods do not need to understand, just exist," said the acolyte, confused.

"Yes," agreed Phex, "but *Sapiens* like to understand." He jumped off the dais and went to get some flasks of water. Kagee joined him, and together they carried them back, handed them up to the sifters and graces.

Phex insisted Missit drink some, too. The god's fingers curled briefly over his, shockingly warm. Intentional, of course.

Flecked eyes examined him. "It was fun, right?"

Phex massaged the ache in his jaw, a memory not of singing but of smiling. Happiness. Had he ever felt a thing like that before?

"You like knowing you can still shock them, don't you?" Phex sipped his water.

"We must make sport of our keepers. Otherwise, how do we survive the cage?"

———

Perhaps to prove his point, that afternoon, Missit tried to sneak out of the building alone and was nearly kidnapped by a fixed.

His bodyguard got him safely back inside, but there had

been reporters present, so everyone now knew what had nearly happened.

Phex was seized with the irresistible, and highly disrespectful, desire to grab the golden god by his shoulders and shake him for no good reason, except that Phex was frustrated and Missit was an idiot. He also thought something was going break open inside Missit soon, and if Missit wasn't careful, he'd burn more than just himself with the molten metal that leaked out.

The pantheon was quiet that night, still carrying with them the aftereffects of that dome. The impact of Missit's recklessness. Like being hit by an asteroid. As if, even though they were performers, they had also, somehow, experienced godfix. The feeling was soporific. A stretched tiredness in the wake of success, edged by euphoria but also so entirely empty of energy that there was no way to be jubilant. Residual jubilance, perhaps. Or maybe just… satisfaction.

Only Berril looked out of sorts.

Phex had no idea why.

He waited with the rest of the pantheon for her to figure out what was troubling her. Berril sometimes took a while to understand her own feelings, especially when those feelings were complicated or unpleasant.

Eventually, she said, "Missit called this a cage. And the acolytes our keepers." She looked at Phex, because technically, that conversation had been between him and Missit. Berril had simply overheard it.

Phex said, "Missit is flippant like that. You know not to take him seriously, right? Even if he is a major god."

"Phex, you are the only person in the whole galaxy who doesn't take Missit seriously," said Kagee. He turned to Berril, encouraging. "Why is that messing with you, birdie?"

"It just made me realize that we really can't leave." Her

eyes were pained.

They were eating dinner together at the kitchen counter, which meant they were mostly looking out onto the nightscape of Divinity 36. The moon was in a rotation that also gave them a view of the planet beyond and the rings they orbited inside.

Berril pointed with her chin at the city they lived in, out there under the bubble on the satellite that was currently their home.

"We will never be able to go out there and explore," she said.

Kagee scrunched his turned-up nose. "Is that something we're likely to *want* to do?"

"Potentials can't leave this building," agreed Fandina.

"No, I mean afterward. Even if we attain godhood. Gods like Missit and Zil don't go strolling about the city, shopping or casually grabbing a bite to eat. Not here. Divinity 36 is all acolytes and worshipers. Gods would be recognized and swarmed or torn apart by fixed. They really are caged. So are we."

Fandina said, "Berril, sweetness, you realize that there is a good chance we would be spotted now, too? Even though we aren't real gods. No one who worships us is likely to be fixated yet, so it would be relatively safe, but it is impossible for any of us to go unnoticed anymore, either."

"Already?" Berril was awed. She looked at the two sifters. "I suppose you two might be able to go out. You're Dyesi. You'll fit right in."

The sifters hissed at the same time.

"We already look like gods," said Fandina, proudly.

Phex cocked his head and stared at them. They looked exactly the way they had when he first met them. Same general colors, teal and blue, same shape, perhaps a little physically fitter from their performance and exercise regimes. But not substantially different from any of the acolytes.

"You do?" Berril was startled.

"Can you not see it?" Fandina raise up one elegant blue arm, examined it with large eyes, was surprised.

Jinyesun said, "It is not visible to them, silly. It is like the dome."

Fandina clicked. "Of course. How stupid of me. I forgot."

Phex put down his chopsticks, crossed his arms, stared pointedly at Jin. "Explain."

"We have been sifting so much and so consistently for so many months, our skin is different now. Sort of like visually stretchy. Other Dyesi can see this. You see, sifter gods have beautiful flexible skin, more so than other Dyesi. It is blatantly obvious and considered very aesthetically pleasing by our species."

Kagee was amused. "Are you saying Phex and I have made you prettier with our voices?"

Fandina was clearly delighted by this assessment. "You could put it that way."

Tyve put down her spoon with a clatter. "Are you two considered *sexy* now?"

"No such thing as one of us being sexy. We are more like impressive art. The more we sift with you, the better we look just walking around. *And* the more obvious it is that we are divine."

"And that's in your skin, so even if you tried to hide it—" Phex was thinking about security.

"Can't be done. Unless we shrouded ourselves head to toe, and why would a Dyesi wear full-coverage clothing unless they wished to hide their skin?" Jin was not offended, just practical. "Down on Dyesid Prime, it wouldn't be a prob-lem, but up here…"

Phex was confused. "Why not a problem planetside?"

"There are very few acolytes and no worshipers or fixed on Dyesid Prime. Even for major gods, it would be different down there," said Fandina.

Jinyesun explained further. "Those of us who stay behind don't care or are too *different* to make it off-planet."

"The helpless, the hopeless, the lost, and the forgotten." Fandina sounded cool and uninterested.

Phex frowned, thinking that must be the Dyesi young, old, and infirm. "That's not kind." Was this the true secret to the Dyesi unwanted? Were they locked down below and denied the stars? Denied the divinity?

"You misunderstand. Dyesi of our life stage who choose to stay on Dyesid Prime? They lack ambition, not capacity," said Jinyesun. "It's not that the divinity doesn't want them, it's that they don't want the divinity."

Fandina added, "Frankly, it was a pleasure to come up to Divinity 36. The caves are boring."

Jinyesun clicked enthusiastic agreement. "Dyesid Prime is excessively dull. That is why we leave it."

"You're not mad about being trapped inside this one building?" Berril looked curiously about. "None of you?"

Tyve shrugged. "Not really. I spent my childhood on a spaceship. This building is much bigger than that."

Kagee said, "I hate other people. Why would I want to go out among them?" Typical Kagee.

Berril looked at Phex.

He thought about it seriously. "I'd like to see the city. Run some of the alleys and parks, explore the local food stalls, if there are any. But I'm not upset by the lack." He wondered why Berril was so focused on this. Were the Shawalee a highly transient species? Migratory, perhaps?

"Do you really desire that kind of freedom, Berril? I

thought you wanted to be a god." Kagee was apparently equally confused by her inability to accept the trade-off.

"I didn't realize gods lost so much."

"Gods don't walk among mortals. They're *gods*. They have acolytes for that," said Fandina, as if this were both obvious and desirable.

"You going to be all right about this, Berril?" asked Phex. Berril looked at him.

"Did you want to explore Divinity 36 that much?" It didn't seem like a particularly exciting city to him, but what did he know of cities? "We could maybe arrange for a tour. Borrow some bodyguards."

"No. I guess not. I suppose I could go home to my world and walk or fly about."

"Not if you're a god," said Jinyesun.

"Why? I'd fit right back in. No one would know. Among the Shawalee, I'm quite plain and ordinary. I assure you."

Jinyesun and Fandina exchanged looks.

It was Kagee who said, "Berril, you know they won't let you stay looking like that, right? They aren't going to leave any of us looking like we do now. Not even Phex. Not if we become demigods. Even Missit gets a full tinting every time he returns home."

Phex touched his ears, offensively shaped, apparently. Too round, too small, sticking out slightly. All of them would probably undergo aesthetic surgery of some kind.

Tyve added. "It's not just skin dye and metallic body pigment. Missit gets injections in his face to keep away the lines, plus hair extensions and body-hair removal. So does Fortew. Gods require regular maintenance. Image isn't every-thing, but it certainly counts for a lot."

Berril nodded. "I won't look like other Shawalee?"

"Probably never again."

"I actually like that idea. I always wanted to be unique. I just never considered the repercussions to my own liberty."

Tyve tilted her head. "If it's freedom you're after, we can earn a different kind. If we become gods, we get to travel, see the galaxy as a pantheon. We will eventually go on performance tours, just like Tillam. We're only trapped here until we become famous."

Berril perked up. "That's true."

Phex looked at Tyve. "Is that why you wanted to become a god?"

"In part. Also, if Zil can be a god, why can't I?"

Phex nodded and resumed eating. He was struck by a realization. Not that he was trapped, because he'd known all along and it didn't bother him. One way or another, his whole life, he'd been trapped. Tamed by systems that didn't want him. To be tamed by a system that did was a nice change. At least this cage of Missit's was a comfortable, golden one. No, Phex was realizing for the first time that the rest of his pantheon were there for different reasons. He'd always known that they desired to be gods, were driven to perform, but now he thought there must be more behind that desire.

"Why do you do it, Jin?" Phex asked. Jinyesun's personality, in a way, was most similar to Phex's. Both strove to understand other people, other cultures. Both sought explanations for actions, for languages, for behaviors. But in this, they would be different. Jin wanted fame, Phex did not. Why?

Jinyesun crested at him. "I want to be the best."

"Or if not the best, better than everyone else," added Fandina, as if this were highly amusing.

"You're after perfection? This is not the right pantheon." Tyve was amused by their logical Dyesi's impractical dream.

Jinyesun looked thoughtful, crests shivering a little. "Maybe it is enough to imagine I might be remembered as special if I cannot be the best. I think our pantheon will be unique."

"So long as we're not remembered for making unique mistakes," said Kagee.

Silence descended for a moment while they all focused on eating.

"Why don't you ask about the rest of us, Phex?" wondered Berril.

"I think I know what motivates most of you."

"Do you really?" Tyve looked predatory. "Explain."

"You want to beat your brother and the other Jakaa Nova without actually having to fight them. Berril wants to be original and represent hope for her species. Fandina wants to be popular and admired, and maybe shake up the divine system a little bit. Kagee needs to prove something to himself. Possibly also to his home planet. Worthiness, perhaps? Value, maybe?"

Kagee gave him a twisted little smile. "How ever did you guess?"

It wasn't really a question, but Phex answered him anyway. "They trained you to do something no one else would because you weren't allowed to do anything else. I've been there. I know that means social rejection."

"Plus, you never talk with fondness of your planet or your past," said Berril, patting Kagee's arm as if that was the worst thing.

"I'm not a refugee or in exile." Kagee was looking at Phex with a pained expression, as if he hadn't expected Phex to understand him at all. Let alone sympathize. Didn't realize that Phex had started to like him. Like him partly *for* his prickly ways. Like him *because* they shared a similar feeling about their past – shame. Either for what they'd once been or once done. Phex was ashamed of the Wheel. He thought

Kagee pretended to be proud of being ex-core, but he was actually ashamed of Agatay, too.

"But you don't want to go back," Phex said, because he recognized that in others.

"Let's just say I've lost too many people to that hellhole. It is a cruel, unfriendly place, my home planet. Plus, there's no Berril to hug me, no Phex to cook, no Fandina to fuss, no Jinyesun to explain, and no Tyve to tease. And no... well, not anymore." Kagee's mouth twisted.

"Kagee, never say that you actually *like* us?" gasped Tyve, in mock shock.

"Don't tell," replied Kagee, stuffing his face so as not to have to talk anymore.

"And you, Phex. Why do you do it?" asked Berril, bright and curious.

"Well, at first because I had nowhere else to go."

"And now?"

"I want to belong."

"You like performing, too. Admit it." Tyve grinned, sharp-toothed and pleased with herself.

"Yes," said Phex, surprised by this truth. "It's nice to be good at something."

"And to touch others with that skill," added Jinyesun.

Phex supposed that they all, both together and apart, had something to prove. To create art. To be heard. To be seen. To be recognized. To influence others. Even he, who had ended up there by accident – who had to defend his right to exist at all. The others maybe felt that a little too, at their core.

How odd, that to justify being alive, they were becoming gods.

15

GODLY SUPPLICATION

Things changed for Phex and his pantheon after Missit sang with them. The acolytes started treating them like gods. There was really no other way of perceiving it. Of course, it wasn't quite the reverence accorded Tillam, but they were certainly being treated differently from other potentials. It was as if they had moved into demigod status already, without exams or performance reviews.

Also, things started going a lot smoother with Kagee. Not because Kagee had changed but because Phex had. Having gotten the extreme of cantor out of his system with Missit, Phex understood his own limits now and was no longer as afraid of his own voice. He had listened to what Missit's voice did to keep him bound, to stop him from damaging the sifters, and he understood it at last. It was something he'd needed to experience to comprehend, and now he could compensate for his own shortcomings. Or he thought he could. It made it easier to trust Kagee. And Kagee, in return, relaxed into the framework of Phex's low cantor and relied on him to act as a color guide.

It helped that they found a way to talk about it. Phex

had learned how to talk about cantor from the Dyesi, so he used Dyesi words in terms of the colors that sound produced. But Kagee understood cantor only in terms of music.

"Were you *taught* to sing?" Phex asked when they were stuck on a cantor moment Kagee couldn't grasp and Phex couldn't articulate.

"Of course." Kagee was confused.

"Not by the divinity. I mean on Agatay. Actual *singing,* not cantor."

"Yes."

"Like music?"

"It *is* music, Phex. I can also play several instruments. High-hold elites are encouraged to be musical at an early age. I kept it up even after delineation."

"Delineation?" muttered Phex, Kagee had used that alien word before.

"Removal from political and inheritance obligations." Kagee waved a ring covered hand dismissively. "My point is, I never stopped voice lessons."

"But what we do here is not really music. It's the dome." Phex sat back on his heels, amazed at the simplicity of their conundrum.

"You make no sense."

"If I talked to you more about the sound you make than the colors and patterns you produce, would that make more sense to you?"

"So much," said Kagee, seeming both surprised and relieved that Phex was identifying the issue so succinctly.

"Communication is such a bother," said Phex, meaning it. He switched to Galactic Common. "So, that note? You're slightly flat and the tone is too lean. Can you put in more resonance? Is that easier to understand?"

Kagee actually grinned. His normally sullen face split wide with joyful comprehension. "So much easier!"

Phex nodded. He would have to adjust the way he talked about sound with Kagee going forward, but that was easy enough. Just another language to learn.

After that, it was as if some new pattern had been turned on for all of them. The cantors were no longer just matched – they slowly became balanced, and everyone in the pantheon could relax because of it.

Despite his strong desire to shake Missit over his disregard for his own safety, Phex would be forever grateful to the god for handing him a gift disguised as a challenge. Missit had given Phex an education on that dais. At the time, Phex had no idea that was happening. He thought Missit was doling out a lesson to the acolytes, reminding them not to take advantage of gods. He didn't realize he was part of it. Missit taught him balance in the course of one godsong. Phex resolved to be more respectful of the golden god as a result. No matter how frustrating he found his behavior outside of the dome.

He'd been letting them, him and Missit, get too casual. Phex needed to be careful. His desire to shake a god for carelessness when it was a god's nature to be capricious did no one any good. The feel of Missit's slight form in his arms when he held him late at night, *even* for only a moment, *even* if it was simply for the comfort of a temporary sun, was too easy and too good. Because it wasn't *even* anything. It wasn't a small, insignificant thing, private to them. It had a reverberating effect. Because Missit was a *god*.

Phex had started to think of Missit as something lesser. A scared little boy, no god at all. But he should never forget the awe Missit was owed for his ability, his experience, and his innate talent. Because Missit was everything and more. Missit didn't belong to him – he belonged to the divinity. That, too, had been part of the lesson Phex learned under that dome. Reverence and safety dictated that one did not go around, hugging gods late at night in practice rooms. It belittled them and disrespected the divine.

So, Phex didn't shake sense into Missit after learning of his near-kidnapping. Instead, Phex ignored him when he visited, and ended each bodyguard practice before Missit could approach him, and tried not to see the hurt on the god's face.

He should have known how futile that would be.

Because Missit was a god, and because gods were not easily thwarted, Missit just targeted Phex's bed late at night instead.

But before that came Phex's first supplication messages.

Which is not to say he hadn't gotten them before, but the acolytes didn't show potentials such missives early on. For some reason, the Dyesi had calculated now was the time for potentials to know something about their worshipers. Supplication messages, like votive offerings, came in many forms – written creeds, video recordings, audio hymns, sacred drawings.

Phex got a lot of recipes.

His pantheon was sprawled about their living area, scrolling through supplications. Berril was perched on the puffy couch, Tyve flopped down by her legs. Phex sat next to Tyve, Jinyesun leaning cautiously against him. Fandina lay on the floor, occasionally batting at Jin's foot. Kagee sat close but did not touch anyone, idly humming something old-fashioned and heretical and tapping the rings of one hand against the other in graces' time.

Berril wiggled her screen at them. "This one wants to form a domestic partnership with me. Says she thinks I'll make a good wife, and someone needs to look after me since it's obvious Phex doesn't want permanence." She stared at them, mouth in a little O of confusion.

Phex frowned. "Obvious?"

Kagee stopped humming and tilted his head. "I'll marry you, if you like."

"I'm only seventeen years old!" protested Berril.

"So? I'm only eighteen," replied Kagee.

"I should get first dibs," objected Tyve.

"*Obvious*?" asked Phex again.

"Don't worry your pretty head about it." Tyve patted Phex's knee.

Phex snorted at her and returned to his own messages. Many of them were in languages he didn't understand, but it became clear after flipping through the ones he *could* read that his supplications *also* included marriage proposals. There was a great deal of expressed admiration for his appearance as well. Weird.

It was his turn to express confusion. "Why not just like my voice? This one seems obsessed with my shoulder blades. Really? Shoulder blades?"

"You do have very nice shoulder blades," said Tyve cheerfully.

"Belief is sacred and specific to the individual's relationship with their chosen god." Jinyesun parroted part of the acolyte code.

Fandina clicked in agreement. "The personality of each member of a pantheon is part of the charm of the whole."

"Are you implying that my personality is in my *shoulder blades*?" Phex accused.

Fandina clicked at him in amused agreement.

Kagee snorted.

"I may never understand the divinity." Phex shook his head and put down his screen.

Reading supplications seemed to be helping his friends – if the relaxed, pleased atmosphere was any indication, but Phex wasn't getting much beyond confused. The adoration permeating the missives made him uneasy. He didn't feel like he'd earned such worship yet.

But Berril was practically glowing. "They really like me. A lot of mine are expressions of support. Quite a few are chiropterans, but there are plenty from wingless folk, too. Several think I'm pretty. Me!"

Kagee, of all people, also seemed touched. Ordinarily, he was so sarcastic and cold. "Me, too."

"You're both very pretty," said Phex.

Kagee threw a pillow puff at him.

Tyve seemed the least affected by their first direct experience of belief. Phex supposed she'd been through this somewhat with Zil. She was probably the best prepared of all of them to handle the religious repercussions of their performances.

"What are yours like, Tyve?" Phex asked, more interested in her reaction than the content of her supplications.

"Mostly sweet. Jakaa Nova have a reputation for fierceness. Zil's believers are rather gentle as a result. Looks like mine will be the same. The type of person who wants to pray at the altar of a god with blades for hands enjoys risk mixed with desire. They covet a fierce god. There will always be a few who are in it for the challenge and the danger, but they are far outweighed by the ones who want the warrior to protect them. We appeal to a very specific taste."

"You're lucky to have Zil to lead the way," said Berril.

"And to come from a species with a fierce reputation,"

added Kagee, probably still smarting over Phex's *pretty* comment.

"Maybe," said Tyve, sounding thoughtful.

"What about you two?" Phex asked Fandina and Jinyesun.

The Dyesi exchanged looks.

"Mostly Sapien. As expected," said Jin.

"A lot of it is sexual," added Fandina, not so much disgusted as mystified.

Phex sneered at his species and their general randiness.

"That's normal," said Tyve. "Sapiens find Dyesi hot. Always have. I think it's considered one of the great tragedies of the universe that your lot don't want to bump around on the regular."

That did make the two Dyesi flatten their crests in disgust.

"Don't be crass, Tyve," chided Phex.

"Well, it's true." Tyve was truculent.

"Probably," agreed Phex, remembering the effect that the Dyesi had on his cafe full of hormonal teenagers. "But truth doesn't have to be voiced." The two sifters shouldn't have to put up with Tyve teasing them, especially as they were already coping with believers dripping with want. Phex himself found that aspect of supplication creepy, even when he wasn't averse to sex like the Dyesi.

Berril jumped in to keep the peace. "I like it when they think I'm sexy. No one has ever found me sexy before."

"Me, too," said Tyve.

Berril nodded. "What about you, Phex?"

Phex stood. "I need to clean the kitchen."

"And that's the end of *that* conversation," said Kagee, annoyed as always.

Phex was still the last one to bed each night. Not because he needed the hygiene chamber alone or for other purposes, not anymore. But because he took comfort in the soft rustles of his pantheon settling around him. He made a point of doing one last sweep about the room, turning down the lights, putting away the throws. Sometimes, he would just sit in a couch puff in the semidarkness, absorbing the silence and the knowledge that the others were all there, each one in their niche, safe and ready to start again tomorrow. The six of them, together in stillness and quiet.

This particular night, he was already in bed, in that in-between state, half-asleep but still somewhat alert. He came awake fast because there were no longer six in the room – there were seven.

Someone had come in through the entrance curtain, making just enough sound and letting through just enough light to drive him upright, adrenaline thumping. Before he had time to jump from his niche, his curtain was pushed aside, and a slight figure climbed into the bed with him.

He was so surprised, he forgot his newly trained body-guard instincts. Plus, the familiar smell and rose-gold glint told him this was no threat but some new need for him to collect.

Missit's need.

"Go away," whispered Phex.

Missit's voice was soft and coaxing and very close to his ear, making him shiver but not with cold. "If you make a fuss, we'll be caught."

"What *we*?"

"Fine. *I'll* be caught."

"Missit!" Phex knew he was growling. But he kept his voice as soft as he could. Some of his pantheon would still be awake. No doubt they could overhear. Was Missit's body-guard out there in the hallway, advertising his presence? Or had he given the cyborg the slip again?

The acolytes were hard to predict, but fraternization was verboten. Phex was pretty darn certain that having a god in his bed was grounds for expulsion.

"Are trying to get me booted?" he asked.

"No one knows I'm here."

"You think?"

"I promise. You know I escape bodyguards easily."

"Missit."

"I won't stay long. I'll leave before anyone wakes."

"In the whole building?"

"Acolytes keep strict schedules."

"How can you promise to wake up before they do?"

"I don't sleep much these days."

Phex hated the implication of that. He didn't ask why Missit was there. He could guess well enough. Missit was cut off from his sun – he would take any warmth he could get, even if he had to climb into some potential's niche to get it.

Phex sighed and scooted back.

Missit immediately crawled under the covers. Burrowed against him. The god made a tiny, discontented grumble and shifted about, pulling and pushing at Phex until he'd arranged Phex's bigger body into exactly the shape he wanted. Phex swatted at him in a token way but acquiesced – this was Missit, after all.

Eventually, the god quieted, curled with his back against Phex's chest. With a final murmur, he reached back and grabbed Phex's arm to drape it over his waist.

Phex gave an annoyed huff to let Missit know that this was against his will, but he didn't deny his own instinct to curve around him. For this weakness he got a mouthful of hair, like silken threads, which he tried to spit out but which were remarkably tenacious. He reached up, gathered and smoothed it away from his lips as best he could, but it was very clingy, rather like Missit himself.

"You should wear it up to sleep," he admonished.

"I will, starting tomorrow night," Missit replied as if this were to become their regular routine.

"Stop squirming," Phex ordered.

"My feet are cold."

Phex lifted his top leg slightly.

Callused, icy toes wormed their way between his calves. Missit sighed happily and relaxed into stillness.

Phex fished more hair out of his mouth but was careful not to move too much so as not to disturb the god in his arms.

When Phex woke up the next morning, he was alone in his niche, and he wondered if he'd dreamed the whole thing. Except he was pushed back against the wall, and normally he slept sprawled in the center of the bed. There were strands of rose gold on his pillow, like fine cracks across a ceramic bowl. The scent of Missit was left behind too, like the scent of coffee beans once lingered on his fingertips. Phex wondered if this meant he was supposed to serve Missit, like he once served at the cafe, or if this desire was simply the residual effect of long-term exposure to a major god.

Phex was relieved to find him gone. Missit had left – unnoticed, he hoped – but Phex's bed was bigger and colder than it had been the night before.

Everyone looked at him funny over breakfast.

"Midnight visitation?" said Tyve, pointedly.

Phex gave her a mournful look. "I'll talk to his bodyguard. It's not like I can stop him."

"Phex," said Kagee, firm and annoyed.

"Have *you* ever tried to stop Missit from doing anything?" Phex defended himself. "It's like convincing Berril not to hug."

"Don't bring me into this," said Berril.

"Like Berril's hugs, you secretly love being the object of Missit's attention," accused Kagee.

"Not so secretly," added Tyve.

Phex thought that his feelings weren't important. He looked at Jinyesun. "Am I going to be in trouble with the acolytes if he's found sleeping in my bed?" *That* was important because it effected the pantheon.

"Just sleeping?" asked Kagee.

Phex thought about Missit's squirming against him, swallowed, and choked out, "Just sleeping."

"He misses his sun," said Fandina, using the informal honorifics for parents with infants, as if Missit were a lost child.

Jin crested in thought, then answered Phex's question. "Not sure. These are extraordinary circumstances. The acolytes currently desire anything that keeps Tillam sane. All of Tillam, of course, but especially Missit. He has the most worshipers. If his comfort leads him into your bed, Phex, the acolytes might even encourage it."

"I don't like it," said Kagee. "I don't think it's fair."

"To whom?" Berril asked. "Phex or us?"

Kagee shrugged.

Fandina's crests fluttered. "There are species that co-sleep. Even a few pantheons that mostly sleep together."

"Which ones?" asked Berril, curious.

"Is that a good excuse?" Kagee was sublimely unconvinced.

"Why is it always about sex with Sapiens?" Fandina wondered.

"If it is not about sex, it is about influence," said Jinyesun.

"Same difference," shot back Kagee.

"Phex?" Berril looked at him.

Phex thought about Missit. Missit huddled in a corner of the practice room. Missit coiled into his hug. Missit curled against him last night. Missit whose breath was hot but only when he whispered. Missit who was an instrument of sunlight but had none of his own. Missit who needed someone else's warmth to stay liquid gold – a molten star. Missit who was scared that being alone might cool him down and snuff him out of existence altogether. Missit who nested against him as if Phex could melt a god enough to fill every part of Phex's own cold, barren existence. As if Phex were some special container made to safely hold the remnants of a star.

Was that sex or influence? And how could Phex explain this to his pantheon? To his friends? Phex who had no words.

Phex puffed out his cheeks, lost. Brought it down to the simplest thing he knew for certain. "He needs me."

What exact form that need would take, Phex might never understand. But Missit seemed to. And Phex could be no more or less than himself in response. So, that's what he gave back, himself.

So, Missit ended up in Phex's bed, and what could Phex do about that but try to hold him without restriction? And, hopefully, without getting caught.

He looked at his pantheon. They had a decision to make about this together. Because if he risked himself, he was risking them. "Do we tell the acolytes?"

Everyone looked at Jinyesun.

"Will it happen again?" asked the Dyesi.

Phex considered. "Most likely."

"Unless Fortew goes into remission." Tyve had clearly

learned more from her brother.

They all looked at her.

"I thought it was Neuro Blue," said Berril.

Phex had thought so too, but they hadn't discussed Fortew as a group, as if a conversation about why a god was dying would somehow endanger their own divine future. But Neuro Blue was a neurodegenerative disorder – there was no such thing as remission. If it wasn't that, there were only a few other possibilities. There were not many diseases that the money and power of the divinity couldn't cure.

"Non-baryonic bronchopulmonary attrition," said Tyve flatly.

"Which is *what* in common parlance?" asked Berril.

"Crud lung," Kagee explained, his tone flat.

Phex found himself inhaling deeply as if to remind his body that it could breathe properly. That despite being born in space and running the blades, his lungs were clean of crud and its endless repercussions. He'd dodged that better than he had the blades.

"But that's so rare these days," said Berril in a tight voice.

"Is it really?" wondered Kagee, small, pointed face pinched.

"Still happens. Mostly in the more violent sectors with older, messier bomb tech. Fortew must have experienced exposure in childhood." Tyve tapped her fat-tipped fingers on the counter and then, as if that were not satisfying enough, extended her claws and clicked them in a cascade of nerves.

"You'll scratch it," admonished Phex.

"Will he get a transplant?" Fandina asked Tyve.

"Zil doesn't know. But I also don't know if he has even asked Fortew. Or if it's possible in Fortew's case." Tyve spoke as if her brother's pain was something that hurt her and embarrassed him.

"Chances of survival aren't great. Lungs are some of the hardest to graft in." Jinyesun was practical to the last.

"And even if he survives, he'll never sing again." Kagee sounded cold and scared and lost. For a cantor who sang for his survival, such a thing was unimaginable.

Jinyesun and Fandina exchanged crest-flutters.

"For now, we wait," said Fandina.

Jinyesun clicked in agreement. "And we hope that Missit is good at avoiding the acolytes before he sneaks into your niche."

"Why aren't any of you asking if Phex is okay with it?" Kagee wondered, tone pinched and sharp.

"With Fortew being sick?" Berril was confused.

Kagee shook his head. "With Missit in his bed. With being the crutch of a god. With being *used*."

Phex thought that question had more to do with Kagee's pain than his own, but he appreciated the concern.

"I mean, Phex is risking his own godhood, helping Missit. And for what? Because Tillam is shaky? Who is he to Tillam? Who are we? No offense Tyve, but they aren't *our* pantheon. We could just bar the door against him." Kagee looked over at the flap. "We'd have to install an actual door, of course."

"No doors!" said Fandina and Jinyesun at the same time.

"Okay. Weird," said Berril, looking at their flattened crests and skin gone opaque. "Do Dyesi suffer from claustrophobia?"

"Dyesi are fine traveling in space, and spaceships have doors," pointed out Tyve.

"Situational-specific door-o-phobia?" suggested Berril, amused with herself.

Kagee slammed his hand to the counter. "Focus! My point is: has anyone bothered to ask Phex if he's okay being used by Missit for whatever dumb reason?"

Phex found himself under the scrutiny of five pairs of eyes and two interested crests. He thought about callused toes worming between his calves and mouthfuls of silken hair. He thought it wasn't really his decision. He'd been chosen by a god. The whims of the gods were paramount. Missit was having trouble sleeping. There had been that little catch in his voice. And his feet had been very cold.

"I'm fine with it," said Phex.

"Eloquent as always," teased Berril.

"Right now, he's mine to care for," Phex explained.

"And that's good enough for you to take a risk this big?" Kagee put down his spoon with a clatter and glared at him.

"I can't think of a better reason," Phex replied, honestly, because he couldn't.

"Of course you can't, sweetie," Berril sounded somehow sad. Why was Berril sad? Who was making Berril sad?

His pantheon exchanged glances. Over his head. About him.

"Okay," said Fandina. "If Missit comes back again, we talk to the acolytes."

"Make sure they know," agreed Jinyesun.

"And that they're okay with it," said Tyve.

"And that it isn't about sex or love," added Berril.

"Or influence," said Kagee, although he didn't seem to believe that.

Phex looked at them, wide-eyed with horror. "Me?" he squeaked. Talk to the acolytes about something like this? How humiliating.

"No," said Fandina firmly. "Jinyesun will do the talking."

Jin looked like it had expected that decision all along and clicked an affirmation.

Phex shouldn't have been surprised when Missit climbed

into his bed the next night at right around the same time and in the same manner. He was, but he didn't show it.

Phex didn't bother to protest or whisper to the god at all this time. Missit's hair was coiled up and he squirmed less. Phex simply arranged himself in the correct position so Missit could curl against his body and warm his feet. It was effortless, and if it pacified a god? Such a simple thing, to hold someone close as if they mattered. Weird how necessary they both seemed to find it.

Phex tried not to think about how easy it was for him to fall asleep that way, and how the act of offering comfort was comforting in turn. What did it mean to want another person like that? To be the cavity into which molten stars were poured? To *want* to be that and not get burned by the desire for it?

This time, he woke up first and early.

Too early.

Phex knew it in that way that the daily pattern of so many months had synced his body up to the artificial rhythm of Divinity 36. The lights in the room and the niches hadn't even started their slow easing into the rosy spectrum of false dawn, designed specifically to awaken sentients in as healthy a manner as possible.

Missit was sleeping against him.

Phex examined the sensation. It wasn't at all like when Berril hugged him. Heavier, for one thing. The god's head had lolled back so Phex could look down into that lovely face. The most famous in the galaxy – achingly gorgeous even when slack and still. Phex had been engineered for beauty, but there was something about the symmetry of his own appearance that was so perfect, it became uncanny. Missit didn't have that. His mouth was a little too wide. The rose gold tinting more rose and less gold over his full lips.

His eyes were bruised by exhaustion. His nose had a tiny bump to it. His eyebrow hairs grew in swirls.

The face Phex saw in the mirror had no character to it – it was sullen and aloof. Yes, the bones were beautiful, but it was like a house that had never really become anyone's home. Missit's face looked *lived* in.

Phex shifted so he could cradle Missit in the crook of his elbow, examine him without getting a crick in his neck. Unconsciously, he raised a finger to trace the lines of eyebrows, nose, cheekbones, and mouth, but he was too scared to make actual contact. He kept his fingertip hovering and moved it slowly, afraid to even disturb the air around Missit's skin. Phex was not surprised that his first desire to touch could be so easily suppressed into the disregard of air over skin.

He wondered if he sang, the sound might have the courage to caress where he did not – something like skinsift between humans. Was the distance between his finger and Missit's face as vast as the space between stars or as short as a breath between notes?

He found the yearning itself a novel experience to be treasured and feared. He'd never thought to ache for another person, want a person like food, like the need to master godsong. Wanting to sink into the liquid gold of Missit was the kind of ache that burned – thirst mixed with fixation.

And *that* frightened him. What kind of monster would he become, fixed on a god? *That* made him scared of Missit as well as scared of the need for him.

The lights started to dial up for morning. The acolytes would be stirring soon. Missit would get caught.

Phex tapped the god's forehead gently with one finger but firm enough to make a noise.

Missit came awake with a start.

He looked up at Phex with shocked, gold-flecked eyes. "I slept?" His tone was amazed but at least he remembered to whisper.

"Too long." Phex gestured with his chin at the brightening world around them.

Missit noted the dawn light. He said a very foul word, tumbled out of Phex's niche like he was rolling off the edge of the dais, and disappeared out the entrance.

Phex blinked, not sure what he'd expected, but it hadn't been that. He let out a slow breath, tried not to smell warm metal and spices. Thought about taking advantage of the hygiene chamber first and alone. Thought he probably wasn't supposed to use it for that purpose. Rolled over and screamed silently into his pillow. Wondered if he should hate himself for conflating lust and comfort and worship, or if that was just where Missit met fate.

Surprisingly, he then fell back asleep.

———

"You wake him."

"No, you do it."

"Why are we all scared of him?"

"Phex is scary."

Silence while, apparently, his pantheon contemplated this truth.

"But it's breakfast time."

"He never sleeps in."

"Is he sick?"

Phex didn't open his eyes, but he said, "Jinyesun is going to need to talk to the acolytes."

"We figured," said Berril cheerfully.

"Can you get up and make us breakfast now?" Kagee

managed to sound plaintive and demanding at the same time. They still ate the standard Dyesi rations for breakfast, but Phex had taken to augmenting them these days.

Phex grunted an affirmation. Cracked one eye. Four faces were staring at him.

"Where's Tyve?"

"Said she was starving and is fixing herself something."

"Tyve is in *my* kitchen?" Phex sat up and scooted to the edge of the niche. "Move," he barked at the rest of the pantheon.

"We should have started with that," said Jinyesun wisely.

"Tyve, get out of my kitchen!" yelled Phex, panicked.

Jin said, "I shall go find an acolyte. This must be dealt with. Phex actually raised his voice."

"Should I come?" asked Fandina.

"No, Berril should."

"Me?" squeaked Berril.

"She is fragile and difficult to conceptualize. She will remind them we are different as a pantheon. Exceptions must be made and all that."

"You are so manipulative." Fandina clearly approved of this tactic.

Phex listened even as he shooed Tyve out of his kitchen. There was something reassuring about the way Jinyesun and Fandina understood divinity from within, because their people had created it. Because it felt like these two Dyesi, alone among their species, were on his side. Phex accepted that and hoped beyond everything else that it was actually true. That if a time came when it was the six of them against the divinity for any reason, that it would still be *all six* of them. He wasn't yet sure of that. But it was nice to know Jinyesun would use its big crafty brain on Phex's behalf, even if Missit was the ultimate reason. The two Dyesi needed their pantheon too. Everyone knew that. But there was a part of Phex that worried about where the divinity ended and the rest of Dyesi existence began. After all, the Dyesi had created the divinity, but it didn't define them. It only defined how the rest of the galaxy saw them. There was danger in that dichotomy because loyalty and trust were not the same thing.

Phex watched Jin lead Berril out to advocate on his behalf and tried not to be terrified that this was only the beginning of how many times their pantheon would be tested by the divine conflict between what was expected and what was right.

He suspected his pantheon would eventually say something to him directly about how it went. He thought they'd send Berril to explain it to him.

They didn't.

Instead, Kagee cornered him in the kitchen one evening about a week later while Phex was preparing dinner.

"Are you and Missit having sex?"

"No."

"But you're close to him. More than friends."

Phex frowned. Was that how he would put it? He wasn't sure. Did one become close to a god? Could gods be befriended? How was that possible if they weren't on equal footing to start with? However, in a strange way, there had also never been a time when he and Missit hadn't been close, from the first moment they met. It was odd because prior to Missit, Phex had never been close to anyone. So, he hadn't realized how truly abnormal it was to have been adopted by a god. Or maybe it was more that Missit wanted to be adopted by him. Phex hesitated to label it. So, he said nothing.

Kagee glared at him, frustrated. "He keeps sleeping here. In your bed. That's intimacy."

Phex nodded. He supposed it must be.

"Are you dating?"

"No?" said Phex, but it was a question.

"What is he to you, then? How do you think of him?"

Phex had never actually asked himself that. He was scared to do so. Because Missit was wicked hope and bundled, vibrating starsong. He was luxury and chance given Sapien shape but not real. Like an old mythological god in truth, he was a concept, not a reality – a being that ran down rainbows to bring messages to mortals conferring serendipity and smiles but never to be trusted. But whether Phex trusted him or not didn't matter to Missit's existence, or to Phex's feelings about him. So, how *did* Phex think of Missit?

"I try not to think of him at all," Phex replied, honestly.

Kagee scrubbed at his face with one fine-boned, grey hand, heavy with deadly rings and disappointment. "Jin and Berril got special dispensation for him to be in your bed. But only because the Dyesi have Missit down as *clingy*. Apparently, that's how he is with Fortew."

"Is it?"

Kagee glared and continued. "So, they think that's all it is with you. Friendship. Some kind of skin dependency or touch starvation. You're just a substitute sun."

Phex wondered if that were true. Skin dependency made more sense than Missit actually liking him and wanting him to be something significant in his life.

Kagee pushed on. "Don't let the acolytes realize it's more than that. More than what they permit. Okay?"

"I'm not sure it is more."

"Are you being willfully obtuse or just stupid?" Only Kagee would be so blunt as to insult. But his bluntness was coming from fear, so Phex forgave him.

Kagee leaned those delicate hands on the counter, a faint clatter of metal on the lacquered surface. He pressed himself forward into Phex's sacred space. "This is *it,* Phex. This is our *one* chance. You get kicked out again, and it's not only you – it's all six of us. We can't go on without you. That's the way pantheons work. Don't risk everything for some god from another pantheon, even a great one."

"He's hurting."

"Yeah, I think we've all figured that out. It doesn't mean you need to risk six chances of survival on one man's discomfort."

Phex stopped his fussing in the kitchen. Turned away from Kagee and the living area and looked out their one big window at the cityscape of the moon. At Divinity 36, the crude grey lumps and bumps that were his home, even though he could not go out into it. "*Survival*, Kagee?"

Kagee took the major step of joining Phex in his sacred space. He tucked in close, slid an arm about Phex's waist and leaned his head on Phex's bicep, as if he were Berril – just more tentative. Less assured of welcome.

Phex sighed, reached across his own body with his free hand to ruffle the long, waving fall of beautiful silver hair.

"I can't go back, Phex. To Agatay. I can't go back after all this – the first of my kind to leave, only to return shamed by failure. I'm not a refugee like you, but I also can't go home. I don't want to go where I'm unwanted. Please don't risk us for him. Not us, when we're so good together. All six of us. Please don't risk our family on his instability."

Kagee, who was so proud, had humbled himself to beg.

Phex felt the weight of it, cool and heavy silver against him. The opposite of Missit's melted gold. More solid, easier to hold on to. But no less desperate in its need.

Phex had neglected to take into account that this private time he and Missit had stolen involved the actions of a god, and the actions of gods always came with consequences for those around them.

16

ALL LOVES FIXATING

Before any of them really had a chance to notice, a year had passed. Somewhere in there, Phex had turned eighteen, maybe. More importantly, the Dyesi issued some kind of paperwork that declared him, by their standards and in accordance with galactic law, an adult. He was no longer a child refugee, the ward of some reluctant government. He was still a refugee, but he was now considered entirely autonomous. The acolytes explained that his status as a citizen of Dyesid Prime was conditional on approval for godhood.

Which was coming up after their final performance review.

Jinyesun never explained exactly how it had happened, but the acolytes tacitly permitted Missit's midnight visitations. Or perhaps it was more that they intentionally overlooked them. Whatever Jin and Berril had done wrought indifference if not support. It was allowed only if Missit's bodyguard accompanied him, which Phex approved. So, they had someone sleeping on their couch puff each night, too. This wasn't the dome – Missit's bodyguard didn't have to stay in the hallway, although Phex had thought this one would. He still hadn't seen the bodyguard's face or talked with the cyborg openly. Of course, it was possible that coming inside to the puff was intentional. To listen. To spy for the acolytes. To make certain Missit and Phex didn't test the no-fraternization regulation.

Not that Phex didn't want to. But it felt wrong, and not because the divinity was opposed to romantic physical contact but because Missit was fragile and hurting. Anything sexual, even a good and ultimately wanted thing, was more pressure on both of them right now. Plus, it was far too much of a risk for Phex. His pantheon was already more than understanding about the weirdness of a god cuddling in their midst. He didn't want to push it.

And then even the possibility of anything had passed.

Between one night and then next, Missit disappeared.

No Missit in Phex's bed. No Missit at Phex's bodyguard practice. No bodyguard came to that practice, either. Itrio had to return to her duties.

Phex could have guessed, but Tyve told them all over dinner. "Tillam is heading back out on tour."

"Fortew is in remission?" Phex asked politely.

"Missit didn't say anything?" Tyve was surprised. As if none of them had noticed that Missit had stopped sneaking into Phex's bed. Which, Phex paused to think about, could be the case.

"I haven't seen him in days." Phex admitted. He wasn't mad about it. Missit's orbit had shifted to include him for a short while. Phex had known from the start that he was an interim epicenter until something better came along or the original could be restored.

"That's cold." Kagee sounded unreasonably angry.

Phex hoped it wasn't with him.

"Zil says Fortew wants to go back out while he still can." Tyve shook her head, sad but pretending confused toughness.

"So, they go on tour, unhappy and stressed, with a dying sun. Why? Why would they do that to themselves? Why not go somewhere beautiful and peaceful, appreciate what little time he has left?"

"Because it's what he wants." Jinyesun stepped in, understanding and compelled to explain.

Tyve nodded. "Fortew is one of those who loves it. Being a god was all he ever wanted, and he became one of the best and most well-known because of his joy in performing. He lives for it."

"Dies for it, too, apparently." Kagee had no tact.

"Phex, are you angry about being abandoned?" Berril asked, because Berril *also* had no tact – she was just a lot nicer about it.

Tyve shushed her, but the question was out there, hovering.

"It's not about me." Because it wasn't, so his feelings on the matter didn't rank, so far as Phex was concerned. They never had.

"And yet you got dragged into it." That was Kagee, still grumpy.

Phex sighed. "It's not about Missit and his coping mechanisms, either." He considered his words carefully and finally added, "Missit will stand with Fortew on that dais until they both fall off of it, if that's what Fortew wants."

Tyve nodded. "All of them will."

"And we can't blame or judge them for it when we are only at the beginning of this thing," said Fandina.

"While they are at the end," added Jinyesun, sounding more thoughtful than sad.

It was assumed by the three remaining potential pantheons that they would all be making it through to demigod status at this point. They had put in the time, perfected the technique, and formed functional pantheons capable of coloring the domes. Unless they spectacularly failed their final performances, demigod was guaranteed. Right?

However, it became clear pretty quickly that Phex's pantheon was being treated differently. The other two pantheons had been told to prepare to move, which they thought meant collecting their stuff to relocate to demigod quarters within the building.

But Phex's pantheon was given no such instruction. In fact, at one point, an acolyte pointedly and somewhat plaintively asked Phex if he really needed so many ladles. Phex wouldn't have thought much of it, except the differential treatment was impacting Fandina's peace of mind and, worse, Jinyesun's.

"Why haven't they told us to pack up our space yet?" worried Jin over dinner the evening before their final exam.

"Do they think we won't pass?" asked Berril, now also worried.

"Are they going to deny us demigod and keep us as potentials for another year? Kick us out? It doesn't make sense." Fandina was twitchy in a way Phex hadn't seen since the sifters figured out their balance.

Tyve said, "There is no point in worrying about it now."

Phex agreed. "Focus on making it through tomorrow."

"There's no call to be reasonable," grumbled Kagee.

"Has Tillam left yet?" Phex tried to sound casual, as if he were changing the topic for their benefit rather than expressing actual curiosity.

Tyve shook her head. "Zil said they're waiting on supplies. Might be something medical."

"Oh, gods. They'll be watching our dome tomorrow, then, won't they?" Berril squeaked.

Tyve nodded, grin spiky and evil.

"Great. That's not terrifying." Fandina looked even more worried.

Tyve snorted. "Half of them have been in and out of our practices for the past month or more already. What's the difference?"

"Fair point," said Fandina.

"Who cares if gods are watching?" Kagee sounded like he was trying to convince himself.

"Who cares, indeed?" Jin sounded awfully glum for a Dyesi.

Phex shoveled extra protein into Jin's bowl. "We'll be fine."

"You always say that," grumbled Berril.

Their final dome exam was different from all the eliminations that had come before. It was almost, although not really, a debut performance. It was by no means a true dais of major gods in front of a massive congregation, but it wasn't taking place in a small dome, either.

Acolytes from all over Divinity 36 as well as the press and members of certain exclusive divine sects were invited to attend. There were moon residents willing to encourage potentials, but also worshipers of other pantheons – carefully vetted and privileged to render judgment on the new crop of demigods. These would be Sapiens and aliens from highly devout sectors of the galaxy, honored by divine indulgence and invited specifically for their favorable support. The Dyesi wanted to see not just what the potentials' dome colors did to other Dyesi but, more importantly, what the godsong did to non-Dyesi. This was their chance to see if the new pantheons truly worked as gods. If their domes could bring about godfix, if they could push casual fans into fully devout worship. That was what the acolytes truly wanted.

Among the devout, there were always those for whom it was a point of pride to be first. The first to worship at the altar of the next major pantheon. The first to believe in a new god. The first to crow about having discovered the next galaxy-wide entertainment sensation.

And, finally, there were a select few who made a point of attending any performance of potentials that they could because there would be no fixed. It was a safe, sane way to experience the dome, even if it was unlikely to be the best dome. As a result, final exams tended to draw congregations who enjoyed divine entertainment but were less inclined to full worship – skeptics. The hardest nuts to crack. The ones the Dyesi really wanted to win over the most.

There was minor buzz about this year's crop of new gods. Gossip had been carefully leaked, as well as select performances and behind-the-scenes footage. Their finals were better attended than most, or so they were told. They were in one of the larger in-building domes, and the congregation was packed. The three pantheons lurked under the dais, each in their own vestry and wearing special costumes, and very nervous.

Phex sat stiff-backed and staring at nothing. He was self-conscious about how short his hair was, aware that there was something wrong with the shape of his ears. He worried that Berril really was the wrong color, that Kagee was too color-less, and that Tyve had an overabundance of everything. They didn't look or act like true gods. They'd worked hard to get where they were, but suddenly he realized how very immature they must seem to those who had attended real domes. To those who had seen Tillam live. To Tillam themselves, sitting out there in judgment. To a congregation pulled off the moon that spawned the best and brightest, who spun songs into divine light.

Until that moment, Phex had never entertained the thought that they might not be good enough. Because they *had* to be. Suddenly, he was struck with the horrible idea that maybe they just weren't. How could he even think of himself as a god, even imagine that he had the potential to become one? A lowly crudrat. What was he even *doing* there?

He looked down at his tight outfit, matched to the others'. Expensive. The most beautiful, and impractical, thing that he had ever worn.

He looked over at Tyve, who was pacing back and forth, practicing her moves in little hand flicks and sharp steps, reviewing them in her head for the hundredth time. Fandina and Jinyesun were sitting completely still and decidedly opaque, crests back, focused and terrified. Kagee was playing with his rings, nervously twirling and spinning them, pushing each one up to the knuckle then back down again. Berril was huddled in a corner, wings curled in a self-hug.

She shouldn't have to hug herself.

Phex walked over and slid down the wall to sit on the floor next to her. He patted her knee bump under the thin membrane of her wings and waited, not at all long, for her to raise her head. He slumped down so she could rest against his shoulder.

They sat like that for an eternity and a split second.

An acolyte appeared in the doorway. "It is time."

Phex helped Berril up. She tucked her wings back. He put his arm around her as they moved up to the dais. The other four followed close behind.

All too soon, they were standing atop it, thousands of eyes on them, the dome grey overhead. Now they had to separate. Sifters in the center, Phex and Kagee to each side, Tyve crouched at the front, and Berril standing, tiny, at the back.

Berril started their performance with a light pattern of soft feet, like rain, until it hardened and slowed into a heartbeat. It was unusual to start a dome with grace, but they'd decided there was no point in them being anything but different.

It was Phex who called the first color to the dome, using the simple, clean power of his triggered voice. Singing out one single note from soft to loud, saturating the dome with nothing but a stunning sapphire blue. Patternless, just color, until Kagee came in, threaded high cantor through Phex's note, giving the color depth and pattern. Berril beat out dark and light textures. Then, suddenly, the cantors were harmonized, and Tyve was moving, and their signature starburst took over the dome. It was a spectacular opening that relied almost entirely on the pristine strength of low cantor and the efficiency of perfectly balanced sifters.

They were singing a recolored version of an Errata piece, but until Kagee began the first verse, no one realized that. There was a surprised rustling as the congregation caught up to the godsong. They'd chosen Errata because their songs were easier than Tillam's, and Phex rarely had to switch cantors. The few times he did in this one, it was mostly for show, and they could hear the congregation gasp in shock when he did it. Phex wasn't sure whether that was positive or negative, so he tried not to worry about it.

He thought they did the piece justice – not true to the original but not corrupted, either. Just twisted with flourishes Phex had already come to think of as theirs. Tyve performed moves that had come from Phex's crudrat training. She played her body into Jinyesun's natural pattern tendencies so that organic swirls dominated the edges of the dome, like fractals unfurling over a sphere. The saturation that Phex's unreal voice could bring to Dyesi skin was allowed to dominate, almost punishing the eyes with its intensity. It made the whole dome slightly overwhelming, so that when Tyve beat in a pause or flipped Berril into quiet and stillness, these were moments of profound relief.

It wasn't a relaxing performance for anyone. Phex thought that their shows would always feel a little like work to any congregation. Slightly too frantic. Slightly too primary. Slightly too surprising and unpredictable. A bit exhausting. When Berril leapt up and her wings burst out near the end, the dome was tinted yellow by an audible murmur of surprise. There were some there who didn't know she was a true chiropteran, and to find her suddenly in flight was shocking.

Phex let Kagee carry the final note while he faded low cantor, turned and ran up the dome, back flipping over Berril, who had glided low to skim the dais. Phex landed with one knee bent, arms and head down. Knew that behind him, Berril had swooped back up, doing a mirror of his flip in the air, only to plummet down from the pinnacle as if dropped. Tyve caught her exactly as Kagee cut his note.

The dome went black with the suddenness of it.

There was utter silence.

Then the dome recovered itself and resumed its dormant pearly grey.

Phex risked a glance down at the congregation. They seemed... fine.

Dyesi, as a rule, were less reactive to the effects of the dome than other species. They also didn't come from a culture that expressed approval with loud cheering or clapping. Generally, it was the height of their crests and the sifting of their skin that indicated focus and interest. From what Phex could see, crests were alert and puffy, and all the skins were showing consistent coloration.

Then he heard someone cheer. There were Sapiens and a few other species in that congregation, and *they* expressed approval in a gratifyingly audible way.

Phex and the others stood and nodded at them, grateful for the support.

The ambient light of the grey dome brightened slightly at some unseen signal or sub-auditory command. Phex glanced around, trying to spot Tillam. But if any great gods sat in that congregation, they were well disguised. He supposed it would be dangerous for them to openly attend, since chances were higher that their worshipers would be among in any given public audience.

As this was an exam, Phex and his pantheon stood rather awkwardly in a row at the front of the dais, looking down at the panel of acolytes, awaiting judgment.

Six judges sat in the middle and toward the front of the congregation. They seemed to be engaged in a heated debate, which was nerve-racking. Normally, assessments of the potentials went quickly.

The audience grew restless and impatient. They had been promised three groups. Why was this one still on the dais, doing nothing?

It happened so fast that, afterward, Phex was grateful for all that bodyguard training he'd put himself through.

A large Sapien nearly as tall as Phex rushed the dais. She moved fast, too, possibly an athlete of some kind?

At first, Phex thought she was going to jump up onto the platform with them, which was nearly impossible. It was higher than her head, and she'd need crudrat training or similar. But then he noticed she was holding something as though about to throw it.

Phex had no idea what it was, but he was certain he should stop her.

She was focused on Fandina and Jinyesun, who were on the opposite side of the dais from Phex.

Since he couldn't get between her and them, he dove off the dais directly at her instead.

He wasn't fast enough.

She'd thrown whatever she held even as he landed on top of her.

The speed and weight of his body drove her hard to the floor of the dome. She was writhing and screaming in a language he did not know. Crazed, hectic screams with an edge of hysteria to them.

Fixed.

What was a fixed doing so close? And how could she have fixated on his pantheon? They weren't really gods. They didn't even have a name yet. How could they have a worshiper gone rotten already?

Phex muscled her over onto her stomach and twisted her arms behind her back. He was already surrounded by guards. Not Dyesi. Dyesi didn't fight. These were hired muscle.

Phex relinquished the fixed to a very annoyed-looking Sapien. Only then did he look back at the dais. Fear curdled his stomach because he knew that he hadn't managed to stop the woman's throw.

Her target had been the sifters, but Berril had leaped to protect them. She'd deployed her wings and wrapped the two Dyesi in the soft membrane of the most delicate shield.

The horrible smell of burning flesh hit Phex's nose. Small spots on those precious wings were smoking slightly, and Berril was screaming.

Phex took a running leap up the side of the dome and back onto the dais. He slid over to Berril, who crumpled to the floor, wings flopped out behind her. She was writhing in agony.

The dome was in uproars. Everyone was shouting and talking at once.

Fandina and Jinyesun were frozen in shock, crests flat back and almost entirely opaque. Oddly, in that moment, Phex wondered if the opacity was a defensive instinct, if it somehow hardened and protected their skin. Because that had been the fixed's purpose. She'd thrown acid at their sifters. Everyone knew acid was the best way to destroy Dyesi skin. It was the fastest way to end the career of a sifter or diminish godhood – in this case, before it even started.

Berril was in too much pain to even take comfort in Phex's arms. He could do nothing more than try to shield her as she writhed. Try not to touch any part of her back or wings that might be burned.

Tyve was yelling at the acolytes to do something.

Kagee looked wildly around for a moment, then said, "Get her costume off, Phex. Anything that might have absorbed the acid."

Phex frantically began to strip what was left of the stupid tight jumpsuit off Berril.

Berril was in too much pain to care or protest.

Kagee jumped off the dais and ran for the water station. He grabbed the huge cask and tried to single-handedly haul it toward the platform, but he was too slight. Several congregation members understood what he was doing and ran to help.

They levered it onto the dais, and Phex, using strength he suspected came from pure adrenaline, lifted the darn thing and drenched Berril with it, in a desperate attempt to flush the acid off her.

Kagee panted from below. "Easier to get *her* to the water."

Phex agreed. He lifted the now-wet and naked Berril into his arms, scared by how still she'd become, and jumped off the dais. Not caring that he landed a little wrong. There were bottles and bags of juice and other liquids in the drinks area, so he took her there.

He and Kagee started opening anything they could and pouring it over her wings and back. They thought only about washing as much of the acid off her skin as possible.

Other hands were helping now. Aliens and Sapiens from the congregation. Opening things, pouring.

Eventually, what seemed like ages later, medics finally arrived.

They took Berril away, curtly informing Phex and Kagee that they were absolutely not allowed to follow.

The two cantors stood there, panting, shivering a little, covered in water and juice and shaking with adrenaline. Phex's skin was tingling. He felt burned in spots too, a sympathetic reaction to the horror.

He looked at Kagee. His grey eyes were huge, like he needed to cry.

Phex glared hard.

Kagee nodded, terse. His face resumed its customary arrogant pout, pointed chin up-tilted slightly. He'd keep up the facade if it killed him. Kagee hated showing weakness even more than Phex did.

Together they turned and looked back at the dais. The platform was now a water-drenched focal point of chaos.

Tyve had gone slightly feral, claws out and teeth bared. She'd taken a protective stance in front of their two sifters, who were still frozen and opaque in shock. Tyve wasn't letting anyone near them, which meant medics as well.

Phex figured that was logical. While he and Kagee had
followed their instincts and training to help Berril, Tyve had
done the same for their Dyesi – knowing their sifters were the
intended target and that she was the only fighter left.

Phex gestured with his head at Kagee, who nodded and
climbed back onto the dais to try and calm her down.

Phex turned and stalked toward the six judges, who were
sitting, frozen in shock, apparently trying to comprehend
what had just happened. He faced them, slammed his hands
down on the table, hoping to surprise them out of their paral-
ysis with noise and vibration.

But the Dyesi judges remained still and unblinking while
everyone else was loud and panicked. Phex looked around,
annoyed, and realized that all the other acolytes were the
same. Every Dyesi in that dome was just sitting still as if
suspended in space and time.

Phex only had one weapon left. But it was a good one.

They were in a dome, and he was surrounded by Dyesi.
And most Dyesi had some ability to sift. He wasn't sure if his
impact on the dome would be enough without trained gods,
but it was his best option.

He picked his most powerful note, the highest he could
achieve at full volume. He started with the judges, blasting
them with sound, and then he slowly rotated it out, hitting all
the sifters there, potential or not, trained or not – even his
own sifters, injured or not.

The dome responded. Going from relaxed grey to hard,
hot, impossibly bright orange – eye-searing and ear-blinding.

By the time he'd finished his rotation and began pulling
back his cantor, stillness reigned – acolyte or alien or
Sapien, it didn't matter. And the Dyesi were no longer
opaque.

Only Kagee seemed unaffected. Even Tyve had retracted

her claws and closed her mouth to stand dumbfounded, staring at him.

Phex cut his note abruptly, not caring if anyone was bruised or burned by the suddenness of it.

He glared at the six judges.

One of them looked like it might speak.

Phex up-tilted his head like Kagee always did, then opened his mouth, threatening another blast.

The acolyte snapped its mouth shut and crested at Phex.

"You allowed a *fixed* inside my dome." Phex's voice was flat with disgust.

"You are a baby pantheon. You should not *have* any fixed." The judge sounded timid, its face speckled with humiliation.

Phex didn't care how embarrassed they were. "And yet my grace just got hurt because you *let in a fixed*. Why did you not vet the congregation? How dare you allow this to happen?"

"How could we know to expect something that has never occurred before?"

Phex dropped all formalities. He was furious. His ears were white-hot and roaring with it. "You didn't screen for insanity?"

"You are *potentials*. You barely have worshipers. You have never even performed under a proper dome before. It is not possible for anyone to be fixated on you yet."

"Then what just happened?" That was Kagee, from the dais. He was using formal Dyesi, but he was also enraged.

Tyve had calmed down and was busy checking Fandina and Jinyesun to be sure they weren't burned by acid or voice. They seemed unharmed. Still shocked, but they were coming out of that. Their complete opacity faded to a normal tinted iridescence, teal and blue.

Fandina recovered first. "What is going on?"

"What happened?" asked Jinyesun shortly after. And then, "Where is Berril?"

Satisfied that they were okay, if confused, Phex turned back to the judges. "Explain to me how you let a fixed into a dome full of potentials. Full of children." He used the Dyesi word, because they might not think of the potentials as kids but he certainly did.

Fandina focused on Phex and the judges. "Why is Phex yelling? Phex never yells."

"Why did he blast the dome? Have you ever seen that done before?" asked Jinyesun.

"Not outside of the caves, not from a Sapien, but that is not the point." Fandina blinked large eyes, as if awakening from a dream.

Phex realized then that the freeze response was so strong in Dyesi, that was why they never fought.

Kagee explained calmly, "A fixed got in and threw acid at you two. Berril shielded you with her wings and was burned. Phex is mad."

"Is Berril okay?" asked Jinyesun instantly.

"Is Phex going to kill someone?" wondered Fandina in a hushed tone.

Phex thought that was definitely a possibility. How dare the acolytes just sit there? He wondered what would happen if he grabbed and crashed those smooth Dyesi heads into each other.

"Not if I get to them first," said Tyve. "You two all right?"

Fandina and Jinyesun clicked in unison.

Tyve jumped off the dais and stood next to Phex. She extended the claws of one hand and pointed them at the judges. "Explain."

"We cannot," said the Dyesi, eyes riveted on the sharp, gleaming threat.

"You should not have any fixed yet," reiterated one of the others.

"Rest assured, we will look into this."

"It proves one thing," said one of the other acolytes.

"Judgment is irrelevant," agreed another.

"Why?" asked Tyve.

"If you have fixed, you are already gods. Our opinion does not matter. The worshipers have acted as proof on this matter."

"One could have hoped they had used less-violent means to express their belief," said Kagee, back to his normal sarcastic self.

"Your chiropteran will be fine. We have the means to repair her easily. However, we would not have been able to heal your sifters. She did the correct thing. Her flesh is less valuable than theirs." The acolyte indicated Fandina and Jinyesun.

"Could I just kill this one?" Tyve asked plaintively.

Fandina, Jinyesun, and Kagee descended from the dais and joined them.

"No one is killing anyone," said Fandina firmly.

"Jakaa Nova. So violent. And what purpose would my death serve?" asked the judge in question, seeming actually interested.

"It might make me feel better," said Tyve.

"Me too," agreed Kagee, looking dangerously smug.

One of the judge's idents chirped. "You can go see your chiropteran now."

"Take us to her," ordered Fandina, sounding like a god.

Tyve sheathed her claws.

They turned to follow an acolyte.

Phex walked backwards, using his peripheral vision to keep pace with his pantheon. "You find out why this happened, acolytes. I want to know where that fixed came from. Why she exists at all."

"Oh, so do we," said the Dyesi, cresting at him intently. As if, on some level, the Dyesi blamed him.

———

Berril was medically asleep when they arrived. She lay face down on one bed with each wing spread over an additional cot of its own. Phex had never before appreciated how truly huge her wings were. They were attached from her elbow up and down over her shoulder blades. Her forearms were folded under one cheek. Patches of gleaming bandages covered her back and fanned out over both wings. Her wounds arched in a crescent, like a massive version of one of Phex's blade scars.

"You can talk. She won't wake up," explained the Sapien medic.

"Will she be able to fly again?" Tyve asked.

The medic looked insulted. "Of course. The color match won't be perfect, but that hardly matters. I understand she was scheduled for texturing, implants, cosmetic surgery, and tinting tomorrow anyway. We'll just get started on that tonight."

"What?" said Kagee.

The medic looked him up and down. "You too, rock sprite. You're gods now. You can't look *ordinary*. We are professionals here. You do realize that?" she sounded faintly disgusted.

"You aren't even going to wake her up to ask permission?" Kagee pushed.

"Why waste the drugs? It won't impede her healing to

begin surgery immediately. And it's not like she has a choice. None of you do."

Kagee frowned.

Fandina grabbed his arm.

"It is in your contract," explain Jinyesun.

"The divinity controls your image," added Fandina.

"You must have known we're required to accept aesthetic surgery and maintenance tinting if we became demigods," said Tyve.

Kagee took a breath, looked at Phex. "Yes, but I didn't think they'd just do it to her like this after what happened."

Phex tightened his lips. "So long as it's safe."

The medic bristled. "As if we risk gods *here*! Don't be childish."

A warm voice spoke from the entrance. "Is everyone okay?"

They turned to see Missit and Zil coming inside, greeting the space.

Tyve ran to her brother.

"I heard you flashed claw, little sister."

"It was necessary."

"Does the enemy still live?"

"Unfortunately."

"You were always a poor warrior." Zil teased gently.

"Wasn't my kill, it was Phex's." Tyve was childishly defensive.

Zil looked at Phex. "Was it? So, you're the failure?" Phex suspected he had somehow earned brotherly teasing too. It was confusing.

Kagee glared. He took Zil seriously. "Because you fight off Tillam's fixed regularly yourself, warrior? Your domes run with blood, do they?"

Zil bristled. "What did you just say to me?"

Missit was staring at Phex. "Fixed? Fixed!"

Phex frowned. "You didn't see what happened?"

"No. The bodyguards got us out the moment someone rushed the dais."

"A fixed threw acid at our sifters. Berril protected them," Phex explained curtly.

Missit rushed at Phex, eyes worried and gaze all over him. He stopped close enough to make theirs a private conversation.

Phex backed away, scared Missit was going to touch him. The god looked like he wanted to. Needed to.

"I'm fine," Phex said quickly, in Galactic Common for some reason.

Missit swallowed, nodded, hands clenching at his sides.

Behind him, Tyve and Zil argued in their native tongue – rapid, low, and glottal. Tyve was standing between her brother and her high cantor.

Kagee should have known better. Jakaa Nova never responded well to being challenged. But Kagee had his rings up.

Missit turned to press against Phex's side, the excuse being he was now looking at Berril's small, still form.

Kagee walked ostentatiously away from Zil and went to stand with their sifters, close to Berril's head, looking down at her patched wings.

Missit said, softly, "I thought she was the weakest of you. Like I am in Tillam."

Phex considered the golden god. "Is that so? And here, I was just realizing that they are the weakest, aren't they?"

"Who?"

He gestured at Fandina and Jinyesun. "The Dyesi."

Missit looked confused.

Phex explained. "They freeze. There's no flight-or-fight response in them, is there? Just freeze."

"Is that weakness or instinct?" Missit had grown up among them, after all.

Fandina touched Berril's temple with three fingers in a kind of benediction. They were listening to him and Missit talk about them, but Phex didn't mind – they were his sifters, after all.

"Does it matter if the instinct is a weakness?" Phex wondered if Missit froze like the Dyesi.

Missit considered, then said, "I think you'll find that the Dyesi are more powerful than you or I could possibly imagine. After all, they are the makers of gods."

"What good is that when one crazed Sapien can render them inert?" Phex wondered.

Missit tilted his head in thought. "I think the acolytes underestimated."

"The fixed?"

"No. You."

Phex wasn't sure if that meant him as an individual or his voice or his pantheon.

"Are you scared of them, Missit?"

"The fixed? Of course. I have more than most. Thousands. I know I give my bodyguards the slip, but only here on Divinity 36. Out there, I do *try* to be careful. You don't need to worry about me."

"Not the fixed. The Dyesi."

"Scared of the Dyesi? No. I'm sympathetic. I, too, usually freeze. Are you?"

"Scared of them? Not yet. Sometimes, I think I should be."

"And which path is yours, Phex? Fight, flight, or freeze?"

"I don't know yet. But I can tell you something."

Missit clicked encouragement.

Phex smiled down at the great god, knowing he was exposing his own softness. "I have good instincts."

"How do you know that?"

"I survived into adulthood."

Missit gave an ironic lopsided smile. Gestured at Phex's pantheon, standing around Berril, worried and injured. "The problem is that now you have to keep them alive, too."

Phex nodded, knowing they were both thinking of Fortew in that moment.

For the first time, Phex didn't see Missit as something he needed to help or protect. He saw Missit as high cantor and member of a long-running pantheon. How had Missit felt, seeing his friend of over a decade lying frail and hurting just like Berril?

Terrible, of course. Especially if he couldn't do anything to help.

What happened when gods became helpless? Did they go insane? Like the fixed?

Phex had gone a little insane back there when Berril crumbled in pain. So had Kagee and Tyve. So, too, he supposed, had Berril, or she wouldn't have leaped to protect the sifters in the first place.

Was madness part of godhood? Or was it part of friendship? And in his case, when the two were now inexorably linked, would he ever know the difference? And did that matter in the end, if the results were the same?

An acolyte entered the room, looked around briefly, approached Phex. "Demigod, there is nothing more you can do here. Leave your grace to rest."

"Demigod?" replied Phex.

"You passed. It's canon," replied the acolyte as if that were obvious.

As if it weren't important.

"Congratulations," said Missit, sounding sad.

But Phex's first thought wasn't of godhood. It was that he could now become a citizen. Being a newly minted god didn't matter as much, in that moment, as belonging to a planet.

For the first time in their association, Phex ignored Missit entirely and focused on something else. His ident band.

He clicked the infonet open and searched for his travel documentation. And there it was, already updated.

Refugee status?
Rescinded.
Citizenship?
Dyesi.

Just like that, Phex was one of them. One of the Dyesi. One of the weak. One of the frozen. One of the sifters. And, maybe, one of the monsters.

"Welcome to the divinity," said the acolyte, loudly, to all of them.

Zil embraced Tyve, slapping his sister's back. Fandina and Jinyesun looked up from Berril, crested with excitement, flushing dark blue with joy. Even Kagee allowed himself a small smirk. Smug, of course. As if he had never doubted it. As if he deserved it. But that was Kagee.

"Phex?" Missit was not accustomed to Phex ignoring him.

But Phex was less interested in being a god when he had become, for the first time in his life, a whole person.

"Jinyesun." It was work to keep his voice steady.

The Dyesi crested in his direction. "Yes, my low cantor?"

"Is there still no such thing as an unwanted Dyesi?"

"All Dyesi are wanted," reiterated his sifter.

And Phex believed it.

fin

What happens to Phex, his pantheon, and Missit next? Find out in *Demigod 12*, book 2 in the Tinkered Starsong series. Join Gail's newsletter, the Chirrup, for sneak peaks at cover art, sample chapters, and more at *GailCarriger.com*

AUTHOR'S NOTE

Thank you so much for picking up *Divinity 36*. I hope you enjoyed the first installment of Phex's story. If you would like more Tinkered Starsong, please say so in a review. I'm grateful for the time you take to do so.

I have a silly gossipy newsletter called the Chirrup. I promise: no spam, no fowl. (Well, maybe a little wicker fowl and lots of giveaways and sneak peeks.) You get to see cover art and read samples first! Find it and more at…

gailcarriger.com

All my love & gratitude to R the refugee I once (oh so casually) adopted who now makes me, and this series, better & stronger.

ABOUT THE WRITERBEAST

New York Times bestselling author Gail Carriger (AKA G. L. Carriger) writes to cope with being raised in obscurity by an expatriate Brit and an incurable curmudgeon. She escaped small-town life and inadvertently acquired several degrees in higher learning, a fondness for cephalopods, and a chronic tea habit. She then traveled the historic cities of Europe, subsisting entirely on biscuits secreted in her handbag. She resides on the edge of the Pacific, surrounded by fantastic shoes, where she insists on tea imported from London.

CPSIA information can be obtained
at www.ICGtesting.com
Printed in the USA
LVHW050749260523
748013LV00001B/60